EXCESS

KATE STEWART

This book is a work of fiction. Names, characters, places, and incidents are the product of the author's imagination or are used fictitiously. Any resemblance to actual events, locales, or persons, living or dead, is coincidental.

Copyright © 2017 Excess by Kate Stewart. All rights reserved, including the right to reproduce, distribute, or transmit in any form or by any means. For information regarding subsidiary rights, please contact the Publisher.

Visit Kate Stewart's website at *www.katestewartwrites.com.*
Cover Design by Amy Queau, Q Designs
Edited by Edee M. Fallon, Mad Spark Editing
Interior Design & Formatting by Juliana Cabrera, Jersey Girl Design

ISBN-13: 978-1546793076
ISBN-10: 1546793070

Manufactured in the United States of America
First Edition March 2015 under pen name Angelica Chase

10 9 8 7 6 5 4 3 2 1

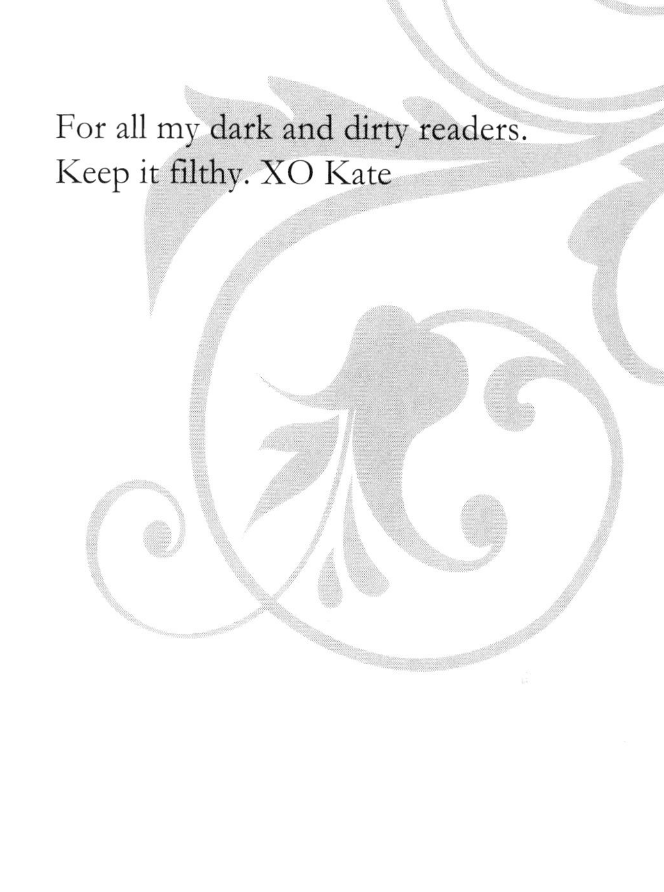

For all my dark and dirty readers.
Keep it filthy. XO Kate

CONTENTS

OPULENCE
Book 1

§§

When I was twenty-eight years old, I wrote my own winning lottery ticket. A simple idea thrust me onto the fast track to wealth, and into a world I had only ever dreamed about. I submerged myself in the unfamiliar, a life that seemed all too alluring…until it lost its appeal.

I made my fortune, built my castle, and then exiled myself within its comforts once reality set in.

Far too late, I discovered I was drowning in a sea of hungry sharks. Given the choice to sink or swim, I chose the latter…and it cost me everything.

Devin McIntyre, the most dangerous shark of them all, was the last nail in my naïve coffin. His beautiful smile and amazing cock tainted me in ways I could have never imagined.

I craved him. I needed him. I loved him.

Miserable with the outcome of my prosperity, I set out to change what disgusted me most—the first decision being to rid myself of Devin. Little did I know that taking that first step would make me a slave to a man far more tempting…or that my addiction to Devin would threaten to ruin it all.

"We have created a manic world nauseous with the pursuit of material wealth. Many also bear their cross of imagined deprivation, while their fellow human beings remain paralyzed by real poverty. We drown in the thick sweetness of our sensual excess, and our shameless opulence, while our discontent souls suffocate in the arid wasteland of spiritual deprivation."

– ANTHON ST. MAARTEN

§§

"FUCKING RIDE IT," he ordered, digging his fingers into my hips. I took in his lusty gaze as he eyed my bouncing chest. His wavy, dark brown hair glistened from his exertion, sweat trickling down the front of his tuxedo shirt. His dilated pupils were a far cry from the dark blue depths that normally mirrored a stormy deep sea. He licked his full bottom lip as he thrust up hard, making me scream out. "This is what *you* wanted," he chided as he battered me with his cock, pounding it in from underneath me as I whimpered through the intensity of his thrusts. He made use of the leather chair he sat on, using the firm cushion to piston his hips upward and bury his length inside of me. He was beyond a skilled lover, and when Devin wanted to punish you, you damn sure knew it.

Feeling him on the brink, I moaned in protest as he pulled out quickly and ordered me to my knees. "Suck me off."

Kneeling in front of him, I looked up to see him eye me expectantly. Without waiting for me to fully open my mouth, he pushed to the back of my throat as he came in hot spurts, and I choked it down willingly. "So fucking dirty," he murmured, massaging up and down my throat with his fingertips as his pumping slowed. He pulled out, rubbing the last drop over my lips.

"Every drop," he demanded, pushing his tip slightly inside my mouth, forcing me to take the last of it in. "Nothing better than you, Nina," he whispered sweetly, though the words were anything but. The truth was, I hated this beautiful man. I hated that I wanted him so desperately. At one time, he'd meant everything to me. Now I longed for the day I could break free, but I craved him like a drug.

I fed his need for dominance; he fed my inner whore.

I pulled up my dress that was now wrinkled from the burden of my knees and looked him over. As usual, he withdrew without a second thought, completely apathetic. This was sex for him, a fix for me. I didn't ask him for more, and he had no intention of giving it. I was a game he had played and won, and I knew it. It had been over months ago when I caught him fucking his wife. That's right, his wife.

He fixed his jacket and ran his hands through his hair, looking flawless as he turned to me with a wicked grin.

"Something on your mind?" I asked, pretending to admire my new eighteen-carat tennis bracelet.

"Why haven't you moved on?" he asked curiously. I knew secretly that was the last thing he wanted me to do. Though he could not care less about my wellbeing, owning me was still a priority to him. He made sure of it with every heart-stopping orgasm.

I walked up to stand by his side then turned my head as I leaned in. "What makes you think I haven't? It's only your cock I crave now, Devin. The sex I still have nostalgia for, and obviously, the feeling is mutual."

"No longer in love with me?" His smirk made my blood boil, but I had learned to hide it well.

"No longer willing to do more talking than fucking," I said dryly as I made my way out of the room. The truth was, I wanted to turn around and beg for the man I met to somehow reemerge, but it would have been pointless. The man I met had always been a shark, had always bared his teeth, but had done it so subtly that by the time he had sunk his teeth into me and brought me down to the bottom, it was way too late.

He was the very last nail in my naïve coffin.

Devin was another price I paid for my wealth, another reminder that with each dollar earned a part of my humanity was stripped away from me. I had joined the elite like Devin when I had still believed in the good in people.

Fucking people.

Rejoining the party, I made my way toward Devin's wife, Eileen, purposefully meeting her eyes as I lifted a flute of champagne off the tray closest to her. She appraised me greedily, her deep hate showing in her eyes. She was perfect in every way: a petite blonde with a tight...everything. I hated her. Not because she belonged to Devin, but because of what she represented. She was the very definition of pretentious.

"Nina, how good of you to come," she bit out as she eyed me over her tipped glass of Krug, the same champagne I had spit out when Devin introduced it to me. He decided it would be better used to shower me in before fucking me mercilessly.

Good times.

"You have no idea," I replied with obvious meaning as I brushed past her, leaving her to draw her own conclusion. I couldn't resist a look over my shoulder and was rewarded as she gaped at me openly. I gave a smug smile and looked behind me to see Devin's eyes grow cold as he realized our word exchange would cost him the latter part of his evening.

Their argument wouldn't be the confrontation that a wife should have with a cheating husband. She wouldn't cry about her broken heart or his complete lack of respect for their marital vows. No, there would be no love lost between them. For that to happen, the relationship would have to be based on love itself. No, this argument would more than likely be a tongue lashing with a few tsk, tsks on the etiquette of extra-marital affairs and a repeat of the do's and the don'ts. And when she says don't, she means me.

I gave Devin a sly wink then quickly made my exit as he rushed to his wife's side to mitigate. Their heated whispers faded into oblivion as I walked down the dock and away from the hotel-sized yacht toward my town car. I texted my driver, Carson, and saw that he was already waiting for me with the door open. I gave him a warm smile.

"Carson," I said with a nod as I made my way into the plush, leather backseat, kicking off my heels with a satisfied groan.

"Ms. Scott, how was the party?"

"Uneventful," I said quickly before he shut the door.

I had taken a huge risk tonight confessing to Devin's wife.

I'd never purposefully started a fire where Devin was concerned, and I was sure the outcome wouldn't be a pleasant one. I tried to ride the high of my deceit but couldn't manage to keep it.

Nothing, I felt...nothing. I purposefully thought about the fact that my latest evil deed might have cost me Devin.

Still...nothing.

Maybe I had finally rid myself of my addiction after all. I didn't have to worry about facing his wrath tonight, assured that whatever the outcome of my play, the circumstances would never change.

So the question remained: Why hadn't I moved on? The answer was always right behind my mind's eye, a whisper in my ear, a tap on my shoulder.

I had become one of them. I had no soul to save. I found pleasure in what used to disgust me. I had begun mingling with the shark's years ago and had the choice to sink or swim.

I had chosen to swim, and it cost me everything.

"A virtuous woman is not moved by big names and flamboyance, but only men of profound wisdom and integrity move her."

– MICHAEL BASSEY JOHNSON

§§

I WASN'T BORN RICH, and I worked for everything I ever had. My wealth had come to me later in life with a simple idea. Once upon a time, I was a housewife to a veterinarian. Sound boring? It was. It wasn't until it all fell apart that I realized that I could have wasted the rest of my life in that cell without knowing any differently.

I no longer had the desire to confine myself to that type of prison, having never felt validated when I was married. It took me years to discover the bigger picture, and it had nothing to do with marriage.

I was a coupon clipping, Pinterest stalking, hobby enthusiast with entirely too much time on my hands. I was always doing what was trending, and eventually, that enthusiasm led me down an insane road: a fast track to wealth I could never have imagined.

I was born in Charleston, South Carolina, where I still lived. My parents were blue collar. My mother was a flight attendant for nearly thirty years, while my father worked as a crew chief for a general contractor. My brother Aaron and I never really hurt for anything, but we didn't live large. My mother's idea of extravagance was dining out on steak. I wasn't gifted a car on my sixteenth birthday. I had to work to buy my own car and was rewarded with an affordable, used truck while my friends paraded around in their gifted BMWs.

I could not have cared less about designer jeans back then, or what labels I wore. Now I had a personal shopper, wardrobe consultant, and I wouldn't be caught dead in a BMW.

The fine lines of class and stature were made clear to me when I was young. The elite of Charleston would shun my mother publicly, though she tried desperately to fit in where she could. One of my first memories was my mother taking me to a community pool in a posh neighborhood a few miles away from our apartment.

We walked into the clubhouse, all eyes landing on my mother. Being the proud woman she was, she grabbed my hand and quickly started to introduce herself to the women gathered. The shrewd women quickly picked her apart as they sipped their martinis in their designer swimsuits. My mother became embarrassed quickly and was on the verge of tears. She guided me out to the pool and let me swim for as long as she could handle their hostile glares.

"Come on, baby," she prompted as what looked like the clubhouse manager approached us.

"Ma'am, if you're not a member—"

"We're leaving," she snapped at the woman who seemed satisfied with my mother's reaction. She quickly wrapped me in a towel, pleading with her eyes. "Let's go to the beach, Ninabelle," she said, drying me quickly. With a smile, I nodded and saw my mother's relief when I didn't throw a fit. When we got into the car, my mother sniffled, and I saw a lone tear trickle down her cheek. She wiped it away hastily then turned to me.

"Promise me, Nina. Promise me right now that no matter what happens, you will be nice to everyone, unless they give you a reason not to be."

"I will, Mommy," I answered back eagerly.

"You are such a good girl," she said, grabbing me and hugging me tightly.

That night I heard my parents fight for the first time as I was tucked in my bed, reading Shel Silverstein with my Strawberry Shortcake nightlight. It was my absolute favorite thing to do, my little indulgence. I was memorizing the poem "Clooney the Clown" for book day at school. I had never heard so much anger in my mother's voice and was too afraid to shut off the light.

"Jesus, Jennifer. What the hell is your problem!?" my father yelled, sounding exasperated.

"This! It's ten o'clock, and you're just getting home! We haven't seen each other in weeks. We both work our asses off and for what? Bills we still can't afford to pay! What do you want me to do?" I heard him say as he shut their bedroom door.

That fight was only the first of many. Their arguing was a constant occurrence that stayed consistent until I finally left home the minute I turned eighteen and could get the hell out that house. I hated the way my mother looked at my father as if she blamed him for the life she was living. To this day, I had a hard time spending more than a few minutes with the two of them. They would never have to fight about money again, but years of arguments had led to a mutual resentment that refused to dissipate.

Money had ruined their marriage. Money had ruined mine as well, but not for lack of it. It was just the opposite.

My husband had decided that new money and philandering went hand in hand. Once I had earned my first million, he had made it his mission to let me know he had supported me for years. It was if he assumed I would leave him. It was a total... fucking...nightmare.

My ex-husband, Ryan, had taken what he wanted off the top and invested it as he saw fit, so much so that there was only middle left by the time I had put a stop to it. Once he was completely cut off from me financially for pissing away hundreds of thousands of dollars, he began to resent me, though I kept him in a lavish lifestyle. I divorced him quickly and found out the hard way that I would forever be in debt to him for those few years he allowed me to stay at home while he worked. I was still paying him alimony.

Bastard.

The day I finally left him, he accused me of letting the money go to my head. I swore then, no matter the circumstances, I would never legally bind myself to another man. If it were love, it would last, regardless.

He never once apologized for the hurt his infidelity had caused, nor did he try to save our marriage in any capacity. He wanted my money, he made that clear. Ryan made it impossible to be excited about my new wealth. He left me jaded and bitter in less than a year of striking gold, and I would forever be wary of trusting anyone else with that much power over me.

And I have rarely been kind to anyone since.

I may have turned my back on the girl who grew up in this beautiful, hidden gem, but I could never turn my back on Charleston. The city filled with cotton candy sunsets, rich history, and natural beauty never grew old to me. No matter what exotic destination my wealth afforded me, I had only one home.

Charleston in its own right was definitely a playground for the wealthy. There was no shortage of culture, nor was there a shortage of places that catered to the rich. I considered it my little, comfortable corner of the world. It was my territory, and though the sharks had their cove, I still entertained the nooks and crannies to escape the world I was now drowning in. On nights specifically like these, I would make it a point to revisit the places that made me feel most humble despite my success.

I pushed the button for the security glass.

"Carson," I smiled in the rearview mirror. He was the one person in the world who deserved what was left of my kindness.

"Right away, Ms. Scott."

Carson was a kind, older man in his sixties with gentle eyes and an easy disposition. I had enough testosterone ramped men in my life, so I welcomed the way he regarded me. He had no personal opinion, and his eyes never offered any judgment against me. He simply did his job well and with ease. His intuition to suit my needs didn't hurt, either. We had a simplistic relationship that was mutually beneficial. It was the only uncomplicated relationship I had in my life. Pulling up to my favorite secluded spot, I slid on my flip-flops as the sun was making its way down, knowing I only had an hour or so before it slipped beneath the horizon. I quickly made my way down the quarter mile of asphalt that led to the large sand dune that had to be tackled before I reached my view. This hour is what photographers called "the magic hour," and it was aptly named. The sky was painted perfectly in soft pinks and varying hues of blue with an underlying burst of brazen yellow. Staring out toward the Morris Island lighthouse, I sat in the sand in my five thousand dollar, Valentino dress without an ounce of concern. A few years ago, I would have never even looked at such an expensive piece of clothing.

I was the woman who swore she would never wear anything so costly, that I would do so much more with that kind of money. I chuckled now at the thought. Just out of spite, I might order a dozen of the same color tomorrow.

Nestled on the beautiful, white sand beach staring at the old, picturesque lighthouse, I could actually feel a familiar pull of something. Something that felt right and different from the everyday heaviness I had grown accustomed to dealing with. Instead of being consumed with thoughts of my next evil deed, or a way to one up the money driven predators in my circle, here I simply basked in the peace that surrounded me. The lull of the waves, the serenity, and infinite wisdom that the sea shared with me was one of the only constants in my life.

Nothing in the game of life really mattered, at least, nothing that I had grown to care about. I was just another hamster spinning the wheel. The world didn't give a shit about my agenda, good or bad. And while money might buy me a better view of the ocean that humbled me, my money didn't matter to the ocean one way or another. How I fared in life's Monopoly game didn't make one damn bit of difference.

Calm and clarity washed through me in that moment. I no longer wanted to be one of them.

I was wasting my life.

I let the air seep through my lungs and reveled in the sand that grew colder as the sun sank beneath the horizon while the tide quickly engulfed the small amount of sand that surrounded the base of the lighthouse. I loved this spot more than any other in Charleston, though I had never been able to pinpoint why. The strange and misplaced bone yard of old, pale tree limbs enclosed me in comfort as I noted the seagulls' cries.

The sudden strum of a guitar interrupted the serenity of my Zen-filled spot, and I looked toward the direction of the intrusion. I heard a deep chuckle and squinted in the direction of it. Shielding my eyes from the setting sun, I saw the bare feet and tan, muscular legs first then moved my eyes up to a pair of cargo shorts. The white t-shirt was as far as I got before the sun completely blinded me from him as the strumming picked up and he began to sing.

"I keep pretending this is all a dream," he sang softly. My mouth fell open at the sound of his voice. I quickly scrambled to gain my senses and mask my shock by retreating in the direction of the sand dune in favor of hearing more. His voice was amazing and whispered over the expertly plucked guitar chords. What was even more alarming was his lazy stance against a tree stub, and the fact that he didn't even seem to be trying. With the sun still blocking the view of his face, I mourned the soulful lilt in his voice as I made my way back to the car. His last artfully sung words brought a shiver down my spine.

"Your misery makes you beautiful," he rasped as I stood at the top of the dune to try for one more look. I had walked too far and was unable to see him from where I was now perched but stood there anyway, listening to him finish his song. Deciding that what my songbird looked like was better left a mystery, I turned away, having felt enough disappointment for one evening.

For a lifetime.

It was very close to dark when I made it back to the car. Carson simply nodded, needing no explanation as to where I wanted to go. I thought it sad my routine had become predictable. Then again, it was what kept me safe and away from those who posed the biggest threat to me.

Pulling up to my circular drive, complete with an obscenely sized water fountain, I smiled to myself. My home was the one thing I could never complain about. I had the most spectacular beach house imaginable. There wasn't one room without a view, and I basked in the fact that I had designed every single one of them, with the right hired help, of course. I had lived in my dream home for two short years and not a day went by that I didn't appreciate every detail put into it. It was rather ostentatious in size. The marble floor of the foyer, the obscene amount of crown molding, the dark metallics and rich woods all contributed to my need to have something tangible from my fortune. No one needed this much room, but the girl who was forced to share a bedroom with her little brother most of her childhood had no issues with the extra space. In fact, she had actually ramped up the original design to make sure there was enough space in every room, even the closets.

Stripping naked in my seven hundred square foot bathroom, I slipped into a whirlpool of soothing bubbles. My phone buzzed with an incoming message, but I ignored it. The good part about being completely independent was that I had the luxury of answering to no one. After a relaxing soak, I slipped on my robe and covered my skin in silk then lay in bed thinking about the orgasm Devin had given me.

Now that was worth mulling over.

When I walked into the party, he made no attempt to hide his smirk. I knew right away I would get what I came for. Making no attempt to talk to him, I made my rounds, never once looking his way. I felt his eyes on me, and the small goose bumps that accompanied my awareness were present with every move I made. He had an effect on me like no other man I'd ever met. I was wet with need for him before he ever came within a few feet. After an hour of being polite, I excused myself to the restroom and was barely able to shut the door when it was pushed open, forcing me back. He stood in his tux with his hand on the frame, and that knowing, smug smirk on his lips. I drank him in, because I had no choice. Tall, lean, and built to perfection, he filled his tux out nicely. His wavy hair was tamed and styled as usual. His deep blue eyes pierced me as he roamed my body with his stare.

"Pretty bold of you to come," he mused as he took a step in and closed the door.

"Actually, it's not. I have more right to be here than you do," I said, opening my purse and turning to face the mirror. I plucked out my lipstick

and looked over my shoulder, trying to mask my arousal as I carefully layered my lips.

"I think you knew my wife planned this event," he said, straightening his tie behind me.

"Well, then you better get back to her," I said, careful not to meet his eyes as I tossed my lipstick back into my clutch then snapped it shut.

I shrieked in surprise as he gripped my hips, lifting me so that my knees were straddling the sink. Once kneeling in front of the mirror, he placed my hands on either side of it and quickly lifted my skirt. I could no longer see him as he pulled my panties down until they were stretched taut on my thighs. I began to pant and arched my back, pushing out my ass, silently begging for it.

"You have to ask," he growled as his heavy hand came down, marking me with a slap as he locked the door.

"Devin," I panted, arching my back further to encourage him.

"Ask, Nina. Isn't that why you're here?" He took a single finger and swiped it through my sex, pausing on my clit only long enough to make me miss its absence. "You're dripping for me, and so fucking warm." His voice was lower, rougher. I could tell he was equally as turned on, but like with all other things Devin, he was disciplined as well as thorough.

"Fuck me," I ordered. Another slap to my thigh had me gripping the mirror tighter as a small sheen of sweat covered my forehead.

"That's not asking," he said, taking a step back so he met my eyes in the mirror as his hand came down again. "Say it."

"No," I hissed, feeling the sting and biting my lip in an attempt to stifle my moan. I crouched slightly to meet his eyes in the mirror.

His breathtaking smile was his reply before he ran his hands from my hands on either side of the mirror down my bare arms. "Nina, I'm running out of patience. Do as I ask." His hands trailed my sides, down my thighs and gripped my panties. He slowly started pulling them back up when I whimpered.

"What's that?" He leaned in, his breath in my ear. "You have something you want to say?" I let out a slow exhale.

"Have it your way."

"Please, fuck me." His response was instant, and I was full of his

fingers as soon as I took my next breath. He was far from gentle as he thrust his digits inside of me. I rode his hand furiously as he gripped me around the waist, plunging them in and out, finding a rhythm.

"I love this pussy," he hissed, pulling me back so my head rested on his shoulder. I watched him fuck me furiously with his skilled fingers as he showcased my sex to me. He stopped suddenly, pulling his soaked fingers to his mouth, and we watched together as he cleaned them with his tongue. I turned suddenly, snaking my arms around him for support and taking his mouth in a fiery kiss. He obliged, just as hungry. I wrapped myself around him, my bare ass on the vanity as I heard his zipper. I swatted his hands away, only too eager to play my part, and gripped him, finding him hard and ready.

"You can't deny me, Devin," I said boldly as I ripped my mouth away, planting my feet firmly on the ground while keeping my eyes on his as I gripped him with my fist. "You want me just as much." His menacing chuckle only worsened my desire to get the best of him. I should have known by now it would never happen. He had never let me win.

"I can stop anytime I want," he fired back, zipping up his pants and taking a step in retreat. God, how I hated him.

"Fine. That's fine, Devin," I replied, pulling myself together quickly. "Gabriel offered to escort me home. I'll be more than happy to see what game he wants to play." I turned back to the mirror, fixing my smudged lipstick and lifting a brow. Devin showed no emotion whatsoever as he grabbed a towel, wiping the evidence of our kiss in the mirror off smoothly.

"Suit yourself," he whispered before placing a tongue-filled kiss on my back and leaving the room. I stood staring in the mirror. All those hours in the gym, all of those fucking fillers, creams, all of those months drinking lunch. What the hell was the point? I could fuck a man like Devin, but I could never keep him. A man like Devin had the attention span of a gnat when it came to women. I was a fool to think I was the only one in our six months of dating. Not only was I fool enough not to know he was married, but I was also sharing him with other women, or so I was told when his wife confronted me.

I didn't have to question why I was still fucking him. I wanted him no matter how bad he was for me. I needed to feel the way he made me feel.

And a part of me loved him…still.

That made me a fool. It made me completely blind. I was lovesick and dickstruck. Judge away, but unless you've been the center of Devin McIntyre's attention and the woman underneath him, you could never understand. Self-respect took a back seat to those few moments with that perfect cock. And before our relationship became only sexual, he'd had me convinced that he was much more than an amazing fuck.

I took one last look in the mirror and made my way out of the bathroom where Gabriel was waiting for me. He was a prime example of tall, dark, and handsome, and I had every intention of carrying out my threat. I was tired of being the one who abstained for a man who no longer pretended to care.

"Nina, you look beautiful," Gabriel offered as he lifted his arm at the elbow toward me.

"Nina, a moment," I heard behind us. I couldn't help my smirk as we both turned to face Devin.

"Don't keep her long, Devin." Gabriel winked at me as he kissed my hand and strode confidently down the hall. I watched him walk away then turned to Devin.

"A bit dramatic, don't you think?"

"Get the fuck in here, now," he ordered as he walked into the room he came from, which looked to be an office.

"I don't think so," I countered, turning in Gabriel's direction.

"Nina." His voice was ice. As much as I wanted to stand my ground, I wanted him more. I took a tentative step in the room and was jerked inside.

Last time, Nina, I promised myself.

"You're not fucking him," he hissed as he pulled my back to his front and gripped my breast, squeezing hard enough to bring tears to my eyes.

"Why not?" I asked shakily.

"You said please. I forgot my manners." He turned me around then lifted my skirt before pulling me with him to the couch where he sat down. He plucked my panties away easily and positioned my pussy next to his mouth so I was forced to straddle his seated body, my sex hovering over his face. With my hands braced on his shoulders, I watched as he buried his

tongue inside of me, making me moan loudly. My whole body shuddered as I rode his face, his tongue taking me furiously with long, vicious licks.

"Oh, God," I cried as he sucked me greedily. "Fuck, Devin," I praised as he brought me close. I felt my release start just as he pulled away and beat furiously on his shoulders. Ignoring me, he pulled me over his lap face down, lifting my ass up to resume his lapping. I parted my lips, taking in all the air I could when I heard his zipper. My sex clenched at the noise, and seconds later, he was sliding his girth into me inch by inch, filling me from behind. I moaned loudly as he grabbed a handful of hair, pulling me off the couch and into his lap as he again sat, impaling me. Leaning back, his shoulder cradled my head, we both gasped for air as he sank deeper inside of me. He gripped my hips, pounding into me furiously while I pushed off his thighs with my hands to match his thrusts. Feeling completely full, I cried out in praise as he tore into me.

"Nina," he breathed as he continued his assault. Turning my head, our eyes connected as I noticed the difference in his regard for me. His eyes had softened considerably, and for a brief moment, I saw the man who had first approached me nearly two years ago.

Don't look at them, Nina. He's a liar.

Devin leaned in to kiss me, and I turned my head hastily to avoid the intimate connection. He gripped my throat in anger and squeezed. I came instantly, my limbs shaking uncontrollably until I went limp like a ragdoll.

"Thank you," I murmured into his neck as I regained my senses.

"Turn around and ride it," he hissed, his contempt for me returning.

Ignoring my phone again, I took up residence in my favorite chair on the balcony that sat just outside my bedroom, listening to the waves roll in and the distant cries of beachgoers.

Summer was approaching, and I gave a small smile at the thought of wading through the waves. The familiarity of the act gave me a small amount of hope. I'd done it every year for as long as I could remember.

Maybe I could be her again one day. Maybe I could be the woman who found pleasure in the little things, the woman who didn't now crave corruption as a pastime, a woman capable of being nice to everyone.

I had treaded too far out into a world I had no business entering. I had become part of a circle where genuine smiles were scarce and the sharpening of claws was a daily occurrence, an active participant in a soulless lifestyle that seemed to have no fucking point at all.

Poor little rich girl, it's lonely at the top.

This was what people wanted? This was what I wanted?

That night, on the verge of sleep, the words my songbird sang to me replayed in my mind.

"Your misery makes you beautiful."

"Don't Gain The World & Lose Your Soul, Wisdom Is Better Than Silver Or Gold."

– BOB MARLEY

§§

SITTING AT MY desk at home the next morning, I cringed when I opened the email from Devin. To my surprise, it was simply my typical morning report of my stock progression. He governed both my corporate and personal portfolios, but I had no intention of keeping it that way. I might've been hard up for his cock, but there was no way I would continue to give him the power to shit away my fortune if he was so inclined.

STEP ONE: Dissociate

I wrote him back, requesting all my stocks be temporarily frozen and transferred to a new firm I had previously arranged. He would be forced to abide.

And I knew this move would be the beginning of the end for me. My phone rang immediately.

"What the fuck are you doing?" he hissed.

"Listen to me carefully, Devin. You've made enough off of me. I want to be free of you...completely."

The silence on his end of the line was deafening.

I started to speak again, but the phone went dead. A knock at my door twenty minutes later had my heart pounding. I closed my robe tightly and looked through the peephole.

Shit.

"Open the fucking door, Nina. I can see your silhouette," he barked.

I opened it quickly, and he barreled past me.

"Devin, listen..." I trailed off, realizing he had no right to be angry. We were over and had been for months. He had omitted a wife, and everything I'd thought about him was a lie.

"What *is* your excuse?" He whirled on me suddenly.

"I don't need one. You're the most dreadful bastard I've ever met. You knew I was new money and you took advantage and you won. You made a small fortune off of my investments. I won't apologize for anything. I want nothing more to do with you. You need to leave."

"I can afford to lose you, Nina, but why now?" I did my best not to look at him. Somewhere inside of me, weakness lingered for him. But he'd come a hell of a long way from the man I met to the man standing before me. The memory of his mouth all over me less than twenty-four hours ago would have to wait.

"I want to move on," I said quickly.

"Your pussy is not my paycheck," he said, taking a step toward me. "It's my pastime."

"Well, find another pastime. I'm done. I should've washed my hands of this as soon as I found out about Eileen."

"Always back to that." He took another step forward, the anger rolling off him in waves.

"I know, how indecent of me to bring up your wife, forgive me," I snapped. He took another step toward me, his blue eyes blazing as he attempted to corner me. If he got close enough, we would be fucking in a matter of minutes. I walked toward my kitchen, putting the counter between us. He said nothing as his chest heaved. He looked genuinely hurt, which confused me, but I was too fed up to care.

"Just what the hell were you thinking last night with that little stunt you pulled?" he asked carefully.

I shrugged, feigning indifference, then changed the subject. "If you can afford to lose me then what is the big deal?"

"I can't watch—" he cut himself off.

"Watch what...? My money?" I was certain that was the case; that I meant nothing to him. He'd spent the last few months proving that fact to me.

I received no reply as he ran his hands through his hair, all the while silently assessing me.

"So last night was a goodbye fuck?" he asked with no emotion on his face. I didn't even recognize him anymore. Secretly I was hoping for some show of emotion, but I knew better.

"Yes," I said quickly. "You may not have morals, but I'm trying to salvage what's left of mine."

He laughed bitterly as his brows rose. "If you aren't mine to play with, you will be someone else's. No one is going to take you seriously."

"Wow, now you're insulting me. Seriously, Devin, is this really you?"

I couldn't believe his audacity. I crossed my arms over my chest, no longer willing to let his cool demeanor or my lingering feelings toward him get in the way of what had to be done. We were over.

"I need a few days," he said, making his way toward the door.

"No, I want you to do exactly as you're told. Freeze it all… now. I will have my attorney on this within the next fifteen minutes," I threatened. He turned back to me, and I walked in front of him to the door, my hand on the handle.

"Nina, I'm asking you nicely here. I just need a couple of days," he pleaded.

"I really don't give a shit what you need, Devin. It's done."

He took a step toward me, his intention clear and evident in his pants. Our little exchange was turning him on. Either that or he thought he could manipulate me with sex. Not anymore.

"Fuck you," I hissed, turning to open the door. He slapped his hand against it, stopping me, his body enclosing mine as he whispered in my ear. "What's wrong, Nina? You want to be my Mrs.?"

"Never," I said harshly. "I just want out, Devin."

"You'll never be out, Nina."

I braved a look into his dark blue eyes and saw that look again: soft eyes paired with a gentle voice. It looked like concern. This man confused me to no end. I braced myself for his clean scent, the familiarity stirring me. My nipples tightened as he stood, still staring into my eyes. I mustered every last bit of resistance I had.

"What do you want, Devin?" He continued to stare at me, leaving me completely confused because I was sure that I had no effect on him. Had I really been that weak? He leaned in and very gently brushed his lips across mine. It had been so long I'd almost forgotten how gentle he once was with me.

"Please don't...just don't," I begged, my resolve slipping slightly. I forced myself to remember everything that had transpired since the fateful day I walked in on him and his wife.

I can do this.

Devin seemed to catch on. His hand slid down the door as he pushed away and released me.

"Let yourself out, Devin. I have work to do," I snapped, tearing my eyes away, too exhausted to fight him further.

He gripped my wrist and pulled me sharply to him. "Watch yourself, Nina."

My lips parted in surprise. "What the hell is that supposed to mean?"

"It means pay special attention to what you do next," he said quietly. "You want to be free of me, fine," he bit out as his fingers dug into my flesh. "But know you are on your own."

"Get out of my house," I said with a shaky voice. His grip loosened and that look returned, the look that told me he cared; the deceptive look that led me to this place. I let him see the very last tear I hoped to shed over him, and I felt his body visibly flinch though his face remained impassive.

"Goodbye, Nina." He let go of me and quickly shut the door behind him. Tears threatened, but I was done. He had come into my life when I was vulnerable and looking for acceptance. At one time, he had treated me better than any man ever had, fucked me harder, and kissed me longer. But I could only swallow so much poison before I got sick. And that's exactly what Devin was: poison packaged in a gorgeous smile and a mouth-watering cock. Our beginning was false, and our end was inevitable.

I decided against working the rest of the afternoon, tasking my assistant Taylor with a long list of things that had to be addressed. Of all the people in my life, she had the last small part of trust I had to give. She worked tirelessly to keep me a legitimate force to be reckoned with. She had an MBA from Harvard, and instead of running her own empire, she had opted to help me run mine. She was a savior and a saint, showing endless patience with me when it came to the details. I was a college dropout without a clue, and she was a powerhouse, a wealth of knowledge, and I would do anything to keep her.

In the last two years, I'd attempted to remedy my complete lack of knowledge by paying attention to the details. Though I would never fully grasp the majority of it, I was getting there.

"You sound sad," she noted on the phone. I looked up at the ceiling and took a deep breath.

"I'm fine," I answered after a short pause.

"Bullshit."

I laughed at her candor. She was a straight shooter. I guess if I had a single friend left in the world, it would have to be her, though we didn't spend much time together on a social level. I pictured her now behind her desk, multiple monitors cued up, feeding her greed for information. Her beautiful red hair would be perfectly pinned up and her dress impeccable. Her phone lines were probably lit up with important calls as she ignored them to weigh my mood.

One friend left in the world, and I paid her handsomely.

With a deep sigh, I resigned to get back to business. "I'm fine, Taylor. It was time to take out the trash."

"Aye, aye, and hear, hear! Finally!" She hated Devin with a passion.

"I moved all the accounts to the Garrison firm. Please follow up and make sure it's taken care of by day's end."

"Already on it," she said, typing at a sorcerer's pace.

"I never fully trusted him," I said under my breath.

"You got out easy. It could have been so much worse," she said simply. "I'll email you tonight."

"Taylor, why do you stick with me?"

She paused since my question was atypical. The first year of our relationship, I had kept it completely professional. The truth was, she had intimidated me a bit at first.

"I'm not ready to gamble yet," she said after a beat. "Besides,

I like to think we are in this together."

"We are," I confirmed as my eyes burned with fresh tears. I needed to hear that more than she would ever know. She must have heard the emotion in my voice because shortly after she offered to come see me. Taylor rarely made house calls.

"I'm fine, I swear. Hold it down for me, okay? I'll be back to it soon. I want to go over the list of properties."

"Oh, have something in mind?" she asked, sounding genuinely curious.

"Not yet, but I'm thinking about it."

"Talk soon. Proud of you, boss," she clipped out before hanging up.

I quickly called my lawyer, and within an hour I received confirmation from Taylor that Devin had indeed complied with my demands. I would spend the next few weeks with my new firm, pouring over my holdings and real estate investments. I wanted to keep things simple, and although Devin used my money wisely, he had diversified me too broadly.

A minute later I got an email. It was a list of the properties Devin's investment firm had purchased with my permission. I looked at the list briefly, deciding to get back to it later. My heart wasn't in it today.

I wanted to be hands on. I had no desire to waste my days away at the spa or fake my way through luncheons with false smiles with friends I didn't have.

Once I was uncovered as Devin's whore, I was kicked out of every circle I had so desperately weaseled my way into the last four years. Now free of Devin, I had nothing. I wasn't sure exactly where to go from here, but anything was better than the life I was living.

This wasn't living. I was surviving.

Making my way upstairs to shower and change, I felt my heart constrict once or twice but refused to humor it. Once dressed in designer, loose fitting slacks and a tight fitting, bust-enhancing blouse, I reached for some pumps. As I was artfully applying my makeup, I was suddenly disgusted with the stranger reflected in the mirror. I went back into the closet, opting for jeans and a t-shirt.

Watch yourself? What the hell did he mean by that?

I brushed my long, dark brown hair and scrubbed my freshly painted face off. I settled for a light dusting of bronzer on my imitation tan, some lip gloss, and a layer of mascara to accentuate my gray-blue eyes.

So this is thirty-one.

Reaching for my favorite pair of Chucks, I picked them up then slid them on. Deciding to drive myself, I relieved Carson for the day. I needed to disappear. I needed a drink. I picked my most inconspicuous car—my Mercedes—and let the top down. It was one of those seventy-degree weather days, not a cloud in the sky. They weren't a rarity in Charleston, but winter had lingered a bit too long. I reveled in the feel of the sun on my face as I drove over the two-mile Ravenel Bridge, observing the beautiful Charleston harbor with Sia singing in the background.

I drove out to Folly Beach to get some much-needed space from my usual scenery. The circle I had just alienated myself from wouldn't be caught dead here. Smiling to myself, I made my way down the busy Folly Road, delighting in the burst of new tourists who were bustling about, taking note of a few changes and recently opened storefronts. Breathing in deep, I caught a whiff of air from the vendor serving fresh boiled peanuts next to me. Folly was to me the essence of a little surfer town, with old school tourist shops at every corner. Local bars buzzed with live music as I drove past. The smells were heavenly wafting through the air. The strip seemed like a small carnival of color and texture.

This was home.

Pulling into the parking lot next to the Tides hotel, I quickly made my way toward the strip. I walked a few minutes, noting the amount of bodies I had to dodge. Charleston was growing, no longer the hidden gem of my childhood. I stood and watched a young street performer tear up the saxophone like he had been playing for well beyond his years and clapped wholeheartedly when he was finished. I leaned in and gave him a large tip, refusing to put it in clear sight. He took the money and shoved it in his pocket with a smile, not realizing the size of it. I winked knowing that later he would get a decent surprise out of it.

I walked into The Mystic bar and quickly took a stool. Having never been there, I noted the cool atmosphere. There was a small stage in the corner with room enough for a small crowd on the dance floor. The bar top itself was shaped oddly and took up the entirety of the rest of the space. It was the longest bar counter I had ever seen, starting at the entrance and leading in a series of waves out to the dance floor with stools on either side. The bartender smiled at me as I looked around. Somehow it worked. He took my order, and I continued to look around as I waited for my drink.

"Wow," I said as he handed me my Blue Moon with an orange slice.

"Yeah, it's different," he said then chuckled.

"Your place?" I asked as I noticed the color scheme of navy, light gray, purple, white, and lime green. Four floor to ceiling lava lamps cast dancing shadows around the bar, creating a glow that surrounded the space. Plants were strewn everywhere. It looked like I had wandered into a pothead's paradise. All that was missing was the incense.

"No, not mine," he answered. I looked up at him, and he was grinning at me. He tapped his fingers on the bar and quickly offered up, "Dave, holler if you need me."

With a smile, I thanked him before giving him a twenty, waving my hand when he offered change. He was young, maybe early twenties, with blond hair and blue eyes. I was sure when he wanted to hold a woman's attention he was more than capable. The bar was practically empty, but it was only 3 P.M. on a Tuesday. The majority of the patrons seemed to be on vacation by the way they were talking. I tuned them out to listen to the music playing. I sighed and took a long sip of my ice-cold beer. Delicious.

No matter how familiar I was with this city, there was always something new popping up. I settled in at three beers and noted the music being played was an amazing mix of old school and new stuff that I enjoyed.

When my next beer was served, I asked Dave to turn up the music.

"What station is this?"

"It's the owner's mix," he said. When he registered my appreciation, he agreed. "I know, he's got incredible taste and has playlists for days. It never gets old."

I smiled and accepted my beer before passing him another twenty. He raised his brows at me quickly. "You sure? I mean, I appreciate it, but you've tipped me enough to drink for days."

Ah, a good guy too. I'd have to tip him more.

"Yes, I'm sure. I'm on the last day of my vacation," I lied. "I didn't spend nearly as much as I'd saved."

"Cool, thank you, really." He seemed relieved. It's amazing what money could do.

"Where are you from?" A voice sounded behind me. Shit. I really didn't want to have to deal with this. I decided to handle it quickly as the stranger slipped into the chair next to me to await my reply.

"I'm really not in the mood for company," I countered as I took him in. He was decent looking, a good build with dark brown hair and a big smile, but I immediately brushed him off. "I'm sorry to seem so curt, but I just came to relax."

"You don't have to do it alone," he said quickly.

"It's my preference," I assured him, my tone growing impatient. He nodded, still holding his smile, though it didn't reach his eyes before wandering off. Four beers quickly turned into six as I watched the bar grow darker around me, all the while entranced by the lava forming and shifting in the large lamps. Realizing I was buzzed, I ordered a few things off their limited menu to try to sober up in lieu of calling Carson for my car. For some reason, I wanted to keep up my rouse to my new bartender friend, Dave, and didn't want to break the illusion by being picked up in my town car. I was someone else today. No longer Nina Scott, successful entrepreneur. I was just Nina.

As the night continued on, the bar grew more crowded, and I found it harder to avoid unwanted conversation. Making my way to a small table in the corner next to the stage, I watched a trio of men in my age range set up their instruments. The stage was dark as they tested their sound system. When I realized I was sitting next to a speaker, I moved to gather my food as the first strum of a guitar rang through it. I looked up to see the stage light and knew my gasp was audible when I saw the man in front of the microphone. He was nothing short of drop dead gorgeous. I cleared my throat, trying to mask the fact I was choking on the carrot covered in hummus I had just taken a bite of.

"Check one...two."

He nodded at the band, and they started playing at his cue. Reaching for the fresh beer Dave had just dropped off, I quickly downed it as I tried to pull myself together. I looked through my glass at the man mere feet from me as he started to play.

Jesus...Jesus! Sweet Jesus, he was beautiful! His body was toned, and his white t-shirt and cargo shorts clung to him like they worshiped him, a pair of well-worn Chucks completing his outfit. His slightly long, blond hair was styled in a spiky mess. I let my eyes drift over his perfectly sculpted, tan calves up to his muscular arms gripping his guitar. A leather cuff decorated one wrist and what looked to be a half sleeve tattoo adorned the other, partially hidden by the arm of his t-shirt. My eyes drifted up further to his neck, and I could see the strain as he began to sing.

That voice. I knew it. I sat frozen in complete and utter shock as he began to belt out an old Pretender's song that I loved.

God, help me.

Closing my eyes, I downed the rest of my beer as Dave approached with another round.

"A shot, anything, something…" I trailed off as the voice and amber eyes focused on my table. "Strong, Dave," I said as I averted my eyes. Dave chuckled as he noticed me visibly crumble.

Who knew I was a groupie?

"Dave." I stopped him as he started to walk off. "Who is that?"

"That's Aiden, the owner," he said, nodding in his direction.

"Don't look at him!" I said, quickly forgetting myself. The bar was still slightly empty, and I couldn't stop staring at the stage. I felt my cheeks flame.

For fuck's sake, Nina!

Dave took in my expression. "He plays on Tuesdays and Thursdays."

"Oh, um, cool," I tried to add with an air of nonchalance, even though it was anything but. Every word sung put me in a trance as I watched his skillful fingers pluck at the strings. After several minutes, I braved another look at his face. Luckily, he was roaming the bar with his eyes before closing them as he sang. When he reopened them, they met mine, and I grabbed my beer again, needing a distraction.

So much for sobering up.

He gazed down at me with eyes the color of freshly kindled flames. I'd never seen eyes of that color and was immediately transfixed by the fire smoldering within them. His face was perfect, cut from a cloth the likes of which I had never seen. The small amount of stubble on his jaw suited his style. He smiled at me then, causing my beer to slip out of my hands before landing loudly on the table. I corrected it quickly, managing to keep it from spilling. He smirked then looked away, working the filling bar with ease. He seemed completely comfortable in his skin, making me wonder what that must feel like. I took in his long lashes as he again closed his eyes, harmonizing effortlessly over the chords.

Dave delivered my shot, and I downed it without hesitation before handing him a stack of twenties.

"Look, I really can't keep taking these insane tips," he said, attempting to push the cash back into my hand. I nodded absently, taking the money back without argument. I had no time to talk. I was busy...lusting after a guy singing at a bar.

What the hell, woman?

Quickly coming to my senses, I turned to Dave who seemed confused by my behavior.

"I was a bartender a long time ago. This is a good day for you. Take it," I said sternly, dismissing him as I grabbed my phone to alert Carson that I would, in fact, need him. I set my phone down, ignoring the two missed calls from my mother. I was in no mood to listen to her rants, choosing instead to do the responsible thing and finish my plate as the band started a new song: Nirvana's "Heart Shaped Box."

Aiden...I wanted him.

When he finished the song, he thanked Dave, who handed him a beer. I watched the entire performance, mesmerized as he wrapped his full lips around countless melodies I adored. His set was a mix much like the music played in the bar, a mingling of everything old and new with some songs I assumed were his. I loved every single thing that was played. The music seemed to drag people into the bar, but when the female patrons noticed the man singing, their reactions were always the same: a dropped mouth and increased proximity to the stage. I chuckled at my stupidity. This man probably got ass on the regular from any woman of his choosing. The whole situation seemed ridiculous and sobering.

Yeah, Nina, you've officially hit bottom.

I got up suddenly, refusing to entertain my stupidity any longer, and walked over to the bar, handing Dave one last tip. He shook his head in exasperation while thanking me profusely.

At least one of us would go home smiling.

As I walked out of the bar, I felt foolish, my heart pounding and my face heated from the alcohol. I'd asked Carson to pick me up in his personal car to keep heads from turning and was about to slip in when I heard that lethal voice.

"Wait, excuse me."

Turning toward the source, I saw Aiden was fast approaching me, and I had to fight to keep my mouth from dropping open.

"Hi, you left your phone on the table in the bar," he said with a smile. The man was devastating up close. I couldn't help the lightning streaking through my every limb, making me even more aware of my attraction.

"You were playing," I said, sounding confused.

"Yeah, well, *they* still are," he chuckled. He held my phone out for me. His voice was deep and tickled all my senses. I grabbed my phone as he held it out to me and could feel my limbs growing weaker.

Nina! Get it together.

All I could think about was fucking him, him hovering above me, my legs wrapped tightly around him as his amber eyes burned a hole through me as I moaned beneath him. I wanted to say something about his voice, to compliment him, but I couldn't help my verbal outburst.

"I think about fucking," I said sincerely.

Oh...my...God.

His eyes grew wide, and he burst out laughing as I attempted to keep the vomit from erupting out of me.

Shaking my head quickly, I tried to deny the words I had just spoken. I chose my next words carefully as he stood with his hands in his pockets and a huge smile on his face, still laughing softly.

"I don't quite know what to say to that."

There was no rock to crawl under, and absolutely no way this conversation was going any further. At least he didn't know my name.

"I've had a lot to drink," I offered, the humiliation in my face burning. "What I meant to say is, I think you're fucking amazing, really. Your voice is incredible. Excuse me, goodnight," I managed, stopping Carson from exiting the car by opening the passenger door. He stared at me oddly but stayed put.

"Don't leave," Aiden said quickly, holding the door open for me as I got in. He looked at the older Carson with a question in his eyes but didn't ask.

"Seriously, your band is in there without a front man," I said with a smile. I saw a few girls clamoring out of the bar, disappointed until they noticed Aiden in front of my car. They turned on their heels and headed back in, making me laugh. I nodded over his shoulder as he smiled wide at my sudden laughter. "I really think you're needed back in the bar."

"Let me buy you a drink," he said before I could close the door.

"I'm all set. Goodnight," I said, closing the door. Carson drove away while I looked in the rearview to see Aiden looking at the car, perplexed, as he slowly walked back into the bar.

"Interesting evening, Ms. Scott?" Carson asked, amused.

"Carson, how long have you been married?" I asked, changing the subject. Never in my life, not even at my most vulnerable point, had I ever screwed up my verbiage so badly.

"Thirty-seven years, ma'am," he answered without hesitation.

"Wow, impressive," I said with a smile. We sat in silence for a few minutes before my stomach started rumbling loudly. I turned to Carson with sudden excitement. "I haven't eaten a carb in two years. Take me to Wendy's."

Carson looked at me with surprise.

"Wendy's!" I ordered enthusiastically with my fist in the air.

"Yes, ma'am," he replied with a chuckle.

"Sorry to burden you on your night off," I apologized sheepishly. "You can take tomorrow."

"Oh, that's all right. Wasn't in the mood for a TIVOed marathon of *Dancing with the Stars*," he said, letting me know I had saved him the trouble of arguing with his wife about what to watch.

"Married life, I remember that," I said, recalling fondly just the simple act of watching TV with Ryan when we were first married. That seemed light years ago.

Maybe I should just get away from Charleston for a while. I had already been to every single bucket list destination I'd wanted to visit. I hadn't exactly been a world explorer, but I had seen enough to be satisfied.

"If I may say, Miss, you seem...off," he said.

"Carson, I'm so screwed up," I conceded, "and it's more than a beer or two. I don't know what the hell to do. My old life disappeared, and my new one doesn't suit me, either. I'm not sure where I belong anymore." I didn't know why I was confiding in Carson. Maybe I just needed to verbalize the truth.

He glanced over at me as if he understood, but stayed silent for several moments.

"Maybe I should take a trip," I muttered absently.

"You'll end up back home," he said, making the turn into Wendy's. I understood what he was trying to say: my issues would still be waiting for me when I got back. Instead of answering, I opted for clapping in excitement.

"The biggest, I mean *biggest* cheeseburger possible. Fries. Large, Carson." I tapped on his shoulder excitedly. Why had I denied myself for so long? "And a big ass frosty! Yes! And whatever you want!" I couldn't believe my excitement at ordering fast food. When we got to the window, I checked my pockets, realizing I had given Dave all my cash and that my credit cards were in my soon to be towed car.

Shit.

"This one is on me, Miss," Carson said with humor as he grabbed the bag then handed the cashier a twenty.

Yep, it's amazing what money could do.

"Everyday is a bank account, and time is our currency. No one is rich, no one is poor, we've got 24 hours each."

– CHRISTOPHER RICE

§§

I MOANED, STILL BUZZED, and completely fascinated with my cheeseburger. I groaned minutes later when my feast was finished. My phone rang as I walked into my house and I answered, not bothering to look at the caller ID in my carb stupor, then heard my mother's voice.

"Hey, Ninabelle, how are you?"

"Mom, I'm tied up in a meeting, can I call you tomorrow?" I asked, feeling bad for my lie, and quickly adding, "Everything okay? Dad okay?"

"Yes, baby, we're fine. We miss you," she said sadly, tugging at my heart.

"Let's do lunch on Friday. I'll take you both," I offered.

"Your father has a tee off time around lunch, but I can come." I knew it was bullshit. She didn't want him to come, plain and simple. I would have to make a point to spend time with him separately.

"Okay, I'll pick you up, and call before I come," I said, adding an I love you before hanging up. Drunk on the phone with Mom and lusting after a bar band, front man...what a day! I laughed as I undressed and crawled into bed in just my underwear, reveling in the ridiculously comfortable sheets.

My phone rang again from my bedside table, but this time I hit ignore, freezing in place when I looked at the screen.

MISSED CALL: Aiden.

Slick.

I couldn't help the slow smile that graced my lips, or the quickening of my heart.

A text came through a few moments later.

Aiden: You ignored my call. That's just wrong. You wouldn't even have that phone if it wasn't for me.

Sitting up, I crossed my legs Indian style as I contemplated whether or not to call him back. Just that morning I had rid myself of a man who had been just as tempting. The pain that shot through my chest was enough to make me drop my phone, and I swallowed the lump that was threatening to emerge. I had cried for months over Devin. I had just freed myself.

Climbing out of bed, I turned off the lights and opened the door to my balcony, listening to the familiar and soothing sound of the waves. It was just cool enough to keep me sated. Half an hour later, I once again lay in bed, but sleep would not come, and I sat up, staring at my phone. Aiden may be nothing like the bastard I had just freed myself from, but I learned a long time ago I didn't have to have a Mr. Forever. It made absolutely no sense whatsoever for me to deny myself. Devin sure as hell hadn't shed a single tear over me. Aiden could be a welcomed distraction from my aching heart. Deciding not to dwell on a simple text, I typed a short reply then hit send.

Nina: Sorry, I was on a call.

I exhaled and sat back, waiting to see if he would respond. What the hell was I doing? Moving on, I guess?

Aiden: I have to know your name.

Nina: Why?

Aiden: Come on, it's a name. I already have your number.

Nina: Well, it wasn't given to you.

Aiden: I only had time to program mine in and text myself. I didn't have time to snoop around. But I will track you down.

Nina: There were at least twenty females in there tonight willing to give you more than their number. I'm sure they would be happy to give you their name and chant yours over and over.

Aiden: I saw you yesterday at the beach and then tonight at my bar. Are you sure you aren't one of those women?

I knew I had heard that voice. My songbird, of course!

Nina: Nina

Aiden: Finally. For someone who thinks about fucking you sure are hard pressed to give up your name.

Nina: Funny.

Aiden: Where are you? It's only ten o'clock.

Nina: In bed, safe, thank you, and very comfortable.

Aiden: Come see me on Thursday.

I laughed. This man really thought he had game.

Nina: I'll think about it.

Aiden: You should...you know, after you're done thinking about fucking.

I laughed out loud again.

Nina: Are you going to let that go?

Aiden: I'll think about it. See you Thursday, naughty girl.

Cocky too, nice.

And for a few minutes before I drifted to sleep I did think about fucking. Those eyes, those amazing eyes, and that voice... But those eyes, they weren't orange but...amber, the color of a low lit fire. His lips were perfectly plumped symmetry, and his smile was insanely boyish, yet his body language screamed all man. My God, just looking at that man had me completely unraveled. I felt giddy and excited, having butterflies for the first time...well, since Devin.

I immediately wished I hadn't texted him.

It was just word play. It meant nothing.

But that voice, it had a hint of southern drawl and was so deep, not baritone, but just right. Up close, he had strong features and was so completely beautiful. Way too flawless. I needed to find one. Next time I saw him, I would make sure to find one.

Next time?

I prayed for sleep to take me. Then I prayed harder that Devin was in some strange universe, sad about the end of us, though I knew better. Was I that insignificant? My husband shed me so easily. Then a man who I'd been screwing for the better part of a year didn't care enough about me to say one word to keep our fucked up arrangement going.

I let the tears finally fall, exhausting myself. That was what I had to do to finally get some sleep.

§§

Wow, it had been a while since I'd been hungover. I sure as shit could not get away with drinking so much anymore. I cursed as my doorbell rang then answered it in my soft suit of sweats.

"Wow," Taylor said, quickly pushing past me with two coffees and a paper bag in hand.

"Taylor, I told you I was fine," I said, turning to look at her after shutting the door.

"Why don't you have a butler or something?" she asked as she rounded my kitchen counter and pulled up a stool.

"I like my privacy," I said, taking the cup she offered as I approached her. I had a service come once a week, but my choice to have a house this size without a staff was out of pure paranoia. Devin and I were very indiscreet sexually, and often we would meet in my home. I was too afraid we would have an audience.

Don't have to worry about that now. And now my house is tainted.

"Well, I figured when we got off the phone you would hit the bottle hard." She chuckled as she slathered cream cheese on a bagel before taking a bite. She pushed the bag toward me and I cringed.

"No thanks," I said, taking a large sip of my tasteless, non-fat latte.

"You know the saying to get over one man you need to get under another?" Taylor said, absently sipping her latte as she eyed my reaction.

I smiled and shook my head in astonishment. "Is that what works for you?" I asked, curious.

"There is absolutely nothing a man can do for me but get me off, and even then he has to contend with me on quality, because I can do that for myself as well." She winked. I stood there open mouthed as she laughed before taking another sip of her coffee.

"Wow, you've never been attached?" I asked, completely awestruck.

"I've never met my equal, but I look for him," she said in a tone, as if to dismiss the conversation. "Now, I would love to tell you that I will leave you in your misery, but besides the obvious suicide watch, I am here on business." She opened a large folder and pulled out a stack of papers requiring my signature, eliciting a frustrated groan from me.

We spent the better part of the day pouring over them. I never signed a damn thing I didn't fully understand.

After Taylor left, I lay in bed the rest of the day, telling myself that it wasn't a pity party, that I was simply recovering from a horrific hangover.

I no longer had lunch at the Anchor Club on Thursdays. I no longer had Fridays at the Preservation Society. There would be no charity functions to collaborate on. And though I had dreaded most of those events, I now had a completely clear social calendar and nothing to look forward to.

Well, maybe one thing.

Aiden: See you tomorrow. Any requests?

Aiden.

I fell asleep with a smile on my face.

§§

The next morning, I awoke feeling refreshed and renewed. I spent an hour in my own personal hell—the gym—working off the prior evening's indulgence. I had worked incredibly hard on my body the last three years, losing twenty pounds and toning it into a figure I was proud of. It was one habit I refused to part with, and though I hated every minute, I loved the results.

Around nightfall, I slipped into a sexy, light blue, slinky dress and matching heeled sandals after spending a large amount of time lathering my skin in clean smelling moisturizer. I left my hair down in soft waves, dusted my eyes with a smoky, dark brown shadow, and finished with a simple, clear gloss.

Walking into the bar, I was a complete and utter bundle of nerves as soon as I heard Aiden's voice. He was singing Eric Clapton's "Layla". I made it a point not to look at him as I walked in, taking the closest seat to the entrance and glancing up to see Dave.

"Decide to stay a little longer?" Dave asked with a smile, though his eyes raked me with inappropriate appreciation.

I did wear this dress.

"Something like that," I said absently. He turned to pour my draft, and I shook my head quickly. "How about a vodka, soda with a lime, please."

"Sure thing." He looked at me oddly, as if he wasn't seeing the same person. That made two of us. After taking two very big sips of my drink, my eyes wandered to the stage. Aiden was sitting on a stool playing guitar, surrounded by eager women. As soon as I drank in his black, long sleeved, cuffed shirt, dark jeans, and motorcycle boots, my eyes shot up to his face. He was staring dead at me as he sang. I smiled and drained my drink, letting the hard liquor soothe my nerves.

I could think of worse reasons to overindulge, but I decided enough was enough and kept my eyes on him. I wasn't some teenage girl with a crush.

I was Nina fucking Scott, whoever that might have been.

When he had done a complete number on the women in front of him, he approached me where I sat at the bar without hesitation, grabbing the beer Dave offered.

"Nina," he said as he appraised me before taking a sip. "I vow to be a perfect gentlemen, but your dress tells me to act otherwise."

"Is that a compliment?" I asked with a grin.

"Well, you had to have seen what you look like before you left the house," he said, leaning in close. He smelled like heaven: a heady mix of clean man, his own special scent. My body responded instantly though I had been trained over the last few years to hide it well. "What are your intentions with me?" he asked in a whisper.

I leaned back, taking in the soft platinum, spiky tips of his hair, his scruffy chin, and perfect lips before losing myself in the intensity of his eyes. This man was walking sex.

"You assume too much," I said coyly, tilting my head and staring at the stool beside me. He shook his head quickly.

"Drink up, we aren't staying." He motioned to Dave who nodded. I reached into my purse to grab some money, and Aiden put his hands on mine. "Don't insult me." The feel of his hands had me jerking my head to look up at him. He was much closer now, and I felt my sex twitch.

For fuck's sake!

"Okay," I replied softly. His answering smile had me trying my best to not slide off the stool.

"Okay." He leaned in closer. "That was most definitely a compliment on your dress. And to think you had me at jeans and a t-shirt." He leaned back as my lips parted. His eyes brightened with my smile, and I realized he was still holding my hands resting on my purse. He pulled one close to his face and kissed it softly, caressing it with both of his before setting it back down.

"Let's go." He gestured as I stood up.

We walked to the Tides hotel and were immediately seated in the restaurant, BLU. I was sure he thought this was impressive to me, and I played the part as we both ordered without difficulty.

"So, Dave said you were on vacation. Where are you from?"

Aha! He thought I was just some tourist he could have a fling with. Perfect!

"And if you lie to me right now, I'll know it," he said quickly.

"What do you mean?" I asked, confused.

"Your area code is 843, Nina. It's a Charleston area code," he said, watching my reaction carefully.

Shit.

"So, I guess the question is," he said, gripping his beer, "why did you lie to my bartender?"

"I..." I looked down at my napkin, folding it over and over, then braved a look back at him. He frowned, stilling my hands.

"I lied," I said, meeting his fiery gaze across the table.

"Okay," he said, lifting the last part of the word and awaiting further explanation.

"The reason is completely ridiculous," I said, grabbing my wine and taking a sip. "I just...for one day wanted to be someone else, that's all. God, it sounds sad, doesn't it? Anyway, I never planned on coming back to your bar."

"But you did for me," he said with a confident smile. "I like that, little liar." He dropped the subject then, and I breathed out a sigh of relief. I stared at him, my own curiosity getting the best of me.

"Why are you singing in a bar?" I asked, then apologized quickly when I realized how demeaning the question came across. "I mean, not that there is anything wrong with it. It's just that you could be on a real stage somewhere. You could be really successful at it." He smirked before taking a bite of his perfectly cooked steak as I awaited his reply.

"I had the chance once. I passed it up." He didn't seem upset at all about that fact in the slightest. Wow.

"Well, I've never heard a voice quite like yours," I said, forking a bite of fish.

"Maybe you just like me," he said, dismissing his talent. I looked up to find him watching me.

"Maybe you're putting the cart before the horse," I said slyly. "Are we on a date?"

"I certainly hope so," he said with *isn't it obvious* humor.

"Well, what are your intentions with me?" I asked boldly, putting my fork down and matching his steady gaze.

"Not sure yet, but when I know, Nina, you will too," he said seriously. After paying for the bill, he grabbed my hand and led me to the tiki bar adjacent to the restaurant then steered me down toward the sand. He bent over, removing my sandals then held them in one hand as he laced our fingers together with the other.

We walked in silence for a few minutes until we reached the edge of the water. The moon was only half full as we strolled through the chilly sea foam.

We walked and talked for what seemed like hours while I spoke freely about who I was before I became a millionaire, blood-seeking adulteress. We talked a lot about music and our preferences, and I told him how impressed I had been with his bar playlist. He kept our hands firmly clasped as we made our way back toward Tides.

"So, divorced?" he said sadly, as if he knew the pain I'd gone through.

"Yes, but it was really for the best," I said, trying to hide the effect of his thumb sliding over the top of my hand.

"Then why are you so sad, Nina?" he asked as he turned to me, his hands stroking my bare shoulders.

"I'm not...sad. Or if I seem to be...I'm fine, really."

"Why am I so comfortable with you?" he asked, his back toward the water. He peered down at me while towering over me, and I damn near gasped at the hunger in his eyes. "Everything in me wants to take your mouth, stroke it with my tongue, snap that dress off with my fingers and bury myself inside of you, but something else is telling me not to."

Holy...Mary...Mother of God! Please listen to the first voice of reason.

"I'm not sad," I repeated.

"You'll have to convince me," he said, reaching in to stroke my chin and lips. I kissed the tips of his fingers and saw him visibly inhale. I no longer felt like talking. Leaning up on the tips of my toes, I brushed my lips against his. He leaned in to kiss me further, but I stopped him with a hand on his chest.

"Thank you for dinner, Aiden. But I don't have to convince you of shit." I heard his laughter as he followed behind me on the walk back to the hotel. I stomped through the sand, certain it was Devin's voice I had just heard demanding that I adhere to him. Another arrogant man who assumed I would bend to his will.

Well, fuck that.

"Nina, stop," he said, still chuckling. "God, you are a pain in the ass already." He laughed, picking me up so I was cradled against him. "Hard to get your name, lying, and now you're making me chase you...again," he added as he hugged me to him.

I pushed at his chest again and swung my legs down. I was forced to look up into his beautiful face to confront him, but I would not let it sway me. "Let me make something perfectly clear to you. A pretty face and good fuck…I've grown immune to those as a way of manipulation. So you might want to do yourself a favor and save yourself the trouble."

"Wow," he said animatedly, and with a hint of a smile on his lips.

"I know how I sound right now, but I'm serious, Aiden. If you can't show me something different, treat me differently, I'm walking. I don't need some demanding horse's ass telling me what to think, how to feel, and when to come."

There you are Nina fucking Scott!

He charged me, backing me up against a post underneath the pier before clamping his hand over my mouth. I uselessly fought him as he whispered in my ear.

"I have a filthy fucking mind, Nina, and I won't apologize for it. The possibilities are endless when I look at you and your ridiculous body. I want you." He ground his hips into me so I felt his erection. "It would seem right now you have all the power." I closed my eyes, trying to stifle my moan as he continued. "But I won't let you ruin an almost perfect first date because of what some asshole did before me. I'm not him." I opened my eyes as he lifted his hand, still holding our bodies tightly together. "I will most definitely never tell you when to come. I won't have to," he rasped out as his breath hit my neck. My entire body molded to his as I slumped against the post, all of the fight in me exhausted.

"And I haven't even kissed you...yet," he said, feathering his fingers through my hair then cupping the back of my head. "Tell me, Nina, when is the last time a man made love to you?"

I laughed nervously as my heart pounded in my chest, his lips a whisper away from mine.

"I thought so," he said before brushing his lips over mine. He pulled away then grabbed my hand, and I immediately felt the loss of his body and groaned inwardly.

It took me the length of a football field to find my voice. "What would have made this date perfect? You said it was *almost* perfect."

He chuckled. "Out of all that, that's what you ask me?"

I shrugged as we got to the parking lot. He turned to me and said, "I was pretty disappointed you don't like Rush. Seriously a great band."

I laughed loudly as he put his arm around me, walking me back to his club.

"I have another set in about twenty minutes. Will you stay?" he asked, sounding hopeful, as we stood outside the entrance.

I almost answered yes, but didn't want to see women ogle

him. I wanted to keep the intimacy of belonging to him for just one night a bit longer.

"I have a long day tomorrow. My *vacation* is officially over." I could see his disappointment, and it thrilled me.

"Hey, I never actually asked you what it is you do," he said, taking a step forward and placing his hands on my hips.

"I cater to the wealthy. I feed their greed," I said with disgust.

"Wow, that seems like a far shittier job than singing in a bar," he chuckled.

I opened my mouth to apologize again, but he silenced me with his finger, then replaced it with another infuriating brush of his lips. When we separated, I was panting, and disappointed, while he wore a satisfied smirk.

"If I kiss you, Nina, I won't be able to stop." I looked around the busy street with an eyebrow raised. "I don't think you would get away with that here."

"Should I be flattered you want to kiss me, or do you want to test my theory and be fucked in the street?" he asked, smiling wickedly.

Wow.

"Goodnight, Aiden."

"Goodnight, Nina." He leaned in, running his hands up my back and gripping my neck with his fingers, stroking the skin softly. I was instantly warm. He did this for several seconds before leaning in one last time and giving me that same chaste kiss. When he pulled away, he said nothing and simply smiled before turning to head into the bar.

I had no idea what I was expecting, but I certainly got a lot more than I bargained for.

And I wanted more.

"Greed is a fat demon with a small mouth and whatever you feed it is never enough."

– JANWILLEM VAN DE WETERING

§§

"WELL, THIS IS beautiful," my mother noted as we stepped out of the car to make our way out onto the rooftop at The Pavilion Bar. I quickly ordered a mojito, officially declaring myself an alcoholic. I'd had a drink every day this week.

"I can't believe you've never been up here," I lied, knowing my mother had been in hiding the better part of her life. I took in her expensive designer dress and perfectly manicured hair and was happy that the latter part of her life had changed because of my success.

"Nope, not once," she said, taking in the three hundred and sixty degree view of Charleston. We made small talk as we ordered lunch, and I was working on my fourth mojito when she decided to drop a bomb on me. "I'm glad you made time for me, honey. I wanted to talk to you."

Shit. I just wanted to eat my salad, drink some rum then leave. Come on, Mom!

"I'm divorcing your father," she said, staring at me as if weighing my reaction. I sat, mouth gaping, as the sun began to burn the crown of my head.

"Can we get an umbrella?" I shrieked at the empty hole in the center of our table. The waiter stared at me as if I was insane before turning to retrieve one.

"Ninabelle, listen, I haven't been happy for some time," she said.

"Trust me, Mom, you have made everyone aware," I said dryly. My poor father, this would crush him.

"Don't take that tone with me," she snapped viciously. I simply nodded, knowing there was no winning this argument. She was the victim, *always* the victim. I slurped my drink, my anger building.

"I won't buy you another house, and you are not forcing my father out of his," I warned.

"And why is that? Because I am finally trying to make myself happy?" she hissed.

"I'm not your meal ticket, Mom. I set you both up for the rest of your life. Make it work," I said, placing my card on the table for the bill.

"Why are you doing this to me?" she asked softly, trying to keep her voice weak so I would be sympathetic.

"No, Mom, why are you doing this to Dad? He's put up with your abuse for years just to be able to stay married to you. Now because you finally have nothing to blame him for, you want to leave him? I solved your damn problem." She gaped at me as I greedily sucked any remaining alcohol from my ice cubes.

Numb. Numb. Numb.

"I will not finance this divorce," I said, resolute.

"Fine," she said, closing down on me the way she always had.

"What happened to you?" I said, staring at her. She simply looked at me blankly. "I remember who you were before you became obsessed with money, and you were a cool lady." My mother stared at me for a beat before she burst into tears. I looked around us, horrified.

"Mom, I'm sorry, but you have got to stop this. *You* are the parent."

She refused to look at me as I threw my arm around her shoulder, leading her to the elevator. She cried the entire way back to her house while I apologized profusely. I knew better than to pick her up. Our relationship had soured years ago, and even more so when the calls started coming in about what I could "do" for her. It made me resent my money all the more.

She refused to acknowledge me when she exited the car. That's when I knew I was in for it. She rarely forgave me easily. Her love wasn't unconditional, and I had just purposely provoked her. I cursed my stupidity for the wrath I would be forced to endure. I would forever be sorry for hurting her, but not for what I said. My father deserved better. I may just give her what she wanted after all to save him from any more suffering.

I put my head in my hands in defeat as Carson drove away.

Fuck. My. Life!

My phone vibrated, and I looked at it, praying for a distraction.

Aiden: Plans today?

I couldn't help my smile at my answered prayer. Then I thought about the state I was in. I had already unleashed on him unnecessarily. He didn't deserve to have to deal with it again.

Nina: I'd make poor company. Another time?

Aiden: 2001 Palmetto Way. Half an hour.

I smiled as I gave Carson the address. I didn't give a crap about appearances. I wanted to drink in those amber eyes, hear his chuckle. I simply wanted him.

Pulling out my mirror, I fixed the smudges beneath my eyes and smoothed down my one-piece, black silk pantsuit. I had on killer heels that wrapped around the cuffs. I was dressed for execution, and that was my plan. I wanted this man. I'd spent the better part of my morning fantasizing about him. I was less than satisfied with my whisper of a kiss.

We pulled up to a large beach house about forty-five minutes later. There was no way around Carson pulling up in my town car. I'd told Aiden I catered to the rich. I could easily say the car was borrowed. My wealth should have no bearing on our dating, but I wasn't ready to come clean just yet.

Yeah, Nina, believe that lie all you want.

His home was beautiful, though it was far more modest than mine. I admired it immediately. It had much more of an ethereal feel. It was surrounded by palm trees and what looked like a private walk to the beach. I climbed his porch steps and shooed Carson away, making sure he was out of sight before knocking.

As soon as I knocked, the door opened. Aiden was standing, bare chested, and in swim trunks, his confusion clear as he took in my appearance. I was equally as stunned seeing the sleeve of tattoos that covered his right shoulder and most of his arm. It looked like half of a suit of armor. After a minute of appraisal, he smiled warmly.

"Hi," he said, ushering me inside.

"Hi, back," I flirted.

I looked around as he closed the door. The house was tastefully decorated in dark woods and pale accent colors, similar to mine. It was nice, far too nice for a bar owner. My curiosity was piqued, but I refused to pry, praying secretly for the same courtesy.

"I was just about to make margaritas. I didn't know if you would show," he said, grabbing my hand and leading me into his spacious kitchen. He had a door open, and I could hear the waves as I noted the spectacular view. The kitchen was slightly messy and had that lived in look.

Now *this* was a home.

I noted Lenny Kravitz singing "Again" from his docked iPod. Aiden watched me carefully from across the counter as I picked it up, scrolling through his library. I loved every single song he had programmed. After placing it back on the docking station, I turned up the volume a little.

I shook my head and looked up at him with a smile. "It's uncanny. It's like you know exactly what I love."

"Does it make you nervous?" he said with a smile. I opened my mouth to answer, but he started the blender. I made a face I'm sure was less than alluring, and he stopped the blender. "What was that?" I started to speak again, but he turned the blender on a higher speed. I rolled my eyes and took a seat at his comfortable breakfast nook overlooking the water.

"Sorry about that. We can't have your sassy mouth ruining another date," he said, bringing me a freshly filled margarita glass.

I licked the salt then took a sip. "I said I was bad company today."

"Oh, but you look so damn beautiful, Nina," he whispered

in my ear before grabbing my hand and leading me out to the deck. I sat in his oh-so-damn-comfortable-where-the-hell-do-I-get-one-of-these lounge chairs and watched the waves with my feet crossed at the ankles. Aiden picked up my discarded Louboutin and raised an eyebrow.

"Fair warning, I've already been drinking," I said, ignoring the obvious question in his eyes, and taking a huge sip of the perfect frozen concoction. "And I plan on drinking more."

"That bad?" he asked sincerely, placing my shoes underneath his chair.

"I don't think you would believe me if I told you *everything*," I replied, staring into my drink. "And I don't want to ruin this... This is amazing," I said, looking around me. I hadn't actually braved a long look at Aiden. I knew if I did it would be impossible not to touch him. I couldn't shake his stare. His eyes were on me, roaming every inch of me.

He's obviously fond of silk pantsuits.

"This could be a bad pairing, you know. A bar owner, a newly ambitious alcoholic," I said, laughing as I finally turned to him.

"Jesus, you're beautiful." His sincerity had me sitting straight up in my seat. I was beyond stunned as he washed me with his stare.

I fought hard to keep in my chair as I made a joke. "Have a few of these before I got here, huh?" It was anything but comical. I was having a hard time breathing as I let my eyes trail down his sculpted chest to the sexy light patch of hair just above his drawstring.

Fucking...yum.

"Well, Aiden, thank you, and you aren't so bad yourself." I lowered my lashes and batted them as I took another drink.

"Okay." He grinned as if he knew I was trying desperately to clear the air. He grabbed my empty glass and came back minutes later wearing a t-shirt. He gave me a wink as I moved my head back and forth to Lorde.

"So I thought I would take you surfing in the morning,"

he said, taking a sip and settling in the chair next to me. I set down my drink and turned to face him, leaving my head on the cushion and tucking my legs behind me.

"I forgot my toothbrush," I said, clearly not giving a shit.

He chuckled and looked at me again. "What's wrong, sad girl? What can I do?"

"Just be here," I said, smiling. "This is good," I said, honestly.

He exhaled loudly but dropped it as we sat soaking up the sun.

§§

I woke up as the sun was setting, and hadn't realized I'd dozed off. Aiden had covered me in a blanket, and I shook it off quickly to look for him to apologize. I found him in his kitchen sautéing vegetables. He had showered, and his hair was still damp and lay loosely over his forehead. I watched him for a few minutes. His outfit was the same: a white t-shirt, shorts, bare feet, and completely and utterly fuckable. He smirked as he noticed me watching him.

"Sleep well?"

"I'm so sorry," I said, mortified. I knew I must look like a mess and suddenly had an unbearably full bladder.

"Restroom?" I asked.

"Around the corner," he said, still smiling. "By the way, you would make a terrible drunk."

"I said ambitious, not experienced," I reminded him, smiling in return. I walked into the bathroom, noting my horrible, mangled hair and the dark smudges underneath my eyes.

First things first.

I reached behind me to pull the zipper down on my pantsuit and found it was snagged. I started jumping around, back and forth, clenching my insides desperately as I tried over and over to work it down. This was bad. I was certain one more minute would have me mopping his floor.

After several minutes, I opened the door, calling for Aiden.

He came to my aid with a laugh as I danced around like a lunatic.

"Please, hurry." I exhaled, using all my willpower to keep from losing control.

"It's stuck pretty bad," he said, carefully trying to tug at the zipper. After a few attempts, I felt the dam about to burst.

"Please, Aiden," I said, my voice in agony.

"Let me go get—"

"Bust it. Please rip it open. Seriously, please just rip the fucking thing open," I begged. He laughed hysterically as I damn near started crying. He finally relented, busting the zipper and pulling it apart with his fingers. I thanked him by slamming the door in his face.

A few minutes later, while I was trying to get the scraps of my outfit around my body, Aiden cracked the door, tossing in a t-shirt and jogging pants. Once I was dressed, I braved my way back into the kitchen, my pantsuit no longer a clothing option.

Aiden was spooning out vegetables as he looked up at me. We both burst out laughing as he made his way toward me.

"Never a dull moment, Nina," he said, taking my pantsuit from out of my hands and throwing it on the counter. He pulled me into his arms then picked up a piece of fajita meat and put it into my mouth.

"Oh, so good," I mouthed around the bite.

He smiled as he released me to continue his task, but I stopped him by thrusting my hands into his hair and pulling him toward me. "Thank you," I said softly before brushing my lips against his. I pulled back and watched the fire light in his eyes. We stood there staring at each other for a brief moment before Aiden finally took my lips in a kiss.

Finally...oh my God.

Aiden didn't just kiss me, he disintegrated my planet. The minute his tongue swept my lips asking for permission, I gripped him to me, opening up as far as I could go so he could get his fill. Our tongues melded together perfectly, and I moaned into his mouth. He instantly lifted me to sit on the counter, never breaking our connection, only stoking the heat as he nestled himself between my parted legs. I moaned again as he ground himself against me, gripping my neck and pulling me closer to him. When he pulled away, we were both panting.

"Fuck, woman, why did you have to declare that you needed a nice guy last night?" he whispered as he leaned in again, taking me completely. I was on fire when he pulled away.

"I only said it to even the scales. Fuck me...right now."

He froze then pulled away to study my face, quirking an eyebrow. "Interesting."

"Aiden, just trust me on this," I said, frustrated. "I'm not innocent."

He gently lifted me from the counter and put me on my feet. "Let's eat," he said, grabbing a platter of food.

"Are you serious right now?" I asked, exasperated.

"Are you going to elaborate?" he asked quickly.

"No," I responded firmly.

"Then let's eat," he said, pulling out a chair for me. I stalked over and took a seat. I wasn't going to beg the man to fuck me.

He sat next to me and started to build his fajita, and I followed suit, watching him with curiosity. Did I have no effect on the man? I was still ready to combust.

"Would you be offended if I opted to go home this evening?" I asked, piling steak onto my tortilla.

More carbs, great.

"Absolutely," he said, taking a mouthful without looking at me.

"And why is that?" I said testily.

He set his food down and turned to me, forearms on the table, a small smile tugging at the corners of his lips. "Because, naughty girl, you aren't throwing a fit with me. I won't allow it. And I can't take care of that ache between your thighs if you flee."

This time my brow quirked as I watched his lips form into a full, panty-dropping, megawatt smile. I couldn't help but mirror his expression.

The food was amazing. I loved that he could cook and asked him where he learned it.

"Food Network," he replied as he pushed his plate away.

"Really?" I said around a mouthful of my second fajita.

"No," he said with a grin and turned to me. "Who exactly are you, Nina? Because from what I can tell, you haven't been honest with me much at all."

I froze mid-bite, no longer hungry.

"Pardon?" I said, wiping my mouth and fidgeting with my beer.

"The first time I saw you, you were on the beach in a dress worth thousands, then you show up to my bar wanting to be 'someone else' dressed for a Grateful Dead concert. Last night you came to our date in a fuck me dress fit for a high-class call girl, and today you show up in a limo dressed like Ivana Trump. It's obvious you don't cater to the wealthy. *You* are wealthy. I guess my question is, why are you trying to hide it?"

I sat stunned and completely...busted.

"Aiden, I—"

"Before you say a word, I want you to think about it, okay? Just think about it. You don't have to answer me tonight," he said, gathering our plates and walking them to the sink.

I remained seated, feeling like I had just been lectured by my father. I couldn't believe he had just done that to me. I picked up my beer, grabbed another, and then headed out to his porch. I had no idea how long I sat out there thinking.

Damn it! All I wanted was a distraction! I had no idea why I hadn't left his house yet. A simple text to Carson would clear me of having to explain myself, or having to explain the woman I'd become and why I was running. I didn't know how Aiden would look at me if I told him the truth. The fact that I cared what he thought was even more disturbing. When I finished my second beer, I headed inside to find him and wish him a good night.

After a few minutes of searching, I found him in his garage

waxing his surfboard. The mere sight of him had me reneging on my decision.

"Running?" he asked as he stroked his board.

"Not yet," I said, making my decision in the moment.

"Good," he said, lifting the board. "Nina, I want to know you. It's not a crime."

"I just can't figure out why."

He shrugged, coming toward me and taking my hand.

Always taking my hand.

"We are waking up early. Let's go to bed," he said, leading us up his stairs to his bedroom. His bed was huge, and he seemed to take his comfort seriously. It sat in a large, tastefully and simply decorated room with an adjacent balcony. He opened the door, and I could hear the faint crash of the waves. I stood, stunned, loving that his routine was eerily similar to mine. "Extra toothbrush in the medicine cabinet," he said, taking leave of the room. I walked into the bathroom, taking a few minutes to clear my head. He had questions? Well, I had some of my own. Like what the hell did he want with me? Why the hell was he so guarded himself? I thought about his kiss in the kitchen and took a deep breath. The man kissed me like he was desperate for more, yet he'd backed away so easily from going any further. I felt the ache growing inside of me and did my best to temper it before I opened the door. Aiden was laying there, his perfect bare chest peeking out beneath the sheets. He eyed me with a smile and lifted the covers on the opposite side of the bed. I slipped in next to him, and he turned his body toward me so we were facing each other.

"Thank you for dinner," I said softly.

He reached out to stroke my face, and his fingers trailed across my lips. I kissed them lightly as I got lost in the fire in his eyes and he pulled me closer to him.

"I don't think I can hang on much longer," he said, stroking my collar with his thumb.

"Why are you?" I whispered.

"You need me to," he said softly.

"Why is that?" I asked, my pulse kicking as his hands caressed me.

"You told me so," he said, taking my face in his hands and leaning in to kiss me. The kiss was gentle and reassuring. He wanted me as much as I wanted him, that I was sure of.

When he pulled away, he whispered "Goodnight" then turned off the light next to him. I spent an hour staring at the dimly lit ceiling before the waves' melody lulled me to sleep. I woke up hours later in Aiden's tender grip. I held his arms firmly around me and stroked them with my fingertips. I hadn't been held like that since I was married. It was the most comfortable I'd felt in years. I'd damn near forgotten what intimacy was like. Devin had never spent more than a few hours with me, and it was never overnight. Did I really think that bastard had treated me well? *This* man had let me into his home and his bed and was somehow trying to be virtuous. I couldn't help the tears that escaped me. I cried softly, mortified of waking Aiden.

You are seriously fucked up, Nina.

Lonely was more like it. I'd made my fortune and built my castle, and then exiled myself in it.

If Aiden wanted the truth, he would have it. I wanted to trust again, though I had no reason to trust a single soul in my life. But what I was most sure of was I didn't want to be alone anymore.

§§

"Wake up, naughty girl," Aiden said softly. A brief whiff of coffee had my eyes opening. Aiden sat on the bed next to me, a steaming cup in his hand. "Surfs up," he chuckled.

"I'm horrible on the board, bra," I said, quickly burying my head under his pillow.

He laughed loudly as he set the coffee on the nightstand beside me. He pulled the pillow away from me, and I peeked up at him. "Seriously, Aiden, this is the most comfortable bed in creation. Can we just hang out here?"

"I'll make you a deal," he said, lifting me to a sitting position. "You come with me for a few hours this morning, and we will do whatever you want today."

I nodded with a smile. Aiden was already dressed in board shorts, his hair styled to spiky perfection and sunglasses tucked into his t-shirt collar.

"I have nothing to wear unless you want me to surf in this." I pulled the waist on his sweats to show him how much wiggle room I had.

"I have a wet suit. The water is still a little cold," he said carefully.

"And you just so happen to have one in my size?"

"I got it off of what's left of your outfit. The shop opened at 4 A.M. I've already eaten breakfast, too."

I grinned. "I would applaud you, but honestly, it's a fool's errand. I seriously have no skills."

"We'll see. The suit's in the bathroom. Hurry up!"

§§

"Son of a bitch!" Aiden roared behind me, "You little liar!" I'd stolen another wave and rode it out. I laughed and lost my balance, diving into the surf. Aiden paddled toward me, cursing.

"You have no manners," he said, sounding agitated. It was the fifth wave I'd taken from him in the last half hour.

"Oh, I have no doubt I lack etiquette seeing as it's six in the morning! Besides, a baby could surf these!"

I straddled my board as he paddled toward me. He was grinning as he waded through the water. He sat up on his board and tilted his head. He looked gorgeous in a wetsuit, his hair scattered around him, his eyes bright and his lashes thick and wet.

"Now is the time to come clean. What other hidden talents do you have?" He smirked, and I splashed at him.

Now or never, Nina.

"I made two hundred million dollars off of a body care program I created." I looked up just as his face went completely blank. I decided to just throw it out there; the worst was over.

"I was sitting at home one day watching that old movie Cocktail. You know the one?" He nodded, still absorbing my admission.

"Well, I got to that part where he explains about the need for the little drink umbrella, and how the man who made it was a millionaire. And it got my wheels turning. You know, create a need, or at least something that people may think they need. I Googled the most lucrative businesses, pharmacy companies, and—"

"Fitness, a multi-billion dollar industry," he finished, urging me to go on.

"I majored in nutrition in college and thought I would try to put it to use. At first, I was just doing it for fun. I was a bit of a hobby enthusiast, you know, just passing the time, and then it hit me. When I told you I catered to the wealthy, it wasn't a complete lie. I researched the habits of the wealthy and learned that at least seventy percent of them exercise. So I narrowed it down even further and decided to design the program for wealthy women. It took me eighteen months to develop. One amazing meeting with the right woman and a few modifications later, and we introduced it to the general public. She convinced me that working class women would spend just as much on their vanity. She was right. Within a year, I was a millionaire."

"That's incredible," he said, running his fingers through the water.

"No, Aiden, it's not," I said with a sigh. "I haven't been the same woman since. This wave is yours," I said, nodding toward the rapidly rolling water.

"It can wait," he said, waiting for me to finish. Instead, I took the wave again as he cursed me.

"Well, I am obviously not going to get any surfing done today!" he screamed as I made my way to shore. I gave him a smug smile as I lay on the sand, teeth chattering. A few minutes later, Aiden joined me. We lay staring at each other, our fingers playfully dancing.

"I think I know what my intentions are now," he said playfully.

"Oh, yeah, now that you know your new girlfriend is loaded," I said in jest.

He frowned. "Is that why you didn't want to tell me?"

"Well, my last boyfriend, and, oh, my ex-husband didn't fare so well," I said, looking at our linked fingers.

"Who says you're my girlfriend, naughty little liar?" he said, leaning over to brush a kiss on my lips.

I tried to hide my embarrassment by turning over on my stomach and running my hands over the sand.

"Aiden, what do you want from me?" I whispered. He pulled me so I was lying on top of him.

"First, I just wanted a date, then I just wanted to have a margarita, and then I just wanted to take you surfing. Honestly, now, I would just love to spread your legs and lose myself for about a day, maybe two."

His mouth was on mine before I had a chance to reply. His tongue stroked mine repeatedly as I moaned into his mouth, hearing his answering groan. When we finally broke away, we sped to the car, racing back to his house. He carried me upstairs over his shoulder as I cried out loudly in surprise. When we got to his bathroom door, neither of us hesitated. He turned me away from him, pulling the zipper down on my wetsuit and I turned around and did the same for him. We both pushed them off our shoulders and let them hit the floor, me naked beneath mine, him in swimming trunks, which he lost quickly. Every single part of him was carved to perfection. His beautiful cock captured the rest of my breath as my teeth began to chatter. He stood, appraising my body. I reveled in the way his eyes lit, burning embers searing my goose bump covered skin. He reached behind him, turning on the shower, then pulled me to him, quickly filling my mouth with his tongue. I traced the contour of his chest with my hands, anxious to get the sand off him so I could explore him with my tongue.

He pulled me into the steaming shower as we worked furiously between long kisses to get the sand off. It was everywhere as we repeatedly shampooed each other's hair, still coming up with a handful of sand. We began to laugh hysterically as we used an entire bottle, finally coming clean. When all traces were gone, Aiden slid his thumb across my lip, and I captured it, sucking mercilessly. The fire was back, and there was no longer a smile on his face. It was replaced with need. He backed me up against the tile wall and held my hands on either side of my head.

"Leave them here," he ordered, pressing my hands against the tile. He took special care, tracing every inch of my body with his hands before replacing them with his lips. He took my nipple into his mouth, sucking with thirst as I arched my back, offering more. When he pulled away, he massaged my other breast in his hand as he spoke.

"Spread your legs." I obliged immediately. He reached up and pulled my hair gently so my throat was fully exposed to him as his other hand slid between my thighs. The brush of his fingertips on my clit had my knees buckling. He pushed me back up against the wall with force as his mouth covered my exposed throat. He stroked my neck with his tongue as he slipped his fingers inside of me.

"Aiden," I gasped as he stroked me without mercy, his fingers thrusting in and out while his thumb circled me. I felt the friction of his fingers as he roamed my neck with his kiss, overwhelming me. Tension built unbearably until I came with a cry as he pulled away from my throat, watching me come.

"Fucking beautiful," he said, slowing his strokes as I rode out my orgasm.

He leaned in and kissed me before turning off the water and stepping out of the shower. He wrapped me in a large towel and carried me to his bed. Still reeling from the pulsing in my body, I was in a daze as he laid me down and began to wipe the water away. He started at my legs, swiping at the moisture, then planting hot kisses on the newly dried skin. I writhed beneath him, aching for his cock. He pushed my hands away as I reached for him, taking special care to dry me and then torture me with long silky kisses on my thighs. He spread my thighs wider as he cupped my ass, pulling me to his waiting mouth. My body jerked, my clit already sensitive from his touch. But his tongue made a fool out of his hand.

I moaned his name as he licked at me long and leisurely. I fisted his beautiful, blond hair, circling my hips as my orgasm built. He looked up at me as he tongued me, the heat in his eyes bringing his name across my lips in a prayer.

"This..." he said, sliding more fingers into me then licking me off the fingers he'd buried inside me. "This is so fucking good," he murmured.

"Coming," I said softly as my body shuddered.

My orgasm seemed to last forever as Aiden continued to bathe me with his tongue. I gripped his hair and forced his head up when he made no move to stop.

"Please, Aiden," I begged.

He leaned down, filling my center with his talented tongue, pressing my stomach as he pushed it in further. I fisted the sheets, my body spilling again for him. When he was satisfied, he brought himself back to me, and I kissed him with so much fever he had to pull away to take a breath. Panting heavily, he looked down at me with need in his expression. I gripped him tightly in my hand, reveling in the naked feel of his impressive cock.

He reached over and dug through his nightstand, coming up with a condom. As soon as he was fitted, his body covered mine once again. He kissed me deeply and thrust himself inside as he invaded my mouth. My entire body arched off of the bed as he pulled out halfway and spread my legs further. He thrust again fully then stopped, letting me feel all of him. He stilled, so my eyes shot to his as he hooked my leg and pushed in deeper, filling me to the brink.

"To be deep inside this perfect pussy is what I want, indefinitely," he said, circling his hips as he pulled out of me and thrust in again. I came, digging my nails into his arms, begging for more. He kept his pace slow as he filled me over and over, his lips caressing my skin, sucking my aching nipples. I gripped his ass, pulling him to me as I wrapped my legs tightly around him. He moaned as I met his thrusts and I felt him quicken and swell inside me. He gripped the headboard behind me, grinding himself into me as I tightened again beneath him.

"Fuck, Nina, baby."

He let go as I shuddered with him. He collapsed in a heap on top of me as I took the opportunity to explore his perfectly toned arms and back. I caressed him as he gathered his breath then he looked up at me with a heart-stopping grin. I smiled back as he took my lips in a soft kiss.

He disappeared into the bathroom and came out with baby wipes. I gave him a questioning look.

"If it's good enough for a baby's ass, it's good enough for ours," he said with a chuckle.

"Sexy pillow talk," I said with a grin.

After a wipe down with the baby wipes, we both collapsed in bed. He wrapped his arms around me.

"You like this," he said, holding me tighter to him.

"How do you know?" I asked.

"Last night, when I held you," he said softly.

"You don't miss anything, do you?" I said coolly, burying my face in the pillow, knowing he had heard me crying.

He pulled me onto his chest and held me tightly to him. "I like it, too." I nodded, trying to tamp down the emotion building as he looked at me so sincerely.

"Just do me a favor, don't say things you don't mean," I said, nuzzling his neck.

"Such a cautious woman, but at least I know why," he said,

his fingertips putting me in a daze. He leaned in and whispered, "Thank you."

"Oh no, sir," I said, placing my hands under my chin on his chest, "I should be thanking you."

"That's not what I'm talking about," he said with a smirk.

"I know," I said, planting a kiss on his chest.

We ate dinner on his deck that night. This time I put my skills to use, and he was more than appreciative. I stayed another night at his urging, not that it took much effort to convince me. Before we went to sleep and after he'd had his way with me, he wrapped my arm around his waist. I guess it was his turn.

§§

The next morning I woke to an empty bed. Apparently, Aiden was an early riser. I had no obligations but knew it was time to make my exit. Freshly showered, I walked downstairs in the oversized t-shirt Aiden had laid out for me. I could only imagine the questions that would be circling around Carson's head as I joined him at the car in sweats and high heels.

"Aiden?"

"In here," he called from the kitchen. The Red Hot Chili Peppers sang "Give it Away" as I observed him plating pancakes.

"Morning," I said with a smile. He looked up at me with a brilliant smile of his own, his eyes roaming me in his oversized t-shirt. The amber globes heated as I stood there thinking delicious thoughts of what we'd done last night. He seemed to be thinking the same.

"It's about time," he said, rounding the counter. "I've been slaving away," he scorned.

"It looks amazing, really, but I don't eat carbs," I said as he crashed into me, kissing me with a greedy tongue.

"I don't give a fuck right now," he said, taking my lips again.

Whoa, he must be fond of t-shirts as well.

He walked me over to the breakfast nook and pulled off my t-shirt. He took a single finger and rubbed it between my thighs, feeling me ready for him.

"Are you on birth control?" he hissed through clenched teeth.

"Yes," I whispered back.

"I want to come inside you," he said as he plunged one, then a second finger inside me. My desire was audible as I panted. "I'm safe, Nina, but I'll wait."

I shook my head. He instantly turned me around to face the table then lifted my leg so my knee rested on it. His hands roamed my back as I waited to be filled, aching and burning for him.

"I woke up craving you. I should have just taken it." I was instantly full as he slammed his cock inside me. He fucked me viciously as I braced myself on the table, moaning uncontrollably.

"I want to be the only man who gets this, Nina. The *only* one." He groaned as his thrusts picked up speed. I came loudly, begging for more as he thrust again and again relentlessly until he came minutes later, filling me in hot spurts. He wrapped his arm around me, rubbing his orgasm all over me, between my lips and up and down my drenched pussy. He circled my clit over and over, continually rubbing his cum on me and into me as he whispered, "I want you with me, Nina. I really want you with me," he said as he kissed my neck and I gave into his skilled hand. "I'll worship this perfect body as long as you'll let me." His hand slowly stopped, and he led me upstairs so we could both wash off. I stayed silent as I thought about what he asked me. Yesterday I'd practically declared myself his girlfriend. Is that what I wanted? And just because he wanted to exclusively fuck didn't mean he wanted a relationship. It was too soon.

I could be sexually exclusive...with Aiden.

"I've called my car. It's probably waiting for me downstairs," I said, pulling on the jogging shorts I'd taken up residence in. Well, besides the nearly twenty-four hours I'd spent naked.

"Leaving?" he said, wiping off his chest.

"Yeah, I have to get home," I said, refusing to look at him.

The truth was, I had absolutely nothing to do, but he didn't need to know that. When I felt strong enough to see him naked without dropping to my knees and thanking him for the weekend with my tongue, I kissed him goodbye. He insisted I wait until he dressed so he could walk me to the door.

"I had fun," I said, kissing him slowly and pulling away with a smile.

"Me too," he smiled. "Talk soon, naughty girl."

"Bye," I rasped out, finding my trusted driver right where he should be. I smiled at Carson and turned back to smile at Aiden, who was looking at me from the door. I sat back in the limo, laughing at my clothes.

"I was getting worried," Carson said. I was touched by his concern.

"Sorry, Carson, I should have texted."

"It's all right if you're all right, Miss."

I smiled broadly at him in the rearview mirror. "Never better."

"A man is rich in proportion to the number of things which he can afford to let alone."

– HENRY DAVID THOREAU

§§

"GOOD MORNING," TAYLOR chimed on the phone.

"Sure is," I replied happily. Her sudden pause on the phone made me giggle.

"Well, someone had a good weekend," she said, not hiding her surprise. Had I really been that dreadful lately?

"I did," I agreed, stretching in my bed as I put her on speaker and walked to my closet.

"I have a few things to discuss with you. Do you have a few minutes?"

"I'm coming in today," I said, feeling guilty for having been so absent. "I'll be there in an hour. Can it wait until then?"

"Sure. The most pressing is an offer on one of your properties. The Garrison firm said they have been pushing for a quick sale."

"Really?" I asked, intrigued. "Send me the outline, and I'll see you shortly."

"Sure thing," she said then hung up. I stood in my closet in a daze, still deliciously sore from the exertion of this weekend. Aiden and I had spent hours familiarizing ourselves with each other's bodies. He hadn't pressed me further about anything personal, and I realized I hadn't asked much about him at all. I didn't even know the man's last name.

I stood, surrounded by the world's most accomplished designers, as I thought of how he'd kissed me, roamed my body with his touch, and promised to worship it as long as I let him.

My phone vibrated as I settled on a Donna Karen sheath dress and smart shoes. I looked to see the object of my intrigue was thinking about me too.

Aiden: Before you go rule the world today, just know I meant what I said. I want to rule your body.

Nina: Well, I have to admit your résumé is impressive.

I carried out the quick task of a shower and couldn't help but to glance at my phone after I dressed. He was already getting under my skin. His hands and mouth lingered on me deliciously.

Aiden: I'll see you soon, naughty girl.

He was both a sensitive and extremely dominant lover. I marveled at that thought alone. I spent the entirety of my time at my vanity, makeup in hand, thinking about his perfect cock and how amazing it felt to be completely full of him.

I wanted more.

§§

On the way to my office downtown, I opened the email listing the properties Scott Solutions held. I scrolled through them, familiar with most of the addresses. I opened a new email and saw the address I had an offer on was in Savannah. Puzzled, I looked at the list Taylor had originally sent me. All of the addresses were in or around the Charleston area. I walked into work and greeted Taylor, who followed me into my office. She looked flawless in a pinstriped pencil skirt and white blouse, her hair perfectly combed into a sleek ponytail.

"This property has an offer?" I said, pulling it up to get a better look on my monitor.

"Two now, actually. I researched it some, and it looks like it's never been developed." She looked at me just as puzzled. I scrutinized the picture and saw it was basically a riverfront patch of grass with a small shed that sat under an old Spanish moss covered tree.

The office phone rang, and Taylor answered as she sat across from me by pressing her headset. She looked at me and rolled her eyes, and I knew instantly it was Devin. I was in far too good of a mood to have him ruin it, but Devin rarely called without a purpose.

"Good morning, Mr. McIntyre," I said as Taylor took her leave and shut the door behind her.

"Regretting your decision yet?"

"Sure am, I knew better than to pick up the phone," I said dryly.

"I need to speak with you privately," he said, as if he wasn't alone. I could picture him now, staring out his office window in a perfectly tailored suit, ignoring some client vying for his attention.

"Sorry, I'm on my way to Savannah," I said, texting Carson to bring the car around.

There was an extremely long pause before he replied. "Oh, what's the reason?"

"Well, apparently I own some land there and have very interested buyers. You should know all about it, right? It was your purchase?"

"It was," he replied sharply.

"Devin, what can I do for you?"

"Meet me right now. I can be at your office in twenty minutes."

I sighed into the phone before replying, "No."

"Listen to me, Nina. I need to talk to you, just wait there." His tone was urgent and demanding.

"I don't take orders from you anymore, Devin." I hung up, not giving his silver tongue a chance to work its magic. I'd already been that fool.

There was no way in hell I was waiting for him. I gathered Taylor and minutes later we were on our way to Savannah.

"I called the realtor. She is meeting us there," Taylor said, obviously miffed at having to waste a workday accompanying me.

"Perfect," I said, pulling out my phone to answer my emails. Savannah was an hour and a half away from Charleston, and I was quite fond of the city. They were similar in origin and build, but very different in atmosphere. Savannah had always seemed a bit more mysterious to me.

Taylor and I spent the time in the car being productive. We

poured over an endless list of things I had neglected in my last week. Feeling accomplished with what we'd done in the short amount of time, I let my gaze drift out the window. I saw nothing but the golden haired, amber-eyed, wet dream that was now consuming all my imagination.

A short time later, Carson announced we had arrived. When we exited the car, I was shocked at the complete understatement of the picture. We seemed to be on the outskirts of the city, and the deserted plot was absolutely gorgeous. Taylor's audible "Wow" confirmed what I was thinking. The view of the Savannah River was remarkable, and the land was completely untouched. The only likeness between the picture and what we were seeing was the small shed sitting underneath a live oak tree dripping with Spanish moss.

I was absolutely taken with it.

This is not for sale.

"Hello, ladies," a pretty blonde greeted as she walked toward us, hand outstretched. "Mrs. Scott?" She questioned.

"Ms.," I answered, my hand grasping hers in reply. She nodded and turned to Taylor, extending the same courtesy as Taylor addressed her. "You must be Mrs. Volz."

She nodded and shook Taylor's hand. "Please call me Violet."

§§

"Well, I have to say, I have been curious about this place for a while now," Violet said, surveying the land with us.

"Why is that?" I asked, intrigued.

"I have brokered the sale of this property six times in the last two years," she answered, looking directly at me. "It always sells quickly and for a decent percentage more than the previous sale. No one has ever taken residence. I've always been a bit curious as to why, though the commission never hurt." She winked.

"See that for sale sign?" She continued nodding over at a rusty, old and barely visible sign. "That never comes down. I see so much potential here. I'm glad to finally see someone interested in more than flipping the property for a profit."

"That's funny you mention that," I said, turning to Taylor whose wheels were spinning. "I've gotten a few offers on this land in the last few days."

"Oh, well maybe I spoke out of turn," Violet said quickly.

"No, no, I think you're absolutely right. There is something great about his place." She smiled as we walked around briefly. She technically had no property to show aside from the shed no one was interested in.

I asked Violet to lunch with the two of us in a gesture of thank you for rescheduling her day around our impromptu visit. She insisted it wasn't a problem, but agreed to join us. I liked her instantly. Like Taylor, she seemed to have thick skin and a tell-it-like-it-is air about her.

A lunch with the two of them might have been exactly what I needed.

§§

Four hours later, we were laughing hysterically as we emptied our fifth bottle of wine. We sat, relaxed on couches on the patio at Opal, a Greek restaurant I frequented when I visited Savannah. A glass chandelier hung between us as we sampled the wine list, filling up on rich dishes. Even Taylor's demeanor had completely relaxed as we wasted the day away.

"Excuse me, ladies, it's my husband." Violet excused herself, lifting her finger up, indicated she would only be a moment.

"Well, this was fun," I said, beaming as I turned to Taylor who sipped her wine while nodding in agreement.

"I like her," Taylor said. "She's real."

I nodded as she made her way back to the table. "I've misbehaved. My husband is coming to pick me up," she said with a wicked smile and a wink.

"We could've dropped you off," I offered, noting it was time to head back to Charleston.

"Oh, I'll be fine," she said with a smirk. I looked over at

Taylor who had a brow raised at Violet. I excused myself to the restroom and checked my phone after washing my hands, finding several missed calls from Devin.

Not a chance.

He never called me this often. Maybe this time I had actually convinced him I was done. Because, for the first time, it was the truth.

When I got back to the table, Taylor and Violet were talking in whispers and stopped abruptly when I approached. I was about to inquire as to what was being withheld from me when a drop dead gorgeous man approached our table.

"Ladies," he said, his eyes fixed on Violet. She beamed up at him as Taylor caught her gaping mouth.

"This is Rhys, my husband," Violet proclaimed proudly.

"Taylor Ellison," she cooed as he smiled at her before turning to me. The man was beautiful but had absolutely no effect on me. At that very moment, I craved Aiden for the first time.

"Nice to meet you," I said, briefly shaking his hand.

"If you ladies don't mind, I will be relieving you of my wife." Violet turned to us, and we said our goodbyes. I promised I would be in contact regarding some future investments in real estate in the area. Taylor watched with piqued interest as they walked away.

"Taylor," I admonished, "as many beautiful suits as you have seen coming in and out of our office, your reaction to this one surprises me." Waving our waiter over, I gave him my card and compliments on his service, remembering all too well the nightmare of serving people for a living.

"It's not him, I mean, it is him, but..." She stood suddenly and excused herself, her phone in hand as if she was taking a call. I narrowed my eyes but let her have her leave.

Taylor insisted on spending the night in Savannah, stating she would be able to find her way back. Hesitantly, I left her there after she claimed she was meeting an old acquaintance. I suddenly wished we had socialized a bit more. I felt very protective of her. I just couldn't demand answers, though.

I rode back to Charleston, thinking about the property and what I could possibly do with it. It was much too picturesque to do anything rash and too far away from civilization to industrialize it in any way, though I wouldn't want to. A camp, maybe?

I smiled as I picked up my phone. "Hi."

"I've never thought myself a perverted man until today. I can't stop thinking about coming on those beautiful tits," he rasped out.

I felt the heat radiate through me and immediately put up the partition as if Carson could hear.

"What, no confession of love? No recited poems? Just a promise of defilement?" I said breathlessly.

"We both know you have an appetite, Nina. You just haven't shown it to me yet," he said.

"Why, sir, I don't even know your age or your last name," I said in mock offense.

"Come over and I'll spell it out for you with my tongue," he commanded.

I looked out my window as we approached my driveway and saw Devin standing next to his Audi, arms crossed. He was furious.

"Shit," I said, breaking our playful mood.

"What is it?" he asked, concerned

"Irate ex stalking my house," I said. "Hold that thought, okay?"

He was quiet for a beat then spoke quickly. "Where are you?"

"Pulling up to my house. My driver is with me. Don't worry, Aiden, okay?"

"You can't expect me to just sit here, Nina," he said calmly, though he was anything but.

"Not your place, Aiden," I said softly. "I'll call you back."

"Fuck," he ground out. "Okay." He hung up, and I knew our next conversation would go a little differently.

Carson pulled around, and I addressed him. "Carson, I would never ask you to put yourself in harm's way, and I don't think there will be an issue, but will you please just keep an eye out?"

"Say no more," he said, eyeing Devin with disgust. No one liked the man.

I stepped out with a smile. "Devin," I said in greeting.

"Where the fuck have you been? I told you I needed to talk to you!" He was beyond angry. In fact, I'd never seen him so upset.

"I'm here, talk," I snapped. "And just so you know, you have no say now or ever in anything that goes on in my life, including knowing my whereabouts and who I'm fucking. We broke up, and we were never really together," I said, looking up at him.

It still hurt. His deep blue eyes studied me.

"Nina, I don't blame you for ending it. I don't blame you for hating me, but this is important," he pressed as he pulled me by the shoulders so I was standing closer to him.

"What?! Damn it, Devin, spit it out!" I said, exasperated.

"The land you saw today, you need to get rid of it. My firm has made an offer. We want to buy it back." In his face, I saw fear quickly replaced by anger. "What the fuck were you doing there anyway?"

"That would be none of your business," I said defiantly. "The land is not for sale."

He jerked me up by my arms, bringing me close to his face. "Listen to me, sell it to me. I'll pay double."

"No." I jerked my hand away. "What are you hiding, a dead body? I know that land has been sold and resold several times. What exactly is your issue with it?"

"You cannot own it, Nina. It's dangerous for both of us," he said, taking a cautious step toward me. "It belongs to Eileen's family, and when she finds out I flipped it for a profit, and you are the current owner it will be hell for the both of us."

"Oh, God, of course the wife." I rolled my eyes. "So this is why you needed a few extra days?"

"Yes," he hissed, bringing me closer to him. I looked up into his eyes and was immediately transfixed. Devin was beautiful in any mood, but especially when he was angry. It turned me on the most. A whispered thought of Aiden drifted through my mind, but I ignored it as the deep blue sea encompassed me. Devin leaned down and brushed his lips against mine, renewing my arousal.

Still a shark, Nina?

"Who you fuck is none of my business," he said, digging his fingers into my shoulders. "I've lost you."

I snorted, quite unattractively. "Don't play concerned now."

"For a smart woman, you really are so naïve."

"Well, how about for just once you enlighten me!" He leaned in and bit my lip, sucking mercilessly before covering my mouth and taking it completely. I pushed at his chest, and he didn't budge as I kissed him back. His kiss deepened and gentled slightly as he thoroughly tasted me. I moaned into his mouth as his arms trapped me to his body, a body I'd seen a thousand times and would never tire of.

"Nina, ask me inside," he said, lifting me slightly so I felt the bulge in his pants.

"I'll be more than happy to enlighten you."

"No," I said, pushing him away and taking several steps back, putting much-needed space between us.

"I am with someone else, fucking someone else. We are over, Devin. Stay away from me."

His face twisted in rage as he took menacing steps toward me, making me flinch. Seeing my fear, he stopped where he was and stood, his hands on his hips, shaking his head as if he couldn't believe my confession. I was no longer his possession. With a deep breath, he looked up at me.

"Sell the property. Please just get rid of it. Save us both the hassle," he pleaded as all the fight left him.

"Why do you stay with her?" I asked for the millionth time

since the night I discovered them together.

"Goodnight, Nina," he said, turning from me and getting into his car.

He sat staring at the wheel before looking back up at me one more time and turning the ignition. I realized then that Devin was just as infuriating to me in his refusal to answer my questions as I had been to Aiden.

Aiden. I needed to call him back.

Devin sped away as I drug myself up to the door, dreading the conversation. Devin would always have a certain effect on me if I let him. And I had just let him. I couldn't in good conscience call Aiden with my head swimming with Devin, his kiss still fresh on my lips. I opted to text.

Nina: Wicked fight, I won. Call you tomorrow.

Aiden: Not good enough.

My phone rang, and I considered ignoring it. But Aiden deserved better. He had been nothing but good to me.

"Hi," I whispered, throwing my purse on my kitchen counter.

"Do you love him?"

"Don't ask me that," I said with a sigh. "You won't like my answer."

The silence on the line lingered.

"He was nothing but a damn bad idea. He's the bad guy, and in some fucked up way, I'm drawn to it. He's a shark, and I let him turn me into one as well. I saw the signs and ignored them. I know that's not what you want to hear. I don't think I've ever made a good decision when it comes to a man. I kissed him, Aiden. But I won't do it again."

More silence.

"Look, Aiden, if you don't want to see me again, I'll understand. I didn't realize how much baggage I was bringing into this."

"Come see me tomorrow," he said and hung up.

"If you want to know what God thinks of money, just look at the people he gave it to."

– DOROTHY PARKER

§§

I SPENT THE NEXT morning thinking about my next move. I should just sell the land. I didn't want to give Devin any more reason to approach me. I was confident Violet could find me a similar plot. After all, Savannah was beautiful and full of places just as captivating. I fancied the idea of owning a small part of it, of developing, contributing something.

That's very unsharklike, Nina.

I smiled.

I texted Devin.

Nina: Have your office send over the paperwork for the sale. One condition, you NEVER contact me again socially or otherwise.

Devin: I'll miss you, Nina.

I laughed as I read it. Prick.

All at once, I felt free. I spent my day at the gym thinking about Aiden and the apology I owed him. I didn't want to lose the small connection we'd made. The sex was phenomenal so far, and I was craving his touch. I hadn't lost sight of how often I smiled when I was with him, how much more of myself I bared to him when we were together. I fucked up kissing Devin. I might have lost the only real shot at a relationship I'd had in years.

But Aiden was still a mystery to me.

§§

I walked into The Mystic and immediately spotted Aiden. He was chatting up a beautiful blonde as they sat at the table next to the stage. I was unsure whether or not to approach him. I opted to sit at the bar and greet Dave.

"Nina," he said with a wink.

"I live here," I admitted.

He laughed loudly. "I assumed as much," he said, grabbing the twenty I handed him as he sat my beer down. "I won't ask."

"Thanks." I smiled, my heart not behind it. I waited ten minutes, only looking over at Aiden once. I refused to let the jealousy seep through me. I had no right. Letting out a sigh, I finished my beer then picked my purse up to leave when I heard his voice behind me.

"Naughty Nina," he greeted with contempt in his voice.

I turned to look up at him. "I'm not playing games tonight, Aiden. If you are angry with me then just say so. You don't have to parade around, flirting with other women. I am well aware you have the power to get laid anytime you want."

"Aiden," the blonde from the booth whined as she walked up. "I didn't think we were finished talking." She glared at me as I stared at her blankly.

I braved a look at him, and my lips parted. His eyes were fire, his jaw set like he was ready for war.

"Karina, I will call you," he dismissed her as he kept his eyes on mine. She stomped off, grabbing her purse from the table and pushing past us as she left.

"I'm sorry, Aiden," I said softly. "It was just a kiss. I am sorry, though. Excuse me." I stood to leave, knowing I wouldn't be back.

Seconds after I walked out I felt his hand take mine as he led me around the corner in the alley behind his club. He positioned me against the brick wall as he stared at me. I looked up at him, completely weak.

"It really is ironic that you think you are a shark, Nina Scott," he said before backing me up, his fiery eyes ablaze with need.

Well, he knows my last name.

"I know I made it clear to you that I wanted to own this body, maybe I should have included this sexy fucking mouth, too," he said, sliding his hand up and cupping my chin. "But you never did give me an answer, did you?"

My panties were soaked. I moaned as his breath hit my skin

with every word.

"No," I answered. "I didn't." His smirk was full of menace. He wanted me to pay, of that I was sure.

"Allow me to clarify which parts I want to own," he said, lifting my skirt slowly inch by inch. A group of people walked by laughing and turned our way. Aiden didn't stop as he lifted it up further, exposing my white silk panties.

"This." He cupped my sex roughly, and I gasped out as the onlookers quickly walked past us. I stood, completely frozen, both mortified and absolutely on fire. I reached up to pull him to me to cover myself as he reached around, gripping my ass and squeezing with both hands. "This," he said, pulling me to him and grinding into me slightly before thrusting me back against the brick.

He pulled open my blouse button by button as I quickly looked around us, realizing we were being watched by every single passerby.

"Aiden," I said, giving him big eyes.

"I don't give a fuck. I'm not finished," he said, completely oblivious. Once he finished the task of opening my blouse, he gripped my breast roughly. "These," he said as I moaned, arching my back into him.

"And most definitely these," he said, biting my lips hard and punishing. I cried out, my eyes watering as he bruised them. He pulled back and ripped the silk of my panties completely away. I slid down against the wall, and he brought me back up. "I think it's time you gave me an answer," he said as he unzipped his pants. He turned us around quickly so his back was against the wall and lifted me up so my legs wrapped around him. I frantically looked around us until I felt the thick head of him invade me. Then nothing else mattered. I bit his shoulder as he slid his rock hard cock into me. Once fully connected, we both stared at each other in awe. My body vibrated around him.

"So fucking good, Nina. Did you forget?" he slammed into me hard as I heard a gasp or two pass us by. I couldn't stop him, and I didn't want to. Aiden slid down to the ground with us still connected.

"I need you to give me an answer, Nina," he said, cupping my head and bringing me in for a kiss. Anyone who saw us now would simply see me straddling him, my skirt covering our indiscretion. He was deep as I writhed on top of him, but he wouldn't move.

"It was always going to be yes," I said quickly. Aiden had just completely claimed me. I didn't need any more reasons to give in. I wrapped my legs around his back against the brick wall as we began to move.

"Fuck, you feel so good. This pussy is so fucking perfect," he said as he eyed my chest. "Still, I'm so fucking mad at you," he warned, gripping my hips and slamming himself into me. I gasped as his eyes lit with satisfaction. He clenched my neck tightly, bringing my lips to his. His tongue traced my mouth before invading it as I got lost in his cock buried deep inside of me. "When you come all over my dick, naughty Nina, just remember you don't deserve it, not tonight." He slammed into me again by gripping my thighs, pulling me roughly to him. He licked his index and then stuck it into my mouth. I sucked it greedily as I rose and fell on his stone dick, the fire in his eyes spurring me on. "But I can't help myself tonight, and I think I might have started a slight addiction of my own." He slipped his hand beneath my skirt, cupping my ass, spreading moisture over my back entrance. I gasped as he plunged his finger in without warning. I collapsed and came with a scream as he clamped his hand over my mouth, bucking furiously as he spilled into me as we both rode it out. When we had both caught our breath, he slowly started buttoning up my shirt as we stayed connected.

"You fucked me in the street," I breathed out, open mouthed and dazed.

"Maybe it's time you start taking me at my word," he said with a sardonic smile.

"Maybe I will," I murmured as he got to the last button and

kissed me gently.

"So what's your last name?" I sighed as he placed a soft kiss on my chin.

"McIntyre."

REVERENCE
Book 2

§§

Devin

I was a prick, but I never hurt anyone that didn't deserve it.
Well…until Nina.

I was a very smart man who made a very bad decision, but the mistakes I was paying for were not just my own.

My behavior toward her, no matter how unforgivable, had always been about protecting her—from me, from my wife, and from the long line of mistakes I would never be able to rectify.

Nina was finally done with me, and I knew it was for the best. I could finally keep her safe from depraved people like me. I needed her as far removed from the situation as possible. I tried to force myself to be content with her decision to move on…until I found out whom she was moving on with.

§§

Nina

My unyielding love for a corrupt man might have cost me the affection of someone worthy.

With Aiden, I had finally discovered a version of myself I could tolerate; then he dropped a one-word bomb that ruined my new sense of self. Instead of listening to my voice of reason, I blocked it out, until it became a scream that refused to be ignored.

Now, I would give anything to quiet that voice.

"...the human animal is a selfish beast..."

– TENNESSEE WILLIAMS

§§

DEVIN

I'M A PRICK, and I'm damn good at it. I've never really hurt anyone who didn't deserve it.

Well…until Nina. My behavior toward her, though unforgivable in some aspects, had always been about protecting her, from me, from my wife and from a long line of mistakes I'd never be able to correct. I'd handled almost every situation in the last few years in one way or another on her behalf, or with her in mind. She was embedded in me, a part of me, and was now the reason I sat behind my desk staring out of my window instead of ensuring my next client's fortune.

I could never forget the surge of need that shot through me the first time I laid eyes on her. Long silky hair, breathtaking eyes, and lips among perfectly contoured high cheekbones. Petite, but completely alluring, her curves mesmerizing with her movements. From leg to lips her body was a beacon of sin. She wasn't oblivious to the effect she had on the men around her, she just didn't seem to care.

Or the first time she walked into my office. She was already a wealthy woman but wore it horribly. She wasn't classless. She was very well spoken. Not completely the white trash, lottery ticket winner I had envisioned. She was easy prey when I approached her at the Admiral's Club. Her dress was as ill-fitting then as it was the day she stood in my office completely clueless and looking to me for answers.

"Ms. Scott, please have a seat." I gestured as she walked in, taking a look around.

"Nice," she said quickly, trying to mask her awe at the size of it. I grinned.

"So the reason I approached you was to see who was handling your investment banking," I said smoothly, pushing my portfolio toward her. "If you haven't had a chance to look online, here is a list of our clients." She

opened the leather-bound folder, eyeing it briefly. I knew she didn't recognize the names on the list. I had researched her a bit. She grew up local, married some douche bag in college, and quit to live the American dream, to become a housewife and mother, though the latter was never carried out. She did not have a child bearing figure. She was petite, her body perfectly tight.

Stay on point, Devin.

"Anyway, those aren't important." I didn't want to embarrass her. My intentions were simple. I wanted her millions, and I wanted to multiply them and hand some of the profit back to her while keeping the rest. "I'm just going to be honest with you, Mr. McIntyre," she said, crossing her legs. "I have no idea what I'm doing when it comes to things like this. Until now, my best tool for utilizing my money was to buy economy size packages of hamburger meat and separate them into freezer bags." I laughed loudly and watched her squirm. Her face reddened considerably, and I knew instantly she regretted saying it.

She studied my face, searching for some sign she could trust me. I didn't give her anything. "Ms. Scott, I simply want to run a few things by you. You can have your lawyer look them over and decide what you think is best for you."

"Fair enough," she said with a smile.

That smile started it.

I knew she had recently finalized a divorce. She was a little thin, and I could see the bags under her eyes from lack of sleep. I felt the need to protect her then. It wasn't subtle, but a sharp lash to my chest. This woman had no clue how to handle her new fortune. I stood up, rounding my desk.

"Nina, I'm going to be honest with you. You need to really look before you leap at this point. I'm sure you are aware of the horror stories of those who come into fortune and lose it quickly."

"Well aware," she countered with a hint of bitterness. I knew her ex-husband had done a number on her. It wasn't my problem, and I couldn't help her with that.

"Just be careful. Don't believe me or take my word for it. Hire someone, someone who knows what they are doing, who can ensure you are protected in every move you make."

"Isn't that your job?" she said, looking up at me, her gray eyes making

me forget my focus. The woman was absolutely stunning.

"Not exactly," I answered, taking the seat next to her. "I plan to gamble a bit with the money you allow me to play with. It's a process. But I can guarantee you are in good hands."

"You're reputable. I did research that much," she said with another smile. My body tightened in reaction. Her long brown hair looked like spun silk lying on her shoulders. I wanted to reach out and touch it, but mostly I wanted those heart shaped lips wrapped around my cock. "So, before you and I start investing, let's get you a right hand to form a corporation. I'll have a friend at another firm make a recommendation so I won't have a hand in the matter." I stood up and heard her faint words.

"Thank you," she whispered. I looked down at her and saw the sincerity in her face. "I know you say not to take your word for it, but I have a feeling it might not be such a bad thing to trust you."

"Make me earn it," I added, "and make everyone else. You've done a hell of a thing, Ms. Scott."

"Thank you," she said, reaching for my hand. I shook hers politely before she turned to walk out. "Beautiful," I said audibly.

I'd never said a damn thought out loud without intention in my life. This woman had just fucked that up.

She paused, so I knew she'd heard it, but didn't say a word as she left my office. And just like that, this prick fell in love.

"Mr. McIntyre, Mrs. McIntyre line one." I cleared the haze and picked up the phone, dreading the exchange to come.

"Eileen."

"Darling, when will you be home?"

Acid curdled in my stomach, making its way up at her words. "I was just thinking about your pretty little head."

"Oh," she said cautiously.

"Yes, I was picturing it under the guillotine."

"I don't have time—"

"I was thinking," I interrupted her, "of how easy Henry VIII had it. The man was onto something." "Amusing," she said dryly. "I need you home tonight."

"Where you sleep is not my home. You want appearances,

fine, but don't fucking call that my house." I was shorter with her than usual today, resentment brewing out of my every pore from what she'd cost me.

I hated my wife. "Fine." Her voice was stern, a sign an imminent threat was coming. "Our anniversary dinner is this evening. Just a few close friends."

"And I need to attend because?" I smiled, knowing I was playing with fire. "Be here by seven, guests will arrive at eight," she snapped.

"When the fuck are you going to let me out of this?" I snapped back. "When you've served your time," she said quickly then hung up.

I'm fucked.

A month ago, I was so fucking close to being rid of her. The satanic slut I called a wife had not only robbed me of the last seven years but was now dangling my livelihood in front of me. Everything I worked for she held in the palm of her hand. And I let her have it. I'm a very smart man who made a very bad decision. And the mistakes I am paying for are not my own. I glanced at my phone.

Nina: Have your office send over the paperwork for the sale. One condition, you never contact me again socially or otherwise.

I deserved that. I knew I deserved it. For the last few months, I've been a complete bastard to her. I had to hand it to her, though. She was tough, and she'd loved me well. Knowing she wouldn't believe the truth in the words, I sent the text anyway. There was no way she would ever deem me sincere.

Devin: I'll miss you, Nina.

I threw my phone down, knowing I would get no response.

She was finally done with me. The pain creeping through my chest as subtle as a heavily swung ax told me I was far from done with her.

"Trust is like a mirror, you can fix it if it's broken, but you can still see the crack in that mother fucker's reflection."

– LADY GAGA

§§

NINA

IT WAS LIKE life had just handed me the golden ticket and said, "Sorry, my bad you didn't read the fine print. You can't have fucked a relative."

I left Aiden that night to start his set at the bar. He didn't notice me stiffen in his arms at the mention of his last name. After a slow tender kiss goodnight, I abandoned him to completely freak out in the safety of my town car. On the way home, I Googled everything I could about Devin. His LinkedIn had a clear business profile but said absolutely nothing about his personal life, including his wife.

Nothing new there.

How could I have been so stupid? I knew him for over a year before I dated him for six months, blissfully ignorant until his wife actually *called* me to let me know I was his mistress, and one of many. And when I went to confront Devin the very same hour she'd berated me on the phone, he was fucking her on his desk. He didn't look surprised to see me in the least, nor did he come after me.

Devin loathed her, this much I knew after the fact. And if he'd had other affairs, it was due to that fact alone. I may not have been the first, but I was most definitely his last. Up until the point I ended it, at least. Pain pierced my chest at the thought. Eileen had him trapped somehow; he'd never cared enough about me to tell me why. I continued to sleep with him out of spite toward her after she'd purposefully ruined me publicly a number of times—and because I loved him desperately, but that was another illusion.

It wasn't until a few weeks later when she'd shunned me at my first social gathering that I realized she'd set the whole thing up. Devin had confirmed as much to me without so many words. I'd watched them a little more closely than other people.

I'd seen him openly glare at her once or twice when backs were turned. Only a fool would believe they were anything more than publicly married. But I was the only one who truly cared to take a second look. After a solid month of endless humiliation at the hands of his cunning wife, remorse turned into anger. I'd taken Devin by the cock, led him into the coat check closet and fucked all my frustration out. Deserving or not, he was all I had, and I used it to my advantage. I lost a large piece of self-respect that night while Devin eyed me warily as he zipped his pants. He didn't question my intent and simply took what I offered him.

I should have known.

Then again, the man lived like a bachelor. Aside from the handful of weekends we went away, we rarely spent the night together. I assumed it was his determination to keep our relationship private. He didn't want anyone at his investment firm knowing he was fucking a client. I'd never held it against him, but it did make me curious. I was too busy starting Scott Solutions to wonder or do anything about it. And he'd made me happy. He'd never offered me more than sex and friendship, and I took it and ran with it. I was to blame for the lack of control over my feelings getting involved, but I never had a chance with him.

Devin was magnetic, raw, hungry, beautiful, and ambitious. Power emulated from his intense, deep blue gaze to his fingertips.

Devin never held my hand after I'd found out, nor did he apologize. As the months progressed, I was reintroduced to him and in a completely different way. I'd let him continue to have my body, treat me as less, and all for the sake of spite, or so I told myself. I'd been cheated on, and no matter how much I loathed his wife, I'd taken part in the affair knowingly and without empathy for her. It was wrong. I was wrong. And still…I loved him.

Back to the matter at hand, Nina.

I'd just been fucked and fucked well by Aiden, and my mind was still on Devin. Would it ever end?

Aiden was new, fresh, exciting, and completely single. I had slept in his bed, dined in his home. He seemed an open book. *I* was the one who had been hesitant to share. Now I had questions, and so many of them I was reeling. I'd jumped into another sexual relationship without asking the important ones.

I Googled Aiden and found nothing but a small mention in an article about his band.

I already knew enough about Devin to know he didn't have any brothers. Even if they were estranged, there was no reason for Devin not to have mentioned it in the time we spent together. Then again, Devin wasn't the most reliable source.

Aiden, Devin, it seemed obvious someone had matched their names purposely this way.

Cousins? I put my head in my hands with a groan. If I asked Aiden and he questioned me, it could be disastrous. Would he be disgusted? Could he overlook it? Could I?

FUCK YOU, LIFE!

I didn't need to jump to conclusions. McIntyre was a pretty common name. They did not resemble each other in the slightest. The confidence they both shared wasn't necessarily a reason to panic. They were both amazing in bed, but I was sure that had nothing to do with genetics.

Okay … so I could ask Devin, except less than twenty-four hours ago I told him I never wanted to speak to him again. How would he interpret my sudden twenty questions? Did it matter? Was it just a coincidence?

I wasn't that fucking naïve. I dialed Taylor. "Boss," she said, breathlessly. "Taylor, did I catch you at a bad time?" I asked with a smile.

"No." She exhaled slowly. "Just working out."

Something in her tone told me different, but as always, I didn't prompt. "I have an issue."

"Okay, hit me," she said, her breath now under control.

"How do I find out if two people are related without asking them directly, or anyone else? I guess I'm asking you if we are able to get a background check?"

"Why are you question-marking the end of that sentence and who are you afraid of?"

"No one," I said quickly. "This is personal."

"Go ahead," she said with humor in her voice. I felt my cheeks heat as uncertainty raced through me. Well, fuck it. If I were going to be in limbo, I would be armed with the right information. "I think I might've bagged a set of brothers."

"Oh God, that bastard has a brother. Lord help us all," Taylor said comically. "I don't think so. I mean, I'm not sure. So can I get one on the both of them?"

"Of course you can. You have enough to buy the info, Nina. I know just who to call. Send me everything you have on them both."

I breathed out a sigh of relief. "You still haven't signed that paperwork on the land. It was couriered over this afternoon."

"I will in the morning," I said as Carson pulled up to my drive.

"It's a shame," she said, sounding forlorn. "It was beautiful."

"And more trouble than it was worth," I said, thinking it ironic I thought the same of Devin. "It belongs to Devin's wife's family. So there's that. I can meet you at the office now." I sat in the backseat, ready to direct Carson to my building. I needed to accomplish something, to distance myself from the situation. I felt like it was a sudden lifeline.

The sooner I got rid of Devin and his wife, the sooner I could breathe easier. "I…"

Taylor had never been speechless. "Taylor?"

"I'm in Savannah," she admitted then sighed apologetically.

"The morning, then," I offered after a brief pause.

"I'll be there early," she replied, guarded.

"I won't, so don't worry about it."

"Goodnight." She hung up without responding.

My wheels were already full speed, so I didn't have time to wonder about Taylor's whereabouts. I sat back in my seat as a message came through.

Devin: You didn't sign the papers.

Nina: You aren't allowed to text me.

Devin: It's not over yet.

Nina: Tomorrow.

Devin: That's tomorrow, see me tonight.

I didn't bother entertaining him and completely ignored the ache in my chest. I climbed out of my car, determined to find more answers.

But the truth was, I already knew somehow they were connected. I felt it in every fiber of my being.

"Your conscience is the measure of the honesty of your selfishness. Listen to it carefully."

– RICHARD BACH

§§

DEVIN

I ARRIVED AT MY anniversary party thirty minutes after eight, and an hour and a half after she was expecting me. Knowing I'd raised my wife's blood pressure considerably before I'd got there was a small victory. Eileen's parents and sister were seated in our dining room and looked at me expectantly for an explanation, which I didn't give.

"I apologize," I said, quickly taking my seat at the head of the table then grabbed my glass. "To my wonderful wife, happy anniversary."

The rest of our guests, minus her sister, raised their glasses in praise of their fair hostess then began to devour the first course. Always in fucking courses with Eileen. She considered dinner an event. It was never a quick bite, just a slow and agonizing task, especially with her choice of company. Our anniversary gave reason to prolong it even further, a celebration of our farce of a marriage. She'd even brought out her eighteenth-century china. As the drab conversation rolled on, I drank, heavily, ignoring the second and third course, opting for a courteous nod or short sentence of reply. Looking over at Eileen, I recalled our wedding day. I was fond of her then, and she was once a tiger in the sack. I was never a man for sentiment, and love wasn't a requirement for me. Love wasn't the reason for my union, though I couldn't deny I'd felt strongly about the possibility when I married my wife.

It was a partnership. I didn't need her money. I wanted to play the game. I was in it for the thrill. I wanted to drive a stake into the heart of the city, make my claim and start my empire. Although I had my partners, I needed the connections she had in Charleston to grow my business. I married her for her name, but it didn't hurt I was fond of her classic beauty and her wit. She was sharp and stealthy when she worked a room, and I needed someone beside me that adhered to the wealthiest appetites, to attract them and bring them in. I was old money, but when I moved here from Savannah ten years ago, I needed a shoe-in, a way to easily marry myself with the elite. Something she could do with her name alone. The world was my oyster at twenty-nine when I married her.

I got that so fucking wrong.

After a few years of ignorant bliss, she started withholding sex at her whim. She'd made it perfectly clear that I was to do as she wished. *Happy wife, happy life.*

I ignored her. I was busy growing my firm and didn't bother to try and save the marriage. She had her agenda: to live and die exactly like her mother. And I had mine. She thought I was weak.

Stupid cunt.

"Seven years, Devin," her mother piped. "It's time for the itch."

She couldn't have handed me a more loaded statement. I caught Eileen's gaze that told me not to go there and gave her a small smirk.

"I have a feeling I will fare well."

Eileen plastered a smile on her face.

The truth was, no one at the table was blind. There was a giant elephant stomping all over the Renaissance style, oak dining table that we all ignored.

Her mother numbed herself with her anti-depressants while her father aided me by taking advantage of my abuse and cruelty with my new ten-thousand-dollar bottle of Macallan, an anniversary gift from my wife.

Her sister, Sandra, glared around at all of us while we ate. She apparently was in a good mood, because insults weren't flying between her and Eileen. When the two were amicable, it usually had something to do with me. There was only one woman I despised as much as my wife, and that was her sister.

Sandra lived in Savannah in what I was sure was a dark cave

where she sacrificed defenseless animals and small children before cleansing herself in their blood. There was no deity worthy of her praise that she could possibly hold in higher regard as much as she did herself. She radiated evil and I, along with my wife, shared open contempt for her.

I would normally question her presence in the house, but it was evident to me Eileen had her here as a subtle reminder of her case against me and to keep me on my toes. Sandra was as much to blame as my dear wife for my predicament.

"Sandra, how good of you to come." I raised my glass, prodding her with my wolf grin.

"Will you be staying long?"

"Just long enough for dessert." She smiled.

"And maybe while I'm in town, visit an old friend or two."

Touché, cunt.

And finally, there was Mr. and Mrs. Theodore Marion, Eileen's closest friends and two of the wealthiest people in Charleston, because it was completely fucking necessary for them to share in our wedding anniversary celebration.

Everything was an occasion. Honestly, I was surprised this was the extent of our guests.

Two years ago, before I'd met Nina, I'd asked my wife for a divorce.

Two years ago, she declared she wouldn't grant me one and swore she'd find leverage to keep me.

Two years ago, my wife had fumbled around blindly in the dark and found that leverage with the help of her sister.

Two years ago, I became a slave to her will.

I had no choice but to trust her out of desperation, and she'd turned the tables, demanding my loyalty and public fidelity in exchange for bailing me out. She kept secrets for me, and in exchange, I had transformed into the puppet she'd always wanted.

One short month later, my salvation walked into the Admiral's Club, and I saw a glimmer of hope. After months of meetings, I'd purposefully avoided a few appointments to avoid fucking her.

I needed her business.

Nina was the key to getting my life back since it had all fallen apart. I rolled the liquid around in my tumbler, thinking of the last bottle I'd savored. My body tensed in recognition. I was christening my sailboat *The Talisman*, with Nina.

I had met with Nina again several times, and over the first year I'd known her, I'd never gotten close enough to where I couldn't resist her.

She had been my biggest challenge.

When Eileen agreed to let me take residence in downtown while she remained on Seabrook Island, I had rejoiced in the prospect of my prison break. My first priority was becoming free of her, and because I was so damned close to my goal, I rewarded myself with Nina.

She was my one and only affair.

Nina had done what I had advised. She formed her company Scott Solutions and had given me millions to play with. I was fine gambling with her money, but never my own. That was my rule. It was also my job.

And when it came to Nina and investing, I could do no wrong, hence the name of my boat. It was named after her, though I'd never told her.

She was my talisman, my charm, my fresh air. I'd never made a single dollar on poor investments, or done a shady deal. Even the flipping of that fucking land and its consistent sale was legitimate, if only a little gray.

No, it wasn't poor business choices that got me here, it was my fucking heart, my conscience, my misplaced loyalty. Things I didn't need to survive. Things that now mattered more than playing the game I set out to win. I had a new agenda: Get my life back, and if the gods saw fit, get Nina back as well.

For now, all I had was a cold bed and cold hearted bitch who threatened to keep it that way. I spent the rest of my meal growing hard underneath my napkin at thoughts of Nina on my new sailboat.

"It's beautiful," she said, turning to me with a wink. "Just how much am I paying you?"

I smiled broadly. "Full disclosure, Ms. Scott. Check your email."

"I think it's safe for us to be on a first-name basis," she said, grabbing my hand as I guided her onto the deck. It wasn't an obnoxious boat, but it was impressive. I had enough to buy any of the fucking boats on the harbor, but sailing was my passion, and I wasn't doing this for show. This was what I loved, and it seemed even more complete with the woman who had just graced the deck. "You look beautiful," I said carefully.

"Thank you," she said, scanning the harbor. It was the start of summer, but the breeze was heavenly and lifted her long hair off of her shoulders. "All right, Captain, I learned a few things. I'm ready to help."

I chuckled as I took her in. She was overdressed in a yellow sundress and sandals, but it was subtle, and something deep inside my chest tugged in the moment she waited on me, her eyes expectant. She had put on a small amount of weight and was glowing. I pictured my mouth on her then, my tongue plunging deep inside her pussy and wondered what her moans would sound like.

"I've got the whole of it," I said, tying off then starting the motor.

"Hey, that's cheating!" she said, watching me steer out into the harbor.

"Well, beautiful, we could spend the day trying to row ourselves out, but we'd be exhausted."

"Oh." Her cheeks reddened. "Shit," she said, further embarrassed.

"Hey, beginner," I said, hoping it helped, "make yourself useful and get me a beer."

"It's like, when I'm around you, what comes up comes out an avalanche of stupid. I can't imagine what you think of me."

I studied her long and hard before telling her what had more than once graced the tip of my tongue without spilling out. "I happen to like it that you are so candid with me," I said as she smiled. "I also think you are fucking beautiful and prefer this view over any I've ever seen. As far as what I think about you, I think you know I do a lot of it."

She swallowed as she handed me a beer and looked around the flawless harbor. "I could get used to this."

"What?"

"You calling me beautiful," she whispered as she looked back at me. I'd seen it a few times since we met, but here she was making it perfectly clear. The feeling was mutual.

"I'm curious, Nina," I said, busying myself around the deck, completing the steps my father taught me, focusing the boom and getting ready to set the main sail. "How did you do it?"

She stiffened as she studied me, using my advice against me. She would make me earn it. "How did I do what?"

"How did a twenty-seven-year-old college dropout become a multi-millionaire in a year?"

She smirked. "I did what you did. I saw an opportunity to gamble, and I took it. Except, I didn't have to seek it out. It came to me."

I stayed silent as I released the jib and set a cleat, urging her to continue.

"I was a fat kid. I think it's ironic now how my past torment is now the reason for my fortune. I was the epitome of an ugly duckling. I learned early on you had to have something going for you, either looks or money, and I had neither. So I made it a point to do something about it. I started young, thirteen or fourteen, I think. I wiped everything out of my diet except for rabbit food, began working out vigorously, and in a year's time… You get it. Anyway, I realized it was my only saving grace. I made it a hobby, I worked my ass off, literally, and it paid off. I was no longer the last girl to get invited to the dance. I was the first. Boys didn't seem to worry about my bank account…then. So when I had to choose a major in college, I chose nutrition. I started to design a program for a class project and the rest is history."

"And you found an investor," I said, watching her skirt tease me as it whipped in the wind with a near glimpse of what lay underneath.

"She found me. Actually, it's funny because that woman hadn't ventured out as an investor in years. I sent it to the market to test it, and she was the first in the pool to pick it up. She was convinced it was the next Atkins."

"She was right," I said, grabbing my beer to join her and take the wheel. She was sipping a glass of the second bottle of champagne she brought. The

first's remains sinking to the bottom of the Atlantic after I gave it a love tap to christen the boat. "And are you happy with the results?" I asked, taking my place at the wheel.

"Yes, no, I mean…" She looked at the heavens, shaking her head. "I'm happy that it helped so many people. I am still kind of reeling from it all. It was definitely a case of too much too soon." She turned to me. "I'm not complaining, and I'm thankful to you for steering me in the right direction."

"You're welcome," I said, opening a fresh beer.

"It's been a ride," she said distantly. "And it's only just begun."

It was then I saw her sadness. The kind of sadness I see in most of my clients when they realize money doesn't solve everything.

Money doesn't solve people, and those were the hardest burdens to bear.

"Nina, you realize that with or without the money, you would still feel the way you feel."

"I should have known he was an asshole," she said quickly. "How could I not see that? And everyone around me, it was like I was a pariah, even to my close friends. The friends I had long before my husband, they made me feel … guilty for the wealth. As if it was my fault they were still struggling. Suddenly we had nothing in common. I didn't have kids, and they were all starting families. I ran out of excuses to call, and they didn't bother to call me. I mean, what the hell is wrong with people?"

Great, I was going to have to give her a pep talk. I sighed as I took in the tourist-filled waterfront park from the harbor. We were in the midst of perfection, and I needed to remind her of that.

"Come here," I said, grabbing her hand and pulling her to me. I'd never laid a hand on her until that moment, and the jolt hit us both. My dick sang its praises.

I pulled her in front of me so she could hold the wheel. She giggled as I draped myself around her and I felt her body tighten as she recognized all my blood was pulsing in my pants in the bulge beneath her. I wasn't about to apologize for it or hide my reaction to her. "This is you now," I whispered in her ear as I cradled her. Immediately, I noted the goose bumps on her flesh, the change in her breathing. "Look at you, Nina, at the wheel. You didn't need your fucking husband to get you here. You didn't need me, either. You don't need their approval to enjoy your success. And I think you know that. You did this yourself. Take control of it and don't ever let another person steer you again. You earned this. Through hard work, and good fortune, you no longer have to compete with anyone. Own it."

"I didn't know it was a competition," she said in a small voice.

"Sure you did," I murmured, brushing my lips against her temple. "It's what got you into the race in the first place."

She gripped my hands around the wheel and pushed her ass against me, and I damn near moaned. I don't moan.

"Tell me what you want," I said, my lips a whisper from the silky skin on her neck. The sun was getting lower and outlined her perfectly as she inhaled deeply and looked back at me.

"I want you to kiss me."

I turned her body fully to me, gripped my hands on the wheel behind her, leaned in, and brushed my lips against hers. I pulled back and saw her disappointment.

I raised a brow. "Not what you wanted?"

"No," she answered, her eyes burning with heat.

"Tell me what you want," I urged as she hesitated.

"I'm not the type of woman—"

"Oh, don't disappoint me, Nina." Pressing my brows together, I studied her perfect mouth. A mouth I'd spanked off to more times than I cared to admit. I wanted her mouth, and I wanted it screaming my name. Encased in golden sunshine, she gave me the permission I wasn't sure I would ask for if she waited much longer.

"I want you to kiss me and mean it." She paused for only a second. "Fuck it. I'll kiss you." She pressed her lips to mine firmly then slid her tongue along my bottom lip. One taste of her tongue and I was gone. I glanced behind her to assess the amount of time I had and then dove deep, sucking her tongue and nibbling her lips. She tasted of mint and champagne, and I couldn't get enough. She was easily one of the most beautiful women I had ever met. I took a risk in inviting her, but it didn't fucking matter the minute I had that mouth. Kissing her was my undoing. Just a kiss in the middle of the harbor had ruined me. Her pussy would cripple me.

I pulled away. "I am not a gentle lover," I warned.

"Oh?" she said, smiling, "Even better." She threw her arms around my neck, pulling me back to her. I sucked her lips dry.

"I'm not sure I can be the man you need," I reiterated, focusing on anything but my raging cock.

Was I, Devin McIntyre, trying to talk a woman out of fucking me?

Pathetic. I was a closer. That's what I did. "Devin, it's what I want. I am not asking for what I need. I've already gambled with that and lost. I just want this." Her murmur echoed as she kissed my neck. "I just want today."

Far be it from me do deny her. And I didn't. What I did do is turn her back around and lift that fucking yellow scrap of a dress until I had her beautiful laced ass in view. Still cradled, her back against me, she arched her body, putting herself on display.

She had every right to showcase her body. It was a work of art. I slid my thumb into the back of her panties, gently stroking her ass as my fingers finally tasted her flesh. Closing my eyes, I breathed in deep as she moaned at my touch, making my dick jump. I gripped her hip with my other hand, pulling her back. As soon as her neck was exposed, I clamped my mouth over it, moving my bruising hand over her hip as the other, still underneath her underwear, cupped her sex.

She was soaked. I was hard. It was simple.

Except it wasn't.

We weren't alone. The harbor was busy, and not only that, I knew Eileen was somehow watching. I wouldn't subject Nina to her. Not if I could help it. I had to make this quick. "Nina, I'm going to make you come," I said, pulling her skirt over my hand to hide my workings as I slid a finger inside her. She bucked a little in reply, completely lost. "But I can't fuck you here."

"Hmmm," she said as a second finger joined the first. She was tight, hot, wet, and willing. I groaned. I do groan, in agony.

"You like being fucked by my fingers?"

"Yesssss," she said breathily. "I want more."

"Do you?" My lips trailed the length of her neck as I pulled the moisture from her pussy, and her body jerked in my arms when I mapped

her clit. "I want my mouth here." My confession came out hungry, causing her to arch further, her breath heavy. She was gone, moaning and meeting my fingers with her eager, sweet pussy. I needed to taste her. I paused my workings as she protested with a hiss and took a finger into my mouth, dipping it right back into her. I savored the tangy taste as I used the same finger to push her over the edge. She came hard and fast and gripped the back of my head as she said my name low and pleading.

"Everywhere my fingers touch will belong to me." It was a promise. I trailed my fingers over every inch of available flesh, her sweet pussy, her thighs, her ass, her stomach, breasts, and neck, ending with her lips. She sucked my finger, turning to look back at me, her eyes full of longing.

My cock jerked again. "I want my mouth here," she said, grabbing the bulk of my cock and squeezing roughly. I couldn't agree with her more. I wanted it there, too, but it would have to wait.

She stayed in my arms until I had no choice but to pull away and ready the boat for shore. She remained quiet on the way back, and I watched the wind pulling her long hair away from her face. God, she was heavenly. Even with a raging hard on, I found myself more content than I had been in years.

"This doesn't have to be anything, Devin. It can end the minute I step off this boat." The look she gave me told me she meant her words. She sensed my hesitance, and I almost told her the truth.

Almost.

"There are some things…things I'm working on. You and I being involved will complicate them." Not bothering to look at her, I was ready for the inevitable.

"I understand," she said without emotion. The mood was broken, and I felt the guilt.

Why had I even asked her here with me? To fuck her? She was my best client. What the fuck was I doing?

Assisting her off the boat, she turned back to me. "It was amazing, and I loved every minute of it."

"I'll take you anytime you want," I whispered, placing a chaste kiss on her lips. "Stay safe, Nina."

Opening my celebratory bottle of Macallan, I took a long drink as

I watched her approach her town car and felt the urgent tug. I couldn't let her walk away. I needed to let her go. The realist in me knew it was for the best. I was forcefully married. She was newly divorced and had trust issues. We were a ticking time bomb, and yet as I watched her beautiful frame disappearing from my line of sight, everything in me screamed for her to stop. I felt like I was losing her already and I couldn't prevent my legs from moving, nor the words from coming out. I caught up with her just as her driver was opening her door. He retreated gracefully, giving us privacy as he eyed me with curiosity. I grabbed her hand, kissing the back of it.

"I want you, in every way, Nina. I think about you constantly. I just don't want you to get hurt."

She looked at me with pleading eyes. "Then don't hurt me."

But I did hurt her, and every fear I had of us being together came true. Predicting the end and the way it would happen didn't make it less painful, and now I was begging her to see me by text. And she wouldn't even fucking answer me.

Still in my suit, I sat on the grass at what was once home, piss drunk with my nearly finished bottle, staring at the pool we'd never used as Eileen approached.

"That was pleasant. I think they enjoyed themselves," she said as she watched me. I ignored her stare as she stood next to me, waiting for an invitation to join me that wasn't coming.

"Do you want to fuck?" I said, making a mockery out of the night. "Dear?"

She scoffed as she tried to take my bottle, but I kept a tight hold on it. We struggled for a few seconds before she gave up.

"You really should see a therapist," she remarked.

I couldn't help the loud laughter that burst out of me.

"I'm not the one living in denial," I said, taking one last swig before emptying hundreds of dollars onto our perfect lawn.

"Devin," she hissed. "Waste."

I looked up at her, noting her freshly applied lipstick. It disgusted me. "You are worried about waste? Good to know, dear wife, because I'm hoping you'll take into account the amount of years we have been in this useless union."

"You loved me once," she said, completely void of any real emotion.

"I tolerated you. I thought you were a good fuck, and the sad part is you are still beautiful. You can have any man you want, but me."

She crossed her arms as she sat next to me. "You made a promise. My mother and father have—"

"Your mother and father do not want each other. They do not love each other. They are fucking institutionalized!"

"Devin, don't raise your voice, please. It's our—"

I stood up, glaring down at her as the dimly lit pool illuminated her features. "Have you been faithful?"

She looked up at me, and I saw it. No, she hadn't.

"Devin, you put me in this position."

There was no reasoning with that kind of stupidity. I wouldn't beg for my freedom. I would earn it the way I had earned everything else.

"I can buy you out right fucking now. Let me out of this, or I'll start over," I hissed down at her.

"Ah, but you can't, can you? With your reputation ruined once I'm done with it, no one will trust you with their fortune. Not with the things you've done."

"I haven't done a damn thing wrong but think marrying you was a good move," I said, walking toward the house, ready to pass out face first so I could live to fight another day.

"I'll have her *hurt*," she said, standing quickly, making the statement to my turned back. She sensed my resolve, and she was resorting to threatening Nina…again. This time physically, though she didn't say the words. Charging her, I held her by the neck. I'd never gotten physical with a woman in my life, at least not this way. I squeezed hard.

"You'll what? Eileen, you have tried the last of my patience. She is out of this. Don't ever speak to me of her again." I let go as her eyes bulged. I knew I hadn't hurt her. I'd only meant to scare her, and it worked. I'd scared her into stuttering.

"I-I-I…" She looked at me as if I'd shot her. "I can't believe you did that!"

"Why is it so hard to believe? I loathe you, you sad, sick, sadistic bitch. I dream of the day your life will end. I fantasize the scenarios." Even after all she'd done to ensure my misery, I tried to reason with her. "We were friends once, sincere friends. We may have a chance of parting the same way. End this now, let me buy you out, and stop the rest of your threats!"

"It's over when I say it's over," she chided as she passed me to get into the house. "And your whore *will pay* for what she's done to our marriage."

"Stay the fuck away from her, Eileen, or I will hurt you," I said carefully. "You can play every fucking card in your hand to ruin me, but if you touch her, I *will* hurt you."

She whirled on me. "Why do you love her? Why, Devin? Why is she so worthy?"

I shrugged out my honesty. "She makes me whole. You only wanted me for half."

Studying me with ever scrutinizing eyes, she shook her head in disgust, closed the door behind her, and locked it before turning off all the lights.

"Happy anniversary!" I yelled at the dark house.

It was never about money. It was about starting my own legacy. I took a shortcut by marrying Eileen, taking years off networking to get clients. Now it threatened to cost me my livelihood. She was right. If she carried out her threat and blew the whistle, I would lose my business completely and had no hope of starting over again. I sure as hell couldn't go crawling back to my multi-millionaire mistress penniless and begging her to house me while I tried to put the pieces of my reputation back together. Even then I wasn't sure once she knew the truth as to why that she could look at me the same.

The damage was fucking done.

I made my way to my car, very aware that I wouldn't make it past passing out in the front seat.

"When I give, I give myself"

– WALT WHITMAN

§§

NINA

WAKING UP TO Aiden's late night texts made me smile.

Aiden: Goodnight, sad girl. I sang for you tonight and went home smiling and thinking about...fucking. I hope you did as well.

No, I hadn't, because I was terrified I had again jumped into the sack with another mystery. It was time to get to know Aiden.

I made my way to my desk in my home office and was surprised to see an email from Devin. It was a bottom line of the amount of profit he'd made me. I had to admit, I was impressed. He was good at what he did. The email was completely impersonal and thanked me for my business. I couldn't help the emotion as I burst into tears he didn't deserve. What the hell was I doing?

My phone rang, but I ignored it.

Devin knew every side of me. That couldn't be helped. Only Taylor and Carson got a glimpse of the woman who still lay beneath…and Aiden. I wiped the moisture from my face and smiled at the thought of him. Then my heart sank. If I were to discover he was related to Devin in any way, would I end it?

I drove myself to work, intent on breaking ties. I would sign over that land and wait for the background checks. It was only then that I would have clear options. Though I was a silent partner in the sale of my fitness program, I'd evolved Scott Solutions into an entity of its own, bringing a direct line from inventor to investor. Taylor had thought of the concept and execution when we began forming our corporation. It gave me a sense of purpose, and it gave young inventors a new platform to cultivate their ideas and bring them to life. It was also fascinating to see what they came up with. We didn't take much from either party, just a small amount off the top, a finder's fee, and a portion of the proceeds aftermarket.

The idea went global within months, and suddenly I was thrust into the spotlight once again with an enormous workload, categorizing young inventors and their creations from not just the USA but all over the world. We brought in a full staff, created jobs, and now had more than my first fortune to manage. I'd been selfish in the indulgences of my personal life and the way it would affect Taylor's already enormous workload, especially when things went downhill with Devin. Taylor deserved far more than she was compensated for and I was changing that today.

When Taylor had mentioned we were in this together, it was one-hundred-percent truth. She'd struck gold with her idea as well and had unfortunately given it to me. I was more than afraid of losing her. I needed her.

"Good morning, Taylor."

"Boss," she said, typing away without looking up. "Boy do we have an agenda today."

"We do, but come see me. I have something for you."

She looked puzzled but nodded and followed me back.

I pushed the contract that was couriered over from Devin's office and asked if she'd reviewed it.

"It's legit," she said, pushing it back toward me.

"And this one," I said, pushing forward another. She read for a few moments and then went deathly still.

"It's time for you to start gambling, Taylor." Her eyes swelled with emotion, an absolute first in the two years I'd known her. I hadn't even so much as encountered a menstrual mood swing since we'd been acquainted. Assessing her now, I knew I'd done the right thing.

"You can't do this!" she said, jumping from her seat. "You are handing me a fortune."

"And a stake in this company and the risk that goes with it. I'm committed, Taylor. I want you for the long haul. I'm a little selfish that way."

"Clearly you aren't!" She shook from head to toe. The

contract promised her a signing bonus of two million, a position as co-chair CEO with endless perks and an automatic twenty-percent share in the company with an option to buy as much stock as allotted, making her a millionaire with the click of the pen.

"I can't accept this," she said, turning ghostly pale.

"I die tomorrow, no one gets it. Well, technically my father will inherit most of it, but he has enough. Taylor, you made this company what it's become. You have organized my life and helped me through endless bullshit. I don't want to be your boss anymore. I want to be your equal and your friend."

She stared at me as if I were insane. I laughed loudly.

"I didn't feel like I deserved the break I got either, but I took it. I want you to as well, and you deserve this, Taylor, you do."

A single tear slid down her cheek, and I sighed.

"And when you're done with your signature, your first order of business will be to tell me why the hell you are hanging out in Savannah."

She sat down again, reading the contract, and took a pen in her hand. I saw her body stiffen the more she read. I told them to make the offer irrefutable. They'd done their job.

She lifted her eyes to mine with a smile. "I'll sign this, but I think I'll keep Savannah to myself, just for now."

"Fine." I nodded to her, prodding her to sign and she did so accordingly at the marked tabs.

"Keep that pen, it just made you a millionaire," I said, repeating the words my investor said to me when my life drastically changed. I hadn't done well by evidence of my recent mistakes, but I had zero doubts about Taylor.

"I don't know what to say," Taylor whispered, looking down at the paperwork in disbelief.

"How about we go over your new role," I said carefully.

She nodded as we both became excited with plans to expand the top floor and build her new office. She would carry out the task of hiring a new PA as soon as possible. It was done.

With Taylor, I felt safe.

I was halfway through my work day when I heard the protest coming loud from Taylor.

"You can't go in there," she said, following Eileen McIntyre into my office.

Suddenly, I wanted my pen back. If not for a weapon, then for a dismissal, but I couldn't seem to find one, and the contract on my desk was the only thing keeping this woman in my life.

"It's fine, Taylor," I assured her as she shut the door behind her.

Eileen stood at the door, scanning my large office. She must have noticed I used Devin's decorator.

Good.

"He has impeccable taste, that husband of yours," I said, ridding my desk of the contract and bracing myself for the inevitable fight.

"He used to," she seethed as she turned her gaze to me, roving my appearance.

We were polar opposites in the looks department. I was dark, and she was light, but in contrast to reality, I wasn't sure which of us light represented. We had both been tainted by Devin and our love for him, and our willingness to keep him.

"Honestly, Eileen, I've wanted to apologize, woman to woman, but I really just don't have it in me anymore. You win. I've ended it. He's your burden. Please just leave me the hell alone."

"I honestly wish you'd made that decision a little sooner," she said, taking a seat as I continued to stand.

"You need to leave. We don't have a damn thing to discuss. I have a company to run." Her sneer was unmistakable in that she had no intention of leaving until she said her piece.

"So self-important. Tell me, whore, how many times have you sucked my husband's cock in this office?"

I looked up in confusion, pretending to count, and then nailed her with the answer, "Two...No, wait…" I turned my head to the side, recalculating. "Three. Yes, definitely three."

"You will pay for that," she said, completely serious.

"I've already paid, and aren't there several others that you should be making rounds to? According to you, I was one in a long line of many," I snapped.

She hesitated, and I saw it. "You lied."

"So what if I did." Her callous indifference had my claws embedded in my palms with a welcomed sting.

I felt the pang in my chest and ignored it. It was all over, anyway. The milk that had spilled and soured was resonating throughout my life. I wanted it over.

"Please, leave," I said, deflating back into my chair, suddenly exhausted at the thought of the circles I'd been running in for months.

She leaned over, placing her hands on my desk, palms flat. "You listen to me. Less than a week ago, you fucked my husband at a party I planned."

"I paid to attend that party, and honestly, it was pretty drab. I needed a highlight." The small tug at the corner of my lips didn't go unnoticed.

"You think because you have money now, street rat, that you're entitled?" I studied her perfectly styled chignon, her blue silk pantsuit, and manicured lips, and felt a small amount of pity. She was truly beautiful, and desperately clinging to a man that didn't love her, had probably never loved her. I wasn't sure Devin was capable, at least the Devin I'd known over the last few months.

Pressing my lips together, I thought hard before I spoke. "Entitled is a word I would only use to describe women like you. Tell me, have you ever worked a day in your life?" She lowered her eyes in a bored glare. "*Earned*. I earned this. That's the word I would use. I'm not a street rat, Eileen. I'm a threat and one you take very seriously. But I can assure you now, Devin and I are no more. You are free to abuse him any way you choose." I walked toward my door and almost had my hand on the handle before she spoke.

"You don't *truly* know him. You never will," she said, now standing. "I came here to warn you, if you so much as contact him again, he won't be able to stop me from *dealing* with you."

I shut the door and turned on her. She seemed taken aback that I wasn't intimidated by her threat. I glared at her as she took a step back at my step forward. "The truth is, I was truly sorry for what I did until I realized what you are. I had no intention of sleeping with Devin again. I had no clue he was married. He didn't act the part, and for that I am forever a fool. But what I didn't count on was your wrath. I'd been deceived and, well, your antics prolonged our inevitable end. I fucked him to spite you." Liar. Okay, I fucked him because I couldn't get enough, either. "And my ending it has *nothing* to do with you. I'm not afraid of you, Eileen, never have been." I leaned in close. "Take your entitled ass out of my fucking office before you're thrown out by this *street rat*."

She pushed past me before turning back and facing me head-on. "People like you can never possess the things we have. You wouldn't know what to do with them. You could never preserve history or covet tradition. Look at you…You can't even hold marriage in high regard. You will never have a piece of my life."

I peeked my head out the door as she walked off, shooting myself with a finger gun in the head so Taylor laughed and relaxed. She was well aware of who Mrs. McIntyre was. Watching Eileen retreat to the elevator, I let out a deep breath and sat down to sign the contract for the sale of 3445 Peach Tree Way, Savannah and stopped my pen and snickered.

Looks like I would *possess* some very important land her family had originally owned. And if I felt like it, I would burn it to the ground. I tore up the contract, knowing I was starting another fight.

And for once, I would be ready for it. I picked up the phone to buzz Taylor to send for our courier.

"Man is not, by nature, deserving of all that he wants. When we think that we are automatically entitled to something, that is when we start walking all over others to get it."

– CRISS JAMI

§§

DEVIN

CERTAIN I WOULD go blind if I stared at the torn scraps Nina had sent me that once resembled the contract on the land, I pushed the paperwork into my trashcan.

I had a consult in twenty minutes, and my head was pounding. What in the hell was she thinking? She'd made it clear she wanted to be free of me and the only thing tying us together was this last shred of business.

Fear crept through me as I thought of the possible repercussion of her action. For a brief minute, it was accompanied by a glimmer of hope.

Did she still want me in her life?

Was this an attempt to prompt me into badgering her some more?

I took a shot of whiskey to even the scales of last night's binge, followed by a thorough teeth brushing, and topped it off with a fresh tie.

Sitting behind my desk, I clicked on a picture I'd kept with me, the last piece of evidence I had left that Nina was once mine.

It was the night she told me she loved me. She was covered in a sheet with just fucked hair and looked absolutely beautiful. She was talking to me when she saw me position my camera on my phone and smiled. I loved everything about that photo. There was nothing between us then, nothing holding us back from simply being us.

No rules to adhere to. She was mine, and I was irrevocably hers.

She'd told me she loved me. I hadn't said it back.

"Mr. McIntyre, your two-thirty is here."

"Thank you, send him in."

I spent the majority of my meeting zoning out as my client

spoke, thinking of all the ways I'd had Nina: angry, submissive, subdued.

I missed her.

I ended my meeting knowing I wasn't doing either of us justice and handed over a large homework assignment of investments to research to keep him stifled until we could reschedule.

My head wasn't in it. I was going home.

I pulled out of the garage, feeling like utter shit as memories swirled around in my head. Her smile, her laugh, her lips, the way her mouth opened slowly into a perfect O before she came.

My need was insatiable for her, and it was only getting stronger as she grew more distant.

I passed my exit, opting to drive. After our sailing expedition, I purposefully scheduled her next appointment for a week later, hoping she was the one who didn't cancel.

"I wasn't sure if you would call," she said, walking in to admire the room again. I noted to give her the name of my decorator.

"I didn't, my PA called yours," I replied as she rolled her eyes.

"Fascinating, but why am I here?"

I sat back in my seat, taking in her perfectly fitted, white designer dress and silver dipped shoes.

I. Had. To. Fuck. Her.

"I wanted to see you," I said simply, offering no more explanation.

"I see." Her brows knit in confusion. "Well, how good of you to interrupt my work week to be so selfish. Have you had a good look?"

"Take off your panties," I said, moving back in my chair so she could see the bulge in my pants.

She gawked at me.

"I'm very serious, Nina. Take off your panties."

She didn't move, but simply stared at me.

"I'll be a good boy and take you home to fuck you properly. I've just imagined you in my office with your skirt up for so long, and your pretty cunt shiny and wet in my face. I really want to make this fantasy a reality. So please, for me, take off your panties."

Her breathing stretched throughout the room, sucking all the air out of it. The electricity crackled between us as she walked over to me. I stayed seated as she slowly slid her skirt up, revealing that she had none on.

It took everything in me not to touch her. I watched her vibrate as she looked down at me. She was perfectly waxed, smooth and silky. I could smell her arousal.

"Tell me what you want," I said, moving my hand to touch her as she leaned forward in anticipation.

"Devin, please," she begged as I watched her shake in front of me.

I slowly pulled down her skirt as she glared at me and pushed my intercom.

"Ana, I'm gone for the day."

"Yes, Mr. McIntyre."

I turned to Nina, who stood confused.

"Let's go." I guided her to the elevator and down to my Audi.

She didn't say a word as I drove like a bat out of hell through downtown, which was damn near impossible, and pulled up minutes later at my house. She didn't bother looking around her as she followed me inside. She was as narrow sighted as I was.

In the last year, I had discovered more about her than her ex-husband was probably aware of. A few office meetings had turned into long lunches. I knew her tastes and food fetishes. I knew the name of her senior prom date. I also knew about her parents' never-ending feud and her money hungry mother. I'd even been introduced to her brother, Aaron, briefly while he was passing through. She'd made it a point for us to meet, which I found flattering.

She wanted to let me in. I wanted to be in. And so I never let on differently.

What I didn't know was what it was like to be inside her, and that was about to change.

I led her to the kitchen where I grabbed a few water bottles out of the fridge and then held her hand as we went upstairs, leading her into my sanctuary.

"I warned you I wasn't gentle," I said, setting the bottles down on the night table.

She nodded.

"I need to hear you say it," I prompted, keeping myself far enough from her to stop.

"I understand," she said, a small amount of fear in her voice.

"You will do what I ask when I ask it of you."

She nodded slowly, pulling her dress up again, this time up past her breasts and over her head before tossing it on the floor. Her breathing picked up as I watched her. Her nipples peaked under her bra as I walked over to her.

"What do you want, Nina?"

"Everything," she answered honestly. I took her mouth with such intensity she had to brace herself on my arms to keep from falling. I kissed, licked, and sucked until her entire frame leaned into me for support. She needed air, and I gave her none.

Turning her body, I pushed her onto my bed. She fell, her legs spreading as she pulled herself up on her forearms, watching me. I undid my tie as her gray eyes pooled with desire. I knew that hunger. I matched it and far surpassed it.

"Spread further. Let me see that beautiful cunt, Nina."

She spread wide, tilting her hips up as she opened for me. I slowly pulled off my tie and then swatted her center with it, making her scream out. She bit her lip, her eyes watering, and looked up at me with confusion and fire. I knew it was in there somewhere. Undressing quickly, her eyes widened and then lingered on my hard cock.

She was impressed. She should be.

I stroked it for her, letting her see all of me, as she'd let me explore her with the same hungry eyes. Crawling on top of her, I felt her gasp as I nudged her entrance. I towered over her, my arms separating our bodies, but our centers aligned perfectly.

"Don't look away from me. I want to see your eyes when I fuck you," I ordered.

Her perfect lips parted as she panted and lifted her hips up, begging for me.

"Just the tip," I taunted as I fisted myself and offered her an inch.

Her tight, wet pussy accepted it with ease as she bucked her hips, begging for more as I left just an inch inside her, coating her folds with her own slick heat. I moved back and forth, slowly fucking her with the head of my cock until she writhed and began to beg.

"What do you want?"

"Your cock, all of it, ple—"

I slammed into her all the way to the hilt while her eyes met mine, and she screamed out in praise. I pulled out slowly, fucking her again with just the tip. Her face burned with desire as she looked up at me.

"Devin," she pleaded, bringing her legs around my hips to pull me down as I hovered.

"I've wanted this a long, long time, Nina. I need to know you've wanted it too."

"Fuck." She writhed underneath me in frustration.

"From the first day, Devin. Please, fuck me. Please!" I slammed into her again, then pulled almost entirely out.

The feel of her was weakening me, but I wanted her desperate, hungry, and for only me. Right before she started to beg again, I thrust, once, twice, and she clenched around my cock, exploding around me in all her beauty, keeping her gaze on me and her mouth parted with her scream.

She gave me her whole orgasm without me having to ask.

She was fucking perfect.

I grunted through my need to let go, fucking her hard and gripping her legs around me, lifting her to sink in deeper. She moaned and scratched my skin, a plea for more as I pounded deep into her soaked sex. I raced my climax and won, drawing several more screams and moans from her before finally pulling out to spill all over her perfect tits.

Not bad for a Wednesday at three in the afternoon.

I'd say that's a good fucking day, Devin.

I reached between Nina's legs, drawing out another orgasm as she murmured to me through small gasps.

Pinching her sensitive clit, her body shot up and I stilled her with one hand on her chest while I tortured her with the other.

"Devin," she whispered, bringing my attention to her mouth.

I slid my drenched fingers into it and watched her suck them. I was hard again but wanted to let her rest. I had far more planned.

I kissed her thoroughly and pulled away. She sat up, pulling the sheet around her.

"In this bed, you remain naked," I ordered. She dropped the sheet with a shy smile. She lay back on the pillow, staring at the ceiling as I offered her water. Her breathing was heavy. It was then that I knew she was nervous.

"Can I be honest with you?" she asked, turning to look at me.

"Aren't you always?" I said with a smirk, taking a long pull of water.

"That was incredible," she whispered, taking slow inventory of my body. "If you only have one speed, I like the setting.

"I don't disagree," I chuckled, putting the water on the nightstand. I pulled her on top of my chest and took a nipple into my mouth.

"Am I sporting a sex afro?" she said, quickly running her hands through her hair, ignoring the effect of my mouth.

I let go of her nipple and howled with laughter. I felt the same tug I'd grown accustomed to when I really looked at her. She had a small mole next to her nose that she covered with makeup. I first noticed it that day on the sailboat and could clearly see it now. I stroked it with my finger, and she turned her head.

Wiping the mascara smudge underneath her eye, I brought her nose to mine. "You look perfect."

"Liar," she whispered as she tried to dismount me.

"You have no reason to be nervous, Nina."

I looked up at her as she tried her best to relax. She couldn't do if for herself, so I decided to help her out twice, once with my tongue, the other with my cock. She knocked out quickly after her fourth screaming orgasm.

Those screams justified my need for her.

I was, after all, a closer.

"In reverent pauses, when we slow down and think about the gift of life, we may briefly touch humility."

– BRYANT MCGILL

§§

NINA

Aiden: Dinner?

Nina: I'm all yours.

Aiden: I'll make sure of it.

HE GAVE ME an address, and I looked it up. It was a private country club close to my home. Standing in my closet in a daze, I realized I didn't know how to continue the budding relationship between us without being deceitful. I'd given Taylor the info on the two men and was assured I would know something before the night's end. I would have to tread carefully until I knew more. I picked a sleeveless tan and teal silk dress whose name brand I didn't give a shit about. I was sure it was expensive, but with Aiden, I didn't have to worry about appearances or wearing last year's fashions.

With him, I could be anyone I wanted. This was new. We were new. I smiled as I dusted my face with powder, seeing the blue in my eyes pop out to match the dress. On any given day, my eyes changed color, going from an extreme stormy gray to blue. Even my eye color cooperated with me on my new agenda.

Do better, *be* better, and make better choices.

I wasn't sure if I would ever fit in with my new peers, but I was a far cry from the hopeful housewife who waited patiently for her husband to come home to have something to look forward to. I had let people ruin my first few years of success, and I was determined not to let their opinion control my happiness any longer. My new identity wouldn't have anything to do with the status quo. I had caught myself in time to keep from truly selling out. I had a delicious distraction who was now showing me just how beneficial it was to be real. And, just maybe, this time I would find myself in a real relationship.

Aiden.

I felt the ache growing between my thighs at thoughts of being filled by him. I was still deliciously sore from last night and embraced the fire spreading through my veins. I'd told him I wanted him to be the good guy, but his torturous fucking told me he was anything but. His dazzling smile and sincerity contradicted that point.

Carson drove me to the club, and I was greeted by a smiling valet as he tried to avoid my subtle cleavage, but failed miserably.

It was a beautiful night and the day's heat was fading quickly. I was led through a large dining hall draped in fabric and chandeliers to a private dining room that could cater to hundreds. Off it was a balcony surrounded by palms and small, intimate, rock-filled fires, comfortable couch seating, and…Aiden.

He was dressed impeccably in a suit and tie that looked just as natural as his jeans and t-shirt. He was looking out at the ocean with his hands in his pockets. His golden blond hair was combed back neatly as if he'd been styling it that way for years. He looked up as the hostess and I entered. Next to him stood an intimate table for two dressed to the nines in glassware, candles, and fresh pink peonies.

"We will have your server to you soon, Mr. McIntyre," the hostess piped with a knowing smile for us both. I held in my cringe at the announcement of his name and thanked her, turning back to Aiden, who now fully faced me, taking my breath away. He looked like a Wall-Street mogul. He was so tall, broad, and lethal in a suit. He smiled and held out a hand, not leaving his spot as he stood next to an open glass door.

I walked toward him, drinking him in.

"You look surprised," he mused.

"I am a little. You clean up nice." Pulling me to him, he planted a slow kiss on my mouth and then wrapped his arms around me, placing another kiss underneath my ear as he hugged me.

"I had a meeting today. I thought I might take advantage of

the monkey suit and show my girl a good time."

I looked around me and shrugged. "This is beautiful, Aiden, but you didn't have to go through all this trouble. I would be happy anywhere." I suddenly felt guilty. It must have cost him a fortune to reserve the room. Once again, the guilt of my wealth threatened to ruin my evening. Dismissing it, I looked around, noting the spectacular view. I watched a cruise ship sail by and looked back to Aiden, whose amber eyes glowed with amusement.

"I didn't go through anything," he said simply. "Come on, let's sit." He pulled out the chair for me, and I took a seat, feathering my fingers through the delicate flowers. "You deserve to be dined properly, Nina."

"That's not important, and unnecessary." Placing my napkin in my lap, I looked up to see Aiden frown.

"I disagree." Seconds later, he was testing a bottle of wine it seemed he previously ordered and nodded once at our waiter after he took a sip.

The white wine was smooth, crisp, and delicious. The formality, the way he presented himself, it all seemed so out of character for him. I suddenly mourned my sandal-clad surfer with a dirty mouth.

"Now you look disappointed."

Taking a long sip of wine, he put his glass down.

"Come here."

I stood and rounded the table as he pulled me onto his lap. "What is it?"

"It's just…you and me, this isn't us."

"*Us* is yet to be determined. I happen to enjoy the ritual of it all, but I didn't realize it would upset you," he said as his fingers brushed over my knee. I turned to face him, pulling him closer and taking in his scent. He was wearing cologne that I was unfamiliar with but smelled incredible. I breathed in deep, leaning into him, letting him stroke my skin.

"I'm sorry. I don't mean to seem ungrateful." I saw fire in

his eyes as his fingers traced my knee in slow, small circles. I lifted his wine glass, taking a sip and leaned in to kiss him. He sucked the wine from my lips, and I moaned, tracing his lips with my tongue. I felt him harden underneath me.

"Are you wet for me, Nina?" His fingers drifted further up my leg, but only slightly, stroking the tender skin beneath my knee.

"Mmm," I whispered, lost in his touch. The door opened, and neither of us moved as our wedge salads were placed on the table. Our eyes were still locked as the waiter disappeared as quickly as he came, closing the door behind him.

"Hungry?" he whispered, taking my bottom lip in his mouth and sucking gently as his finger eased up my thigh underneath my dress, stopping at the skin just between my thigh and the hem of my panties.

"Very," I said, leaving no doubt of the source of my hunger. My arm wrapped around his neck as I opened my legs further, welcoming him.

He pulled my dress down, covering my exposed skin and let go of my lip. Frowning in frustration, I made my way to my seat and returned my napkin to its rightful place. I cut a portion of salad, not looking up, because if I did, I knew I would beg him to take me. I was ravenous for him, for the release. I wanted to get lost in him so I didn't have to think about anything. He was trying, for me, and I owed it to him to do the same.

"Tell me more about you, Aiden. I want to know everything," I said, picking up my wine, noticing he hadn't touched his salad. I paused with my glass halfway to my lips. "You aren't eating."

"I thought we were passed this…the hiding." His stare was debilitating and beautiful, and I wanted nothing more than to ease his mind.

"We are."

"We're not."

Smirking to lighten the mood, I finally brought my wine to my lips and inhaled the glass. "We seem to be arguing a lot tonight."

"Tell me what happened." It wasn't a request. It was an order.

"Discussing our exes, isn't it a little soon?" My smile seemed to trigger his anger.

His fist came down hard on the table, making me jump. There was a slow burn in his eyes, and his chin was set in determination. "I want your attention, *all of it*, and someone has taken that ability from me. I want to know what happened."

Sitting motionless, I saw the demand in his stance. He was running out of patience, and I was screwing this up.

"I unknowingly got involved with a married man. I trusted him completely, and I fell hard, really hard. And I can honestly say we were happy. He treated me…" I paused, terrified of saying the words to the man who was doing an incredible job of trying to make me forget.

"He made me happy. We were happy."

Twisting the stem of my glass with nervous hands, Aiden picked up the bottle, filling my glass as the doors again opened and she crab soup was delivered to the table. When we were alone, I continued bracing myself for his judgment.

"When I found out he was married, I continued sleeping with him, but…he'd changed. Not only did he betray me, he started treating me like a possession. Our connection was broken. It continued for months. I was miserable and decided to do something about it. I finally broke it off…" I paused again, fear racing through me, "…the day I met you."

"You didn't leave him for me," he said, matter-of-fact, spooning his soup.

"No, I—"

"I wasn't asking. So he's barely a ghost in your bed."

I felt the chill emulating from him. He looked up through a spoonful of the rich, creamy soup, and I nodded.

"Okay," he said quickly, nodding at me to resume my eating. I grabbed my spoon, relieved that much was out of the way.

"Your turn."

His eyes matched the flame that flickered between us in the dark room as the sun disappeared from view.

"I'm a habitual bachelor. I've never been married, and I don't want children. I don't find it at all appealing. Marriage to me—" he shrugged his shoulders and swallowed his soup "—it's not something I'm capable of. I don't know, maybe the right woman. I'm thirty-five, so I really don't see changing my mind. Maybe. I've had two serious girlfriends, both when I was in my twenties. Both relationships ended amicably."

He's thirty-five. Devin is thirty-five. They aren't brothers. I smiled broadly and damn near sobbed into my soup.

"What is it?"

"Nothing, tell me more." I picked up the wine, refilling our glasses with enthusiasm as he studied me oddly. I was acting like a jackass. I would have to try harder to salvage our night.

"Not exactly the reaction I'm used to when I declare that I'm a permanent bachelor."

"It doesn't bother me. I just got out of that nightmare. I'm relieved you are this way. I won't ever marry again, Aiden." I felt a shiver down my spine as I said the words, more certain than ever of the truth of them.

I had business sense. When it came to a hard cock, I had no sense. Only one of these things defined my future. For now, I would revel in the fact that I was a ravenous slut with an insatiable need, and this man seemed to want me just as much.

He sat back in his seat, pushing his bowl away. "I look at you and I see differently."

I felt my cheeks heat at the sudden pressure of his words. "Aiden, I—"

"Hear me out before you panic."

"Okay."

He grabbed my hand across the table. "I'm not declaring my love. It would be a lie. I'm not promising anything. But what I will tell you is when I'm with you, there is a new kind of calm in me. One I didn't realize existed until you came along. I like it. I want to keep it around." He lifted my hand to his lips and brushed them over my knuckles. That act alone had my pulse thumping between my thighs. Stroking a thumb over the top of my hand, his eyes turned molten. "And you have the most perfect tasting pussy I've ever had my mouth on. I don't think I can wait past dinner to get another taste."

"Then please don't wait," I whispered.

"Take this finger," he said, stroking my index with his, "and put it inside you."

Without hesitating, I did what he asked, gasping at how much I needed to be touched, needed *his* touch. My clit was throbbing, begging for attention. Sensing me straying from his orders, he stopped me.

"Don't, that belongs to me. Now bring your finger to my lips, Nina." Obliging, I lifted my hand over the table to his mouth and moaned as he sucked my finger eagerly. Kissing the pad of it, he let go, placing a chaste kiss on the inside of my palm, and then resting his cheek in it.

"I can't say that you openly admitting to loving another man won't make a difference. You say you are done, and I choose to believe you. With any other woman, I would walk away. With you, it makes me burn."

"I didn't know you existed." My voice was small as I studied his perfect lips.

"And now that you do?" he asked, pulling his face from my hand and making room for the plate of perfectly cooked tenderloin with béarnaise set out before us. The waiter disappeared, and I couldn't help but hope we stayed uninterrupted. I was on fire for him, every muscle in my body tightening. The longer his eyes lingered on me, the more desperate I became to keep them there.

"I wanted you from the minute I saw you, Aiden. That's something. I won't promise you anything, either, but I want the same. When I'm with you, I feel more like me."

"So we agree we give this a chance?" I nodded, my body

reacting to his stare and peaking for him. My breasts felt like a heavy burden, and my nipples ached.

"Aiden, I need you." My voice was hoarse, filled with desire. He stood abruptly and walked over to the banquet double doors, locking them. He took my hand, leading me out to the private balcony and sat on the couch. I straddled him at his urging as he slid his hands up under my dress and cupped my ass. He looked at with me with reverence. My chest expanded with an ache for only him.

"Aiden, please, I can't wait." Towering over him on my knees, I stroked his full lips with my tongue, watching as the last of the sun's rays danced off his golden hair. His fingers found purchase as he slid them through my drenched folds, his eyes never leaving my face, lighting a fire. Pushing me to sit over the hard bulge in his pants, he pulled out a heavy breast and sucked on the nipple eagerly then grazed his teeth back and forth over the taut flesh. Close to the edge, I grabbed the back of his head, grinding my pussy into his hand, my body begging as I breathed heavily. Riding his skilled fingers, I was near climax and just about to burst when he stilled them. "Stop," he ordered as he withdrew from me. I paused on his lap. He moved underneath my dress, releasing his long, thick cock. I gripped it with my hand with the intent on guiding myself down on him.

"I want your mouth," he said just as I aligned us. "Now, Nina, put my cock in your mouth."

Searching his eyes, confused and near combustion, I sank down on my knees on the unforgiving wooden deck, licked and parted my lips. Pulling roughly at my chin with his hand, he opened my mouth wide and shoved his entire length inside. I gagged through it as I looked up at him, sucking and gasping around his girth. He was hard, really hard, and his eyes told me he had no intention of relenting. He gripped the sides of my head as he fucked my mouth, thrusting up and choking me slightly. I regained control, gripping him with my hand that he swatted away.

"Use your mouth, not your hand." Scolding me further, he gripped my hair and the back of my head, forcing it down over his impressive length. It was animalistic and cruel, and I loved every minute.

"When I get you home and you lead me to your bed," he grunted pumping further into me, "I'm going to rip that fucking dress off and hurt you with this cock. Show me you want that, too. Suck it."

He thrust deep on his last words, and I moaned, my eyes watering as he battered my throat, gripping me hard and shooting his orgasm in my mouth without warning. He pulled my hair harder, forcing me down to his root, and slung his hips one final time as his salty cum coated my throat.

I gasped as he pulled out of my mouth, wiping it with the back of my hand, and looking up at him with surprise. He pulled me back into his lap, cupping my still exposed breast and pulling at the nipple with his teeth. Stifled by my reaction to his cruelty, I tilted my head back.

"Dined like a lady and fucked like a whore."

Knowing the truth in his words, I stopped moving my desperate body against his. He cupped my chin, concern in his eyes.

"Is this what you need?"

I nodded without admitting it with words. I was suddenly ashamed of my hunger, my thirst for this type of sex, and I had only had it with one other man.

"Why did you try to hide this from me?"

"I don't know. I was this way for him. I felt like it was wrong to be the same with you."

"It's preference," he said simply, "and it's what you need. I can satisfy that desire thoroughly and as often as you need it."

It struck me then. I was a fucking fiend, and he *knew* it.

He was going to leave me hungry. I felt a small shift in power.

Was I really capable of giving the power to him?

"Can we please just finish our dinner?" I asked, straightening my dress.

He nodded, adjusting his beautiful dick back in his pants. Standing, I turned to look at him, the moon now shining bright and full above us, the fires around us burning steadily. We stared at each other for long moments, understanding passing between us in silent agreement. He had claimed me once again with his declaration of power.

Aiden moved past me, kissing the top of my bare shoulder. It seemed we had relaxed more as dinner progressed. We shared dessert back on the patio and laughed as we finished another bottle of wine on the loveseat near the fire pit.

"What made you get into music?" I asked, then added another question. "And you said you were offered a deal, but why didn't you take it?"

He seemed deep in thought as he moved his fingers between mine playfully.

"It didn't appeal to me, endless hours in the studio, the unforgiving road. I'm happy with the small crowd."

"You are immensely talented, Aiden. It's kind of a disservice to the world." He chuckled as he pulled me closer to him on the couch.

"I wouldn't go that far, but I'm flattered you think so."

He wrapped his arms around me as we settled in, staring at the fire pit in front of us, the flames licking the air in a greedy dance.

"Thank you for dinner. It was excellent."

"You're welcome."

Looking up at his chiseled features and full lips, I sighed. "So the girl that you said you would call, the one you were talking to before you took me in the street, should I be questioning you about her?"

His slow smile told me he was pleased with my question. "She used to tend bar at The Mystic. She wanted her job back. I didn't call." I nodded, watching his fingers lace with mine. "I think I like you inquisitive and slightly jealous."

"You started this, Aiden. Can't take it back now." His chest rumbled with light laughter.

"I wouldn't want to."

He pulled me closer and attached our lips, slowly opening our kiss into something more. I tasted his smooth, playful tongue fully and pulled away.

"Aiden, I like what you do to me, no matter how you do it. Please know that."

"Listen, Nina." He twisted my body to make sure I heard him.

"I'm not worried about who's had you or who you've had. What matters now is I want you. I want you and I want to give you what you need. Fuck the rest of it. It will all fall into place the way it's supposed to."

I nodded, my eyes filling with emotion.

"Come on." He stood up, cradling me and gently lowering me to my feet.

"I'll take you home."

He kissed me deeply again, and we stood wrapped up in each other, listening to the soothing melody of the Atlantic.

"I'm convinced we have each been endowed with a beautiful heart. We may not always see it. We may not even believe it. But it's a gift that came with birth and, every time we act selflessly, it grows a little."

– STEVE GOODIER

§§

DEVIN

"YOU ARE NOT concentrating," Walker said as I recovered from his last blow. I was furious now. I lunged toward him on the mat at neck-breaking speed and landed a hard blow to his chin. He flew back but recovered quickly, sweeping my legs out from under me.

"Getting mad about it isn't going to help your case." He chuckled, hitting me with a right and then a left on the ground before springing back to his feet. I was on my feet in seconds. I purposely slowed my breathing, blocking everything out.

With the help of silent clarity, I stepped forward, waiting for Walker's inevitable slip. As soon as he dropped his knee—a telltale sign of a right punch—I dodged it and brought my gloved fist around, resuming my fury. I landed one after the other, pounding my coach into oblivion.

"Fuck," he declared, spitting a mouthful of blood on the mat before narrowing his eyes. I braced myself for his body shot and took it with a grunt before he nailed me once again to the mat.

"Is it a woman, McIntyre? Oh, what the fuck am I asking. Of course it is. Is the missus set on a summer in the Hamptons and you wanted Europe?"

Jesus, this idiot had no clue. He was a roughneck from Detroit and apparently thought talking to me like that was rough speak to us *privileged folk*. I didn't have the strength to tell him that it was my ex-mistress, not my wife, and chuckled at the thought right before he backhanded me with his glove for the fuck of it.

I deserved that hit. She wasn't just an ex-mistress.

And he was right. My head wasn't in it, but that didn't keep him from punishing me for the last five minutes of our session.

"You make me regret taking you on," he said, grabbing his

water and spilling half of it over his face and chest.

"I pay you, so your opinion really isn't that important." I stared at Adam Walker as he looked back at me with no humor. He wasn't happy. Well, that made two of us.

"You have shit going on, understandable, but this is where you are supposed to twist it to your advantage. Dig deep."

"Do I get brownies and milk with this after school special speech?" I took my gloves off, disgusted. I'd never landed so few punches.

"Seriously…" Adam walked away. He knew he wasn't going to get anywhere. "Bring your A game or don't come back next time, McIntyre. I've taught you better, and I need a partner worth sparring with."

I grabbed my bag and sped out of the parking lot, heading toward downtown. Eileen had called twice, but I had no intention of returning the calls. The threat was always there. Maybe tonight she would ruin what was left of my life, and maybe I'd fucking let her. I was so over the whole thing. I could stack my chips, cash in, and let the rest scatter around me. I wasn't even interested in my current clients and found no thrill in rolling the dice for them. What had been my driving force for so long, the reason behind my inability to keep Nina, now appealed to me less and less. What did it really matter if I couldn't do what I "loved" anymore if I could no longer look at it the same.

Pulling up to my home, I was greeted by a stack of mail before heading to the bathroom for a hot shower. I was completely useless these days. I wasn't doing a fucking thing to further my career because all my thoughts were occupied by a woman who'd made it clear she wanted nothing to do with me. I had a decision to make. I could fight for her, or move on.

I could get laid. That would help. Fuck some stray, make her come, make myself feel better. The only problem was, my dick only got hard to thoughts of her. I stood in the shower, letting the hot water hit me.

Nina, fuck.

I gripped my cock, thinking about the first time I saw her out after we'd slept together.

It was at a charity auction. Some fucking half-assed attempt for one of my partner's wives to do her good bidding for the year. The items up for bid were strange and morbid, and I had no interest in any of them. I was there to support my partner's wife, and possibly get a little networking done. I hadn't called Nina since that day, though it had been less than a week. Seeing her, I instantly felt guilty. It wasn't that I hadn't wanted to. I just didn't want her getting used to it. We'd made no promises. I was already worried about the repercussions of that day and how much I'd wanted her since.

One look from her as she gathered her paddle let me know she wasn't interested in excuses. I gaped at her in a floor-length, off the shoulder red gown. She was fucking stunning. I walked over without hesitation, thankful my wife had a headache. I didn't know how I would handle it when we all came face to face. I would have to tell her the truth and soon.

She plastered a smile on her face as I approached.

"Devin, how are you?"

"Don't. Don't do that," I said quickly.

"Do what?" she replied, absently looking around us.

"Don't pretend to be happy to see me when I fucked up. And get that fake fucking smile off your face. Your real smile is much better."

She stared at me with daggers in her eyes, and I smirked. "I knew you were pissed."

She turned away from me, and I began to panic. Only she elicited that feeling from me.

"I've thought about you every day." This time I was looking around for the pussy who said that. When I realized the pussy was me, I cleared my throat.

Her eyes burned with anger when she looked back at me. "How convenient for you to admit as much now," she hissed as she leaned down toward the silent auction tables in front of us, pretending to inspect the items for bid, picking up the pen to make and offer here and there.

I cleared my throat again. "Actually, this is very inconvenient, my partners are here. Can I see you after this?"

She scoffed as she leaned in again, penning another offer.

"Nina, you won't make friends by throwing your money away."

"I'm trying, Devin, okay." She looked around, keeping her voice low. "I've done everything I can think of. I've joined their fucking clubs, given my money, offered a free hand. I don't know what else to do." She was out of her element and completely unsure of herself. I hated it.

"Come," I said, taking her politely by the arm. I brought her over to another client, knowing in the back of my mind it was a bad idea. Everyone knew my wife.

"Nina Scott, this is Victoria Stoddard. She is the chair of the Admiral's Club. I don't believe you told me you've met. Nina owns Scott Solutions." Victoria looked at me assumingly, and I handed her more ammo. "Nina is with my firm. Please excuse me, ladies. I have to make a call." I walked away quickly before Victoria could ask about my wife's whereabouts. I considered leaving, but when I looked back from the bar, Victoria had already left her side. She probably smelled the fear on Nina, who was searching the crowd for me. When her eyes landed on mine, I saw the relief. I ordered a drink, and when I looked up, she was gone. The lights flashed, signaling the auction was beginning. I went inside, seeing her red dress to the right of me. I didn't brave a glance. I was painfully aware of how far she was from me. I was playing a dangerous game. I didn't give a fuck, though, because I wanted her.

"Okay, ladies and gentlemen, our first item…" I wasn't paying attention as paddles flew up around me, the bidding getting more intense as the items dwindled down. I studied Nina, watching the emotion cross her face as she studied the goings-on. She wanted in so badly, she just wasn't sure how to do it. Most of my life, I'd been wealthy. I never had to fight for a seat at the table. I didn't know what it was like to feel like an outcast. Staring at her now, I knew it was painful.

Looking at her, I knew she didn't belong.

She found me in the sea of faces, and I saw the resolve cross her face and knew that she would be bidding on the next item and that she would win.

"Okay, ladies and gentlemen, next we have an eighteenth-century

rubbing board. This particular piece of history..." I looked down at the auction menu and cringed.

Oh, fuck.

I saw her paddle go up at the bid for ten-thousand and heard the snickers around her. She looked around at the faces of the people openly musing at her, and I saw her lips press into a firm line. She had something to prove and had no intention of backing down. I was thankful when Mark Thompson lifted his paddle at twenty thousand, but knew Nina had no intention of losing. The bidding went up to a surprising twenty-five thousand, and I had no choice.

"Twenty-six thousand to the man in the black tux." A collective sea of black tuxedos laughed with the crowd, except for one woman who was openly glaring at me. I shook my head in a firm no, pleading with her not to bid further, but of course she did, making the useless, ancient artifact worth a false thirty-five thousand. I lowered my paddle at forty grand, giving up. Nina looked back at me with a smug smile as the gavel was smacked. I closed my eyes, my head shaking back and forth, and ran my hands through my hair.

"The lady really wanted that rubbing board, folks." The crowd burst into laughter as Nina lowered her head at the attention.

I was suddenly angry with her, with her inexperience, and her inability to read a situation. I fucking hated the crowd laughing at her and wanted to go and yell at her for the embarrassment she'd just brought upon herself. When the auction was over, I joined her and pulled my checkbook from my pocket.

"Let me get this," I said quietly as she looked up at me with a smile.

"I own it. I bid on it. I won."

"Nina, please, just let me get this," I said more sternly.

"I've got it, Devin. Surely you know I can afford it." It took all the strength I had not to scream at her in line.

"Nina, I—"

"Forty thousand dollars won't make up for it, Devin. You can't buy yourself back into my good graces." She leaned in further. "Or back into your bed."

She took another step forward as the line moved, and the auctioneer smiled broadly. "Oh yes, the rubbing board."

I leaned in and whispered so only she could hear, "Congrats, you are now the proud owner of the world's oldest dildo."

She froze and stilled her pen, her smile falling from her face. She looked up at me in question as I walked off and out into the parking lot. She deserved to be made to scrape the shit she'd stepped into off of her own foot. I couldn't keep holding her hand. But damn it, I wanted to. I wanted to help her, but at the same time, I wanted to keep her separate from this world.

"Devin, I'm sorry," she said as she caught up with me in the parking lot. Without thinking, I turned and wrapped my arms around her, pressing her to me. "For what?" I took her lips without giving her a chance to answer. I kissed her long, hard, and thoroughly. I hadn't lied. I'd thought about her every minute of every day. When I pulled away, her lips parted as I licked mine, savoring our kiss. Suddenly her features darkened as she forgot my hold on her, her voice low with shame.

"You were just trying to help me. God, I've never been so embarrassed in my life." She buried her head in her hands, and I pulled them away.

"Stop it," I snapped as she stood, stunned. "Those fucking people aren't worth your worry. Most of them have never done a selfless act in their life. You don't need to compare yourself to them."

"So easy for you. Tell me, Devin, why are you surrounded by them? Aren't these your partners? Your friends?" she huffed, still reeling from my kiss.

"They are my bread and butter, Nina. They are necessary for me. I don't have a choice, but you do."

"I'm just trying to fit in," she said in a soft voice.

"You don't belong here. Not with them. I'm sure there are plenty of nice *wealthy people out there, but..." I pointed to the hotel we had just exited. "Those people I know, those people I do business with, and they are not those nice people."*

"What would you have me do, Devin?" Trembling beneath her red gown, she confronted me head-on, a storm brewing in her gray eyes. I gripped her hand and pulled her into my Audi. She didn't resist as I turned the ignition and took a deep breath. She stared straight ahead as I looked over at her.

"Nina." Grabbing her hand, I held it in mine. Trembling beneath my hand was hers, soft and small. I held it tighter, completely unsure of what to do. I felt somehow responsible for her. I'd only fucked her once, but somehow I knew it had nothing to do with it.

"I'm completely alone, Devin." She looked at me then with unshed tears in her eyes, and I felt my entire body go weak in visceral reaction. I pulled her to me in a soft kiss, exploring her perfect mouth as she moaned, her tears falling down her cheeks and onto my hands as they cradled her face.

"Nina, alone is exactly what you will be with a crowd like that. Come on, let's salvage our night."

"Where are you taking me?"

"To the water," I answered as I buckled her belt then mine.

"I love the water," she said softly.

"I know." I grinned at her with a wink. She winked back and returned my smile, wiping her tears away.

I drove to the Isle of Palms, and we removed our shoes as we walked along the beach. I grabbed her hand as she stayed silent, still upset, but with each passing minute, I could feel the water working its magic, calming her. She'd told me a long time ago she grew up a water baby. All of her favorite memories were held at the beach. I understood the allure. I felt the weight of the world shift slightly as the water traced the shore. It was becoming warmer.

She laughed out of nowhere as she turned to me. "How did you know what it was, the rubbing board?"

"History major," I said, chuckling with her. "Though that wasn't in any of the books. I can't believe that was up for auction." I smirked, turning to her. "Planning on using it?"

"Absolutely not," she said with a childlike giggle. "I wouldn't even begin to pretend to know how. I should demand full disclosure. It looked like some sort of, I don't know. It's made of brass and wood, how would they even begin to…" I gestured with my fingers how the women would impale themselves on the board, facing each other as Nina's large eyes rounded and her mouth formed an "Oh" of understanding.

We walked a bit longer, and I felt her hand relax in mine.

"Feel better?" I asked as she turned on me at the same time with a question.

"Why didn't you call?"

"I can't give you more than sex and friendship." She didn't hide her disappointment, and I didn't offer her more. "A friend would call," she said, stepping toward me.

"I was planning on it."

"I was holding my breath," she mouthed as she eyed me carefully. Her dress outlined her body as the excess material flew in the wind, and I felt the pull, as I always did, to have her beneath me.

"What are you thinking?" She smiled as I let my eyes appreciate her.

"I've never let a woman so damn beautiful have this much effect on me."

"Well, what are you going to do about it?" She put her hands on her hips, an awkward gesture for the dress she was in, but that was Nina, a square peg trying desperately to cram into the round hole.

"I'm going to eat your perfect ass." She took a step back and burst out laughing.

"You won't be laughing while I'm doing it." Catching the lust clear in my eyes, she stopped her laugh abruptly, her eyes wide.

"I don't like the way you make me feel," she said, unsteady on her feet.

"No, you love it, and that scares you more." I pulled her to me, tasting her and fucking her mouth with my tongue. Pulling away, she searched my eyes, and I gave her nothing.

"Let's go." She nodded and bit her lip. I scooped her up, running with her down the sand we had just walked. She laughed hard, wrapping her arms around my neck.

"Thank you," she said as I slowed, lowering her to the ground.

"For what?"

"Trying to save me…again."

"One day I may succeed."

She smiled as I held open the door for her. "One day I might let you."

In the now freezing shower, I fisted myself over and over, thinking about that night and the number of ways I had violated her, carrying out my promise and doing much more. I stilled, letting go as I spilled over, the burn in my chest staying with me.

§§

NINA

Aiden decided to take me home in his Jeep with the top down, but not before pulling up next to Carson in his monstrosity and honking obnoxiously. Carson rolled down his window, his eyes wide.

"I'll be escorting Ms. Scott home tonight, sir."

"Please, call me Carson."

"Will do," he said, knowing full well the spectacle he was making. "If I may, Miss," Carson added quickly, "please fasten your belt." My heart squeezed at his concern as I pulled the strap away from my chest and showed him the inch that it gave. Aiden took off like a bat out of hell, and I saw Carson's face pale before Aiden raced us out of sight.

"Hey, you want to get along with me, better get along with my sidekick."

Aiden smiled as he pushed shuffle on his iPhone. "Will do, Miss." He pulled the cuff of his shirt out of his jacket, straitening it out to tease me, and I punched him in the arm.

"Damn, woman!" His eyes bulged.

"I had a little brother. I had to condition on the regular," I warned.

"I'll keep that in mind as well." He rubbed his arm in mock pain, and I rolled my eyes. We stayed silent as we drove through the night, the moon low and surreal as the breeze whispered through the cabin of the Jeep. The Church's "Under the Milky Way" came on, and I thought it fitting. It was absolutely perfect.

"Do you know where you are going?" I asked as he picked up my hand, kissing my fingertips.

"Yep, we are going for a drive. We can't waste this moon." I nodded in agreement as he avoided stoplights and continued to drive over every bridge in Charleston. We rode for some time,

Aiden always the perfect maestro, seducing me without words and a simple playlist.

"It's unreal what you do to me with music," I whispered in his ear, leaning over into his seat and stroking his lap suggestively.

"Time for bed." He suddenly exited, heading back toward the direction of my house, and I laughed loudly as I gave him directions. Minutes later, he looked over at me, and I saw his need and leaned over again, kissing his neck briefly before pulling away.

Looking up at the larger than life moon, I lifted my phone and took a snapshot. I frowned at the picture. It wasn't a damn thing like what we were seeing. Aiden noticed my frustration after several attempts.

"Some things are to be lived in the moment only. They can't be captured." I looked over at his golden hair as it played in the breeze, his tender smile, and understood immediately.

I was going to fall for this man.

§§

At home, Aiden stayed silent as he surveyed the expanse of my house. He didn't seem impressed and walked through it with me, opening each door as I guided the tour. I finally let out a long, loud breath after several minutes of silence.

"Well?"

"I'm going to bet you only use two or three rooms in this house on a daily basis." He looked pointedly at me, and I nodded.

"This isn't the right house for you," he said, dismissing it.

"Well, I designed it, and I happen to love it."

"No, you don't," he said, studying me as we stood in a spare bedroom. "You defend it. If you loved it, you wouldn't try so hard, and you wouldn't be asking for my approval."

I rolled my eyes, and he closed the distance between us. "Don't do that, beautiful. I'll make you cry."

"What?" I said, looking into his fiery eyes.

"Don't roll your eyes at me. It's disrespectful."

"Respect is earned," I muttered as I rounded the corner of the room into the carpeted hall, still on edge because of his assessment. I heard the air whoosh next to my head before I realized I was on the floor with my hands pinned above me. I looked up as Aiden towered over me. "And you are about to earn mine."

I giggled as I fought his hold in vain and he held my hands with his one as he tore my dress away from my chest. I paused, hearing the material rip, and looked up at him in shock. He snapped the strap of my bra away and pulled the cups down, revealing my peaked nipples.

"Still not taking me at my word, Nina?"

I fought him hard, then turned my body and ripped my wrist free as I attempted to crawl away. He held on to the material as I struggled to move from him, my back and thong covered ass now bared to him as he won the war with my now ruined dress. I felt the sting of his slap on my thigh and screamed out.

"Aiden!"

He lunged for me just as I was about to break free, pressing me down with one hand on my back while tearing away my panties. Seconds later, I felt his hand separate my legs easily as he lifted me on all fours. I was dripping as he landed another painful slap. I looked back to see him removing his jacket and tie as he held me in place with his hand on my hip, his fingers digging in painfully. I moved to get away when he stopped me with the boom in his voice.

"Don't even think about it. I already owe you for the first time."

I lay my head on the carpet, my ass in the air, waiting for my punishment. I felt the ache to be filled as I panted, unsure of his next move. A sudden burst of cold air hit me as I realized we were under an air conditioning vent. I moved slightly to keep the chill from my skin and screamed as Aiden bit me hard on the back of my neck. Pain washed over me just as he thrust into me from behind. My body exploded in sensation as I called out to him. Overcome by the sudden intrusion of his long, thick cock, I twisted my ass to try to accommodate his size.

I felt the strap around my neck before the squeeze as he tightened his belt, thrusting into me full force.

"If you want out of this, Nina, you tap the floor with your palm, understood?" His voice was raw, angry, and full of lust. "Let me see you do it," he pushed out through clenched teeth.

I tapped the floor with my palm, and he rewarded me by tightening the belt. I was leashed now as he pounded into me, pulling on the belt for leverage. He slowed his thrusts and tightened it further, cutting off my air, but only for a few seconds before releasing the hold to slam in again.

Thrust, thrust, squeeze.

Thrust, thrust, squeeze. I bit my lip as the orgasm built deep inside of me. I was dizzy with lust, only able to feel him. The powerful thrust of his hips forced me to collapse forward, and I was rewarded with the painful squeeze of the belt and another hard slap on my now bruised ass as he again lifted me back to my knees. With one more push of his punishing cock, I came, and he squeezed and slapped as the current raced through me, leaving me completely drained. I fell forward again, unable to care about the consequences. The belt was released, and I was turned over in time to see Aiden's eyes blaze.

"I'm going to treat you so nice," he whispered, tracing my neck with tongue-filled kisses while his fingers eased in and out of me, pulling the moisture from my orgasm. "I'm going to need to fuck this pussy well and often."

"Yes," I breathed out in reply. Succumbing to his touch and his promising words, I shuddered as he traced my folds softly with my slick juices. He pulled away, catching my eyes as he drew back, pulling my legs up around his shoulders, hooking them behind his neck while lifting my upper half off the floor. He slid into me slowly, so slowly, as I choked on a gasp, completely full of him.

"Aiden," I whispered hoarsely.

His hand slid down my chest over my breasts, caressing them as he made his way down to my aching clit. "I know, baby, you still need me."

I nodded, knowing how desperate I seemed, knowing that no matter how good it was, I was insatiable. No matter how hard I came, I would always want more. I was addicted.

"Watch it, baby. Watch my cock," he murmured soothingly. I followed his eyes to where we met intimately, and I watched his length go in and out, coated with my orgasm. He pushed in deep, his reach slightly painful, caressing the spot deep inside stroke after stroke. The sight of his cock covered in me had me coming again instantly, and he sped up as we both watched ourselves connect. My skin was on fire as I watched his coat of armor tattoo flex with his exertion and admired the sharp contours of his chest. There was nothing but the menace in his eyes as he punished me with harsh licks over and over, pushing me to the brink. His knowing smirk was sinister, as if he knew exactly what I was feeling and how to take it away.

If this man was my knight, I had no doubt he was hiding the dark horse he rode in on.

My body still halfway between the floor and wrapped around his shoulders, he pounded into me, slowing only to readjust his grip before rearing back and really punishing me. I felt every inch of him, and he made sure of it, his body taxing mine. I felt him harden further as he rubbed me deep and I held out for him as he pushed in one last time.

"Aiden…" My voice lifted as I came in a scream and he gripped my thighs tightly, pinching the skin as he poured into me with a rough, "Nina."

§§

Halfway between a shower and the bed, we found ourselves in a tangled mess in the kitchen, and I was suddenly face to face with a very hungry and exasperated Aiden. I laughed as he threw a fit over the type of food I kept in my house.

"There is nothing here!"

"There is plenty there. I just went shopping," I said, crossing my arms with a smirk.

"What the hell is this?" He held up a bag of low-carb wraps, and I burst out laughing.

"It's bread."

"The birds wouldn't even eat this shit," he griped, finding a container of raw peanut butter and grabbing a spoon.

"It's healthy."

"Iphts shbit," he said through a mouthful of peanut butter, making a face of complete disgust when the taste hit him.

"Yeah, I should have warned you that's not exactly sweet." He glared at me as he downed his water, chasing a mouthful of flax seeds and raw peanuts.

"I'll be more than happy to send Carson to get you a Happy Meal, cry baby," I taunted, naked aside from his boxer shorts that I rolled around my hips after our last bout of sex.

"No, it's fine," he said, seemingly unsatisfied, his nose wrinkled. He looked gorgeous in his dress pants and bare feet, his hair still covered in product but thoroughly picked through by my greedy fingers. His skin was perfectly kissed by the sun, his hands battered from his guitar. I wanted him again as I watched his face contort with each new item he studied and tasted. "I'll just eat this," he said, pausing to read the label, "carrot and hummus healthy snack pack."

"Good for you. A wise choice at three A.M.," I said, shaking my head in mock approval.

"Listen, I'm all for keeping that beautiful body of yours in shape, but this has got to suck," he said, eating one carrot covered with hummus and tossing the whole thing in the trash.

"It's how I do it. It's to stay small *and* healthy, Aiden. It's not just about vanity."

"Cook for me, then. Make me something out of all this shit in here, and I'll be the judge if it's edible."

"You want me to cook for you, now, at 3 A.M., half naked

in my kitchen?"

"Why not?" He looked at me expectantly.

"Unless you walk on water or you just replicated your penis and now are the new King Tut, you are asking too much."

He stalked toward me, and I chuckled as he sat me on the counter in front of him.

"My cock is not enough for you?" His voice was low, threatening. I looked into his eyes filled with hunger as he watched my nipples draw tight.

"I think you know exactly what your cock is to me," I said, leaning in to kiss him. He pulled away, dodging my kiss.

"Someone is cranky when he's hungry." I leaned in, kissing his chest, tonguing the dark, black pattern that shadowed his pectoral, and trailed my kiss up to his neck. "I love the way your skin tastes." I saw the bulge in his pants and looked into his eyes.

"I've fucked you six times since we walked through that door, Nina." I couldn't read his expression, but I knew it wasn't good. I backed away, giving us both space to breathe.

"I don't know what to say." I lowered my head. "It's the way I am."

He looked me over carefully. "He conditioned you."

"Sorry?" I was completely confused.

"Your old Dom—"

"Dom?" I laughed and shook my head. "I've never had a Dom."

"Yes you have," he said, completely convinced. "Look at you, Nina. The minute I step forward with a commanding sentence, a look, a touch, your body responds. You've been conditioned, and really well."

What...the...fuck?

"Nina, I leashed you tonight, and you didn't object. Most women would panic or at least question their lover."

I sat stunned as he looked at me.

"It's second nature to you."

Anger rushed through me as I pushed him aside and

jumped off the counter then turned to him. "Fuck you and your assumptions."

"Nina," he countered, moving toward me. Putting my hand up, I threw his shirt at him.

"Aiden, I think it'd be best if you left. I have to work tomorrow. Playtime is over."

Put that in your pipe and smoke it.

He stood stunned for a brief moment before gathering his clothes. I pushed his boxers off of me and turned to walk away.

"I'm sorry, Nina, but it's the truth."

"Goodnight, Aiden."

I pulled myself up the stairs and closed my bedroom door, completely baffled. A million sexual scenarios ran through my mind as I recounted my time with Devin.

And we had done *it all.*

I dove into bed, burying my head under the covers. As soon as the chime alerted me Aiden had left, I locked the door from my bedside remote.

Dom?

"The opposite of love is not hate, it's indifference.

– ELIE WIESEL

§§

DEVIN

MY WIFE WALKED into my office, unimpressed by her invitation. "What is it, Devin? I have an appointment."

I slid the folder in her direction. "I'll make it quick then, dear." She looked up at me, annoyed as her eyes drifted over me and then down to address the folder in front of her.

It was her instant recognition that told me *I had her.* "It went up for quick sale this morning. I've already put in an offer, on your behalf, of course."

She fingered the paper with adoration. It was an offer she couldn't refuse tied up in a nice shiny bow. A plantation she'd dreamed of owning that had never been for sale. She'd often spoke of it and the possibility of owning it when we still shared the same bed.

"Devin, I don't quite have enough," she said, her face paling at the thought of losing.

"I agree you aren't quite liquid enough right now, honey. I can remedy that."

I pushed different paperwork in front of her, and a check I'd cut over a dozen times already. "If we hurry, I'm sure we can push the sale through before Mrs. Marion gets wind." I had her attention. I had the perfect bait. If she signed the paperwork and accepted my check, I would regain controlling interest of my company, and in return, she would own the plantation she'd wanted since she was a child.

"Of course, if you're not interested, I could give Mrs. Marion a call." She glared at me openly as she picked up the pen. "This and nothing else, Devin. You get nothing else." I rolled my eyes, knowing that getting my company back was half the battle and with her signature, I'd just won. I tried to hide my wolf grin as I sat back in my chair but failed.

"This isn't over, and this means nothing," she hissed as she stood up and walked out of my office.

I didn't bother to reply.

In the end, I would have the last word.

§§

NINA

After hours of tossing and turning over Aiden's declaration, I decided sleep wasn't coming and beat Taylor to the office. I opened my email in a sleep-deprived coma, literally inhaling my coffee as I drank it. I didn't need another man coming in with a blazing cock proclaiming he knew what was best for me. I wanted a playmate and someone who was genuinely interested in getting to know me. I was hard on Aiden by throwing him out, which I felt guilty for, but at the same time, he needed to know his place, and it wasn't quite at the head of the table. Not yet. I wasn't sure agreeing to start a relationship was the best idea, either.

Dom. Dom. Dom!

Devin had never once had to explain his actions in bed. We'd never used a safe word. He'd never…

But he had. He'd had me in every way imaginable, and I'd never once stopped him. Because the truth was, I fucking loved it, just as I'd loved being leashed by Aiden and the cruelty of his fucking.

The whore in me celebrated my luck in finding two men capable of sating my appetite.

Shut up, whore.

Aiden was a versatile lover while Devin, though clever with charming words, had never once made love to me.

Do I embrace this? *Naughty Nina.*

I shivered in my seat. I'd spent way too much time thinking it through already, and it was always the same conclusion.

I was a greedy nymph, and when I was hungry, moral conscience didn't come into play.

In all the night's activities, I'd forgotten about the background check and opened the email from Taylor she'd sent sometime during my dinner with Aiden. I read through both files with a fine-tooth comb.

> Devin Alexander McIntyre, born October 28, 1979, age 36.

Thirty-six? *FUCK.* I fought hard to remember when I'd asked him his age. He'd had a birthday and didn't tell me. Of course he hadn't.

> Father, Eric McIntyre, age 63.
>
> Mother, Genevieve McIntyre, age 61, born in Germany.

It was a simple summary. No siblings, which gave me a breath of relief. It was a complete timeline of his life and career. He'd been valedictorian of his high school, and a track star. He went on to Brown to double major in business and history, eventually graduating with an MBA. No criminal record. Married Eileen Greer, May 15, 2008. Wow, the happy couple just had an anniversary.

Fuck them.

I moved onto Aiden.

> Aiden Elliot McIntyre, born March 26, 1980, age 35.
>
> Father Elliot McIntyre, deceased, age 34, Suicide.

Oh no! Pain spread through my chest thinking of my own father and how I wouldn't have done well without him. I needed to spend time with him. I would make it a priority.

Poor Aiden.

> Mother, Juliana McIntyre, age 59.

I read the rest with my mouth hanging open. If Devin was impressive on paper, Aiden was a golden child. He made All-

American in football. His achievements were endless. He'd gone to Harvard, graduating with a doctorate in psychiatry and onto graduate school for business communications.

I stared at my screen, completely useless. Taylor walked in as I blinked rapidly at the screen.

"Well, I see you got my email," she piped, handing me a fresh latte.

"He's a bar owner," I said, scanning through the rest of the information.

She sat across from me, unaffected as she spoke. "Who better to serve you beer than a neighborhood shrink?" I pushed away from my desk and started pacing.

"We went to school together," Taylor added. "I remember him." I cornered my desk, arms crossed.

"And?"

"And nothing. I saw him at a few parties, nothing special. I remember he was hot. I never had a conversation with him. My roommate was in love with him. That's the only reason I took notice."

I nodded. "Did she ever date him?"

"No, she gave up and settled for some grease monkey her second year."

I pulled at my lip as I absorbed the fact that I was dating another scholar out of my league. It was no longer a mystery why he was so intuitive, so quick to voice his opinion, so quick to dish out advice.

So quick to diagnose me as a fiend.

He was a certified doctor of the fucking mind who had leashed me like a dog last night and fucked me for seven straight hours. I sat down again, banging my head on the desk as Taylor chuckled. I looked up to see her beaming at me.

"Someone's happy. What's your story?" She was practically glowing, and it was anyone's guess why. Maybe she had finally watched every episode of Jeopardy and had all the correct answers, maybe she had gotten our coffee buy one get one free, or maybe, just maybe she had finally found a man who could do a better job of fucking her than she could.

"Not as interesting as yours," she said, dodging my question once again.

"Taylor, come *on*."

"Well, I will tell you this…" She raised a brow just as there was a knock on my open door. "Excuse me, ladies, the server is down. We are delayed half an hour."

Taylor jumped up, her demeanor changing in the blink of an eye as she followed the head of the tech department out the door, barking orders. I chuckled as I watched her follow him to the elevator, handing his ass back to him in a paper sack before he escaped.

That's my girl.

I spent the rest of the day digging in deep, finding the strength to make it through without face planting on my desk. By the time I was finished, my body ached for a bath and my bed, and I couldn't think of anything I wanted more. Making my way out of the building, I found Carson had the door open for me. I slid in and jumped when I saw Aiden waiting for me in the car.

I peeked out, giving Carson the evil eye as Aiden yanked me back in before closing the car door.

"I told him you were expecting me." I sat, silently staring at him. "Talk to me," he whispered as I looked out the window.

"So you can gloat?"

"I'm not in this to hurt you, Nina." I turned to look at him and saw him freshly dressed in jeans and a t-shirt, holding a bouquet of pale peonies.

"You seemed to admire them at the restaurant." He handed them to me, and I closed my eyes.

"I'm sorry." It was all I could say. I wasn't ready to admit that he was right. I'd let him violate me so easily last night, no questions asked. That was not normal behavior. He grabbed my hand and held it as I stayed silent. When we approached my house, I turned to him.

"Where did you go to college?"

"Harvard." I nodded, thankful for truth. "You don't seem surprised, Nina."

"I'm not." I didn't give him anything else as I climbed over his lap and let down the window, addressing Carson. "You are dismissed for the evening. Have a good night." I pushed the button without waiting for his reply or looking for his approval.

"You researched me," he whispered as I took my seat across from him.

"Yes."

Instead of being offended, he seemed amused. "And what did you find out?"

"You're an Aries," I muttered dryly as I faced him with a hard look. "You're an Aries with a golden arm and the IQ of Socrates…Oh, and a shrink…What the fuck, Aiden?"

"Does this impress you?" He was completely unaffected. "Yes and no. What are you doing? And why haven't you done more?"

"More as in what? Waste my life away behind a desk? Work my entire career, graying and slaving to other people as a servant? No thanks, I'm not fond of people." The cabin filled with a tenseness I wasn't used to when it came to Aiden. He didn't like being on the defensive, of that I was sure. His face darkened, and his lips quirked, as if he had tasted something bad.

"You are a shrink! I would think people are your thing." I crossed my arms as he remained completely calm as he sat across from me.

His voiced was laced with anger as I stumbled with my thoughts. "I won't apologize for my education. That's ridiculous. I would have told you things eventually, but you went looking for them. Why are you so upset? Did I ruin your ambition of slumming it with me?"

"That's not fair," I defended. "I was happy you were a bar owner. I was happy I didn't have to pretend with you. I thought you were living in the real world, but I just dove into your own personal world of make believe."

"How so?"

"You don't act like a scholar. You don't present yourself in a way—"

"That suits society? I know. I'm proud of myself." His grin was contagious, and I couldn't help but answer it. "I believe the word you're looking for is humble. I have no reason to list my accomplishments to anyone. I have nothing to prove. Those are things I did for me." We sat across from each other for long moments as I drank him in. His t-shirt was form fitting and clung to him in all the right places. His jeans fit him well, and I couldn't stop staring at his pronounced Adam's apple. My lips itched to trace it. It was sexy as fuck. He looked fresh and beautiful and insanely fuckable.

He hadn't lost a wink of sleep, either. *Asshole.*

This is your drama. Keep cool, Nina.

"How did you know?"

"About your sexual preference? I studied it. I actually did my thesis on sexual behavior." He paused only briefly before he added, "I also practiced it."

My eyes shot to his, and I saw a fire brewing.

"Well, contrary to what you might think, I'm exhausted, so you won't be able to snap your fingers for a snack today." I moved to get out of the car.

"If I wanted to fuck you, Nina, I would already be doing it," he snapped, gripping my wrist.

There it was again, that instant longing. My chest rose and fell with the command of his voice. Was he doing this on purpose to fuck with me? I was aroused when I was supposed to be offended. I had more questions for him but decided against asking them to give myself a chance to get my shit together.

His grip loosened. "I'll stop chasing you, Nina. If that's what you want." Hurt spread through my chest as I looked up at him. I saw sincerity and a twinge of worry. We'd started this too soon. I wasn't ready for commitment, and now I knew it. I was still healing from the loss of Devin. I shouldn't have entertained the situation, but it was too late. He had his hooks in slightly, and I loved the feel of them.

"I'll come to you," I murmured, grabbing the flowers he'd brought me and kissing his lips briefly. He nodded, seeming satisfied, and I got out of the car, barely making it through a shower before passing out in my bed. I woke up twelve hours later to a text from Devin.

Devin: We need to talk.

For fuck's sake.

"Art and love are the same thing: It's the process of seeing yourself in things that are not you."

– CHUCK KLOSTERMAN

§§

DEVIN

"HANDLE THIS OR I'll do it for you." The phone went dead in my ear, and I rolled my eyes.

Another day, another threat.

At least I'd won the majority of the war with Eileen, a situation I would never get myself into again. These days I was less the predator of the rich and unassuming and more of an unwilling puppet.

I'd let it go too far, especially with Nina.

Another unanswered text let me know it was time to let her go. I couldn't force her to listen and she damn sure wouldn't forgive me. Pride was not a factor in this. I had no choice but to try to get her to keep her word and sell the land back to me. Now more than ever, the risk was high, and it was only a matter of time before she would be pushed into the fire.

It couldn't happen. I wouldn't let it happen.

Did I expect her to forgive me? The tragedy was, she would never know that I loved her. That I still love her, that I would always love her.

I'd been a coward, and I'd lost the girl. I was paying penance.

Eileen had come into my office guns blazing and threatened me with every available source at her fingertips when she discovered my affair. My career, my reputation would all be disintegrated in hours. I had no choice but to take her seriously and play along. The result was a visit from a jaded and hurt Nina a month later.

"Devin, good to see you. How's the family?" She walked past me, her speech rehearsed.

"I should have told you," I said, mentally nailing my feet where I stood to keep from going to her. A thousand times I'd picked up my phone, a thousand times I'd put it back down. I had no excuse. And the one I had would not be the one she wanted to hear.

In this fucked up scenario, I should have been apologizing to my wife, not my mistress.

"Yes, you should have, but that's not why I'm here." Her voice cracked. She was trying so damn hard, and I saw it in the way she carried herself. I'd hurt her. I'd hurt myself. It was for the best. Eileen was unpredictable. If she'd gone far enough to take off her clothes and pose for Nina, she meant business. I hadn't seen her naked in years.

Manipulative, conniving cunt.

She knew I was in love with her, and looking at Nina in front of me, I knew it had never been more true.

"Okay, why are you here?"

"This." She pointed to a piece of property on a single sheet of paper she'd pulled from her purse. "I want to purchase it for my mother. I need to know if it's a sound investment."

"You could have emailed," I countered as false hope spread through my chest.

"I should have," she said weakly. She stood and walked over to my office window in a daze.

"I never wanted to hurt you, Nina. That's the truth, but I know it's shit."

"Do you love her?"

I didn't answer. It was best if I didn't. If I told her the truth, it would give her hope that things could turn out differently.

"I can't do this. I can't pretend you didn't ruin me." She looked at me then with tears in her eyes, and my chest cracked. "I told you I loved you, Devin. Did that mean anything to you?"

I loved her enough to tell her the truth. "It can't."

She nodded. "Okay."

"Nina—"

Not meeting my eyes, she cut me with her words. "I said okay. Call Taylor and let her know when you've researched this. She'll be the one you speak to from now on."

I nodded, standing at my desk with my hands in my pockets.

"I miss us, you know. I thought we were happy. You seemed happy. But I guess that was a lie, too." She looked to me to agree with her as I stood

there like the fucking coward I was. "Right. Goodbye, Devin."

She walked out that day, and I was sure it was over, until a month later when I fucked her in a coat closet. My wife had forced her to retaliate, and I was Nina's tool. I'd been cruel to her, forcing myself to act in a way so I could avoid the hole inside of me that festered when I looked at her. She'd changed as well, acting ruthlessly with her new friends. Friends I'd introduced her to. She carried herself well with the chip on her shoulder I'd caused, making moves against her peers out of spite, and watching their reactions with glee. I'd seen her exhibit some of the same behavior as my wife. I was disgusted by it and took it out on her every chance I got. This was not the woman I fell for, and I wound up resenting the monster I'd created.

I was ruthless with her as well, hoping that she would have the courage to once and for all rid herself of me and the chain that I was attached to. All the while, I'd never refused her sexually and taken every chance I could to have her, just one more time.

I was forcing her to give up.

And then she did.

And now it was my turn to let her go.

"The best way to find out if you can trust somebody is to trust them."

– ERNEST HEMINGWAY

§§

NINA

I WALKED INTO THE bar with new resolve. Devin was my past, and Aiden was a possibility. He didn't seem capable of hurting me the way Devin had, and I would no longer punish Aiden for the mistakes I'd made.

I was ready to try, to hope. Months of being Devin's fuck toy had paralyzed me into believing I couldn't be anything more. It was my fault. I'd waged heartfelt war with a woman incapable of feeling anything. I'd challenged Devin's wife and had only seemed to aggravate her while I fell the fuck apart.

It was over.

Being capable of love was an entirely different story, but that wasn't what Aiden was asking for. And for now, I wasn't capable of doing it, though I saw the potential. He was worthy of the feelings I had wasted.

This would be me moving on. Aiden was a host to everything I truly needed, and I would take full advantage. He wanted to possess me sexually and know me spiritually.

I was open to that. Guarded slightly, but open. I sat in my spot, nodding as Dave handed me a beer. Aiden looked at me, and I saw a small, satisfied smile pass his lips as I sat in front of him. God, he was beautiful. He was sitting on a stool with a black acoustic guitar in his lap. He looked even more sun-kissed in a black t-shirt and dark jeans, his hair a golden, gelled mess. Looking down, he struck his guitar, and I mourned the loss of his amber eyes but admired the sharpness of his features—the broadness of his chest, the rhythm he kept with the nod of his head as he started his song.

I didn't recognize the song, but it was beautiful. He sang it unaccompanied by the other guys and looked directly at me as he took turns strumming out the chords and tapping the side of the guitar for beat.

I was lost instantly when his deep voice moved over the words. It had a painful, soulful lilt that moved me in a way that could only be felt. He sang about attempts to steal a woman's heart away from the wrong man. And how it confused her and she could never figure out how to truly love. I sat trying my hardest to fight the emotion brewing as he sang directly to me that I was beautiful and different and worth so much more than I gave myself credit for.

When the song finished, I kept myself seated, tears streaming down my face as he gave me the come here finger. I flew from my seat into his waiting kiss as he held me tightly to him, cat calls coming at us from every direction around the bar.

I kept my arms around him as I pulled back and questioned him, ignoring everyone around us. They didn't exist. "God, that was beautiful. Did you write that for me?"

"No, that one belongs to Lil Wayne." My eyes widened as he chuckled.

"The rapper?"

"Yes, I'm pretty sure he wrote it for a stripper." Aiden laughed loudly as I slapped his chest playfully.

"Don't be so judgmental, woman. Look at you, you're a mess." Wiping the tears from under my eyes gently, he showed me the evidence. I smiled as he kissed me again and I turned around, finally acknowledging the crowd with a bow.

I stayed until he finished his set and he joined me at my table.

"You keep singing to me like that, and I may make a habit of coming out."

"That's the plan," he whispered, kissing me sweetly before cupping his beer and taking a sip.

"I'm here to ask you for a date." My hands were all over him, caressing his chest, playing with the hair on the back of his head. I couldn't help but notice the hint of a knowing smile tugging at the corners of his mouth.

Okay, so I'm a fucking fiend. I get it.

We made small talk as I told him about Taylor and how I was excited about the expansion of Scott Solutions. He listened intently, his smirk deepening with each subtle touch I gave him, a telling sign of my need.

"Nina," he said after half an hour of my rambling and stroking his beautiful skin. "Do you need me to take care of you?" Instead of hanging my head in shame, I nodded. Aiden took my hand, leading me down a hallway into an office. The walls and ceiling were painted pitch black. There was a laptop, a chair, and a lone decoration in the form of a poster on the wall of the Foo Fighters.

"I love the Foo Fighters," I said nervously. Aiden's expression went from humorous to dark and lustful as he shut the door and I attacked, jumping into his arms and licking his lips. He captured my tongue, sucking it eagerly as clothes began to fly around the room. Naked, I stood waiting as he looked over me and I did the same. He was tall, perfectly cut, and broad. Between his thick muscular thighs lay my salvation, if only for the moment. He licked his lips as he eyed my stiffening nipples.

"What do you want?" Pain shot through my chest at the question. It was Devin's question. I pushed it aside quickly, my need for the man in front of me growing with each passing and naked second.

"Hard, really hard." That was an answer.

He gripped my neck and spun me around, pushing me against the wall.

"Spread your legs." Aiden was in rare form as I leaned back, gripping him in my hand. He pressed my face hard against the rough surface. "Did I say you could touch that?"

"No." I smiled through the pain, loving the way his voice sounded. He moved from my grip and slapped my ass in a way so that I parted my legs further. He tested my arousal and groaned, seeming satisfied.

"Always so wet, naughty Nina. Tell me, do you think it's enough for my cock?" I forced my wrist behind me as I again took him in my hand and felt his huge thickness. I moaned at my assessment, and he thrust into my hand once.

"She wants it hard," he whispered into my neck before biting my shoulder and thrusting his fingers inside me before sliding them between my ass cheeks. I let out a surprised gulp of air as he rimmed me with his soaked digits.

"I'm going to fuck you everywhere, in every way." He pulled my hair so I was forced to look up. "Do you hear me?"

"Yes," I gasped, my arousal dripping.

He pulled the rolling chair over and turned me, binding my wrists to the handle. When I looked at my now secured hands, I could see the guitar string digging into my skin.

Resourceful guy.

With a slap on the ass, he pushed the tip of himself inside me, rubbing it over every part of me, and then pushed the chair away so I was stretched painfully on my tip toes, just short of falling forward.

"Aiden, please."

"I love it when you beg." Without warning, he pounded into me full force, pulling the chair back to him as he covered my hands on the handles. The sensation of being full was magnified as he used my body to deliver his cock with so much force I was screaming.

"Keep it down, or I'll make it hurt."

I ignored him, my body ripping with pleasure as he impaled me inch by inch, thrust by thrust.

"I warned you." He slapped me hard, only intensifying the pleasure and then painfully shoved three fingers into my ass. I came hard and loud, hearing the slickness of my orgasm as he continued his assault.

"Quiet, Nina, or I'll make you pay." I lay my head in the chair, biting my tongue as he fucked me ruthlessly with his dick and fingers, bringing me up again to a furious orgasm before I floated away. Aiden was relentless as he continued to pound and pound, his heavy balls slapping my clit furiously. I felt him stiffen with his oncoming orgasm and he pulled out of me quickly, putting the tip of him inside my puckered entrance before coming with a harsh breath. I shrieked at the sudden intrusion as he slid in further, his second wave filling my ass with his hot release and pushing in the rest of the way. I cried out as his fingers found my clit, thumping once then twice as I came again, his dick still filling me and keeping me full. It didn't stop as Aiden continually thumped my clit as it pulsed and aided my orgasm, making it last and last.

I praised him over and over as he pulled his softening cock from me, rubbing the slick hole with himself.

"You like being fucked in the ass?"

"God, yes," I said, no longer ashamed of my need. "Anywhere, everywhere," the whore in me told him.

"This is mine," he reiterated, sticking his once again hard cock into my backside.

"Oh, God, yes, Aiden," I said as tears streamed down my face. "I fucking love it."

He pulled out of me, untying my wrists and sat in the chair, pulling me onto his lap. I sat there catching my breath as his hardness between my open legs tickled my clit.

"I would love to see if you can come this way, but I think were out of time," he whispered, cupping both my breasts from underneath my arms, enclosing me as he stroked my sensitive skin.

"I came here to ask for a date, not sodomy," I giggled.

"Well, you can have them both. When is our date?" He nuzzled my neck, and I stood up to gather my clothes.

"Tomorrow night. Do you have a tux?"

"I have one, yes."

"Carson and I will pick you up at seven." Pulling on my jeans, I appreciated his beautiful body as he reluctantly dressed.

"You could skip the set and make me scream again," I said, looking at him from underneath my lashes. He moved toward me, tilting my head for a long slow kiss.

"You should probably sneak out unless you want to witness my first standing ovation."

§§

I made it home and spent hours in the gym exhausting my ridiculous new libido. Even in my sated state, I wanted more. I knew this could eventually be a problem, but for now, I would choose to ignore it. I would start asking questions and getting answers from the source. I still wasn't sure that the two men who consumed me were in any way connected, but our lives seemed so separated, I put that worry to bed along with thoughts of Devin, who seemed to be getting irritated by my refusal to see him.

Devin: Talk to me or I come to you.

It was a threat I needed to take seriously. Hearing from him in any capacity still set my heart beating faster, my chest rising and falling with memories both sweet and sensual. He'd been everything I needed, everything I thought I'd wanted, but I'd ignored all the warning signs.

With Aiden, I would do better, try harder, attempt to make the intense sexual relationship into something more. I owed it to myself to be *someone's*, not someone's whore.

Aiden seemed to embrace my sexuality and handled it like a pro. I didn't have time to worry if he would tire of me. I was busying myself with happy thoughts as I drifted to sleep while we texted each other.

"Where excess lies, usually someone had to give something up for the other to get it."

– A.J. DARKHOLME

§§

NINA

AT SEVEN SHARP the next day, Carson and I pulled up as Aiden opened his front door. He turned to me as I was exiting the limo. He looked dashing in an old school, black, perfectly fitted tux and a bowtie. I damn near stumbled toward him in my new Jimmy Choos as he descended the stairs, doing a little dance reminiscent of some Broadway show and nailing it with ease.

The man was brilliant, beautiful, talented beyond words, and had a cock that could silence a porn star.

I sighed as he took my mouth in a kiss that promised me much more as the night progressed.

"You look beautiful, Nina." He pulled my hands out as he admired my sea colored dress that hugged my body perfectly and flowed loosely from mid-thigh down. I wore my hair up and left my neck bare, but cuffed my wrist in diamonds. We slid into the cab of my town car as Carson drove toward the venue.

"You don't mind slummin' it with me tonight?" I asked as he kissed my palm.

"I'm a chameleon, baby. I can handle any situation."

I quirked my brow. "I believe it."

"I was raised knowing where the proper fork is. I did indeed have a mighty large silver spoon."

"Tell me about your parents," I asked, knowing a part of the answer. He stilled my wandering hand on his thigh.

"My father died when I was young, my mother…I rarely hear from her." He didn't seem affected by it.

"That must be hard." I pulled my feet up beneath me on the comfortable seat as I tuned in. He leaned back in his seat, straightening his already perfect bowtie.

Another dark expression, one I hadn't seen before, crossed his features, but it wasn't sadness. It looked like resentment.

"My father killed himself. I never thought it bothered me, but I guess it stuck with me. I researched a lot about emotions and the human mind. That's what got me interested in psychiatry. I was looking for answers."

"Did you find them?" He nodded his head, looking out the window. "Yes and no. I got some insight, but in truth, he would be the only one who could truly answer them. My mother refused to speak of him."

"I'm sorry, Aiden."

"It was just a way for me to cope, I guess. I never really wanted to be a shrink."

"You never really wanted to be anything, did you?" I laughed. "You have all these amazing talents, degrees, and you just…"

He leaned in with a grin. "To you, it's a waste, but why? For money? You of all people know how tainted that point is."

"I do," I agreed wholeheartedly, but added, "You could be helping people with your expertise."

"Point made, but, Nina, I'd rather lift them with music, not listen to them suffer. I'm not so sure there are magic words to help the human condition. But I'm beginning to think there are magic people." He fingered my cheek as his molten brown eyes moved over my face. "You do things to me."

Ignoring the intimacy of his statement, I opted for humor. "You do things to me, too," I said on a laugh. "Pretty raunchy, Mr. Shrink. What would Freud say about the way you fuck?"

His grin set my heart racing. "He wouldn't say anything. He would take notes and do the same to his woman."

We laughed as the car slowed, and I pulled out my lipstick for a quick fix. "One hour and we are out of here. I'll take you for a Happy Meal."

He stilled my movement. "If you hate these things so much, why are you here?"

"I joined *everything* in hopes of making some new friends when I became wealthy. I was chair on a couple of committees due to my overly generous donations. I've stepped down and ducked out of everything in the last six months. I no longer give a shit. I've hated most of these functions, but this is one cause close to my heart." I nodded out of the window and smiled as he saw the sign for the Charleston Aquarium.

He nodded as he exited the car and reached out his hand for mine. We bypassed the carpet at his insistence and were greeted by an ambiance of soft lights and live jazz music. I immediately grabbed a waiting glass of champagne and handed one to my beautiful date.

"It's my job to get the drinks," he cooed in my ear as we sipped champagne, hands clasped.

"Come on, I want to show you something." I walked him past the first two larger than life-sized aquariums filled with tropical fish, and he looked on, admiring them along with me.

"It's way more fascinating to me than art. It's alive and beautiful and ever changing." He squeezed my hand as we walked along the colorful and contrasting wall of fish. I weaved through the crowd, intentionally not making eye contact with anyone. I was here with Aiden, and that was all that mattered. For once in the last two years, I had someone to entertain. I wasn't being hidden, a kept secret. For once I was being revered as someone important. At least to him.

"Want to dance?" I asked quickly. Aiden seemed distracted as he looked around us.

"No, not here. I'll dance with you some other time. I promise." He squeezed my hand, and I let it go.

We circled the aquarium, stopping in a quiet room filled from floor to ceiling with sharks. I stood in awe, staring into the tanks with the same fear that always struck me when I saw them. I swam among them in all aspects of my life, but I respected them greatly. I watched as a six-foot blacktip swam past me, touching the reinforced glass as it slid along side of me.

I loved the sea and all its creatures and was fascinated by its intricate ecosystem. My plans were to help expand the aquarium, making it one of the east coast's biggest and best. I stood for several moments watching the beady-eyed, smooth skinned predators glide along the water, changing directions without warning.

Suddenly there was a whirlwind of activity. They began to circle faster as more sharks joined the mix, causing my pulse to pick up with the flurry of activity in front of me as they raced around, held captive only by a few inches of glass.

"Aren't they incredib—" I was cut short by the sight of Aiden facing Devin in the center of the room.

I stood paralyzed with fear and jumped as a shark tale tapped the glass next to my head. The two men were completely silent in what looked to be a standoff. Terror crept through me as I realized these men not only knew each other but hated each other as well.

I stood motionless as fierce blue eyes met molten lava. I could literally feel the hate static mounting between them and cringed. I'd never seen Devin so livid, his jaw set. I couldn't see Aiden's face clearly, but his posture told me his look was probably eerily similar.

Breaking my immobility, I walked up next to Aiden and grabbed his hand.

"Let's go," I prompted, starting to walk as Aiden gripped my hand hard, telling me to stay in place.

Devin turned his glare from Aiden to look at me and seemed to suddenly realize I was standing there, a physical jerk moving through him, his glare turning to disbelief. Aiden caught on quickly and turned to look at me for confirmation, asking the silent question, *"Is this him?"* and I nodded quickly as he dropped my hand.

My heart ripped at the loss as my eyes stayed glued between the two of them.

"Fuck you, I'm not doing this tonight," Aiden hissed at Devin through clenched teeth. I looked to Devin who had murder in his eyes, his gaze shooting back and forth between us.

"Nina, when you *fuck* my cousin, does it remind you of me?"

I was crippled in that moment. Devin looked at me with a *"Well?"* as I stood there, completely powerless to stop the next few minutes of my life. Aiden turned to me, confrontation clear in his features.

"Research."

My defense was weak and worthless.

"I wasn't sure. I didn't know. I swear I didn't know."

I cowered away, terrified of the two of them.

"We're leaving," Aiden snapped as he came toward me in a blur.

"You aren't going anywhere with her," Devin hissed as he walked forward in an attempt to block him.

"Devin, do yourself a favor and walk away," Aiden countered, sliding his hand around my hip.

"The fuck I will!" Devin yelled as I stood in front of Aiden.

"You have no say in anything I do, Devin. I came with Aiden, I'm leaving with him. This wasn't intentional. It just happened. Aiden can attest to that."

I turned on my heel, heading toward the exit with or without Aiden. I knew I should be throwing myself at his feet, at his mercy, but I couldn't do it. Not with Devin standing there.

I clutched my purse and dug deep for my emergency bottle of Xanax, taking one and downing it with a glass of champagne from a ready tray. Minutes passed as I waited on Carson to bring the car around.

Suddenly Aiden was hot on my heels as he exited the building. Carson pulled up and opened the door for us, concern written all over his face. Once seated, I popped a hot bottle of un-chilled champagne I kept on hand, taking a long sip. It was awful, but it would get the job done.

"I didn't know. We didn't exactly disclose our names until the night I asked. I was just as surprised as you are now. When I found out you weren't brothers, I didn't think much more of it. I figured he wasn't a part of your life."

"You fucked up," he said tightly. "You figured wrong."

I felt a chill sweep through me as a stone-faced Aiden failed to look at me. I lowered the glass partition.

"Mr. McIntyre will be returning home."

Carson nodded as I put the partition back up, cradling the warm bottle of champagne in my arm, wishing at that moment to be anyone but me.

"What can I say? Please, Aiden, tell me."

Aiden sat perfectly still, his body language screaming violence. I wanted more than anything to ask what had transpired between them but knew I may never get the answers. Carson stopped in Aiden's drive, and for the first time Aiden looked at me, and in his eyes, I saw what I'd feared.

"If I would have asked you—"

"We would have never begun," he said, matter-of-fact. "This can't happen, Nina. I'm sorry."

He exited the limo, walking past his porch steps toward the side of his house, down the beach path, motion lights beaming on to guide his steps. I blindly followed him, my insides sinking as he made his way out to the surf, untying his bowtie. He stood as he reached the white foam, the only light hovering over us coming from the back porch of his house.

"Aiden, please talk to me." I heard my voice shake and took a deep breath.

"You knew," he said as a statement. "You surprise me sometimes. I think I have you figured out and then you pull the rug out from under me. It was what I loved about you most. Now I think it's what I like about you least."

"Fuck, please don't do that. Don't jab at me. You came after me that night, remember. I didn't do this intentionally or to spite him."

"It can't happen. I'm sorry. You need to leave." He walked away, leaving me on the beach holding a hot bottle of champagne and my face covered in running mascara.

§§

I was pulled from sleep by the rumbling of my cell phone. I quickly texted Taylor that I would be into the office in the morning, then lay in bed with my eyes shut tight.

Did that really fucking happen?

I had no reason to believe Devin would show up to that event. It wasn't something he would be interested in, and no matter how hard I'd pushed the case, none of the women on my other committees were remotely interested in helping with the expansion of the aquarium.

He'd made good on his threat and come specifically for me.

And now you know. Cousins.

I saw it and ignored it. Same last name, similar upbringings, Ivy League educations. It was clear it was a connect the dots scenario. I knew, and I'd ignored it. I wanted Aiden. And deep down, I still wanted Devin. Fresh tears crippled me from moving out of bed as I christened my pillow over and over. Devin was furious. Aiden was done. And I was once again alone.

Who exactly was I crying for?

I wiped my face, but the tears wouldn't stop, my body aching with my deep-seated need for the man I loved and loathed, and the good man I'd lost and wanted desperately to keep, the pulse between my thighs making me aware I could never have either.

I'd let sexual thirst rule my life, and now as I shuddered with sobs to grieve both men, I was all too aware of my arousal. The need was distinct and unavoidable. My nipples peaked with thoughts that should be anything but present, and I pinched them hard in frustration. I moaned out as the pleasure broke through the pain, my sex becoming heavier with need.

Disgusted, I turned on my stomach and buried my head in the pillow as my hand drifted down toward the throbbing. I cried out when my fingers reached the tip, tears still coming down as I gave in to my need. I stroked myself hard without giving my body a chance to open.

Punishing my clit with rough fingers, I strained for release and came up empty. I cried in frustration, bringing the wetness from my middle to the top, rubbing furiously and moving my hips for friction. Still gasping and straining, I came up empty and moved my head to the side for more air, and I froze.

He stood next to my bed, his eyes on fire with lust as he watched me cry in frustration and heartbreak, trying to reach my orgasm.

Slowly his hand reached toward me, pulling the comforter off the bed, revealing my naked skin. I waited as his eyes appreciated me and he stayed planted next to me, his fiery depths beckoning me to continue. I began to move my hand again as he watched me cupping my sex beneath me, still pushing for release and failing.

Sobbing, I planted my knees on the bed, lifted my ass and ground furiously into my hand as he watched, lips parted, his erection straining in his pants. I worked tirelessly for release, sweat beading on my forehead, hard heavy breaths coming out with my cries. My heart thrummed hard inside my chest. He palmed his hard cock, watching me intently.

I needed relief. I needed him.

"Please, I can't do it…please!"

He moved lightning fast, his hands covering my ass, stroking the back of my thighs. I felt his tongue trace the contours of my backside before he buried his thick tongue inside, fucking my pussy with it. He licked me from bottom to top as I gripped my pillow, writhing in agony. Suddenly I was turned over and forced to watch him as he shed his clothes. I kept my hand low, rubbing furiously, his hungry eyes my encouragement.

"I'm sorry, Nina," he whispered as his lips trailed warmly up my neck.

I reached out to him, but he gripped my forearms, pinning them next to my head as his hard cock nudged my entrance. My chest lifted in asking as his mouth covered one nipple, pulling and biting before moving to the other.

With one solid thrust, he was buried deep, rubbing me exactly where I needed him and I came, pulsing and praising.

He moved inside me slowly, kissing my face, my eyes, my brow, nose, chin, and neck. I cried against his lips as he took my mouth sweetly and completely as he made love to me. Minutes later, I orgasmed again as he stroked me deep inside, so much so I felt an aching part of me start to heal.

"I love you, Nina," he whispered to me as he came, pouring himself inside.

I opened my eyes, staring deep into the dark blue depths and whispered the name my heart held sacred.

"Devin."

HINDRANCE
Book 3

§§

Nina

Storms are a funny thing. Most people ignore the warning signs: a strong gust of wind, a lightning strike on the horizon, the distant rumble of thunder.

My head and heart had been at odds for the last two years because of Devin McIntyre, and my relationship with Aiden had only complicated matters. Still, I craved both men. Just when I thought the decision was taken from me, a choice between the two became inevitable. The two men I had attached myself to emotionally and physically had already told me everything I needed to know.

Although the dark clouds were gathering overhead, I ignored the lightning, played deaf to the thunder, and let the tempest push me toward them both. I ended up in a whirlwind of secrets, a vortex of deception and depravity I never imagined possible. I was drowning again, but this time … this time I would be ready.

Or so I thought.

Nothing could have prepared me for the coming storm.

"The truth is rarely pure and never simple."

– OSCAR WILD

§§

PROLOGUE

MY HEEL SANK into the pluff mud, and I left it there, swiftly relieving my foot of the other. Turning my head toward my idling car, I reassured myself that it was still there, the door left open in case I needed to escape in a hurry. Hearing another bloodcurdling scream, I walked toward the dim light. Fear shot through me in waves as Shel Silverstein's words fumbled around in my head, "Clooney the Clown" a horrific internal monolog resounding through my frightened mind. My senses heightened with each step I took toward the cracked door. There was soft music playing in the background. I knew the song but could not make out the words. It was upbeat and a little jazzy, and totally unfitting.

I could hear the crunch of crisp grass under my feet, and then another scream echoed in the night. Reaching into my purse, I fumbled inside and let out a way too audible breath of relief when I felt the cold steel.

Another scream, louder, more desperate. Pain…this was pain.

"Enough!" It was a loud boom of a familiar male voice.

I recited the poem over and over in my head, the way I used to when I heard my parents fighting, and yet I knew that what I was about to see was far worse than what I used to hear. I took another step forward, and a motion light came on, alerting my presence to those inside. Sweat from the humidity, along with adrenaline from fear, had me dripping, my now soaked blouse clinging to my torso.

Terror raced through my every pore as I gripped my gun and took aim in front of me.

A dark figure appeared out of the door, but I instantly knew who it was. He came toward me in a black blur, yelling my name as I squeezed the trigger with a scream of my own.

"A man when he is making up to anybody can be cordial and gallant and full of little attentions and altogether charming. But when a man is really in love he can't help looking like a sheep."

– AGATHA CHRISTIE

§§

DEVIN

NINA LAY ON her stomach, facing away from me as I traced the curve of her spine with my fingertips from her neck down to her lower back. We both lay quiet after I'd made love to her then fell asleep. When we woke this morning and she realized I hadn't left, I saw the surprise on her face when she opened her eyes. She turned away from me as I continued to stroke her. I was sure my confession and my tender touch had stifled her into this silence. She finally turned to look at me, and I saw confusion and pain in her cloud-filled eyes.

"I'm leaving her." Emotion crossed her features in what looked like a hint of relief, but it quickly disappeared. Before I could say anything else, she rose from the bed and shut the bathroom door behind her.

I'd left her alone to shower as I sat in her bed admiring her beautiful frame while she polished her face in the mirror.

"I meant it when I said I loved you, Nina. I meant it. I think you know it. I think you've known it."

"Devin, why are you doing this? If this is a pissing contest between you and your cousin, I'll be the first to break the news. He broke it off the minute we left the fundraiser."

I tried not to show my relief, but she was watching me closely, and it was evident.

"You don't belong with him." I pulled at my pants, trying to hide my growing erection from simply watching her. Now was not the time.

She turned in her chair to face me, a makeup brush in her hand. "And I don't belong with you. Sex is all we've ever had between us."

"Bullshit."

"Really?" She stood, walking over to stand in front of me. "My shrink told me you conditioned me this way. Is that true?"

"Your shrink." I sat slightly stunned before realization hit me. "Fuck that, Nina. Of course he would speak ill of me. With every breath he takes he lies."

"Seems to run in the family. Besides, *we* didn't speak of *you* at all, because I didn't know for sure the two of you were connected until last night. I would ask you what your beef with him is, but I'm pretty sure it would be another lie."

"My beef?" I tried to mask my chuckle. I wanted to grab her and ravage her again, but her body language told me I was about to be thrown out. When I discovered the door unlocked last night and found her in bed writhing and needy, I thanked God, Santa Clause, the fucking lucky leprechaun, and whoever else was responsible. Walking away was not fucking happening and touching her again felt like returning to heaven after a long stint in hell.

In the back of my mind lingered the thought he'd tainted her, but I wouldn't let him have her. I'd never let him have her.

The minute I saw that son of a bitch clasp her hand, all bets were off. She was mine. I would make her mine again. I would prove my worth, my love, my devotion. I would keep her safe and to hell with the consequences. She was worth losing it all.

Looking at her now as she stood in her silk camisole and matching shorts, tapping her brush on her thigh, it was clear I should have made the decision a lot sooner. Still, the jealous bastard in me had to ask.

"Was it intentional with him?"

She watched me in the mirror as she circled a soft brush on her cheekbones. "I'm no longer capable of being that callous."

"So you are telling me this is just coincidence?" *Unfuckingbelievable.*

She nodded once, as if she didn't care one way or the other whether I believed her. This was going to take work—a lot of work.

"Why do you two hate each other?"

When I hesitated, she noticed, but I stayed silent, trying to figure out how to tell her the truth. She was looking for a quick explanation I didn't have. The contempt she had for me at that moment told me it was definitely not the time. The truth would only push her further away. It was over between them. That's all the mattered. "As much as I love *not* getting any answers from you, I have to get to work."

"It's complicated, but I promise to tell you everything. Just let me have the deed to the land and I'll—"

"What?" She was shrieking now.

Not good.

"Fuck you, Devin! Are you serious? Is this why you're here? Jesus, couldn't you have let me have my meltdown in peace? I can't be manipulated like that anymore, haven't you learned?" She was furious, and I felt my balls creep up slightly at her glare. I stood, coming toward her.

"You don't honestly think I'm here for that, and you know it. You're just scared." I knew I struck a nerve when she threw her brush at me.

"Get out. Seriously, get out." She pointed toward the door. "He wanted to love me, to make me happy. He want—"

"Don't finish that sentence, Nina. He can't have you!" I felt the rage rush through me as I clenched my fists. "Stay the fuck away from him."

"I intend to, as I do you. The land is not for sale, and if your cunt of a wife wants it, she can come get it herself."

"So this is once again about your war with my wife." She flinched as I said the word wife. The woman that loved me was in there somewhere. "As much as it pains me to say this, you are no match for her. I don't know what lengths she will go to. Just let it go."

She stomped into her closet and pulled a dress off the rack before throwing it over her head.

"Tell me what you want so I can tell you no," she huffed.

"I want you."

She stopped her busy hands to utter a quick "No." She

stopped at her mirror, checked her lips then grabbed her purse. "Let's go."

"I came here to tell you that I'm sorry. That I cared, that I still care, and that I was wrong." Fuck, that was hard but long overdue. My heart was in her hands, and I could already see her twisting the knife in.

My eyes implored hers as I gave her the long overdue words. She had built a solid wall, and I had my sledgehammer ready.

"You know I can't forgive you."

"I know."

"So how could you possibly get me?"

"Time, effort, and orgasms." I gave her a wolfish grin, and her flying keys caught me in the jaw as I cursed the same fucking leprechaun who brought me into this room. Okay, maybe charm wasn't the best tactic. Reminding myself that losing my temper may set me back, I tried again.

"I didn't sleep with her that day. You walked in right after she threatened to ruin my career and you. She told me you were coming and if I wanted to protect you, I had to play along. She got naked, and I let her. You saw what she wanted you to see. And in a way, I wanted it to happen because I wasn't fucking strong enough to let you go. I wanted you as far away from me and my bullshit as possible. I wanted to protect you. I was ambushed and made the quick decision to go along with it. I was a fool and a coward." My balls were shrinking as the leprechaun kicked them repeatedly. "What I did, the way I acted after you found out, you know that wasn't me."

"I don't know you at all."

"You know me better than any woman ever has." I saw the words strike her and one brick fall, but the wall remained standing.

She stopped at her doorway and turned to me, giving me a hard look. "Doesn't matter."

"I've loved you for as long as you've loved me, Nina."

She dropped her shoulders, tears quickly springing in her

furious eyes. "Two weeks ago, I would have forgiven you!" She walked up to me, slapping me hard as she screamed. "Two weeks ago, I could have worked to forgive you! I've always known she had something over you, Devin. I'm not a complete idiot. You didn't trust me, and you didn't love or respect me enough to let me in. Instead, you treated me like a useless whore, and I let you because I loved you that much. No more! Two weeks ago, I started dating your polar opposite, and I wanted that, Devin. I *wanted* Aiden. I deserved him. And now you've taken that from me, too."

I gripped her arms, shaking her slightly. "Stay the fuck away from him, Nina, or I swear to God—"

"Or you'll what?"

"Jesus, who are you exactly?"

"You should know. You helped shape me into…*this*."

"No, you did that all on your own," I snapped as I gripped her harder. "You turned into a ruthless bitch all by yourself, and it disgusts me."

"But it was okay that you were always a lying, cheating bastard!"

I deserved that. Letting go of her arms, I shoved my hands into my pockets, our eyes staying connected.

"We were happy. You can't deny it anymore than I can. It worked, and we worked in and out of the bedroom, no matter how fucking wrong I was with the way it started."

"We can't go back, Devin."

The searing pain in my chest silenced me as I followed her out her front door. I wondered just what the hell I was thinking as Carson pulled up, his contempt for me clear in his eyes. She was completely shutting down and time was running out.

"Please, Nina, give me a fucking chance here." I ran my hands through my hair as she watched me carefully. I saw her decision before she spoke.

"You have no right to ask me for anything." Slipping into the car, I saw her resolve as Carson slammed her door, preventing me from speaking further. I opened the door and slipped in with Nina just as Carson took his seat up front.

"Carson, please excuse us."

He looked back to Nina, who was staring out the opposite window, and she gave him a quick nod of her head. As soon as he shut the door, I attacked, gripping her wrists and pinning them next to her head.

"Okay, I tried the nice-guy-I'm-sorry-for-the-things-I've-done shit. Didn't work, and thank God for that. It won't happen often, so let's do the I-still-know-how-to-make-Nina-listen part." Her eyes widened as I knelt down in front of her on the floorboard, still holding her wrists.

"Let's pretend for just *one* second I am capable of being sincere." She rolled her eyes, and I gripped her tighter. She stared at me blankly, and I let go of her wrists, leaving them at her sides and smoothing my hands over her skirt down to her thighs just beneath her dress.

"Go to hell, Devin." I heard the ache in her voice. She still loved me, and it was up to me to remind her.

I licked my lips, and her breathing picked up as her gray eyes beckoned me to do more, fuck her senseless…and then go to hell.

"You think I never cared for you?" I ran my hands up her thighs, softly brushing her smooth skin and watching her reaction to me. I gripped the thin sides of her panties, pulling them down slowly and discarding them. "Answer me," I snapped firmly.

"No," she whispered, keeping her eyes locked with mine.

"That is a fucking lie." I pushed her knees apart, and she didn't stop me. I stayed still as she watched me expectantly. "This is just sex, right?" I licked the pad of my finger and slowly swiped her sex, her arousal coating it. I watched her study it along with me.

"Yes," she said carefully, her chest heaving. "You taught me the difference."

I pulled her bottom half toward me, spreading her wider as

she looked on, her lips parting with want.

"Wrong again," I said, letting my breath hit her sex. Her nipples drew tight underneath her thin silk dress as I strummed her creamy smooth thighs with my thumbs. "I didn't know the meaning of the words, Nina." The air was thick with expectancy as I looked up at her. "You showed that to me." I leaned in, swirling my tongue over her clit once, twice, and then began lapping her slowly.

"Devin," she rasped out as her body began to quake.

"You're so close already, and you think this is just physical," I reminded her as I moved my mouth away. "I could tongue you and fuck you all day every day for the rest of my life. I'll never stop wanting you, and I'll never stop wanting you to need me. And only because it's much more than this and I'm going to need you to admit it *now*." I leaned in and licked her smoothly once. She gripped my hair, pushing her soaked pussy toward me. "You taught *me* the difference between just saying the words and saying them because you mean them." I saw the emotion cross her features as her lips trembled. "And you're the only woman I have ever really meant them with, and I can't let you go. I won't, Nina." I buried my tongue inside her, tasting all of her as she silently cried and moaned my name. Sucking on her clit gently, I looked up and watched her body shudder.

"Devin," she pleaded as I pulled my mouth away reluctantly and looked up at her. Her body vibrated her release waiting with just another swipe of my tongue.

"I know everything there is to know about you, Nina Scott, and it's mostly because you never shut up while we were together. You've changed me, whether I wanted it or not."

I pushed two fingers inside of her as her eyes widened, filled with passion, heat, and the love I knew was just under the surface. "I'm completely enamored by you, and it has nothing to do with this," I taunted, licking her with a lazy tongue. "But you see it's so fucking good I think I'll take it all." Her body went rigid as she reached the brink and I pulled away, watching her face twist in agony.

"It's not too late. I can make this right." I slid my fingers in and out of her as she let her tears fall silent and moved her hips, searching for her release. "You *will* let me make this right." Continuing to taunt her with my hand, she thrust her hips desperately.

"Devin." She said my name, but I heard please. I wanted her to scream it, to realize her need for me on both levels. I had to have her confirm she felt the same, and that I hadn't completely lost her. I was asking too much when I had given so little, and I didn't give a fuck. This woman had consumed me.

Reaching up, I freed her breast by sliding the silky material of her dress off her shoulder. I took my fingers from her center and soaked her nipple with her arousal before leaning in. Just a breath from devouring her puckered, taut flesh, I whispered, "I don't want to go back. Here, now, this is enough." I pulled hard on her nipple, sucking mercilessly as she gripped my head, digging her nails into my scalp.

The car got warmer with each passing minute, but I kept my mouth latched onto her as I took off my jacket.

"Devin, please." I stopped my assault and sat back on my heels, caressing her thighs.

"You still love me, Nina."

"Don't do this, Devin." She shook her head as her hand made its way down in an effort to relieve her ache. I grabbed it and kissed it front and back.

"I waited a year to touch you, knowing it was wrong. Knowing that I was a married man and all I had to offer you was a hard on and a headache." I leaned in again, knowing she was still on the verge, and spread her gently, licking up one of her folds and down the other. "You see, I know how to fuck, and I know how to please a woman." I darted my tongue around everywhere but where she needed it. "But I've never been so fucking satisfied as I was when I had your perfect cunt trembling around my cock." I darted my tongue on her clit and took it off right before she came. Her tears were coming fast now, out of frustration and hurt. "It didn't take me long to figure out why it felt so good, so different, and so totally fucking perfect. Can you tell me why?"

She was in no shape to answer. "Take out my cock, Nina." She lifted up, slowly unbuckling my belt and unzipping my pants, freeing me and stroking me with our eyes locked.

"Why, Nina? Why did it feel so fucking good when I was inside you?"

Her face was burning with heat, her eyes darting to my mouth as I whispered, "Why? Tell me why."

Her tears continued as I gripped the top of the leather seat behind her shoulders. Eyes still connected, I sank into her, filling her tight, wet, greedy pussy. She grabbed my hips, trying her best to control my thrusts as I remained still, throbbing, eager for more. "Answer me!"

"It was love," she cried. "It was love." The defeat in her voice fueled me as I kept a slow pace, punishing her without her deserving it. I leaned in, taking her mouth, moving my tongue against hers in sweet fluidity as I pushed deep. I hooked my arms under her thighs, pulling her closer and circling my hips so I could feel all of her.

"And why does it feel so good now, Nina?" Face straining with her impending release, she dug her nails into my arms. Need built, but I fought for control as I stilled again. "Nina," I ordered in a menacing plea of my own.

"It's still love." She wrapped her arms around my neck as I pulled her off the seat and onto my waiting lap. She lifted up and down achingly slow as we got lost in each other. I braced myself as she came, wanting it to last. I pulled her bottom lip in between my teeth and gripped her ass, impaling her as her orgasm continued on and on until she broke in my arms.

"It's still love," she whispered again as her limbs shook and her insides twitched. Gripping me tighter, she hugged me to her as I continued stroking deep, her clit rubbing along my hardness as one orgasm led to another and another until she was limp in my arms. My arms wrapped around her and I held her tightly to me as we both let out moans of appreciation.

Refusing to give in to myself, I pushed deeper as I pulled her hair so she was forced to look at me. Seeing a small slip in her resolve, I reached in and sipped her lips before my next confession, still driving into her as hard as I could.

"You are all I want." I licked the shell of her ear. "You are all I will ever want." With one last push, I gave her the rest of me. "It *is* love, Nina."

Leaving us connected, I twisted us around so I was sitting on the long, leather seat and she was resting on my lap. After a few quiet moments, she looked up at me, her face stained with mascara and her hairline damp, a sign of her exertion.

"How could I ever trust you again?"

"Just give me some time. I'll try to be the man you deserve."

Her small laugh had me looking at her in confusion. "Devin, no offense, but you aren't exactly the white picket fence type of man."

"And that's neither what you want or need from me, is it?"

Looking at her, for the first time in forever, I saw a new future. She lay curled on my lap, vulnerable and raw and absolutely beautiful. This was the woman I fell for.

"Why now?"

I brushed her hair away from her face then gave her the truth. "I never saw a way out, until I realized what I feel for you was my way out."

"What does that mean?" Her voice was still a whisper.

"I'll show you." She seemed relieved that I was offering action instead of words. It was the only way to prove it to her. She moved from my lap and straightened her dress. I pulled up my pants and grabbed my jacket. "No more closets, no more scandal, and no more hiding. Until I can give you that, I won't touch you again."

A whole new expression crossed her face as she mulled over my words. When I was satisfied she'd really heard me, I took her lips again, moving my tongue slowly over hers, closing the kiss when we both were struck with renewed arousal.

I smiled down at her, knowing her wheels were turning with new scenarios. She looked back at me, her lips slowly turning up at the sides before her expression evened out. She was still fighting it and probably would be for a long time to come. I both expected and respected her for it. Regardless of what she thought, I knew her strong appetite never really outweighed her reasoning. She saw her hunger as a weakness, but it only made her more irresistible to me. In my eyes, only a truly strong woman could acknowledge her desire to be dominated and admit her thirst for it. She'd become more accepting of that, and I couldn't help but wonder if that motherfucker had anything to do with it. I let her see the anger flash in my eyes. I'd unleashed the hunger in her, and I had no intention of letting another man reap the benefits. It relieved me to know Aiden was no longer a threat. He'd ended it.

Smart move, motherfucker.

Regardless, I wouldn't let him near her again.

"Wait for me," I implored one last time before I took my leave of the limo. She didn't give me an answer, but she didn't need to. Her refusal to do so fueled me all the more.

I drove off in my Audi with a renewed sense of purpose. I had moves to make.

"Man is not what he thinks he is, he is what he hides."

– ANDRÉ MALRAUX

§§

NINA

OVE.

Devin.

Loves me.

And I fucked him. I fucked him…again. I stood in the shower for the second time this morning in a daze. Devin's words circulated through my mind, his touch reverberating throughout my body as I stood stunned. My mind was at war with my heart, and both were in complete upheaval. My heart ripped through the grave, gasping for air as my mind continued to shovel dirt on top of it, both with their own screaming opinions, leaving me eager for silence.

That was Devin: a perfect storm of everything I did and didn't want. And I'd given him hope and found myself hoping as well.

"I'm leaving her."

Oh, God, if that were the truth, what did that make me? Next?

Even if I didn't believe Devin was capable of doing the same thing to me, even if I believed his intent, could I respect myself for trying with him? It had never been an option for me before. That option had flown right out the window the minute I saw Eileen naked on his desk. And even before that, he'd warned me we could never be more.

Wake up, Nina!

What the hell had I done letting him back into my bed? Jesus help me if I didn't want him there now. Devin promised me answers and a better version of himself before that would ever happen. He'd never so much as promised me I'd see him again when we were dating, and now he was asking for a future.

And you believed him?

If there were an award for self-loathing, I would wipe out

the competition. I climbed back into the limo, noting it was still fairly early, and I would make good time to the office. All that drama and my day hadn't even really started yet.

"Carson, play something, anything."

"Yes, Ms. Scott." Relief washed through me as classical piano came drifting through the speakers. I didn't recognize it but was thankful it didn't have the ability to jog any memories.

He loves me. *Now* he loves me. *Now* he's sorry. Now that he knows I'd been fucking his cousin. Was this some sick competition? I'd been so desperate for release, I'd begged him to fuck me only for it to turn into the most intense lovemaking I'd ever experienced, and by a man who reassured me time and again he wasn't capable. I closed my eyes, trying desperately to erase his lips from my neck, his gentle tongue, his tender touch as he explored me. Those eyes, those beautiful eyes that coveted me, worshiped me. Why was he doing this to me? Why was I letting him?

"FUCK!"

Carson jumped in his seat, keeping his hands on the wheel as he eyed me in the rearview mirror. I put up the partition to avoid further embarrassment. Carson was no fool to my behavior after several of my encounters with Devin. He'd seen me silently cry, seen the evidence of our relationship in my appearance and behavior. If he hated Devin, he had a right to. Taylor had caught on as well. These people cared for me and showed as much in their contempt for him.

And once again I'd let the devil have my body, lie to me with his gold dipped tongue—an upgrade from silver due to this morning's thorough showcase.

No, I wouldn't believe him yet. I refused to. My mind won this round. But my pounding heart reminded me seein' is believin' and if Devin made good on his word…well, I would cross that bridge when I came to it. Even if it made me the biggest fool, even if it ended the rest of me, I was still very much in love with that man.

And he loves me.

Even obsessing over Devin, I felt the sadness creep in for the man who had accompanied me last night, held my hand, and promised me a dance I would never receive.

Aiden.

I shook my head in denial with the way it played out. Aiden hadn't even given ending our relationship a second thought. But he was in the right.

And I had, after all, just this morning bedded his cousin.

Was I even capable of being faithful anymore?

And even if I had denied Devin, I would have been faithful to a memory. Aiden ended it. I had no one to be faithful to. And yet, it still felt wrong. But being with Devin in those moments had never felt so right.

Aiden wanted me, treasured me, and treated me so beautifully. There was a definite connection between us, sexually and emotionally.

But I had to face the truth. Aiden and Devin were connected as well. And though I was dying of curiosity, I would probably never get the truth out of either of them. Devin had promised to tell me everything. And then asked that I hand over the land.

Bastard.

Was this what he was after? Jesus, would he go to such lengths to get his way? I wasn't for sale. He could keep his sordid fucking tale, and he and his cousin could fight it out on their own. I would hold onto that land until my deathbed. It was priceless to me now. If Devin's virtue were true, then he would have to prove it around his fucking agenda. I'd set this test and sit back.

Yes, by all means, show me, Devin.

I felt the bitterness surface. This was me jaded and afraid of myself, of him, and the damage of giving him another chance. I had no choice in my racing thoughts now, and my tortured heart felt completely ripped, torn pieces cracking continually for a different man. Is it even possible to love two men at once?

My mind thought it incomprehensible, but my heart disagreed as it beat in my chest, reminding me that they both had a piece of it. I'd only scratched the surface with Aiden; perhaps that's why I felt such an ache for him. With Devin, I'd learned what I'd lost, what I thought was an imaginary bond we shared. And this morning he was trying his best to convince me it was real.

God, it felt so real. I scrubbed my face in disgust.

Whatever game this was, in order to play, I had to get a grip.

The sick, needy nymph I had turned into was ruling my life. My anger at myself brought me to one conclusion: love should not be this complicated. Fuck them *both.* I needed neither of them!

Says the sated Nina.

I took Carson's hand as I stepped out of the limo, making my way into my building and stood frozen in reception.

"AARON!" He turned with a knowing grin in my direction, and I went running into his waiting arms.

"Oh, God, if you only knew how fucking happy I am to see you!" I wiped my tears away with one hand while hugging him furiously with my other arm still clasped around him, unafraid of my use of language. Genuine relief swept through me as I surveyed my brother. He looked so much better than the last time I'd seen him. He'd been heartbroken, and as a result, his smile hadn't quite reached his eyes. But that all seemed irrelevant as his eyes beamed down at me now. It gave me hope.

"What's a matter, mutt?" He chuckled as he pulled away. Aaron was the spitting image of my father, thirty years younger with a Roman nose, blue eyes, and dark brown hair that was cropped short. He was a full foot and a half taller than me, but with a thin frame. I soaked in his favorite attire: collared polo, golf shorts, and loafers, which he lovingly referred to as his "gear." It was a look he had mastered and hadn't bothered to change since his teens.

"Why didn't you call?"

"I just got in this morning. You were my first stop." Aaron

lived in Florida. He'd followed his college sweetheart out there when she landed her first real job, and when they broke up he'd stayed, claiming he loved it. I had begged him to come home, but I think it was more or less an excuse to stay away from our parents, and the fact that he'd held onto hope that they would reconcile.

"Let me check in with Taylor, and we can leave. Come with me. You have to meet her." We boarded the elevator, and I looked over at him.

"How is Florida?" I asked, eyeing him suspiciously.

"Sunny all the time," he bit out quickly. I would never get him to change his mind.

"You've returned every check I've sent you. Accounting keeps asking me why I bother." I nudged him roughly so he would look at me.

"I don't need you to take care of me. I'm just so grateful you got Mom situated, though you shouldn't have."

"I did it for Dad." He nodded. "I know." When the elevator door opened, Taylor was waiting on it.

"Morning, bos—Nina." She smiled, and I felt my brother stiffen next to me. I didn't need to look at him to know he was fixated. Taylor was breathtaking. Today she wore a little racier attire. Her thigh high skirt accentuated her beautifully toned legs, along with killer heels. Her hair was left down and was the perfect shade of deep red that matched her lipstick. I had to admit, even I was taken aback by the siren who greeted us. We stepped out, and when I introduced them, Aaron was just slightly more formidable than a drooling idiot. Taylor gave him a small smile and boarded the now empty car.

"Nice to meet you. I assume you will be spending the day with him?" Guilt quickly settled over me that again, I would be neglecting work.

Taylor gave me a knowing smile. "You have nothing pressing. Go. I'll reschedule the PA interview. I know you need this."

"Taylor," I offered in apology.

"Door's closing," she said, winking at Aaron who turned to me.

"FUCK ME, FUCK ME, Nina. That is the most beautiful woman I have ever seen. Why the hell didn't you tell me?!"

"Tell you what? I have a hot assistant. Well, she's technically not my assistant anymore. I made her partner." Walking into my office, I looked back and saw my brother staring at the closed elevator. "She's out of your league, bro."

Hearing an indignant "hmpf," he turned and took a seat in my office. "Thanks for the vote of confidence."

"It's not that, it's that she's really …" God, how to describe Taylor … "Independent."

"I dig that in a woman."

"Aaron, she's not your type," I said, trying to close the subject.

"That's not what I just saw." Ignoring him, I opened my email and answered a few that had to be dealt with. I wasn't losing this precious time with my brother.

"I'm proud of you, Nina." He was looking right at me as I peered over the screen.

"Don't be, if you only knew what I've turned into." Swallowing the lump in my throat, I continued. "I'll make you proud."

Frowning, he pushed out a breath. "What's going on, Nina?" Shaking my head, I hit send on my last email and looked up smiling.

"Nothing."

"We are getting nowhere fast. You are as elusive as Mom right now." Narrowing my eyes, I scolded him.

"Don't ever compare me to her." It wasn't a request.

"Okay, well, stop pretending everything is okay when it's not and talk to me."

"Geez, don't you want ten minutes of normal? What about you? Why the sudden visit?" Shrugging, he stood up and walked around my office.

"I don't have another tournament for few weeks and wanted to see you. Do I need an excuse?" Aaron was a semi-pro golfer, and in his spare time, he worked odd jobs. He had a carefree life, and I suddenly envied that about him.

"No, I'm sorry. I'm so happy you're home." Turning off my PC, I gathered my purse. "Come on. I'm all yours today. What should we do first?"

"I have tee time at Dunes in two hours. I didn't want to pass it up. How about breakfast?"

"Come on! How long are you here?" I put my hands on my hips as he walked past me, knowing he was in the shit house.

"Until Tuesday, so back off." He pulled my arm off my hip to drag me back to the elevator. "We'll hit the waves too while I'm here."

Aaron and I shared a deep mutual love for the water. We spent a good amount of time every summer at the beach together until I left for college. Still, I couldn't help but feel the small tug in my chest at the memory of my last time in the water with Aiden.

Twenty minutes later, we were seated at Poogan's Porch, sipping coffee on the patio. It was just cool enough to be comfortable.

Aaron looked over the menu with clear prejudice.

"They have eggs and bacon, simpleton," I piped as he gave me a wary eye.

"I just don't think it's necessary to add all this shit to eggs."

"Then order eggs with no shit." His lips curled up at the sides, and I knew I had him. I felt deep relief with my brother's presence. Now this was a man who *knew* me. The uncorrupted pre-millionaire who was more preoccupied in bettering herself and whose hardest choice of the day was what to cook for dinner.

We'd always got along. Instead of sibling rivalry, it was typically us against our parents. Though we'd had our fair share of fights, our collaboration of damn near emancipating ourselves from our parents was our common bond. We mutually agreed our mother was the true villain, but together blamed our father for not liberating us from her altogether.

Aaron had developed a stammer when he was younger as a result of her. The more intense the house became with all the arguing, the worse it became. I coped by reciting the poem "Clooney the Clown". Together we were a nervous poem reciting, stammering, fucking mess. To this day when I was truly terrified, I'd recite that poem. I also had an unnatural adverse reaction to any sort of sudden loud noise or yelling, hence my emergency stash of Xanax. I often wondered what lingering effects that hellish house had on my brother.

Eventually, we became resentful enough to fight back with our indifference and tried to completely dissociate from them. It was just us, and we raised each other. As much as our father tried to keep the monsters at bay, his anger would win out and we would be stuck in the middle. We'd eventually forgiven our father and made a nonverbal commitment to simply tolerate and appease our mother for his sake. Secretly, I'd always hoped she would turn back into the loving and tolerant woman I'd known. A woman Aaron had never met. I knew her temperament for me now was money induced. Her kind, term of endearment "Ninabelle" made me cringe.

Aaron had come a long way from the little boy who had frequent accidents in bed. He'd once been so terrified he couldn't talk himself out of my mother's wrath.

I shook away the image of my baby brother trying to explain to my mother why he couldn't get to the toilet.

"M-M-M-Mommy, I'm s-sorry!"

She would grip his arm hard, jerking him into the bathroom, screaming at him as she cleaned him. I physically cringed at the memory. I looked up now to the man across from me, thankful he'd never used her behavior as an excuse to treat others poorly, and never excused her behavior once he was old enough to know better. My brother was one of my heroes.

"Stop staring at me. It's fucking weird." He looked up with a harsh glance as he sipped his coffee.

"You're so grown up," I mused at him with pride.

"Nina, I'm twenty-seven years old. I hit that mark a long time ago." Rolling his eyes, he held out his cup to the waitress who filled it then sat back, looking at our limited view of Queen Street. "Okay, so spill it. Setting down his cup, he folded his arms on the table.

"Nothing you need to know, honestly. A little man trouble, but nothing I can't handle."

I was such a fucking liar. Still, this was my brother, and my shit had no place in his head.

"Man trouble," he snickered. "Well, I can't imagine why, Nina. You pick the absolute worst men to fall for."

"Not true," I defended as our plates were set in front of us.

"Your first boyfriend was a total ass clown. What was his name? Trevor?"

"Terry. He was nice, and if I remember correctly, he gave you one of his dad's golf clubs."

After situating my coffee, I looked up and realized he was frowning about the food. "They put shit in my eggs." I burst out laughing as he eyed the cilantro that had ruined his breakfast. He continued his assault on my history as he scooped the green off his plate. "Then there was your first serious boyfriend. I can't remember his name. Oh yeah, it was 'Oh, Nina. I love you, Nina. Oh, Nina."'

My face burned with the memory of my baby brother bursting into my first real make out session. Thank God we were still fully clothed.

"Can we not dredge up the past, please?"

"I hated Ryan, for the record," he stated of my ex-husband, ignoring my plea and opting for toast, bypassing his eggs completely.

"What about you, brat? It's not like you have a great track record." I stopped myself. His last breakup had hurt him in the way that can't be joked about, and I apologized.

"Me too. I shouldn't have brought up Ryan." He looked sincere, and I nodded, stirring my coffee with my spoon. "Is it Devin?" When I had introduced the two before Devin and I got involved, I could see he assumed there was something going on. "I liked him."

"You met him once."

"Even so, is it him?"

"No," I lied. "You know, Aaron, maybe we are destined to—"

"Don't even say it, Nina. We aren't *them,* and we will never be."

Smiling, I agreed again without words. "I'll buy you a house here." He was shaking his head as the first two words spilled out. "They won't even have to know."

"Nina, I love you. You are the most important person in my life, but I refuse to live off of you. I want to find my own way. And hey, I'm not doing so bad, okay. Don't worry about me. You will always have me, just not here. It's Florida, golfer's paradise."

"I'll come to you then, and soon, okay. No more every six months shit. And we can't count Christmas, except for last year when you sprinkled weed in Mom's batch of Christmas cookies. That Christmas counts."

We both exploded with laughter as we recalled her sleeping the entire day, suddenly "exhausted" while Dad, Aaron, and I drank on the patio playing Yahtzee, free from her reign. It was the best Christmas ever.

I paid the bill, and Aaron shoved money in my purse, cursing while giving me a disapproving eye. When we exited the tiny picket fence leading out into the street, I saw Aaron's face contort in fear as he yanked at my arm hard and I was pulled off my feet. All I heard was a crunch and explosion of splintering wood. I felt an unbelievable throb in my side as I stared up at the blue sky, completely confused. I saw one head come into view then two, and soon I was screaming in pain.

"Fuck, did you get the license plate?" one guy shouted to another.

"No, they took off."

The next voice spoke directly to me. "It's okay, ma'am. We just called an ambulance."

Panic caused my next scream to be directed toward my brother.

"Aaron! Aaron!"

"I'm here." It was faint.

I turned my head to see him lying on the ground a few feet away from me, his leg partially impaled as a result of a piece of wood from the fence. He looked at me helplessly as the burning in my hip spread. I was filled with panic as he closed his eyes and I begged him to keep them on me, which he did weakly.

Sirens approached minutes later, and I was screaming again in discomfort as they lifted me into the back of the ambulance. As the doors closed, I tried searching for Aaron, but instead, I saw *her*.

Sitting up without thinking, I pushed through the pain to get a clear look at her until the medics pinned me back down.

"That which does not kill us makes us stronger."
– FRIEDRICH NIETZSCHE

§§

NINA

HOURS LATER, I was sitting at Aaron's hospital bedside as the doctors informed him his surgery would consist of inserting pins and screws, and they went into further detail as to how it would proceed. Fixing his mangled leg might require two surgeries and months of recovery. I cried as my brother's worst nightmare was realized. He wouldn't be golfing for a very long time. Even a month away was a nightmare for a golfer. As it turned out, my injuries were minor. The fall had knocked my pelvis out of place, and there was severe bruising, but I managed to escape with both legs and a prescription for strong pain medication. Tears trickled one by one as I apologized to my brother for his pain and the part I played in taking away what meant most to him.

"It's not like I won't recover," he said dryly. I was nowhere near being as comforted as his words tried to make me.

"I think my ex's wife did this." He eyed me carefully then exhaled slowly. "I think she tried to kill me. This is my fault. Jesus, Aaron, she could have killed you." I sobbed as he listened to me tell the tale of Devin and his diabolical wife. He asked a question every so often but mostly just listened. I felt like I was finally coming clean to someone who had the right to reprimand me.

When I finished, Aaron was thoughtful for a long moment before he spoke. "Nope, sorry, even if that's true, *you* didn't do this. You didn't even see the fucking car. I'm glad I was there. It sucks…" He winced in discomfort, adjusting himself on the bed. "But, Nina, that hit would have killed you."

I continued to beg his forgiveness as he comforted me as he laid in the hospital bed.

"Nina, have you ever heard the saying 'Every day is a Monday?'"

"No." I sniffed into his bedding.

"Well, dear sister, when I was bingeing on Jack Daniels to get over Danielle, I swore the next day I wouldn't do it again. And the next day I would, and I would swear to start over. This lasted for about six months. I treated every fucking day like it was a Monday, and when I fucked up, it became Sunday again. I just kept at it, some days knowing it was a lost cause, some days more of an optimist. Eventually, that day came."

"I get it," I said, wiping my nose.

"You didn't do this to me. And tomorrow is *your* Monday."

"I'll feel guilty about this until I die."

"And one day I may use it against you when it's funny, but right now it's not."

After the cops showed up and questioned us for their mandatory amount of minutes, Aaron's meds kicked in and took him into a peaceful sleep, after I assured him I wasn't leaving. Some part of him thought I might be delusional about the incident being purposeful, but the part that believed me wanted me safely next to him, so I promised I'd stay until we figured it out.

I lied.

Exiting the hospital, I went from devastated to murderous in minutes. I called Devin's secretary under false pretenses, stating I had an emergency and found out he was dining with his fair wife at The Chophouse. His secretary and I got along well, and I was sure this would be the last favor I asked.

Rage swept through me as Carson pulled up and I exited without his assistance. Pushing through the waiting crowd, I spotted them immediately in the center of the room, and they weren't alone.

And in no universe would it have mattered.

Neither of them saw me as I approached. I gripped the fine linen that covered their table with my fists and pulled the entirety off it off as they stood crippled with shock and covered in their feast.

"Goddamn fucking bitch! Do I have *your* attention!" She looked around the table with pleading eyes, paling with my every word. "Tell them what you've done, Eileen! Tell them what you've done!" She glared at me over the table as I rounded it to get closer.

"Nina," she hissed over the commotion, "I'm quite sure I have no idea what—"

"She proved her love today for you, Devin," I raged, not looking his way, my eyes zeroing in on his wife as I inched closer to her. "If you ever come near me or my family again, I won't have to make it look like an accident! I'll do my own dirty work."

Devin stood, mouth gaping, as I let out my fury without worrying about the consequences. Maybe I'd played right into her hands with my public outburst. Then again, she'd expected me maimed or dead. Picturing my brother in that hospital bed caused me to take another step around the table. Devin walked toward me, clearly confused.

"Your wife put a fucking hit on me, Devin! Who the fuck actually does that? But just like everything else in her life, including her marriage, she failed." Eileen looked around the room terrified as several of the staff came toward me to halt my scene.

I used my time wisely and stood face to face with her. "You want him? Have him! And please, by all means, make sure he stays the fuck away from me. You are right, sweetheart. I *am* a street rat. And there's something you should know about rats—" I slapped her hard, and she flew back, her hand on her swelling face, playing the victim perfectly "—we can fight just as dirty as we fuck. Come at my family or me again, and I'll show you how bad it can get."

Disgusted, I turned to Devin, tears of rage in my eyes.

"She almost killed my brother today to get to me. She almost killed Aaron!" He took another step toward me, reaching for me as the rest of the table looked on at the spectacle.

My arm shot out, stopping him as I gripped my hip, the

pain starting to throb unbearably. I must have looked a complete mess, my clothes torn, my face streaked with tear stains.

"Nina—"

"Please, I'm begging you to stay the fuck away from me. You are not worth it."

To make sure he got my point, I said it again, my eyes locked on his. "You. Are. Not. Worth. It."

His eyes filled with something I'd only seen in brief glimpses over the past few months. Remorse quickly turned to rage as he looked over to witness his wife's breakdown.

She reached out to him, and I turned on my heel, leaving without looking back.

§§

Shaking in the back seat of my town car, I dialed Taylor. I'd wondered if the police were looking for me due to my behavior at the restaurant. I wouldn't be a bit surprised if Eileen painted herself a victim and sent them for me. Someone had the decency to return my purse to me at the hospital, minus the cash in my wallet, of course. They took a couple hundred in twenties but managed to spare my six hundred dollar phone.

Idiots.

She picked up on the first ring.

"Boss."

"I need to talk to you now, privately."

"Okay."

"In person."

"Okay, I can meet you. Where?"

"Downtown, somewhere public."

"Should I be worried?" Her tone let me know she'd heard the desperation in my voice.

"Meet me at the market, the first closest to Bay." I hung up without waiting for a reply. I knew she would be there. The Old Slave Market was situated in the heart of downtown Charleston. The hideous name came from the fact that it was supposed to have been where the buying and selling of slaves started in the 1600s, but the locals knew better. The real location of the slave trade was actually a few streets over. The market had since been remolded into a main tourist attraction where hundreds of vendors of art, jewelry, and other local treasures were sold.

Carson let me out in front of the first of four long buildings that made up the market. Taylor was waiting, her expression unreadable. I started walking next to her toward the entrance, and when I was sure we weren't in earshot of anyone, I started barking orders.

"I want a new alarm system in my house and at Scott Solutions tonight. I don't care what the cost is. Bribe them. I want a security team for me personally and stationed at Solutions all day, every day."

She nodded. "Now we have people we are afraid of?"

I stopped and turned to her. "Devin's wife tried to kill me today. I can't prove it, but she was there. I didn't see the car, but I saw her after, as if she was trying to confirm I was dead. My brother was with me and got me out of the way in time, but he was badly injured. It's time to be cautious. I don't know when or if they'll be coming for me again. It might be best if you lay low." I couldn't believe the words coming out of my mouth. I was still in shock this was the situation.

"Jesus, a hit. Who the hell does that?"

"I said the same thing when I bitch slapped her in The Chophouse twenty minutes ago." Taylor burst out laughing, but I could see the hint of anger in her eyes.

"Good for you, and I will carry out all of that. Give me five minutes, and then you and I are going for a drink."

"Taylor, it's not safe to be with me right now." We walked from one building to the next as the vendors began to break down for the night. The crowd was thinning. It was time to leave.

"You trust me with the livelihood of your company. I need you to trust me for five more minutes."

I nodded as the pain from my hip became impossible to ignore. I leaned against a vendor table, pretending to sift through hand woven scarves as the reality of what today had brought set in. As much as I hated to admit it, I should have taken Eileen's threats more seriously. My brother was hurt, and for the first time in my life, I was afraid I wouldn't live to see another day. No matter how brazen I'd been, I was now scared shitless.

Taylor returned minutes later, motioning for me to walk with her. I had her accompany me back to Carson then took the prescription for my medication out of my purse, asking him to fill it and pick me up in an hour. Taylor nodded in agreement with my timeline and walked me over to Henry's House, a pub across the street from the market. I winced with every step as we made our way to the busy bar. It was too painful to sit, so I stood as she took a stool.

Once we'd both had a shot of something strong—whiskey, I think—and a beer in hand, Taylor turned to me. "Okay, so I think it's time I explained a few things to you."

I nodded, intrigued.

"I was raised in situations like this. I'm not afraid, and I don't want you to be, either."

I waited because I was still too absorbed in the situation and the pain in my side to reply.

"Tomorrow, we get you a permit, forty-eight hours later, a gun."

"No," I dismissed her suggestion, wincing at the pain seeping through my every limb. "Taylor, I'm not the type of woman—"

"Today made you that type of woman," she deadpanned, and I nodded. "This might be shocking to you, and I get it, but from where I come from this is just another day in the park."

"Where did you come from, Taylor?" I looked around the bar, fear creeping in as I thought about the fact that I might have been followed every minute of today, my new reality still impossible to fully grasp.

"Dirt and metal grass."

"Always so cryptic," I scorned as I looked right at her.

"Today's not the day for my story." She nodded over my shoulder. "Security is here. I want you to do what he tells you to, and I'll pick you up tomorrow."

"Taylor, I don't know what to say."

"You're welcome, and it's still my job, at least for the next few weeks. I'm glad it was me. I think this might have scared the new applicant." She smiled, and I returned it half-heartedly.

"Is this really fucking happening?" I shook my head in disbelief as Taylor led me to my new saving grace.

"It is." I looked in the direction she was heading and saw two men. One seemed to be waiting at the door for someone outside, and the other was looking right at us. I paused mid-step as I took him in, but Taylor gripped my arm, nudging me forward. "Nina, no matter what fuck up she hired, he can't compete with this guy."

He didn't have an earpiece liked I'd expected, or a men-in-black suit on. His jeans were tattered, and his t-shirt was wrinkled and worn. His head was shaved smooth, and he was covered in tattoos. His knowing smirk at Taylor had me on edge.

"Nina, let him help." I nodded as we approached. "I'm Cedric. I'll take good care of you, Ms. Scott." He extended his hand politely, despite his rugged appearance, and I accepted it, thankful for the help.

"Tomorrow," Taylor reminded as she walked out of the bar, leaving me in Cedric's hands.

"Ex-military, eight years, some Special Ops, and I've been guarding now for four years. You will sleep like a baby." Even as he spit off his résumé, I doubted the truth of his words on my sleeping capabilities. "Thank you for coming on such short notice." Nervously, I sputtered out the situation, giving him entirely too much information as we walked back through the market to await Carson.

"Did you tell the police?" he prompted.

"Yes, everything I'm telling you." He couldn't hide his smirk.

"Might want to shorten the story in case there is a next time."

"I'm sorry. I'm nervous. The wife, Eileen, she's so well-known and respected in this city. I know it will be her word against mine. I just can't imagine they will do a damn thing about it. And she knew it. It was pretty fucking bold of her to actually be there when it happened."

"That kind of cockiness is sure to catch up with her at some point, but it's also a good reason for you to take the precautions you are taking. I'll be investigating this on my own, as well as cooperating with the police when needed. Do you have an issue with that?"

I shook my head no. My pain level had increased to ungodly as Carson finally pulled up. Cedric had kept me behind the brick building as we waited then guided me to the car as I told him I was going back to the hospital. He agreed it was for the best until they got a clear idea of the type of security I would need at my house. I slipped into the car and was surprised when he joined me.

"You and I will be spending a large amount of time together for the time being." I had no choice but to agree. I had no idea what I was in for.

Carson eyed Cedric as he introduced himself. Carson's reaction to the events of the day was nothing less than fatherly concern. He'd refused to take a much-needed vacation at my urging. He couldn't hide his disappointment that I'd left him in the dark and he'd said as much on the way to the hospital. Cedric escorted me to the room but not before requesting Carson's presence once he was parked.

And just like that, my whole life had gone from semi-fucked up to out of control with no end or relief in sight. Somewhere outside of the hospital walls, there were people possibly plotting my death. In the last few hours, my life had been completely turned upside down. And though I wanted to blame Devin, I knew this wasn't his doing. Still, I prayed he'd really heard my words and stayed the hell away from me. And even as I thought it, my heart told me I'd die a thousand deaths to feel the way he made me feel this morning.

He. Loves. Me.

And that fucking love almost cost me my life.

"Confront the dark parts of yourself, and work to banish them with illumination and forgiveness. Your willingness to wrestle with your demons will cause your angels to sing."

– AUGUST WILSON

§§

DEVIN

I STARED AT MY wife entwined with her lover in our marital bed. I'd left the restaurant immediately after Nina and started making phone calls knowing I wouldn't get any answers from Eileen. If I'd stayed with her a minute longer, I would have lost all control. I felt the hope from that morning slip away from me with Nina's parting words. She was furious and had every right to be, but she'd meant them.

And that had changed every rule of fair fighting.

As I stared at Eileen sleeping soundly with one of my partners, I had to stifle a laugh at the fact Thomas wasn't wearing his hairpiece. It amazed me they had become that comfortable. He was so vain about his appearance. I reached into my pocket and took a snapshot with my cell phone before dropping my suitcase loudly on the floor.

They both jumped as soon as they saw me and shot out of bed, scrambling for cover.

"Devin," Thomas offered in a low voice as an apology. I ignored him, my sights on the woman looking back at me in shock.

"What are you doing here, Devin!" She gripped a sheet to her chest as if I would at all be interested in seeing anything underneath it.

"Good morning, honey," I chimed happily. "So fucking good to be home. I see Thomas was kind enough to keep the sheets warm." I gave him a sly grin. "Thanks, pal. And now that there's a vacancy, I'll just get settled." I opened my suitcase and dumped the contents on the floor. It was an entire week's worth of suits and just enough to have her gasping in disbelief.

"Devin, you can't possibly think you—"

"See you at the office, Thomas," I said warmly as he threw on his suit coat. He stopped just short of the door and turned to me.

"Devin, I don't know what to say."

"See you soon, Thomas." I couldn't give a fuck about his presence, but it was good to know he would be shitting himself the rest of the week worrying about my retaliation. I may just give him a run for his money. He was, after all, fucking my wife. I couldn't care less, but then there was that matter of respect. Though I was positive she'd painted me a pretty villain to Thomas, I decided I would make sure her prophecy came to fruition.

"Devin, get out! Get out of this house!"

Ignoring her demand, I removed the canvas off the wall. "You know I always hated this painting." I gripped the Renoir and opened the window next to her bedside table. I pulled a sharp pen from my suit jacket and ripped through it, hearing her screams. It was her prize possession. I threw it out the window, and it landed just short of hitting an escaping Thomas.

"Sorry, buddy," I called as he jumped out of the way. "Safe travels."

I turned back to Eileen, who was now pounding on my chest with her fists. "I own your plantation too now, bitch. You really aren't very good at the game of Monopoly. I now own Park Place and all the hotels, and you have just landed your ass in jail."

She stopped her pounding and looked up at me.

"The paperwork, I read it."

"I forged your signature on the real initial contract. It's the first shady deal I've ever brokered, and it was fucking worth it. It got you into closing where all the lawyers were present, and you signed it away to me with a smile."

"Get out of my house," she ordered with a pointed finger as she sat on the side of the bed, dressed in only a half-slip.

"Call it off," I countered. "You have gone too fucking far!"

She looked up at me, judgment clear on her face. "*I've* gone too far. And what you've done you won't have to answer for?"

"I don't care what happens to me anymore. Can't you see that? I. Don't. Fucking. Care. I'm here, call it OFF!"

"I already have." With false confidence, she stood then walked toward the bathroom. I gripped her arm and pulled her to face me.

"Sorry, honey, but I'm going to have a bit of a hard time believing you. At least you've spared me the argument of admitting it. I'm going to need proof."

"I warned you," she snapped. I shook her hard and let go as she started sobbing before falling back onto the bed. "And I warned you, Eileen. Don't make me this monster, because, for her, I will be. I'll fucking kill you right now!"

"Please, Devin. I saw you leaving her house yesterday and I—"

"Another man just left your bed, Eileen. Spare me the jealous act." Holding her down on the mattress, I hovered over her. All I saw was fear. "I'm back for good. You've taken away my only chance at happiness. You get your wish. This will be a marriage again, but I can't say the nature of it will be desirable." She looked away from me as I gripped her chin, forcing her to look at me, her eyes wide as I hovered. "The minute she dies, you do, too. Now tell me, honey, do you believe me?"

"Devin, I'm sorry. I only wanted you to stop seeing her. I told you, you can have indiscretions, just not—"

"Unh uh, Eileen, now I only want you." I slid my hands slowly down her sides and gripped her hips, sure I would leave bruises. She began sobbing hysterically, and I let her go, without an ounce of remorse. The switch had been flipped, and I couldn't shut it off. She cowered under my glare as I nailed myself to her mentally. "You're done, you've sunk yourself, it's over."

She wanted me as a husband, well by God hubby was home.

"Appear weak when you are strong, and strong when you are weak."

— SUN TZU

§§

NINA

AFTER AARON WAS situated, comfortably recovering from surgery, I messaged Taylor to meet me at the hospital entrance. I had hardly slept, too revved up on pain meds and the aftermath of the day's events. I'd spent the better part of my night pacing the floor at Aaron's side. At four A.M., a nurse took pity on me, sliding a second bed into the room and making me comfortable enough to lie down. I still hadn't managed to slip off, constantly looking outside the glass in the door for Cedric. I'd managed only a few hours on exhaustion alone.

I walked outside of the hospital against Cedric's request. I needed the air, due to the constant noise inside of the busy entrance making me more anxious. The thunderous rumble of an engine had me jumping out of my skin as a long, sleek, blacked-out muscle car came into view before stopping suddenly. I looked to Cedric who seemed perfectly calm, sure he was misreading the situation, and felt the dread overwhelm me when I unbelievably watched Taylor exit the driver's side.

What in the hell?

She stood with the door open, tapping her fingers on the hood. "Come on, boss." I was sure this was some sort of joke but played along, taking a seat beside her. We shot out of the parking lot, minus one Cedric, who assured me I was in good hands.

"Taylor," I said, lifting the ass end of her name in question.

"Boss," she answered back with a smile. "Open the glove compartment."

I did as prompted and saw a gun the size of a small cannon nestled comfortably in black velvet.

"That's Leroy Brown," she introduced. "And I'm sure you know his rep."

"Baddest in the whole damn town," I finished for her. "Is this a joke to you?"

She looked at me seriously, momentarily taking her eyes off the road. "Not at all."

"She tried to kill me, Taylor." I was irritable and in a lot of pain. Popping two more of my pills, I decided I would need a shower sooner than later. My mouth was dry, and I could feel my skin starting to crawl.

"So what, someone makes an attempt on your life, and you go crawling under a rock? Not happening."

"Well, I sure as hell am not going to walk around with a target on my back!" Taylor was speeding, and I buckled my belt, making her chuckle. "What's with the Knight Rider?"

"It's my taste," she offered simply.

"Okay, correct me if I'm wrong here, but isn't this like, a man's car?"

"I'll forgive you for that … eventually. We're here." She pulled into the parking lot, and I looked at the sign. It was a sporting goods store. "First we get your license then I teach you how to shoot."

"Taylor, I don't feel comfortable with a gun." She pulled opened the glove box and grabbed her pistol then pointed it right at my head.

"Are you fucking crazy!" I sat still, completely sure that my time was up, that I had somehow mistook Taylor for someone I could trust. Trembling from head to toe, her face gave away nothing as I braced myself for certain death. After only a few seconds, she questioned me.

"Now, would you feel more comfortable with a gun?"

"Jesus Christ, you're fired!" I shrieked, pulling my head away from the barrel. She turned it to the side, examining it.

"Safety was on, and you can't fire me. I'm now your co-chair. You wanted to know who I am, well, this is part of it. I'm not going to sugarcoat shit, and it's time you took better care of yourself. Lesson one: when someone is threatening your life, make sure you have a big goddamn gun, and you know how to use it."

"That was unforgivable!" I yelled, my adrenaline still pumping through me at an all-time high.

"Nina, you are not a weak woman." Furious, I sat as she tried to reason with me. "Do you want to rely on others to take care of this situation, or do you want to have a say in your own fate if push comes to shove?"

Stunned, I sat, twisting my hands in my lap as she continued. "You leave your fate in the hands of other people, they are bound to let you down."

Don't I know it.

"Who let you down, Taylor?"

She smiled and gave me a wink. "Nice try."

Still a bit furious with her scare tactic, I followed her into the store, completely terrified by my new revelation, and just a little bit in awe of my new partner. Clearing my head, I focused as much as I possibly could as I filled out the necessary paperwork while Taylor browsed through a glass case catalog of shiny protective metal. I'd never really had an opinion on guns, never had to. Never thought I would be in the situation to form one. Suddenly I was pro shiny protective metal. She looked up at me every once in a while in reassurance. I took deep breaths as the clerk walked me through the various pieces of information as Taylor ordered several guns she thought would be a good fit for me.

A gun for me. A fucking gun!

Back inside Knight Rider, I felt a little more at ease and began to relax for the first time in twenty-four hours.

"Taylor, what am I missing here? Why would Cedric leave me with you?"

"I've known him all my life. He knows if I can't outrun them, I can outshoot them."

"Where the hell are you from?"

"Tennessee." I barked out a laugh as she gave me a stern

look. "Trust me, it was the Wild West."

I frowned, completely lost in my thoughts, and found myself drooling on her car window as she slid to a stop in front of the hospital. I'd slipped off somehow and was now cupping the drool from my chin to gather myself. I turned to see Taylor amused.

"Well, thank you, Taylor, for a terrifying yet informative experience." I turned to her with a wink, my hand on the door handle.

"I would never hurt you, Nina." Pressing my lips together, I attempted to stifle my tears but failed. Her eyes softened slightly.

"Trust Cedric, steer clear of the office until he gives you the okay, and try to rest. Your brother needs you. The office doesn't."

"Does it ever need me?" I smiled as she chuckled. "Get out, your brother needs you." I watched her speed away as Cedric escorted me back inside.

"Tennessee was the Wild West, huh?" Cedric simply smiled as he led me back to Aaron.

And that was the completion of day two in an alternate universe.

§§

DEVIN

Every second that ticked by was agony. I waited for a report from a few men I'd hired to watch over Nina. They'd made me aware she had hired guards of her own. She was doubly protected, and it did absolutely nothing to help me. She wouldn't leave Charleston, I knew that much. She wouldn't leave her brother's side.

All of this was on me. I was dealing with it, but it didn't make it easier to stay in this house, sleep next to Eileen, and watch her every move. I didn't let her out of my sight, not even for a private moment. I'd confiscated her phone the minute I'd returned home. It was beginning to wear on her, I could tell. Eventually, she'd give in and want her freedom back, so I bided my time.

"Going somewhere?" I peeked around my newspaper and stared at her as she scurried down the hall to reach the front door. She would never be fast enough.

Shoulders slumped, she faced me. "Devin, I have an appointment. You can't keep me prisoner in my own home!"

"Sorry, dear, those are the breaks. Besides, I've invited your mother over for lunch."

Sheer terror covered her features as she raced through the house, making sure it was perfect. She barked orders at the service staff as I finished my coffee.

Eileen had a sick and deep seeded need for her mother's approval. I was sure it was what had ruined her and her sister, corrupting their stability. I was positive it was what made them into the monsters they had become. Sandra had proven as much with her actions. They were both unredeemable as human beings.

Eileen came to a halt only when she saw the smile on my face. She believed I was bluffing.

"You are a cruel bastard."

"And you are a heartless bitch. I could do this forever, darling." She walked toward me slowly and took a seat next to me at the table. She feared me now. I knew I could use it.

"What do you want?"

"I want you on camera admitting you hired someone to kill Nina, how much you paid, and exactly who it was."

"You can't be serious," she scoffed. "Devin, I'm not that stupid."

"Yes, you are, wife dear. You were, in fact, at the scene of the fucking crime and have been questioned by police, have you not?"

"You think I'm going to admit to hiring someone to kill your mistress on tape?"

"Yes," I said, turning the page of my paper. She sat staring at me as I ignored her successfully.

A knock on the door had Eileen looking to me, horrified as she got up to answer.

It was, in fact, her mother.

I wasn't bluffing.

Yes, indeed, hubby was home.

"Those who restrain desire do so because theirs is weak enough to be restrained."

– WILLIAM BLAKE

§§

NINA

Nina: I'm sorry, Aiden.

I'D SENT THAT text a week after the "accident."

Three words, I texted him three words he deserved. I'd been deceptive to a fault, and I deserved his silence. As I sat admiring the lighthouse from the shore, I realized it had been three weeks since the attempt was made on my life. Aaron had been discharged from the hospital, and after several lengthy arguments and a horrible visit from my mother as a reminder of what life would be like under her watch, he had returned to Florida to finish his recovery. Leave it to Mom to keep her children safely at bay. This was my mess, and I wanted Aaron as far away from it as possible. He'd fought me every step of the way, but in the end, with the help of Cedric's and my coaxing, he'd returned home. I'd hired a full-time nurse to help him and paid all his medical bills. I'd also arranged for his condo to be paid off and an ample check to be delivered each month. We would fight about that later.

My mother hadn't uttered a word to me other than what concerned Aaron. She eyed Cedric with interest but was too determined to keep her conversation with me short to prod further.

And I was relieved.

As I'd watched her leave the hospital, I called after my father, asking to have a word with him. He ignored the protest of my mother as she glared at him before exiting the sliding doors with a matching glare for me.

"Dad, just go. I don't want to cause trouble."

"She'll get over it. She always does." He looked tired. What had once had been a handsome man full of funny jokes about life's vibrancy had now turned into a defeated shell of a man who no longer had the strength to fight.

He guided me to the waiting room, and we sat as I gathered my words as best as I could. The truth was, I was scared. If somehow another attempt was successful, I was worried about what would become of him. Aaron would try to an extent, but he was no match for my mother. He seemed to read my mind as I started in.

"Dad, if she leaves you—"

"I used to pray for that day," he whispered. "I wanted it to happen. Then I would look at you, Nina, and you brother was so damn lost, and no matter how much *I* wanted to leave, I couldn't. She would have found a way to keep me out of your lives." He lowered his head, as if ashamed. Stunned by his admission, I waited for him to continue.

"After so many years of struggling with that woman, I taught myself to feel…nothing. It was the only way I could survive the marriage. But saying it should have never happened is like saying the two of you should have never happened. I'm not proud of the environment I raised you in, or the woman I let mother you, but I am so proud of you both. I'm sorry…" He looked away, trying to hide his tears as I hugged him to me. "If that car would have killed either of you, I don't think I'd be able to handle it, Nina. I…" He pulled the moisture away from his eyes then looked at me. "Just be careful with yourselves."

Aaron and I had agreed before our parents arrived to keep the facts surrounding the "accident" to ourselves.

"Daddy, I'll take care of you. You'll never have to worry about anything."

"Sweetheart, you have done so much for us already. I'm so proud of you. I would have never agreed to you doing what you have if it weren't for her."

"Listen to me, Daddy. I need you to really listen to me, okay?" He looked at me fully. "She's a lost cause, and you know it. I want you to let her go." I was crying now as my father's shoulders slumped with emotion and rapidly shedding tears.

"It's not too late to start over. I want you to take this one last thing from me. Just this one thing, okay? For me. Not for you, for *me*." He looked up and held me tightly to him. "Okay, Belle, whatever you want."

That was the moment I knew I had ended my relationship with my mother.

In that moment, I had my revelation that some people, no matter how much you may think you need them or can't live without them, leave you no choice but to do just that. My mother was a dark cloud that had hovered over me my entire life, and the only way to opt for sunny skies was to refuse her presence and end the torturous relationship. And the same applied to Devin.

With Devin, it was simply circumstance that never seemed to change. I'd always love him, but would be forced to do it from afar. Not because he was the dark cloud, but because he brought his own with him, one that stifled my life, just the same as it did his.

Sitting on the beach now gave me some small semblance of normalcy after weeks of living on edge, wondering if my life would be cut short. Isolation had taken on a whole new meaning, one way more miserable. I'd finally made the decision to free myself from the fear inhabited prison and rejoin the world. I'd gone back to work the minute Aaron left for Florida.

Taylor, true to her word, had taken me to a shooting range several times to teach me the ropes. And suddenly, I was comfortable with a gun and now owned several.

This life of mine was strange, and I was a stranger in it. But I was getting there. Day by day, I was finding a way back to me, even in my new reality.

It was a fight for stability, and I had the mindset to win. Every day was Monday, and I was determined to try again. I ignored the sexual thirst my body had built and eventually it had careened into another type of emptiness, one I could tolerate.

I sat for hours just staring at the waves as they calmed me. After a refreshing day in the new summer sun, I stood to walk toward the large dune and saw Aiden pause mid-step as he noticed me. Seeming to make a decision, he made his way toward the beach, and toward me. I had just reached the point of being able to walk without pain. Now, seeing him, I wanted to run. I felt the burn in my throat and couldn't help the watery emotion building in my eyes.

I'd missed him.

He stood in front of me now, his beautiful, fiery chocolate eyes telling me nothing as he watched me carefully.

"Nina," he said low, almost as if he was sorry he'd said it.

He seemed to be bracing himself for the worst. I'd done enough to him and decided I would make this easy on him.

"Hi." There was no way I was leading this conversation.

One long look at him and I was a fucking mess inside. I pushed it down far, letting the bite in my throat stifle it. Maybe it was his strength that was so alluring or the strong arms that could shield me for just a few minutes from the nightmare I'd been sleepwalking in. I'd been dealing with the threat on my life alone, trying hard to be the strong woman Taylor had told me I was. I'd almost begun to believe her.

Looking at Aiden as he towered over me, his beauty overwhelming, his strength emanating from him, I wanted to admit defeat. I wanted those arms around me, to feel the comfort of his touch. But I had no right to ask it of him and I wouldn't.

His normally full lips pressed into a thin line as he watched me try not to crumble in front of him. After a minute of silence, I couldn't handle it anymore.

"I was just leaving. You look well, Aiden."

I started to walk past him as he gripped the side of my sundress, gently holding me in place.

What could I say? What was there to say?

He gave nothing as he kept his hold on me. The pain from the loss of him more present than ever, I felt his rejection all over again. He was truly beautiful in every way. I'd somehow held onto hope the way I always had when any of my relationships ended. I could see clearly now that it was in vain. It was time to accept it. The way I had with Devin.

"I'm sorry. I really am." I tried to move, but he kept his grip. "Please let me go."

"I'm sorry for the way I ended things. You deserve an explanation if you haven't received one already."

He stared at me intensely for a moment, seeming to read my face carefully. He was asking if Devin had shared. I felt a small ray of hope.

"No, he didn't, and I don't deserve it but tell me anyway." I tried to smile and failed.

Aiden's scent drifted over to me, and I felt the longing to be near him. I'd missed him, and I told him as much because it was the truth.

He grabbed my hand, and I whimpered at his touch before pulling my hand away. "Please don't."

"Okay." He stayed quiet for a few moments and sat in the sand, looking out at the water.

I joined him as he stared straight at the calm sea.

"Devin and I grew up together. We have a long history. We are cousins but were raised like brothers. We were pretty close until high school, and then sibling rivalry reached a whole new level." I nodded, urging him on.

"I guess the breaking point would have been a few years ago. We had a serious argument over something trivial that blew up into something entirely different, and we haven't spoken since."

"You two, the way you looked at each other, it scared the hell out of me."

"We can be pretty intense." I'd seen fighting like that my whole life. Some people just don't mesh. Case and point, my mother and father.

"Believe it or not, I get it. But, Aiden, if he's not in your life, why would you end it with me?"

He looked at me suddenly, anger covering his features.

"I was pissed, Nina. I was pissed I'd comforted you over a man you told me you were in love with. *He* was that man. I handled it poorly. But I'm still angry with you." His next words were spoken low. "And I'm even more pissed that I still fucking want you."

His amber eyes blazed with emotion and need. He was dressed in his usual cargo shorts and a light blue t-shirt that read *Green Day*. He looked even more sun-kissed than the last time I saw him, his beautiful, silvery blond hair tousled by the wind.

"I still want you, too, even though I don't have the right. I wasn't sure if you were connected, and I didn't want to chance losing you, but I did anyway."

I looked behind me to see Cedric watching us closely and gave him a wink. He was somewhat far away, so I wasn't sure if he saw my gesture.

"Is there a reason you are winking at the man behind us after you just told me you wanted me?" His voice was dangerous, but I saw the humorous tug on the sides of his mouth.

"Yes."

He leaned in with a chuckle, coming close to my lips. "And that reason is?"

"He's my bodyguard. I didn't want him tackling you into the sand in case you tried to kiss me."

He leaned in, placing his hands on the sand. "And what makes you think I want to kiss you, naughty Nina?"

That one line had my heart soaring, and it quickly took a nosedive with my next confession.

Today is Monday.

"I slept with him, Aiden…since." It was if I had burned him. He jolted back, standing up to glare down at me. I jumped to my feet to join him. Completely clueless as to what to say, I made a worthless plea. "You left me alone on that beach and told me we were done."

"We are," he said, turning, making his way to the large sand dune that led to the parking lot.

"Aiden, damn it." I stood, watching him leave and tugged at the ends of my hair, emotion choking me. I walked the opposite direction, refusing to watch him walk away from me again.

"Today is Monday. Today is Monday," I repeated over and over.

Being honest had its downfalls, too. At least when I was corrupt, I felt justified in my manipulation. Maybe today *was* finally my Monday. And I hated the fucking day.

I could be in Aiden's arms right now, kissing his mouth, feeling his warmth if I'd only lied.

And then suddenly I was. He caught up with me and turned me to him, his mouth coming down hard. I moaned as he thrust his velvety tongue inside, tasting me endlessly, sliding it over mine in a deep, sensuous kiss. I melted into him as he gripped me hard, stroking my face and neck with his fingertips, torturing my senses. When he pulled away, I saw anger.

"Why the fuck can't you stay away from him!?"

I looked at him with another honest answer. "I told you why."

Fire glowed in his depths as he released me and put his hands in his pockets.

"I wasn't ready for a relationship then, Aiden, and I'm not sure I can handle one now. But I think I wished you into my life. I saw whatever it was between us becoming more…something good. I wanted to try. I think we had a chance, but a large part of me will always love him, and I hate it that he got here first." I held my hand over my chest. "Because I think if you had been first, I'd never have room for him."

Aiden stayed silent as I pushed the ball into his court. He glared at me, unforgiving, as I put my hands on his shoulders and kissed his cheek, whispering in his ear, "Some things are live in the moment only. I totally get that now. Thank you for teaching me."

I nodded to Cedric, who was waiting patiently, and watching with hawk eyes. Geez, talk about lack of privacy.

"Why do you have a bodyguard?" I hid my elation at his questioning. I was sure he would let me leave him.

Oh, fuck…How do I tell him this?

"Nina," he warned.

I squared my shoulders, wishing it were Sunday. "Your cousin's wife tried to have me killed."

Aiden looked skyward as if answers would come pouring out of it. "You can't be serious."

"Oh, I am…very. And so is Cedric." I gave him a salute as he gave me an awkward wave, eyeing Aiden curiously. We'd become a team, Cedric and I, with one common goal. Keep Nina alive.

"So…" I jumped at his voice then turned to Aiden, who was staring at me intently. "Not only would I have to forgive you for him," he said, his eyes blazing again as he glared at me, "but I'd also be putting my life in danger."

I opened my mouth to speak but closed it. His words were truth; mine were useless.

After several long minutes, his frame shook with his chuckle as he closed the distance between us.

"Never a dull moment with you, Nina." Before I could speak, he pulled me into his warmth, surrounding me. I wrapped myself around him, holding him tightly to me as he raked his fingers through my hair and stroked by back.

After a long moment, he stuck his finger under my chin, lifting my eyes to his. "It seems your life really sucks without me."

I shrugged in mock defense. "Hey, I'll have you know Cedric is quite the gentlemen. He enjoys staring, waiting, and aerosol cheese."

Aiden laughed as he looked down at me still in his arms.

"Can you forgive me, Aiden?"

"No, but I can buy you a drink."

"I'll take it." We walked up to Cedric, and I introduced the two. Cedric followed as I rode in Aiden's Jeep with him to The Mystic. Cedric remained outside as we walked into the club. I cursed the giddy girl in me that was jumping for joy.

You don't need him, Nina.

He sat next to me at what I thought of as our booth at The Mystic as I told him about the last few weeks. I kept Devin's name out of my mouth as Aiden asked a question here or there but mostly let me talk. Aiden never touched me after our kiss on the beach. It was if my revelation had fully sunk in and he'd made his decision. I didn't blame him.

With each hour that passed, I became more certain he was just being the good guy that he was, talking to a friend who'd had a rough couple of weeks. I envied his ability to keep his distance as my eyes lingered on his lips while he spoke. He asked me to stay for his first set, and I agreed, knowing it would be pure torture to see him in his element and that I could no longer have him.

You don't need him, Nina.

His first song was Tom Petty's "You Got Lucky," and I knew he had intended it for me. It seemed his whole set was situated toward the two of us, or at least it seemed that way. He never sang directly to me, and I mourned that, thinking about the very open display we'd had the last time I was here. He was magnetic as he sang, drawing in a larger crowd, and my chest ached in longing for him. I watched his ticks as he sang: the tapping of his foot, the wetting of his lips, the ease in which he controlled the crowd. And I was smitten. By the time his set was near its end, he had a standing room full of screaming women, and I found myself eyeing the more aggressive predators with distaste. I was jealous. Of course I was jealous.

God, I fucked up.

When he started his own version of Bruno Mars's "Gorilla," the bar literally went up in flames as he tore the song apart with his vocals. I felt the low-lying, recently absent ache start to brew between my thighs and crossed my legs as I watched him, mesmerized. Seconds later, my chest heaving, I gripped the sides of my seat, lips parted as he finally looked up and right at me.

His eyes smoldered as he watched my reaction to him. He saw my arousal and gave me a wicked grin.

This was punishment.

You don't need him, Nina.

I took a long sip of my drink, gripping the cold glass tightly. Memories of Aiden buried deep inside of me pulsed in snapshots to the beat of the music, his voice demanding I remember how it felt to be thoroughly used by him.

Motherfuck me.

Aiden sang every note perfectly, seducing me to the point of frenzy. I slowly took my hand off the table and slipped it into my panties, pausing only to make sure he saw it. He raised a brow but gave nothing else away as he continued to sing, letting his eyes dart to the crowd and then slowly back to me. If anyone took a good look at me in the dimly lit bar, they would clearly see what I was doing.

Fuck it. I was, after all, naughty Nina.

No matter how hard I was trying to do better, this part of me remained dominant. If Aiden wanted to play, I was up for the challenge. I feathered my clit with my fingertips, completely drenched with need. My body responded with a small jerk and the heave of my chest. Aiden licked the lyrics with precision as I did the same with the flick of my finger. With a small nod of his head, I opened my legs further and began to massage myself slowly under the table. Feeling the thrum of the music pulsing through me, I quickened my pace and kept his attention, my vision tunneled on him. I tilted my head back slightly, lips parted as the pressure built below. I was close.

Aiden gripped his microphone, his eyes lit to a new level of heat, need covering his features. He gripped his t-shirt at his chest and twisted it, flashing a small amount of abs. His presence on stage was animalistic as he brought the song to such a static level that hunger filled the air. Every woman in the room was fixated on him, at his mercy, and I was no exception. With one more flick of my wrist, I came hard, our eyes locked.

He owned my orgasm. I gave it all to him willingly. Appreciative breath left me as I straightened myself, grabbed my purse, blew him a kiss, and made my way to the door. I looked back before exiting to see his eyes still fixed on me, his lips twisted into a sinister grin as the song came to a close, and the bar blew up in applause.

Maybe the fat lady hadn't sung on my time with Aiden just yet.

The truth was, I didn't *need* Aiden. I wanted him, and that wasn't going to change.

I'd left the door open for him in invitation, but I walked through it alone.

"Nobody can hurt me without my permission."

– MAHATMA GANDHI

§§

THE NEXT MORNING, I woke up determined that no matter the case with any man in my life, I'd find a little piece of me by repeating old habits. Habits I didn't have to question at all if they were good for me.

I was exhausted after two miles on the treadmill, a personal low in all the years I'd been working out. I refused to beat myself up about it. I was in recovery. Glancing at the clock, I dreaded waking Cedric. The overwhelming need to feel the sand beneath my feet and go for a quick swim in the Atlantic before work took precedence. I braved the trip without him, submerging myself in the warming water as the sun rose. I swam, stretching my unused muscles until I was sure I wasn't overexerting myself. Making my way back to shore, my smile faltered as I noticed Cedric standing near my towel.

"I had to do it." His stern look told me that if he could speak freely, his words would sting. "I'll wake you next time."

"That's all I ask. You know when you feel the safest is usually when they use it to their advantage and strike."

Wrapping the towel around my body and fastening it, I huffed. "Well, *you* are a buzz kill."

Another hard glance from Cedric had me cowering with a peace offering.

"Okay, okay. Let me make you breakfast?" He seemed surprised by my offer. "It's the least I can do. You have to be bored out of your mind by now."

He followed me inside with a huff of his own. "You don't want me busy, Ms. Scott."

"True."

Opening the fridge, I gathered ingredients for omelets and used the time in an attempt to drill him on Taylor. It was wrong, but my curiosity was piqued. She had refused to reveal more than she had the day we went gun shopping, and I couldn't force her friendship, though I knew if I were patient it would pay off.

I worked with her side by side every day, and as always, she was the meticulous professional, nowhere near the outlaw she was when she had picked me up from the hospital.

"How did you and Taylor meet?"

"Middle school," he said carefully, on to me already.

"Oh, childhood sweethearts?" Chopping chives, I tossed them into the pool of eggs as I braved a look at him.

"No."

Great, one word answers.

"So you went to high school together?"

"No."

Fuck.

Cedric hadn't been open about himself, either, only revealing that he had a sister in the Charleston area and a niece I could tell he adored. I served him his omelet, which he thanked me for, devouring it in a mere minute and letting me know he would be waiting for me when I was ready.

Unsuccessful in my attempt, I showered then checked my phone.

Aiden: I went surfing this morning without you.

A welcomed warmth spread throughout my chest as I texted him back.

Nina: Should I be hurt by that?

Aiden: Yes.

I laughed in my closet as I pulled out a white dress that dipped low in the front and clung to my midriff, ending high on my thighs. Wanting to feel sexy, I paired it with some red soled, heeled Mary Janes, topping the look off with my lengthy diamond chain and studded earrings. I pulled my hair up after curling it then brushed bronzer on my now naturally tanned skin.

As I climbed into the limo, I answered Aiden's text.

Nina: That was a hell of a show you put on last

night.

Aiden: Likewise.

Nina: I have no idea what you're talking about.

Aiden: Encore?

Nina: I have meetings all day. Meet you after?

Aiden: My place.

Nina: See you then.

As quickly as my elation came at the possibility of rekindling that spark with Aiden, the underlying threat of stoking the fire with him meant furthering myself from Devin to the point of no return. There was no going back anyway. Not after what had transpired. I wouldn't hurt Aiden again. Not that way. Not if he gave me the chance to be a part of his life again.

Swallowing the harsh burn of betraying Devin, I made my decision. Now it was just a matter of living with it.

§§

Aiden answered the door with a small smile, leaving it open for me to enter and follow him into his kitchen. A few scented candles were burning throughout his house as Portishead played in the background. The atmosphere was completely relaxing, and I basked in the comfortable feeling.

"It's stir fry, no carbs," he said, glancing up quickly. I felt the guilt spread over me. He was truly trying while I remained deceptive.

"Aiden, I…" I trailed off, unsure of how to apologize again as I watched him chop vegetables. He looked up at me, and I flinched as I saw him slice through the pad of his finger.

"Fuck," he muttered, grabbing a paper towel and wrapping his injured digit.

As I rounded the bar, I noticed a visible change in his

demeanor as he studied his bloodied finger, the evidence of his arousal growing in his pants as I approached. His eyes drifted down to his hard cock and back up without apology as I moved forward, taking his finger with a smirk.

"Little masochistic, isn't it?"

"Pleasure and pain, you know all about that." His eyes burned with his statement.

"Unfortunately for me, doctor, I'm addicted to it," I said in the worst German accent. "But for you, maybe it's good." We stood facing each other as I gripped his finger, squeezing to make it more painful. I was fascinated by the rigidness of his body and failed to stifle a giggle. His amber eyes seared my mouth shut as he pulled his finger away.

"You'll pay for that."

"I hope so," I flirted, wrapping his finger tightly with the towel.

"You really are a beautiful woman, Nina." He was watching me as I searched his cabinets for a bandage, coming up empty. I turned to him in question as he continued. "And really fucking dangerous for me."

Suddenly, all the humor was sucked out of the room as Aiden turned back to his cooking. Scrambling to gain some balance back, I offered a hand, which he refused. Minutes later, I could still feel the heaviness as we dined in silence. I glanced at him as he studied his plate, refusing to look at me.

"I've hurt you and ruined this," I said, waving the white flag. "I mean, I know you're trying, but I ruined this, haven't I?" I pushed my plate away, suddenly sick. "I should go." I looked up to see Aiden gripping his towel that rested on his shoulder. He moved it to wipe his mouth then grabbed my hand.

"I just don't see a way around it," he bit out, as if we were having a conversation I was just joining. "Around making you pay." His eyes flared as I swallowed slowly. Playful Aiden was gone, and I found myself afraid of him for the first time. I knew he wouldn't hurt me, but somehow I knew our dynamic had changed, and I didn't know if we would ever get it back.

"Aiden, I want so much for us to be okay again. I do."

"I don't think I can be the nice guy you want me to be right now. I'm pretty fucking mad."

"I'll just go." I reached over and kissed him on the cheek. He slammed his fist down on the table, making me jump, the sudden noise ruining me and putting my already torn nerves on high alert. I braved one last look, and he struck out, gripping me tightly and pulling me into his lap.

"I didn't know. I swear I didn't know he was your cousin. I knew you weren't brothers and that was enough for me."

"And when you let him fuck you?!" I flinched. He pushed me down to the bottom of his thighs as he freed his throbbing cock from his sweatpants. I licked my lips, feeling the instant longing then looked up at him.

"Where should I put my cock tonight, naughty Nina? In your lying fucking mouth, or you treacherous pussy?" I wanted to shy away from his anger, but instead, I was turned…the…fuck…on. I slapped him anyway, feigning offense, and saw the small smile form on his lips before disappearing. He gripped me roughly as he pulled me off of his lap, pushing me toward his kitchen island.

My mind scrambled as his glowing eyes burned into me. "I'm supposed to forgive you for letting him have this," he hissed as he cupped my sex over my thin, white shorts. I ground my hips, wanting to feel the delicious friction. I gripped him back, sliding my hands up and down the smooth, soft skin that covered his hard, thick muscle.

"Put it anywhere you want, Aiden," I invited, my chest heaving fast. He saw my fear and called my bluff.

"Big mistake," he snapped, ripping my shorts free, and not bothering to hold back his contempt for the rest of my clothes as he shredded through them. I was face down on the counter, bracing myself for the worst. I felt the burn in my scalp as he held me there, his hand fisted in my hair. I felt the violence threatening to escape him in his fucking. It was tangible in the air as I waited, pussy dripping in anticipation.

"You're a ready whore," he hissed as I jerked my head up, but he forced it down. "I cooked the dinner. Dined like a lady and fucked like a whore, remember?"

"Then shut up and do it," I hissed back, suddenly unafraid and ready to fight, angry at his power over me. Sensing my fury, he let me up. I whirled on him, clawing his now bared chest.

"I was Devin's whore, now you proclaim I'm yours? Fuck *you*." His eyebrows shot up as he stopped my assault. Pressing his forehead to mine, he wrapped his arms around me as we stood naked in his kitchen. I tried to wriggle free as he held me tightly to him.

"I'm sorry. I didn't mean that. I didn't mean to hold it against you. I'm sorry. We all have our weakness, and right now mine is you."

I stopped fighting as I looked up at him. He seemed sincere. I surprised myself with my next words.

"Punish me." His eyes widened. "Please, Aiden." He took a step back and grabbed my hand, leading me upstairs. When we reached the top, I held his hand tightly as he led me to his bedroom. I felt the familiar stir of memories of all the times he'd had me and looked at him with longing.

"Can we really do this?" I had unintentionally spoken my thought aloud, and he paused as if to let me know I had to answer the question for myself. I began to breathe heavily as I looked at the beautiful man still trying to handle my indecision. I was hesitating because of Devin, and somehow I was sure he knew it.

Fuck. Fuck. Fuck.

Making a quick decision, I sank to my knees, gripping his hard cock and licking my lips. He jerked my chin up to meet his eyes as I readied my mouth.

"You look at me with every fucking twirl of your tongue and move of your lips. The minute you look away, I *will* punish you."

I nodded, taking him into my mouth, our eyes locked. He stood perfectly still as I sucked him mercilessly, scraping the top of my nails over his thighs and then purposefully digging them into his skin to draw blood. He bit his lip in approval as he glared down at me, my mouth working frantically to soothe the hurt I'd caused him. I felt his length harden further as a burst of pre-cum invaded my mouth, and it spurred me on.

I let my eyes water, taking him deep, but never closing them so he could see my apology. He pulled himself out of my mouth as I dove back in, trying to recapture him. Standing me up, he gripped my throat then pushed me onto his nightstand, my back knocking off the lamp.

He invaded me without pause, thrusting into me furiously as I screamed out his name. He stopped briefly to throw the lamp on the bed, using the cord to bind my wrists over my head, securing them around the post. I heard the thump of the lamp behind me as it hit the headboard with each solid push of his hips. The sharp end of the stand bit into the top of my back as he filled me over and over. He lifted my legs and hooked them over his shoulders as he fisted my breasts painfully. I lifted my hips to match his movement, unbelieving of the build behind it.

Feeling the orgasm start around his cock, I shuddered with pleasure just as he robbed me of it by pulling out. "No!" I cried as I lost the sensation. He gripped himself, bringing it back to my mouth, I opened wide as he shot into me, unforgiving. His eyes told me not to protest as I licked the last of him and took it inside. He unplugged the lamp, untied my wrists then pulled me to his chest. I couldn't hide my disappointment as he laughed at me openly.

"Wow, you are such a sore loser," he said, grinning down at me.

"You might want to let that loss sit a little better. I have the rest of my punishment to dish out."

I looked up at him with wide eyes. "You can't be serious."

"Oh, you thought punishment meant pleasure. Well, that's

the point, isn't it, naughty girl? You see, I'm in charge of your pleasure. It's time you learned that. Get on the floor, all fours."

§§

Hours later, I was out of my mind as Aiden tortured me with his cock, his lips, and fingers. I was aroused beyond repair, and still, he hadn't freed me, knowing exactly when I was on the verge and taking it away as soon as I was close. He'd slapped my hands hard every time I tried to touch myself.

"You haven't earned it!"

Frustration rolled off me with every knowing smirk he gave. I would *never* ask Aiden to punish me again.

We lay in his bed a tangled mess as he chuckled at me pouting into his chest. My face was on fire with heat and need, and I couldn't stop moving. I tried my best to get away from him, but he knew exactly what I would do.

I was a broken mess, turned on to the point of tears as he held me tightly to him. I looked up in anger as he continued his endless release of humor at my expense. When I caught his eyes, he was back. My Aiden was back, and suddenly it didn't matter what state I was in.

"Hi," I said, holding him tighter to me, kissing the underside of his tattoo, slowing my kiss at his nipple, biting it softly with my teeth.

"Hi," he said, catching on.

I felt his forgiveness as he looked down at me. We spent the rest of the night talking as he kept me from leaving the bed until I fell asleep.

§§

I woke with my legs parted and Aiden's tongue bathing me. I smiled down at him as his fiery eyes turned my greeting into begging.

"Jesus, Aiden, please let me come." I gripped his blond hair in an attempt to keep his mouth where it was as he chuckled, slightly sucking on my folds before pulling away.

"We'll see." I let out a loud, frustrated groan as he licked and sipped on my swollen pussy until I was at that point and pulled away.

"Fuck, fuck, no, Aiden, please. I'm begging you!"

"And you will continue to until I see fit." I slapped at his chest, my frustration getting the best of me as I wriggled beneath his huge muscled frame, the sight of him hard and ready only angering me further. He pinned me beneath him, sucking my nipples as he taunted me with his cock playing between my legs.

"Stop, please. I can't take it anymore." Closing my eyes tightly, I tried to avoid what his coaxing touch was doing to me.

"Open your eyes, Nina." I kept them closed as he licked down my stomach.

"Now," he ordered in a sharp tone.

I opened them reluctantly, only to be met with the sexiest version of him imaginable. I studied him, taking in his features and his taut, muscled arms braced over me, the small amount of stubble growing on his chin.

I had done so much begging I had no choice but to stop. I was defeated.

I was punished.

Aiden stopped his assault as if he sensed the small break in me. He took my hand, pulling me to him and leading me to the bathroom. We showered together then went downstairs. I stayed silent over breakfast, my emotions still getting the best of me as I watched him eat.

"Eat your breakfast, Nina," he chided before taking a sip of his coffee.

"I told you I wasn't hungry." Wow. Even I recognized the childish tantrum I was throwing. I waited a patient and respectable amount of time before excusing myself.

"I have to get to work."

I couldn't even pretend to be civil at that point. I was burning, every muscle in my body screaming for release.

"Not so fast." He stood, turning me away from him, wrapping his arms around me.

"Today, I want you thinking of me filling you with this." He pressed himself into my backside, and I realized how close I still was. So fucking close.

"And when you finish your day," he whispered into my ear, licking the shell and then pulling at my lobe, "choose the place and I'll meet you there and give you the best orgasm of your life."

He turned me to him, pulling slowly at my lips until I relented, letting him taste me fully. He pulled back, closing our kiss, his eyes intent on mine.

"No touching. Don't do it and I promise you it will feel like your first one."

"Okay," I agreed as he smiled warmly at me.

"I'm trying, Nina."

"I know." I wrapped my arms around his neck. "I think we should get away, you know. Just go somewhere. No past, no future, just the present."

"I couldn't agree more." I felt my heart flutter with excitement as I took his slightly larger lower lip into my mouth, sucking greedily.

"Where are you thinking?" he asked, taking his lip back and tucking it in his mouth.

"Hmm, how about I let you decide."

"I'll think about it today." He swatted my ass, dismissing me.

Walking outside, I sighed happily with a greeting. "Good morning, Cedric."

He looked at me sideways as I greeted him. If he was expecting some sort of walk of shame, he would be sourly disappointed. I buried the guilt associated with Devin as we drove back to my house so I could shower and change.

When I reached the office, I kept busy throughout the course of the day, my needy sex pulsing constantly as a reminder of what was to come. I'd never been so excited. I thought about the ways he'd taken me last night, as an assured lover whose skills were phenomenal, especially in the area of knowing my body well enough to keep me in this state. By midday, I was tapping my foot underneath my desk, trying horribly to cure the unrelenting ache. As if sensing my discomfort, Aiden texted me.

Aiden: Don't fucking touch it.

Nina: I really hate you right now.

I hit my phone. "Taylor, when is our last meeting?" Breathless, I needed this to end. I had no patience left.

"Our last meeting is downtown at four. I arranged it there because of the construction." Our floor was currently undergoing serious renovations due to Taylor's new position and our plans to expand.

"Give me that address."

I texted Aiden with orders to be there at four-thirty.

It dawned on me suddenly that in my hours with Aiden I hadn't once feared for my life, or worried about the state of it. I'd simply been living it. It reminded me of a happier time. A time when…

I was so done going there.

"Oh, what a tangled web we weave...when first we practice to deceive."

– WALTER SCOTT

§§

DEVIN

I LOOKED UP FROM my phone to see Eileen hovering over me on the porch. Hanging up, I looked at her with bored and impatient eyes. For three weeks, I'd been in this hell. Three fucking weeks all I'd known about Nina was that she was a prisoner in her own home, alone, and without Aiden. That much was comforting.

"We need to make an appearance at the Admiral's Club for the Marions' birthday party."

"No, *we* don't."

"Devin, for Christ's sake, I haven't been out of this house in three weeks!"

My head was splitting with the shriek of her voice. I needed the space as well. We were close to finding out exactly who she'd hired, and as soon as that was solved, I would have my freedom.

Glancing at my watch, I addressed her. "Ready to confess?"

"Don't be ridiculous," she scoffed as I followed her from the patio to the kitchen, pointing to the island barstool.

"Sit." She hesitated before taking the seat.

"I want it on tape, Eileen. A video of you confessing to hiring a hit on Nina."

"Devin, I told you I called it off." Her posture was that of a spoiled teenager, and I couldn't help but reason this woman was not well. She clearly had more going on than I'd ever cared to understand. I almost felt bad for what I was about to do.

"This is a divorce decree." I laid the paperwork in front of her. "This is the title for the plantation. I've signed it over to you. You can have all of our assets except for my boat. It's all there. I'll call Byron over, and we can finally finish this."

She looked at me as if I was an idiot. "You want this in exchange for my confession that I tried to kill your whore? Devin, it won't happen." She crossed her arms confidently across her chest after pushing the paperwork back in my direction.

"Yes it will," her mother snapped behind her. "Stupid, stupid girl, did I teach you nothing?"

Eileen froze in her chair, sweat instantly beading on her forehead. Her mother had always been her kryptonite. I cursed my stupidity in my earlier attempts to sway her on my own. My greatest ally was the woman who had ruined her. It took very little to convince her mother about Eileen's latest evil deed, which is why she decided to intervene, for the sake of reputation. I'd only lightly threatened to take the ordeal public in an attempt to persuade her. In exchange for my freedom, I would take away my wife's. Eileen would be spending the next ninety days under observation at the Charleston Mental Institute. When bargaining with her mother, I agreed to complete discretion as she "sought the help her daughter so desperately needed." Eileen looked at me with tears in her eyes.

"Take the plantation, marry Thomas, and let me go." She looked at her mother, wide-eyed and full of excuses.

"He's speaking nonsense, Mother. His claims are ridiculous."

"Give him what he wants, Eileen. Clearly, you have failed him." I felt the snap in Eileen then; it was tangible. It was also a beacon of hope for me. She picked up the pen and put it down, swiping her hand in the air.

"No, I'm not doing this again. Not without—"

"Byron," I called as he entered the kitchen. With her mother and lawyer present, I was free. I had no doubts but stayed as my wife unraveled, apologizing to her mother, and refusing to look at me.

I grabbed my keys as I heard Byron's briefcase click shut. A celebratory drink at the club may just be what I needed.

Game over.

A text came through, making my blood boil.

She was at his home last night.

And I was so close to gloating.

I sent a text of my own.

Devin: YOU CANNOT HAVE HER.

"Deceiving others. That is what the world calls a romance."

– OSCAR WILDE

§§

NINA

I FINISHED MY MEETING with ten minutes to spare. Preparing the conference room, I frosted the privacy glass, turned on the radio, and ordered chilled champagne. For some reason, I was nervous as I waited on Aiden. I opted to do the deed where my meeting was held, a comfortable lounge with plenty of seating. I'd suffered through twenty-five minutes of ass kissing only to hand over money I would have willingly given without prompting. Aiden was all I saw, his attempt to keep my attention solely on him had paid off, and I was just about to show him how much. I wondered where he decided we would escape to.

Getting away with Aiden was becoming more appealing by the second as they ticked by. Adjusting my skirt, I smirked knowing I was pantyless underneath. There really was no point with Aiden.

Lying back on the oversized, leather couch, I closed my eyes briefly. Moments later, I felt his fingers trail up my leg, keeping my eyes closed, my slow smile revealing to him I was awake.

"Hey, beautiful, keep them closed." His voice moved over me like a warm blanket, and my body instantly responded. I did as he asked, his touch sending a welcomed shiver down my spine in anticipation. "Have you thought about me today?"

"Yes," I replied, my voice heated.

"And," he said, prompting for more.

"And what?" I breathed out as his hand pulled away. I could feel his presence sitting on the table next to me then heard the pop of the champagne.

"And how did I fuck you?" Two glasses were poured as he waited for my reply.

"The first time, from behind and hard, the second time, laid out in your bed. And it lasted much, much longer. The third time…"

"Tell. Me."

"Aiden, *please* touch me." I was already writhing.

"Tell me, naughty Nina." His hand resumed its strumming on my legs, and I opened them in invitation, which he took. He paused when he realized I was already bare then slid his fingers through my drenched folds, feathering my clit then thrusting them inside. My body arched up at the intrusion, but he pushed me down then caressed my pebbled chest through my dress.

"So naughty," he breathed into my ear. "This has been waiting for me all day." I could hear the evidence of my arousal as he fingered me viciously. "And the last time I fucked your pussy, Nina, how did I do it?" Rough fingers explored me, my eyes still closed as I reveled in the feeling, still on the verge of explosion. "Tell me."

"Lower."

"And you will have it all. Keep them closed." He pulled me to standing then led me across the room, placing my hands out in front of me until they touched the glass wall that surrounded us. Slowly lifting my skirt up, he kept it bunched around my waist, smoothing my thighs with his hands before pulling me back and stretching me before him.

"Keep them closed, or you won't get my cock, Nina."

I nodded. Panting, I spread my legs further for him without him asking. I heard the zip of his jeans and my adrenaline spiked, kicking my need into overdrive.

Please, please, please, please.

"You sure you want this?"

"Aiden," I warned.

Just as soon as my warning was heard, I felt the burn in my scalp as he wrapped his fist in my hair and buried himself to the hilt in one long thrust.

"Oh, God."

"Keep them closed," Aiden rasped on a promise of more. I pounded my hands against the barrier as he fucked me hard and fast, the build growing intense and unbearable.

His thrusts were frantic, hungry, and animalistic, and I welcomed each one with my moans. His hand came down hard on my ass as he pulled my hair, keeping us tightly together with brute force. Another whack at my skin and I was bucking back onto his cock, my body trembling with the need for release.

Thwack. Thwack. Thwack. Thwack.

Each slap of his hand became harder than the last, and it sent me reeling. As I screamed his name, I felt the rush of orgasm. Aiden gripped my hair even tighter, making my eyes tear up as he pressed my face into the glass.

"Open them."

Blinding ecstasy ripped through me as I shuddered and pulsed, completely unaware of my surroundings. I screamed in pleasure as wave after wave hit me, praising his efforts, and losing myself completely in my body's release. It continued on and on as Aiden reached around, massaging my clit in quick strokes, spurring it further, making it last.

Slowly Aiden massaged my singed skin as I focused my attention on the sight before me. Realizing Devin's eyes were on mine, I cried out in surprise then jerked back in revulsion before looking up to Aiden, whose eyes were trained on Devin. Devin was sitting alone in the lounge adjacent to the conference room, a drink in hand, and completely focused on me. Unshed tears lay heavy as Devin watched me scramble to cover myself, pulling my skirt down.

"Oh my God," I breathed, watching Devin's expression go from surprise to devastation.

I looked to Aiden for answers and saw the glass remote in his hand. "Aiden…why?"

He looked down at me with a smirk. "Shall we go face the music?"

Incredulousness turned to rage as I watched him physically gloat, his eyes remaining trained on Devin. "How could you fucking do that to him?"

Aiden's eyes drifted to me in mild surprise. "You chose this place. And, baby, I thought I told you I'd claim you anywhere." He pulled me to him as I punched at his chest furiously.

"How could you do THAT!"

He gave me an odd look. "It was pretty fucking perfect, don't you think? Weren't you the victim when he was fucking his wife on his desk? Isn't that what you told me?" Looking between them, it dawned on me.

"This isn't about justice for me, though, is it?" Aiden looked down at me with contempt.

"It wasn't about him. It had nothing to do with him until you brought him into it!" he countered.

"I didn't invite him here!" I whirled on Aiden. "You thought I wanted this? That I am *capable* of this!"

"You didn't plan on having him out there when I fucked you?" He seemed genuinely unbelieving as I studied him.

"Jesus, Aiden, and you would go along with it? This is who *you* are?"

I looked back to Devin, who was now standing, drink in hand, an odd expression passing over him. Grabbing my purse, I walked out to him, unable to deal anymore with the look on his face. "I didn't know, Devin. I swear to God I didn't know you were sitting there." I couldn't look at him as I pleaded my worthless case. I heard glass shatter, looked in that direction, and saw the splintered remnants of Devin's glass had fallen short of Aiden's step out of the conference room.

What was I thinking having Aiden meet me at the fucking Admiral's Club where Devin and I met? I was sure Devin would think this was purposeful.

Everything went in slow motion from that moment on as Devin rushed Aiden in a bloodthirsty rage. It dawned on me then that the look I saw on Devin's face was resolve; he intended to kill him. I heard the sick crunch of bones as I braced myself for war. Devin landed blow after blow as Aiden took the first few in an attempt to taunt him.

"Come on, *cousin,* you can do better than that," Aiden urged as he took another solid blow to the face.

I screamed as they crashed through the glass table in front of me, Devin getting the better of him before Aiden—who had him in both weight and size—landed a hard blow to his midsection, knocking him off balance. Devin recovered in mere seconds, unfazed as I rushed to him before he went back in.

"Please, Devin, stop. Please. Stop. I'm so sorry, stop!" I was pushed out of the way as he roared, moving toward Aiden, his intent clear. I screamed for help as a bloody and now defeated Aiden took blow after blow, his face reddening with each one. Several people came running in from what looked like a private party to aid in breaking them up. Devin was uncontrollable, as it took five men to finally pull him off. I stood, mouth gaping, at the animal Devin had turned into, his eyes fixed on Aiden. Cedric came in moments later, sheer panic written on his features.

"YOU'RE LATE!" I screamed at him as he gave me a sharp nod in guilt before pulling me away. I looked to a bloody and battered Aiden who seemed pleased with himself for getting the best of Devin's temper, while Devin looked to me completely broken. I let out a sob as Cedric pulled me out of the door.

§§

"Where were you?" I was berating Cedric as I tried to wrap my mind around what had just happened.

"Downstairs with Taylor. I was only there for five minutes. You were safe inside the room with Mr. McIntyre."

"Not really," I said, the adrenaline crash making me dizzy as Carson drove us home. "I'll never be safe with a McIntyre, and that's the sad truth of it."

Aiden thought me capable of being a monster, and now Devin saw me as one, as I had him. I ignored my emotion from the look on Devin's face as I purposefully numbed myself.

No more. It was all over, and I did not intend to entertain any of it further.

Aiden *wasn't* perfect and his only flaw that I knew of lay within his contempt for a man I still loved. It made him the bad guy, and I'd had enough of the bad guy. I took a trusty Xanax from my purse and saluted Cedric with the bottle while throwing my phone out the window and into the Atlantic as we crossed the bridge.

"You are going to be so bored." I toasted him as he took the bottle away, allowing me my one pill.

There was absolutely nothing to think about or mull over. I was completely done with both men. I had never been more certain.

As I slipped into a medicated sleep an hour later, I was thankful for the pull into darkness.

"In the depth of winter, I finally learned that within me there lay an invincible summer."

– ALBERT CAMUS

§§

ONE MONTH LATER

SIX MILES WAS a personal best for me, and I had hit it every morning for the last week. I was in the best shape of my life just by pushing a little harder. Cedric high fived me as we slowed ourselves to a stop. He was in amazingly great shape. He'd started joining me in the ocean and in the gym. We'd actually gotten to know each other pretty well in the last month. Though he refused to give up aerosol cheese, I had talked him into making better food choices. My health was a priority and hobby, and I felt amazing.

It had taken absolutely no time for me to accept that every day was Monday. All my emails were filtered by Taylor, and I made sure I had absolutely no knowledge of whether or not either man had tried to contact me. I changed my phone number, and no one was allowed past my newly installed gate. This isolation had been by choice. I alone created the poison, and I alone created the remedy.

And of the latter, I was proud. It had been completely quiet as far as the threat on my life. Cedric had mentioned they were close to catching the driver of the car, and I knew it was just a matter of time. I still had some trust left, and my greatest allies were Taylor and Cedric.

Taylor had been absent lately, commuting back and forth from Savannah. My guess was a man, and after a thousand attempts to pry it out of her, Cedric told me as much.

Finally, Taylor has a man. Was that so damn hard?

I still hadn't decided what to do with the land, though I knew by ridding myself of it I was all the wiser. I could no longer afford to care about the mystery behind it. When I wasn't busy enough and was forced to think, I spent my time wondering what had caused so much hate between family.

And I thought mine was fucked up.

Realizing there were answers I would never get and would never seek, I'd decided I was better off not knowing. I had convinced myself of that. Somewhere deep inside and only late at night when sleep evaded me, a part of me that I wouldn't let surface cried without tears. I'd cut her off completely from my daytime persona, and only when I lay in bed, weak with worsening thoughts, did I let her come out to remind me of Devin's face twisted in agony at the sight of me, or Aiden's promise to give me all that I needed before turning our relationship into a cruel joke on Devin.

Little by little, the woman who wished for a different outcome discarded her feelings subtly, like Andy discarded the rocks from his wall in that movie *Shawshank Redemption*. Little by little, I was moving a big mountain a few rocks at a time.

I went to bed after the first month, feeling accomplished. Being alone for the first time wasn't so damned scary, and it wasn't intimidating. It was just life. My life.

I looked to Cedric, who was still heavily winded, and smiled proudly as I walked out of the gym.

All I had to do was clear the air of my obvious distractions to see clearly. I was an ambitious, determined, wealthy woman with a strong, insatiable, sexual appetite who needed to take control of her life.

And so I did.

And you know what I found out? It was way harder to be weak.

§§

Deciding never to set foot in at the Admiral's Club again, for obvious reasons, I sipped a Tom Collins on the rooftop deck overlooking the sunset when my phone buzzed.

"Nina."

"Hey, Taylor. I just got done with the meeting with Jones. He's a weirdo. Like seriously, his inventions might be amazing, but I won't see him again without Cedric." Cedric, now an integral part of my world, had left me alone last night, confirming that they had found the man who attempted to take my life. I was celebrating my first night of real freedom and was excited to finally be back in control. "Come see me. I'm at the rooftop deck of the—"

"Nina, shut up and listen."

"Okay," I said carefully. "What's your problem?"

"In Savannah, I've been frequenting a club called The Rabbit Hole."

I sighed. "You know, Taylor, you finally want to talk about your shit, and I'm finally over asking."

"Please shut up."

"Okay," I said, sensing the seriousness in her voice.

"It's a sex club. Do you know what I'm saying?"

Shocked at her admission, but willing to share, I admitted, "Yes, Taylor. I've had a Dom." Well, actually *two.*

"I know because he's here."

"Who?"

"Devin," she answered in a hushed voice.

I watched the sun drift beneath the horizon as the Ravenel Bridge lit up. The birds danced through the air in sendoff, as if to tell the sun goodnight. So many things had changed, and yet my love for this city remained the same. I stood still, admiring the harbor as I buried my emotion, playing immune to Taylor's confession.

"Taylor, nothing surprises me anymore. Seriously, we really need to clear the air between us, you and I. And why should I care?" I continued in vain, already speed walking toward my car.

"I just thought it strange him being here."

"Well, he *is* a newly divorced man and needs a new sub."

The news of Devin and Eileen's divorce was unavoidable. It had been in every local paper, and our scene at the club only added to the already wagging tongues. I had managed to keep the media out along with everyone else in my life, including my mother turned stalker who had been the only one who'd almost successfully broken into my solid barrier.

Devin had actually done it. His divorce was finalized, and his ex-wife was MIA, rumored to be vacationing overseas to avoid the embarrassment.

Godspeed, crazy bitch.

I got into my Mercedes and turned on the ignition as I spoke. "Let's say for curiosity's sake—"

"I'll text you the address."

"Taylor?" She'd already hung up.

I broke every speed limit between Charleston and Savannah as I rode down U.S. 17.

Whatever Devin had been hiding, I was positive it had to do with that damned club. I cursed my stupidity for the laws I was breaking to spy on a man I swore I was done with. I had to justify to myself over and over that I was attempting to get answers I rightfully deserved. I had suffered a lot for little satisfaction and remained even less knowledgeable than when we'd started our affair.

If he was able to move on with another woman so quickly after he'd claimed he loved me, something inside of me had to see if for myself.

I thought of every conversation we'd had, and searched our dialogue for every clue, but not one led me anywhere. Devin had grown up in Savannah, that much I knew. He'd mentioned a few places he'd wanted to take me, none of them being a sex club. As much as I'd been reluctant to admit it, and as subtle as it had been, I was Devin's sub. His *willing* sub, as I had been Aiden's. This both fascinated and infuriated me. Why wouldn't he just admit to being this way? I'd granted his every wish, and denied Devin *nothing* sexually.

Taylor's apparently a member of the club, too. Hence the reason why she's been so damn secretive. I should have guessed it. Was the entire world hiding behind a daytime mask? I knew I was. It simply made everything easier. My night demons were still haunting me, and as much as I tried to move on, memories played on a continuous loop. I needed answers.

"And thus I clothe my naked villainy
With odd old ends stol'n out of holy writ;
And seem a saint, when most I play the devil."

– WILLIAM SHAKESPEARE

§§

ARRIVING AT THE club an hour and twenty minutes later, I cautiously pulled into The Rabbit Hole, noticing the parking lot was full. Staring at the oddly carved doors, I realized they reminded me of the movie *Alice in Wonderland.*

Fitting name.

I wondered briefly what the inside of places like this were like before the reminder of why I was here in the first place burst through the double doors. Devin was hightailing it out of the club and running to his car like his life depended on it. I slumped in my seat, knowing he hadn't seen me, and relieved he was alone.

Nope, nope, nope, nope, Nina. NO!

I waited for him to start his car, knowing if I didn't catch him as soon as he pulled out I would never catch him. He was in a hurry. I turned on my lights and pulled up behind him just as he was turning out of the parking lot. He sped out as I followed him as closely as I could without seeming too obvious. When I started to recognize the route, I slowed behind him considerably, giving him more space. And with his final turn, I stopped altogether. He was on Peach Tree Rd.

The land. My land.

I'd only been out here one other time, just after I'd obtained it, but I had come alone, spending my time sitting next to the water, soaking in the beauty, and hoping I could make some use of it, though no idea ever stuck. Now I felt the dread in the pit of my stomach as I killed my lights a quarter mile away in the dark night, praying my silent Mercedes remained that way. Rolling down my windows as I approached, I noted Devin's car parked next to the small shed. It was lit from within, and I felt my stomach roll.

That's when I heard the first scream. I jumped in my seat, suddenly paralyzed as I hit the brakes. Waiting and listening for another, I prayed to God it was a figment of my imagination.

It wasn't.

Another scream, followed by another, ripped through the dark night and the serenading of the crickets. Even they seemed to quiet after the next piercing howl. I picked up my phone to dial for help and realized I had no signal.

I had to help her.

You can do this, Nina.

My heel sank into the pluff mud, and I left it there, swiftly relieving my foot of the other. Turning my head toward my idling car, I reassured myself that it was still there, the door left open in case I needed to escape in a hurry. Hearing another bloodcurdling scream, I walked toward the dim light. Fear shot through me in waves as Shel Silverstein's words fumbled around in my head, "Clooney the Clown" a horrific internal monologue resounding through my frightened mind. My senses heightened with each step I took toward the cracked door. There was soft music playing in the background. I knew the song but couldn't make out the words. It was upbeat and a little jazzy, and totally unfitting.

I could hear the crunch of crisp grass under my feet, and then another scream echoed in the night. Reaching into my purse, I fumbled inside and let out a way too audible breath of relief when I felt the cold steel.

Another scream, louder, more desperate. Pain…this was pain.

"Enough!" It was a loud boom of a familiar male voice.

I recited the poem over and over in my head, the way I used to when I heard my parents fighting, and yet I knew that what I was about to see was far worse than what I used to hear. I took another step forward, and a motion light came on, alerting my presence to those inside. Sweat from the humidity, along with adrenaline from fear, had me dripping, my now soaked blouse clinging to my torso.

Terror raced through my every pore as I gripped my gun and took aim in front of me.

A dark figure appeared out of the door, but I instantly knew who it was. He came toward me in a black blur, yelling my name as I squeezed the trigger with a scream of my own.

§§

Devin went down, gripping his shoulder with a string of curses as I pointed the gun at him.

"What did you do, Devin?!" My voice was unrecognizable even to me; it was laced with fear and confusion.

"Nina, fuck, don't shoot me again." He tried to stand, but slumped down again next to the shed door with a wince, still gripping his shoulder.

"What the fuck did you do, Devin!" I roared as I moved closer, refusing to believe that my weapon would keep me safe. I was shaking, and my gun looked like it was on vibrate. I pointed right at him as I approached the door with no choice but to either shoot him or go around him to get to whomever he'd hurt.

"Is she dead?"

"Nina, listen to me. Really listen, okay? Don't open that fucking door." Devin stood slowly on shaky legs, holding his shoulder as I pointed the gun at his head.

"Step back!"

He took a step back, his eyes pleading as he begged. "Baby, please listen to me. Don't open that door!" The gentleness in his voice betrayed me, jogging my memory as tears fell at random, ignoring my need to be strong and in control.

"What did you do to her?" It was a hoarse whisper.

"Nina, I'm begging you. Don't go in there." He took a step forward, and my hand stiffened at my head's command.

"Step back, Devin!"

He took another step and stayed silent, accepting that I wouldn't leave until I was satisfied.

I opened the door.

A dark figure appeared out of the door, but I instantly knew who it was. He came toward me in a black blur, yelling my name as I squeezed the trigger with a scream of my own.

§§

Devin went down, gripping his shoulder with a string of curses as I pointed the gun at him.

"What did you do, Devin?!" My voice was unrecognizable even to me; it was laced with fear and confusion.

"Nina, fuck, don't shoot me again." He tried to stand, but slumped down again next to the shed door with a wince, still gripping his shoulder.

"What the fuck did you do, Devin!" I roared as I moved closer, refusing to believe that my weapon would keep me safe. I was shaking, and my gun looked like it was on vibrate. I pointed right at him as I approached the door with no choice but to either shoot him or go around him to get to whomever he'd hurt.

"Is she dead?"

"Nina, listen to me. Really listen, okay? Don't open that fucking door." Devin stood slowly on shaky legs, holding his shoulder as I pointed the gun at his head.

"Step back!"

He took a step back, his eyes pleading as he begged. "Baby, please listen to me. Don't open that door!" The gentleness in his voice betrayed me, jogging my memory as tears fell at random, ignoring my need to be strong and in control.

"What did you do to her?" It was a hoarse whisper.

"Nina, I'm begging you. Don't go in there." He took a step forward, and my hand stiffened at my head's command.

"Step back, Devin!"

He took another step and stayed silent, accepting that I wouldn't leave until I was satisfied.

I opened the door.

§§

I CAME TO WITH a tap on my window. It was Cedric. Shooting up in the seat, I looked around me, recognizing where I was. I was safe, and Aiden was insane.

Aiden. Oh, GOD, AIDEN!

Rolling down my window, Cedric eyed my gun in the passenger seat.

"You didn't check in. I was worried."

"Well, I had a reason." With the flick of his chin, he asked permission to join me in the car. I nodded, feeling my heart crack with thoughts of Devin. Was he okay? Did they hurt each other? Should I care?

"Pick up your gun?" He gestured at the shiny metal, and I placed it in my lap. "Okay, Nina, tell me what happened."

How long had I been out?

I knew he wanted me to tell him what had happened, but my mouth couldn't form the words. Instead, I dialed 911. Yes, I cared, and if Devin was left to bleed to death and I could have prevented it…I couldn't live with that. After I called the police and gave them the address of the injured man I shot—conveniently leaving that part out—I hung up.

"And you shot him?"

"Yes, out of fear. He was standing when I left." I took several calming breaths before I questioned him. "How did you find me?"

"Tracking device on your cell and cars. We discussed that, remember?" I nodded, very much in the same state of mind as he was when he'd told me about it months ago. He sent a text as I looked around us, suddenly terrified I'd never feel safe again.

"Oh my God," I cried into my hands. I couldn't stop shaking. I reached in my purse for my emergency Xanax, but Cedric stilled my hands.

"Okay, Nina, before you medicate, let's switch seats, and I'll drive you home, okay?"

I looked down at my hands, sure I would see blood on them, but there was nothing. I pulled at the rearview to look at my face and realized I had makeup on. Makeup, how trivial was makeup? Why the hell did we try so hard to hide our flaws? What was the point? Anyone who truly knew you would see them; no amount of paint could truly cover up the ugly in someone.

Suddenly the dim light from the parking lot showcased every flaw I had. I began wiping at my face furiously to erase them.

"Nina," Cedric said calmly. "I need you to listen to me. I want you to get into the passenger side, okay? I'll give you a few more minutes to collect yourself, and then you will need to tell me what happened." I nodded, still not really hearing him, but moved to get into the passenger seat, keeping my gun close.

I buckled my seatbelt, but Cedric stayed where he was as he waited for me to talk. It was a little over ten minutes before I was calm enough to relay the story.

"He was…mutilating her. With her consent!" I closed my eyes, trying to erase the image of the bloodied girl from my mind.

"He's in the one percent."

"Pardon?"

"I'm sure you have heard of BDSM."

"Oh, God, not the Dom shit again!" Despite my comment, I perked my ears up because I knew whatever he had to say might actually be on point.

"The community has a small amount that practices extreme BDSM. It's not news to me, and honestly, if I stumbled upon it, I would have to take action. It's some sick shit, consensual or not, and highly illegal. If you could find the victim, we could have him arrested. She wouldn't even have to press charges because the state would."

"I have no idea who she was. She left and actually refused my help before she did."

"That's how he gets away with it, and it's typical. Some of these people have serious issues. Some of the women either enjoy the abuse or find release in it. They are like cutters, but to the extreme." He glanced over at me, and I shook my head, disgusted. I remembered the girls moan in between screams and shuddered.

"Look," I told Cedric, pointedly, "this may not be news to you, but my life, my childhood, my upbringing, and what I thought was nightmarish about it was pretty fucking normal. This…shit…is not normal."

"It is to Aiden."

I felt the nail drive through my heart at the loss of who I thought he was. "He's a monster."

"Very much so. But to him, it's pleasure."

"How do you know so much about this?" I turned to Cedric, who eyed me with concern. "I've become aware in a few situations I've had to get involved in. Nothing as extreme as the one you've described."

"So there is nothing we…I can do, to put him away? To stop him?"

"Yes and no. It would be extremely difficult."

A few minutes of silence lingered as I let my mind wonder. All I felt was dread at the thought that Devin might be lying there. Aiden had called us his hindrance. Without Devin, how far would he go?

"I have to know if Devin's all right. I just left him there!"

"I have a confession," Cedric said suddenly.

Oh, God. I eyed the gun I still held in my lap and he smirked. "Nothing you'll need your gun for, Nina, but you really are improving on awareness." I let my shoulders slump as the calming effect of the Xanax kicked in. I gave him a *What is it?* look.

"I've been working with Devin to find the man who was hired to kill you."

I snapped my attention to him. He lifted his fingers up and straightened them in an *I know* gesture. "At first I was suspicious, but when he gave me the number that Eileen texted to carry out the order, I followed up. That's how we found him. It turned out to be some drunk living here in Savannah that Eileen knew from high school back in Charleston. He wasn't a professional. He was just down on his luck, needed quick money."

"Why didn't you tell me?"

"Because I wanted to make sure he was our only threat. I didn't fully trust Devin, and I didn't want you relieving me until I was sure."

"And now?"

"He was found in his garage in his car last night, dead. Apparently, Eileen didn't pay him, so he gassed out."

I felt nauseated as I eyed him.

"Hang in there, Nina. The hard part is almost over."

"Oh, there's more," I said as I opened the car door, retching onto the cement. When I finished emptying myself, I closed the door then locked it.

"Yes," he said calmly. I hated that he was so calm, but one of us needed to be. "Isn't there always?"

"Seldom, very seldom, does complete truth belong to any human disclosure; seldom can it happen that something is not a little disguised or a little mistaken."

– JANE AUSTEN

§§

A LOUD KNOCK ON my car window made me jump. It was Devin. He looked like hell and was ghastly white. I turned on Cedric.

"What the fuck are you doing?"

"Nina, I just had to tell him you were safe."

"You son of a bitch!" I honked the horn, garnering the attention of the restaurant goers who turned to look at us as Devin got into the back seat.

Cedric addressed me with caution. "We are not going to hurt you."

I pulled my gun from my lap, pointing it back and forth between both men.

Cedric spoke again. "Nina, you can exit the vehicle now, and neither of us will follow you. You are free to go."

I looked at Cedric and then back at Devin, who looked at me with alarm before spouting off, "I really would love it if you would put that FUCKING GUN DOWN!"

"Don't yell at me!"

"Stop shooting me!"

Cedric grinned at us then turned on my ignition.

"Where the fuck are you going?" I squeaked, suddenly sure I should've taken him up on his offer to exit the car. Cedric took the barrel of the gun and pointed it at him. "Keep it on me, Nina, okay?"

I was completely out of my mind as I lowered it, choosing to see how this night would play out.

"The Barracks," Devin instructed.

"Sure you can make it, man?" Cedric looked in the rearview, concern written on his features.

"It's just a deep scratch." I looked back at Devin, who was already looking at me. "I never wanted you to see that."

"Well, I guess I was meant to," I answered, still terrified. "What is The Barracks?"

"Give me ten minutes, and I promise you'll know everything." Devin stared out the window, dread covering his features. "And then you can finally be rid of me."

We rode in silence, and I peeked at Devin as the shadows from the passing lights moved over his features. He was so insanely beautiful, even at his worst. He remained silent during the trip as I watched him, trying desperately to make sense of it. He finally looked at me as we pulled up. I turned my attention to the shack they had taken me too and went stiff with fear. The building was boarded up, but I could see "arracks "on the sign that was covered by one of the boards. The entrance was lit, but it was completely abandoned. It was absolutely terrifying.

"So this is where I die," I mumbled.

Both men chuckled dryly as Cedric got out of the car. Looking at Devin, he said, "I'll give you two a minute."

I gave Cedric a puzzled look before he gave me a nod. "You are so fucking fired."

"You don't need me anymore anyway. You are safe, Nina."

I sat stunned, wanting to yell at my new best friend some more as he walked away from the car. I turned on the air conditioning, enjoying the cool air as I finally rested my gun in my purse.

"I pictured a lot of things when I met you, Nina Scott, but never in a million years did I picture us in a car with me at gunpoint."

"Things change, people too, wouldn't you agree?" That was the Xanax talking. I hoped he was as impressed with my calm demeanor as I was.

Devin, sensing my inability to no longer tolerate any more bullshit, started without hesitation. "Our parents started this club. Our fathers were brothers." I looked forward, briefly studying the heap of wood, trying to picture the building in its prime.

"It was the first club in Savannah for the sexually promiscuous, and they overcame a ton of hurdles to open it."

"Lovely, really, Devin. A little gasoline and a match could do wonders for the place."

Devin chuckled as he always did at my sarcasm. My treacherous heart betrayed me as it reminded me I missed that.

"Are you high?" he asked, still amused.

"Yes."

"Good." He paused again, looking at me for a moment. "I've missed you so fucking much, Nina."

"That's not what I came to hear." I didn't believe my own voice as I said it. He nodded before he continued.

"Aiden's family was the richest in Savannah, or rather his father once was. He had a huge hand in real estate. Their family home was built on the land you own."

"It was never Eileen's."

"No."

I shook my head, pressing my lips together to keep from reacting before I heard the rest.

"You can imagine growing up in an extreme BDSM household is kind of strange. My parents hid it from me mostly, while Aiden's parents didn't…at all. I would spend most summers at Aiden's house and watch the odd goings-on. I never really thought of it as wrong. I'd witnessed it since I was very young. Women tied to chairs half naked at the dinner table, different men dragging women around the house by their collars at parties. Sex was spontaneous and everywhere in the house. Aiden's parents took us a time or two inside the club when mine were out of town. By the time we were old enough to play, we weren't playing cops and robbers. We had imaginary subs of our own."

I cringed as I looked at him, but he seemed unaffected. "Jesus, Devin."

"My home was…more normal, I guess you can say, while Aiden grew up in the dark. Literally. The older we got, the more we…well, I realized how wrong things were, and it didn't change as we grew up. They never hid it, and never planned to.

Aiden's mom was a junkie and wasn't around much anyway. And soon after the club opened, she stayed there most of the time "keeping the clients happy." We were told to keep our "fucking mouths shut" by Aiden's father, who slapped him around a little to drive home the point. He was a real son of a bitch, and he treated his subs horribly.

"As things progressed in the house, I noticed subtle changes in Aiden. He would go away when I spoke to him at times, simply dazed, just not paying attention, but he would always come back. One time I found him bound and gagged in the closet. His father had done it and left him there for an entire day. He was covered in filth. He was only eight. I went home that night and told my mother and the next day my parents took Aiden away, threatening his father with everything under the sun."

"You were both raised as Doms."

"I guess you could say that. My father was strict with my mother. I noticed the behavior, and I knew it well. I wasn't immune to the power he held over her. But I still knew it was consensual between them. Still is.

"Aiden adjusted perfectly at home with us. It was pretty awesome for me to have him around since I was an only child. I'd suddenly gained a brother. His father never came for him, and if it bothered Aiden, he never showed it."

I nodded, trying my best to remain silent as Devin stared out the window and into his past.

"When we were sixteen, I caught Aiden getting rough with his girlfriend. She left the house crying, and Aiden closed up for a year after that. I think he was searching for a way to control his urges and thought he'd found it in her. He seemed heartbroken by it."

"You mean he's capable of love?"

"I don't know. I'll never really know." Devin continued to stare at the building.

"Needless to say, when he started dating heavily in high

school, I became concerned, constantly on his ass, riding him over how to treat girls. We fought a lot, mostly out of my fear he would do it again. I loved him, but I was afraid of what he'd do even then. I could see it in him. He was a lot like his father, but I never voiced the concern to my parents. High school ended without incident, but what I didn't know is that he'd spent his senior year experimenting on Eileen's sister, Sandra."

"What?"

"Aiden's first victim was Sandra, my ex-wife's sister. She's a fucking monster in her own right and encouraged him in his sickness. I never knew of the connection until after I was married. This was hidden from me."

I nodded.

"After graduation, Aiden came to me one night, completely covered in blood and crying for his soul. He was talking out of his mind, and I kept asking him whose blood it was, but he refused to tell me. I was sure there would be a dead body or something by morning, but nothing ever came of it. And he never confided in me again after I went running to my mother. I was freaked out. I didn't know how to help him. My mother made excuses for him, and less than a week later, it wasn't even an issue. I knew then he might be a lost cause.

"When we graduated high school, we parted ways, two different men. After years of only holidays together, I began to notice Aiden coming back into himself. He seemed better, happier. I was happy for him, no longer afraid of the monster he might become. When I decided to move to Charleston, he came with me. He was the first investor in my firm. I felt like I had my brother back. He'd told me in school he'd treated himself by learning about his urges and learning to control them. I saw what you saw when you met him."

My heart was pounding as he continued. He let out a harsh breath. "Two years ago, and a month before I met you, Aiden mutilated the governor of Georgia's daughter."

"Oh, God, Devin."

"Aiden was fucked and was actually forced to relinquish his fortune to buy his way out of it. He was forced to sell his shares in my company to pay the good governor, who took the loss of his twenty-five-year-old daughter's innocence and turned it into profit. When Aiden came to me to liquidate his shares in order to pay him off, I flipped my shit, going to the governor myself, pleading for him to do the right thing and hold Aiden accountable. Aiden found out, and we had a blowout. He'd just cost me my company and ruined his own life.

"At the time, I had just asked Eileen for a divorce. She was determined to find leverage on me, and her sister gave it to her. Sandra is the one who sets up the meetings between Aiden and the women he tortures."

I felt my stomach roll again as I twisted my hands in my lap.

"Anyway, Aiden encouraged Sandra to tell Eileen, knowing the damage it would cause. Eileen jumped on it and offered to bail me out with her father's money, and I took it. She also agreed to keep quiet about my help in the cover-up. No one would invest that amount of money in a company. It was either sink or swim."

Don't I know that saying.

"You didn't cover anything up, Devin. You were just aware."

"Isn't it the same?" Guilt covered his face as he finally looked at me. "I may not be the monster, but I'm the monster's cloak. I've thought of a million different ways to handle the situation better since having met you."

I let my tears fall as he looked at me the way he always did when he was sincere. I just didn't realize it until that moment.

"You fucked my entire world up, too, but in a good way." He winced and covered his arm as his lips turned up in a smirk. "You were so damned crazy with a need to fit in, you didn't see how fucking immaculate you were *as is*. I fell in love with you our first meeting, and have regretted it ever since." He chuckled as I narrowed my eyes at him.

"I'm not a good man, Nina. The things I've done have

ruined me from ever being truly good for any woman, but I couldn't shake the way you made me feel. The way you looked at me. I wanted to deserve it. I lied about my marriage, I hid these things from you, and you had every right to flee." He faced the window again.

"I think Aiden witnessed his father's sickness vividly when he was young, and something happened that he never confessed. He had a thirst, and he was ashamed of it, at least at first.

"A few months after Aiden was taken from him, his father was found hanging in that shed. He'd burned his house to the ground before he did it. Aiden's mother was already long gone. She'd run off with some junkie from the club, and Aiden inherited all of his fortune." He cleared his throat, as if to keep his sadness away. "I lost my brother a long time ago. I should never have let it go this far. Part of me didn't think I should be responsible for *his* shit. I told myself I wasn't his keeper. I ignored it, acted like it had nothing to do with me. I had a life to live of my own. I had broken all ties with him personally, but once I saw the two of you were involved, there was no escaping it. And you wouldn't let go of the goddamned land." He shook his head slowly back and forth with a small smirk.

I stayed quiet as I pieced together my time with Aiden. He was every girl's dream, and he'd made it that way, making it impossible to believe anything different. He'd played his part so well, I couldn't help but wonder if any of it was genuine.

"Why didn't you just tell me," I cried as I trembled, knowing the truth.

"I wanted to protect you from the truth. I didn't want it to taint and change you the way it did me. I did everything I could to prevent it from happening again. I paid off every employee at The Rabbit Hole to tip me off if Sandra and Aiden ever met there. I closed this place down," he said, pointing to the boarded up shack, "to keep him from meeting contacts here. That's how I discovered him tonight. I didn't realize that shed is where he took his victims until the governor's daughter told me. And it was his sick ritual to do it there. I forged the deed and sold that fucking land, continually flipping it to keep it from him, keeping him in the dark as to who owned it so he couldn't strike. As soon as the owner became public record and Aiden could track their whereabouts, I'd resell it. You were on record as of this morning as the owner. He knew it and took full advantage, brokering a deal with Sandra tonight at The Hole. He pays Sandra serious money, and Nina," Devin deadpanned, "the women go willingly."

I shuddered at the sound of her screams. I could still hear them so clearly.

"You'll never be the same after seeing that and knowing him…intimately." I cowered away from his stare. "I had you watched. I warned you away. I'd only discovered you started seeing him again forty-five minutes before I saw you at the club. I was already looking for you. I was going to tell you about Aiden then."

I saw the pain etched on his face at the memory of seeing Aiden and me together. "If that's what if felt like seeing Eileen on my desk, I deserved it."

More tears fell as I let the emotion overwhelm me, sobbing into my hands. "I want so much to touch you now, Nina, but I can't." I nodded into my hands.

"That day at the club, I got in touch with Cedric and told him everything. I didn't want you near it. It was my mess to clean. He worked day and night to find the man responsible while keeping you safe. I knew Aiden couldn't touch you. That's all it's ever been about, keeping you away. I was so fucking selfish to start this." He ran his hands through his hair.

We both stayed silent, so many questions swirling through my head. I asked none. Finally, Devin spoke with gravel in his voice. "I owed you the truth, and now you have it. You would have gotten it much sooner, but I knew you needed time. I'd already put you through so much." I looked up as his face fell. "I love you. I'll always love you, Nina. But I never deserved you. Your love saved me, though, in that I can throw it all away without regret now."

My voice was a whisper. "What are you going to do?"

"Tell the fucking truth."

Cedric opened the car door, and I jumped at the intrusion.

"Hospital," Devin said quickly.

I looked over his damaged shoulder and saw the bottom of his sleeve was soaked with blood. He looked up at me with a small smile. "I took a bullet for you. Let's see the next guy top *that*."

My chest cracked wide open as I looked him over. I reached my hand back to grab his, and he gripped mine loosely. "I'll live," he said, assuring me.

"I won't."

He stared at me for a long moment before looking back out the window. "You will."

It was a sad statement, but a final one as he let go of my hand. Cedric sped down the highway and minutes later we were at the hospital. Devin got out and thanked Cedric then turned to look at me.

"I won't bother you again, Nina." He turned and walked through the sliding doors before I had a chance to reply.

Tears multiplied by the thousands as I watched the road pass by me in a blur. I let go of a month's worth of tears, pent up frustration, and now grieved the truth. Cedric practically carried me upstairs and stayed with me as I crawled into bed. It didn't take long for the darkness to take me.

"There are two tragedies in life. One is to lose your heart's desire. The other is to gain it."

– GEORGE BERNARD SHAW

§§

SO FUCKING BEAUTIFUL, Nina. Don't move."

"Devin, wait. I'm a mess!"

He lifted his phone and took a picture as I flashed a quick smile. I was sitting in his bed with his sheet wrapped around me, my hair a mess and my skin sticky from hours of sex. Even a hot mess, he'd made me feel beautiful. I looked across at him as he smiled at his picture of me.

"I love you, Devin." He froze in place, holding his phone as I repeated it. "I love you. I'll take your damn friendship and sex, but that's how I feel."

I didn't let him say anything as I pulled myself into his lap. I refused to meet his eyes as I kissed him feverishly. It felt amazing to let the words out after feeling that way for so long. I didn't look at him as I busied myself, latching my lips to his perfectly toned chest. He didn't say a word as he ran his fingers through my hair, softly tugging at the ends, prompting me gently to look up at him. I kissed his chest, ignoring the soft pull as he continued to ask me for my eyes. His touch was so gentle, I cursed the burn in my throat that led to the stinging of fresh tears.

I finally braved a look at him, letting my eyes drift from his sculpted chest to his Adam's apple, then his smiling lips. I returned his smile before I reached his eyes. "I'm not sorry I fell for you," I said, finally lifting my gaze to his. His eyes were filled with emotion as well. It looked like confusion and happiness. I allowed myself to be satisfied with it.

"So, I was changing the subject," I said, gripping his hard cock. He was gloriously naked along with me, and I traced every inch of his body with my greedy fingertips.

His smile turned wicked as he continued to stroke my hair, my nipples peaking underneath the sheet still covering me.

"Nina—"

"Yes?" I cut him off, stroking him hard, the way he liked. Whatever excuse he had for not returning my affections, I didn't want to hear it. I'd said what I'd wanted to say. I wouldn't ask him for more than he told me he could give. I took his lips, sucking greedily, and began to rub my pussy along his stiff cock.

I wrapped my arms around his neck and tilted my head back, getting lost in my own seduction as my orgasm built from the friction of simply grinding myself along his length. He captured my neck in his mouth, moving his tongue up and down its contours, and along my collarbone as I arched my back, moving at a faster pace. He still wasn't inside of me, and it amazed me he didn't need to be to drive me to the edge.

"Oh, God, it feels so good," I panted, just on the brink. My whole body shivered in anticipation as Devin, typically full of filthy talk, remained silent. I looked up to him to see a passion so intense that it pushed me over the edge, and I came hard, calling his name.

"Devin," I murmured as he captured my lips and pushed me down on the bed beneath him. He kissed me softly before pulling back to look down at me with kind, gentle eyes.

"I'm not good enough for you."

"Really? I like it. It's a lame excuse, but I like that you're working that out for yourself. And just so you know, this is love, Devin. This… us…This is love."

He landed a string of intimate kisses down my neck. It wasn't like him to be so gentle.

"I want it hard." My confession seemed to surprise him. I knew he wasn't capable of sharing his heart with me, and I couldn't bear the thought of living through his lovemaking. I'd fallen hard, and his unrequited love would be the end of me if I felt his affection in his fucking.

Without warning, he pulled away from me, grabbing the belt from his pants on the floor. Coming back to the bed, he fastened my ankles together with it, leaving me bound.

"How about deep?" He gave me a sexy smile as he pushed my ankles up and lifted my lower half, so it was resting on his knees. I couldn't see him around my legs but felt the tip of him invade me, making me moan.

"Fuck, Nina, you are ruining me."

"I want you to come in my mouth." My voice was so hoarse with arousal that I didn't recognize it.

"What am I doing, Nina?" he rasped as his length slid into me.

"Taking what's yours," I moaned back.

Because of the way he'd bound me, the sensation was amazing. He was deep, so deep, and the friction was surreal. It was torture not being able to see his blue depths as he fucked me hard and deep. I heard his grunts match his exertion as he lifted up higher, bending my knees so my feet rested on his chest and we were finally eye to eye. Our lips parted further with each thrust, and suddenly our mouths were praying out to each other in appreciation.

"I want you so much, Nina, all the time. You are all I see." I came hard, feeling the explosion through my limbs as he pulled out, unfastening my ankles and slipping between my legs, massaging the back of my calves and thighs.

"Devin, please come in my mouth," I protested as he slipped back inside of me.

"No," he whispered into my ear as he kept his pace hard.

"Why not?"

"Because I want to hear you say it again when I come."

My heart jumped in surprise as he looked down at me, and as soon as his cock jerked in release, I looked right into his beautiful, blue eyes and repeated the words to him.

"Wake up." It was Taylor. I rolled onto my side and away from her, trying desperately not to fall apart as I recalled the rest of that day. Devin had taken me sailing again, teaching me the basics. We dined on oysters and cold beer, then tortured and soothed each other's bodies on his boat until the sun rose, neither of us willing to break away. We missed work and spent the day sleeping, talking, and fucking until we were forced to go back to reality. It had been absolutely perfect. Though he'd never said the words back, I knew he loved me too. He'd loved me all along.

"Taylor, the next time you have a hot tip on where my ex-boyfriend is, please keep it to yourself."

"I'm so sorry about what happened. Why didn't you come inside or at least fucking call me! I would have blown a hole through that fucking psycho."

She was referring to Aiden.

Aiden, the psycho. Jesus.

I couldn't help the pain that spread through me. The loss of who he was like a death to me.

"I handled it, along with Mrs. Leroy Brown." I sat up, covering myself in my sheet as I looked over to Taylor. She regarded me with sympathy and concern, and I shrugged my shoulders.

"I'm going to be all right."

"This much I know, but honestly, if you wanted to fall apart, I would understand." She turned away from me so I could grab a robe. I excused myself to the bathroom, and when I came out, she looked up at me.

"I'm sorry, Nina. I don't know what I was thinking telling you about Devin. I was just so fascinated. When he walked in, he didn't see me, and I wondered what the hell he was doing in there. I was so stunned, I guess I had a teenage moment and wanted to gossip."

I walked into my closet.

"Nina, you have to know I had no idea about any of this."

"You think I thought this was some conspiracy?" I poked my head out of my closet to eye her.

"Nina, with what you've been through, I can't imagine you being able to trust anyone. Cedric has a new black eye, by the way."

I walked out of my closet with wide eyes. "You shouldn't have."

"Son of a bitch deserved it, keeping me in the dark. Apparently, he and Devin are new best friends."

I let out a small chuckle. "It would appear so."

"Do you want to talk about it?"

"Not really," I said, surprised. "I'm getting really good at coping with unbelievable circumstances." Taylor nodded, her red, sculpted ponytail falling over her shoulder. She was looking down at my carpet with what looked like remorse. She seemed vulnerable, something I wasn't used to seeing on her. I didn't like it.

"Taylor, I'm not angry with you in the slightest."

She nodded once. "I'm sorry I've been so fucking evasive. I know that you are just trying to know me, to be a friend."

"Well, the offer still stands."

She looked up at me with a smirk. "You know, I'm almost crazy enough to trust you with the truth. I need a friend too, Nina. I've been alone for a very long time."

"And what about this new boyfriend in Savannah?"

"Cedric's other eye will match," she spit out with disdain.

"He didn't really tell me anything. I assumed as much. So are you in love?"

She laughed as she pulled at her red hair with her fingers. "No, not in the slightest. Actually, it's not one man."

"Really? I should warn you that can be dangerous."

"When we met Violet after she showed us the land, she confided in me that she met her husband, Rhys, at the club. I guess she smelled the Dom in me."

"You are a Dom?"

"No." Taylor smiled. "I just hate referring to myself as a sub."

I laughed as I took a seat next to her on my bed. "Of course you do."

"I wouldn't put myself in any category, but I saw the opportunity to play around a little, and I've kind of let it get out of hand."

"Oh?"

"I've just been…experimenting." She winked. "Anyway, that's what I've been doing. Nina, I'm truly sorry for what happened. I'll hire more security."

"You know, I think I'll keep Cedric." She looked up at me with surprise.

"But he kept you in the dark."

"It wasn't his truth to tell. Besides, he knew me well enough to know I could only handle the truth in small doses like Devin did." Saying his name brought that same burning lump to my throat.

"I misjudged him."

"So did I," I said.

"What will you do?"

Cedric's knock on my door had us both staring at it as if the boogeyman were behind it.

"Nina, channel six," he called from the other side of the door.

I raced to my bedside, clicking it on, and sat next to Taylor as we watched.

"Business mogul, Devin McIntyre, came forward this morning with some shocking news. Apparently, he took part in a cover-up for a scandal involving Georgia's governor, Ronald Matheson. Jeff Talbertson, our field correspondent, has the story."

"Thanks, Sue. Devin McIntyre has come forward stating that on February 13, 2013, he was an eye witness to the aftermath of the brutal beating of Matheson's daughter by his cousin, Aiden McIntyre. Allegedly, Aiden practiced some very dangerous sexual ritual and coerced Matheson's daughter into taking part. When the situation escalated, Jenna Matheson went home to her father to have McIntyre arrested. This is where the story gets interesting. Instead of having McIntyre brought up on charges for his daughter's assault, the governor agreed to take a large lump sum from Aiden McIntyre to help fund his 2014 campaign.

"Devin McIntyre states that he never intended to be a part of the cover-up, and that he did not participate in any of the events. When asked why he was coming forward, he simply stated his cousin 'is a sexual predator, ' and he 'wants to avoid anyone else falling victim to his crimes.' So far, much of this is speculation. As of now, Governor Matheson's camp has declined to comment. We will have more on this story as it develops."

"Thanks, Jeff. Can you tell us a bit more about Aiden McIntyre?"

The story went on, profiling Aiden and his accomplishments as I let the noise drown out. Devin had told the truth, exposing Aiden and possibly ending his sick practice for the time being. But deep down I knew there was no hope for Aiden. No help for him, either. He was a lost cause, and I'd seen it firsthand.

I felt my entire stomach drop when they showed a picture

of Aiden smiling. He looked gorgeous in a t-shirt with the beach in the background, and I was thankful he wasn't looking at the camera. There was no way I could suffer looking into his eyes.

"Devin will lose all his clients. He'll go bankrupt," Taylor said, her eyes still on the screen.

It dawned on me then that this was the leverage Eileen used. Aiden's sickness had cost Devin his business, his freedom, his livelihood…and me.

I felt my heart break again as I looked at Taylor.

"He did nothing but protect me."

"Like I said, I misjudged him, and that's so rare." She seemed thoughtful as she looked at the TV.

"But he's a bad man, right?"

Taylor looked at me, seeming to form an answer and then stood. "I am in no position, nor will I ever be, to dish out this type of advice."

I laughed at the stunned look on her face. "It's okay, Taylor, really. I'm good with the occasional tough love and how to paralyze a man with a bullet kind of advice."

She smiled at me with a wink. "I'm going to go have a chat with Cedric."

"Take it easy on him, Taylor. I need him whole."

"You got it." She looked at me one last time. "I'm proud of you."

"For what? I was scared shitless and shot the wrong man." We both laughed a little.

"You know why."

I nodded, and she shut the door behind her. I looked up to see Aiden's picture splashed on the TV again and turned it off.

I looked at my bed, tempted to let it consume me, to drown out the noise and give in to the pain pulsing through my veins and continuously pumping through my heart. Instead, I grabbed a bathing suit and took it out on the waves of the Atlantic.

"Forgiveness is alchemy of the soul in which the feeling of possibility returns to the human spirit."

– JAKE DUCEY

§§

A WEEK LATER, I was sitting at my desk at home writing out a disbursement schedule for charitable funds for the upcoming year. It was Sunday night, and I was at home working—my new normal—and was okay with that, but the gnawing in my chest wouldn't go away. As much as I tried to concentrate, I heard the voice.

"Nina."

It was Devin's voice that whispered to me through the silence. I set down my pen and leaned back in my chair. This was guilt. Sure, I would feel a little guilty about what had transpired. Okay, a lot of guilt. The man had proven his love over and over. But he was right, it was his mess to clean.

"I'm a bad man."

"No you aren't," I argued with him as I sat alone in my chair. "You're a liar, and selfish, and calculating, and so damn stupid. What you did was stupid!" My chest heaved as I heard my name again, a whisper on his lips.

"Nina."

"And controlling and manipulative." Twin tears slid down my cheeks as I continued to berate him. "And adolescent. Your temper is ridiculous." An image of his dazzling smile surfaced. "And brilliant and beautiful and so damn sexy." I was sobbing now. "And I still hate you."

"I love you."

"Devin," I croaked in my chair, turning it around, away from the door, and burying my face in my hands.

"He's gone." I jumped at Cedric's voice. "Last I heard, he was leaving on his boat."

"Cedric, we are going to have to set some privacy parameters," I sniffed out, trying to mask my obvious breakdown.

"Sorry, Nina, I was just walking in and heard you." I wiped my face, turning my chair to face him. It was so evident Cedric cared for me.

"I know, Cedric, and I'm thankful I have you watching out for me."

"I'll be checking the system out if you need me. We've made some adjustments." I nodded, pulling my seat back to the desk and picking up my pen. Cedric lingered in the doorway, and I looked up at him in question.

"Yes?"

"Nothing," he said, moving toward the living room.

"Say it," I snapped, resuming my scheduling. "We both know you have some sort of bromance going on with him." I looked up and gave him a wink.

"I respect the guy," Cedric defended.

"Okay."

"You could do worse." Cedric walked off, making his way out of the room.

"I have," I whispered before getting back to work.

§§

DEVIN

I lay on my boat, looking up at the night sky. Tomorrow I set sail for the Keys. I'd been making preparations for a week and had everything a man could possibly need. All I had to do was pull up anchor.

That had proven to be the most difficult.

Leave it to me to hold out hope Nina would come around. It was asinine to think as much. In the last few months, I'd been as strung out as a lovesick puppy that just had his first good piece of pussy. And even now as I lay there, I wished for her to be next to me, talking my ear off about anything trivial.

There is so much healing in the right woman's kiss, and for me that woman was Nina. She had done that for me. All the sordid and sick parts of me were healed when her lips met mine. My affection for her and the way she regarded me had once again shown me the difference between right and wrong in a world of fucked up. And my weakness for her had finally fueled me to do the right thing and let my cousin drown in his demons while I exposed them.

Acceptance was a painful bitch.

When I'd first met Nina, I'd accepted the fact that I had to love her from afar. As time went on, I had to accept the fact that I could have her, just not the way either of us wanted. The next bitter pill would be the acceptance that I had to once again deal with the first.

The silver lining was she was safe.

Aiden had left Charleston, and I'd made sure of it. He'd abandoned his club and his home. Apparently, hiding was something he was extremely good at. He was being investigated by both Charleston County and Savannah. A woman had come forward claiming to be a victim. If he ever returned, there was a chance he would be brought up on charges. Slim was better than none. My parents weren't speaking to me, and I found that easier to live with than hiding the truth.

My mother was to blame for Aiden's coddling. She never did fully grasp the idea of Aiden's demons. He had perfected the art of deception by being completely believable. Even I had been deceived for a short time. The only way of ending it was to bring it public. I'd always known that and the fact that Aiden had chosen to damage the governor's daughter made it news. It was my only chance, and though I was years too late, I took it. I'd done my part in helping, but it didn't help me sleep at night.

It would be a long road to sleeping peacefully.

I was fine with the way things went down, except for what Nina had to witness. I'd meant it when I said I regretted falling for her. It led to her losing a piece of herself in the shed that night. Or maybe her meeting Aiden was just fate's cruel way of reminding me what I had to do.

Either way, protecting her was motivation enough.

And now it was time for me to leave.

The boat swayed gently, reminding me I wasn't quite finished with my prep. I was leaving in the morning before the three-day storm rolled in, which would only delay me further. I made my way to the bow, unpacking the rest of my supplies as I heard a loud thunk. I looked to my right and on the deck was a large tote I didn't recognize.

"I packed two bikinis and my gun, but I'll let your behavior determine in which order I use them."

§§

NINA

Devin froze as I continued on. "You really aren't good enough for me. You're arrogant, selfish, and you have a horrible bedside manner. Were you even planning on saying goodbye?"

Devin turned to me, casually pulling the insides of his shorts pockets out, showing me the lint. "You really aren't the best for me either, Nina. I'm bankrupt, homeless, and disowned. Oh, and you shot me." I drank him in as he slowly walked toward me in his fitted t-shirt, his wavy hair a mess. He'd never looked better.

I waited patiently for him as I stood on the dock. When he finally stood, looking down at me, I bit my lip.

"I never did apologize for that. Sorry...for shooting you."

Devin tilted his head with a frown. "That didn't really seem sincere."

"Well, maybe one day I'll mean it."

"Ouch," he said with a chuckle.

"So do you have room for me, cowboy, or were you planning on riding into the sunset alone?"

He held out his hand, and I took it as he helped me onto the boat.

"I have room for this body, but we can leave your mouth in Charleston," he taunted as I looked into his eyes. They were burning with relief and love.

"I'm sorry, Devin, that you lost your life to this," I said

sincerely. "And because of him."

He cupped my face, rubbing his thumbs over my cheeks. "I think my life before all of this made me a little worse off, don't you think?" I nodded. I saw the emotion in his eyes change to doubt. "Can you really do this with me?"

"God, Devin, if I could keep myself away *and* from loving you, it would be my greatest accomplishment. I'll always be thankful I shot you at least once."

His body shook with laughter as his hands stroked my face.

"I love you, Nina."

"I know."

He raised a brow. "You could have left the gun at home, you know."

"I'm just being cautious. Sharks die by bullet."

He would never get my metaphor.

He leaned in and took my lips. "So I guess you are a regular Annie Oakley now."

"Who?"

"Jesus, have you ever opened one history book?" He looked down at me with a frown.

"Are we fighting already?" I asked with a smile. He took my lips again, kissing me softly before deepening the kiss, his velvet tongue moving slowly and seductively over mine. When he pulled away, I saw the fire in his eyes.

"Nina—"

"I have a present for you, but I can't really give it to you until tomorrow."

I saw the wheels turning and stopped him.

"It's not that kind of present."

"I'm intrigued," he whispered, flicking his tongue out to taste my bottom lip. My already wet sex clenched as his hands molded to my shivering sides.

"You'll just have to be patient," I mused as he stopped his assault, pulling his hands away.

"Okay."

After securing the deck, he guided me downstairs. It housed a large bed, a two person kitchen, and a single stall bathroom. Some of our best memories were made here and it was a damn good place to start over.

I studied the tiny bathroom, shaking my head at the tight space. I was a space snob now and had no problem admitting it. "Seriously, we are going to need a bigger boat."

His arms snaked around me, and he leaned in, breathing in deep. "We'll fit fine, you'll see."

I turned in the tiny space, kissing my way up the arm of his soft t-shirt, and started tracing the pink scar I'd left. Devin sighed as he watched me whisper kisses over the damaged skin.

"Devin," I murmured.

"Yes," he said, placing a kiss on my temple.

"What the fuck are you waiting for?" He pulled back, confusion on his face, then let the fire back into his eyes. Seconds later, we were both naked and furiously kissing. His tongue tasted my mouth, my neck, my nipples as he barked orders. He turned me around, his hand coming down hard on my flesh, and his fingers fucking me ruthlessly. I felt my body spark back to life when his thick cock brushed my entrance. He stopped suddenly as I stood, lost to his touch, waiting for him.

"Devin?" I waited and got nothing.

"Devin?" I turned to face him to see his eyes swimming with anger and pain. He was thinking of Aiden. I didn't need to have him clarify. I could see it in his broken features. It was the same look he gave me when he saw us at the club. "I'm sorry." I stood, bared before him, seeing the deep hurt I'd caused him. ". *He* wasn't you."

"No, Nina," he scolded as his eyes closed tightly. "Don't."

"Open them, Devin."

He opened them slowly, and I saw the rawness in them. "I should have believed you. I should have listened, and I should have waited when you asked me to." Devin punched at the wall behind my head and kept his angry face an inch from mine.

"You gave your body to him!" He started to pull out of my arms as I gripped him closer.

"I'm sorry. I love you, Devin." His eyes swam as he gripped my throat, smearing his thumb over my lips.

"What the fuck did I do to us, Nina?"

"You tried to save me…*again,* and I made it hard…*again,* but I am asking you not to stop, Devin. This time I'll let you. I need you to save me. I need you to help me remember who I am."

"Did you love him? Do you?"

"He wasn't you." And it was the truth. I'd never let myself completely fall for Aiden. It had *always* been Devin, and it always would be.

He took my mouth in a passionate kiss and kept us connected, laying me down on the bed. I writhed under him as he moved over me, positioning his cock at my entrance. I moaned as I traced his chiseled chest, admiring the lines and curves of him. He hovered above me, not trusting himself with his anger still raw.

"Do it," I begged. With one thrust of his long, thick cock, I was at his mercy. It was time for punishment, and with Devin, I would take anything he dished out.

"Fuck…fuck, why, Nina?!" he pushed out, his voice twisted in agony, thrusting into me harder and harder. I could see the emotions fighting in him. Anger, hurt, love, lust, all played a part as he tore into me, punishing me, loving me, forgiving me.

He gripped my neck, forcing me to face his wrath and his angry fucking. I let go, bursting at the seams and reaching for him. Gripping my hips, he slammed our bodies together, and my orgasm escalated as I screamed his name. It lasted forever, and I felt like I would never come down. Devin turned me on my side and joined me on the bed from behind, lifting my leg and pushing into me again, massaging my clit. I reached my arms back, grabbing onto his head and pulling him closer as his thick, hard cock pulsed and filled me to the brink. I would never get close enough. He kept his lips on me, kissing me furiously as he fucked me slowly, his arm circled around me, pulling me tightly to him.

"Feel that cock, Nina. It's yours, you own it, and I own the pussy that's holding it."

"Yes," I murmured as I tilted my head up to kiss him. He darted his tongue out, and I met it with mine as they entwined and danced, his cock twitching, his release coming fast.

"I need all of you," he said, pulling out and rubbing my back entrance.

"Please, Devin."

His finger plunged into my soaked core, pulling out an orgasm as he slipped inside, filling my ass with his girth.

"What am I doing, Nina?"

"Taking what's yours," I said heatedly.

He quickened, his hand still teasing my clit. "I need to possess it all. All of you."

"It's all yours." He came hard at my words, a loud rumbling moan escaping his chest as he continued moving through it. I took his release as my body shuddered. He pulled away from me long enough to turn out the light then returned, wrapping himself around me. After a few minutes of silence, he spoke first, "Fuck, I thought I'd lost you."

"I thought I'd lost me, too."

"You are ready and able to do beautiful things in this world and you'll only really ever have two choices: love or fear. Choose love. And don't ever let fear turn you against your playful heart."

– JIM CARREY

§§

I WOKE UP TO the sway of the boat, knowing we were well on our way. I joined him on deck, and his smile was devastating and welcomed. He pulled me into his arms as I looked around us. There was nothing but sea.

"How far off the coast are we?" I asked as he rubbed my nipples through my thin shirt with his thumbs, completely uninterested in my question.

"A few miles. We'll stay close."

I looked at the brightening horizon, excited about our trip, and for the first time, our future. I turned to Devin, who gave me an inquisitive look. "What?"

"Are you ready for your present?"

"Sure?" He lifted the question as he looked at my t-shirt and shorts, noticing I had nothing on me.

My gift didn't have a damn thing to do with any material possession. It had nothing to do with the past or our history. It was no sentimental trinket that represented our time together. It had nothing to do with wealth or lack thereof. It was a simple thing, really. Just an honest reminder that no matter what the hell you've done, there is always a chance to make things right as long as you have breath in your lungs. My present to Devin was a new chance for us to start over, to live in the now without the burdens or guilt from what we'd done. I was sure he would declare me crazy when I announced my gift was "Monday."

SNEEK PEEK AT PREDATOR AND PREY SERIES

§§

TAYLOR

THOSE EYES…THOSE FUCKING dark eyes were the reason for my trip, but if it didn't pan out this time and I didn't get his attention, I was giving up.

Look at you, Taylor Ellison, obsessing over a man.

And I should be ashamed. I'd done everything in my power to get his attention without being too obvious. When Violet had introduced me to The Rabbit Hole, I'd been excited about the prospect of having my own Rhys. I'd been working my ass off for so long I'd almost lost sight of having a life completely. I needed more than an impressive bank account and a fast car. Though I'd reached my goal, I knew I needed more to be satisfied. Months of worthless visits to The Rabbit Hole had turned my excitement into dread. I had frequented it in hopes of finding a man to suit my sexual taste. Nothing too crazy, but just to be sated would be enough for now. I'd fucked a few too many that led to dead ends.

I'd all but given up until I saw him.

He was there each time I went, often alone at a table, sipping his drink, sometimes with friends. I'd seen him come and go but never take on a member of the club. While there, he'd never visited the private rooms. The first time we made eye contact, I saw the recognition in his. There was a spark, an amount of heat. *Something* was there.

Maybe I was obsessing out of boredom. I closed my eyes tight in frustration as I sat in my car, looking at the double doors.

This was it. If it didn't happen, you might have to find a date the old fashioned way.

But that was part of the problem. I didn't date. I wasn't

good at the getting to know you aspect of the evening. I liked the fucking portion and had always preferred to get to that. I very much had the dating mentality of a twenty-one-year-old man; casual sex and nothing serious, no attachments, that sort of thing. I wasn't against those in love and actually saw myself going down that road a time or two. I'd been hurt by a man I had affection for, and I was sure I would eventually try that again with the right man. But now I was just restless. I needed a partner who understood my needs, my body. I'd been settling for far too long.

In my most figure revealing dress, I walked into The Hole and was greeted by Tara, a nice enough bartender who had often tried to strike up a conversation with me. It was obvious she swung both ways, which was fine, but not for me. I had serious issues when it came to women. I couldn't stand ninety-nine percent of them. I guess you could say I was a tad bit of a misogynist. I preferred, and have always preferred, the company of men, whether as friends or fuck buddies.

It had a lot to do with my mentality. I don't find the conversations interesting or the unnecessary drama appealing. I didn't talk feelings or revel in a good pair of shoes. I'd tried, really I had, but women weren't especially receptive to my brand of honesty, the kind that isn't sugarcoated and saves time.

The only woman I had let even remotely close to knowing me was Nina. She was the exact type of woman I most loathed when I met her. Pretentious, all about appearance and image, and she had an unnatural fascination with shoes. I never saw us becoming close, but since everything went down, and because she had been so genuinely good to me, I had let her in a little. She had changed so drastically in the two years I'd known her. Sitting at the bar now with a crisp chardonnay, I couldn't help but be happy for her, if not a little envious.

He wasn't here.

He'd always taken the table in the corner behind the frosted glass. The first time I'd seen him, I'd rapidly drank him in. He was tall, his inky long hair was ear length and cradled his ridiculously beautiful face. He had naturally dark skin. I guessed him to be of Spanish descent. His attire was impeccable. He was always in a double-breasted suit. His pleasure at the club seemed to be to sit back and observe.

I pushed out a disappointed breath as I sipped my wine. It was time to let Mr. Mysterious go. The last time I'd seen him we'd locked eyes for several minutes, neither of us turning away until he was approached by a beautiful brunette that left his table shortly after she stopped. I refused to believe he was gay. I couldn't see it, couldn't fathom it. Not *this* man.

This is boredom. Go home and watch a CSI marathon.

As soon as I'd convinced myself to leave, he appeared at my side on a barstool, and I smirked into my wine as he spoke.

"I think it's time we introduce ourselves."

§§

EXCERPT FROM SEXUAL AWAKENINGS

§§

FALL

I LIT CANDLES ALL over the house in only the scents he would tolerate. I covered our topiaries with soft, clear lights, and arranged fall flowers and large cornstalks into vases around the living room and porch. I loved fall, and by the way the house now smelled and had been transformed, it showed. Grabbing my pumpkin spice latte, I sat in my reading chair on the porch, watching the leaves sway in the cool breeze. I was already cold but refused to go inside, wanting to soak up the last of the sun as it made its way behind the trees, basking in the feeling in the air. Everything seemed clearer, crisper, and cold days were rare in the south this early in the season. Receiving an incoming message on my tablet, I tapped it, finding nothing new. He wouldn't be home for dinner. It was a good thing I hadn't bothered to cook. I knew better. A year straight of eating alone will do that to a woman. I opted for another night of wine and my vibrator.

Once inside, I chose my favorite bottle of red and poured a healthy glass. Surveying my beautifully decorated home, I rolled my eyes. What was the point? Maybe he was right. The last time I had decorated for the holidays, my husband had asked that same question.

"We don't have any children. We hardly have company. Why even bother?"

Prick. We didn't have children because he had a vasectomy three weeks after our wedding without telling me, only for me to find out in the first of many vicious arguments that ensued. We didn't have company because he was too occupied keeping his own, busy with his constant need to stick his dick in their throats. It wasn't enough for my husband to have one affair; he was in the midst of two.

I was not a woman scorned. Fuck that. I was a woman who had been freed, and too lazy to leave him, having no desire to start another relationship or leave my beautiful home. Alex was never here, ever. What was the point of giving up my life for a ghost I barely lived with? I took my wedding ring off months ago. He never noticed because, in all honesty, I couldn't recall the last conversation we had.

And then I remembered.

"You never loved me, did you?" I asked as he entered the house after another late meeting.

"Sure, I love you. Why are you acting so out of sorts?" He ran his hands through his hair, a signature move on his part that I used to find sexy. A stranger to me at that point when we had originally been so close, he stared at me as if I disgusted him, and I returned it. We had been best friends before we were lovers. We'd shared everything. I didn't even recognize the man who now took his place. There was not a damn thing wrong with me or the way I looked. All his fucked up issues about infidelity were his own.

"I'm not an idiot. Don't play innocent, Alex," I snapped.

"Drink your wine, honey," he said dryly, pushing past me.

That was our last conversation. When he was home, he called his mistresses from his office. I heard every word, because I listened. I listened to strengthen my resolve. I had already decided to ask for a divorce after Christmas. New year, new life, I guessed. He would let me keep the house and I would let him keep most of his money. He had plenty of it, due to old money passed down from his parents, and his newfound success at his advertising firm. I supposed he thought that since I wanted for nothing, I should just accept my circumstances as a good little wife, go shopping, get pampered. The truth was, I mourned my relationship with my husband, or at least the man I knew before things fell apart. The most frustrating aspect was he refused to admit anything was wrong; the man that had proposed to me knew something was wrong with me before I did at times. He was attentive and nurturing and…human. My tears saddened him; my smiles and laughter fueled him. He'd loved me.

I shook off the small amount of pain making its way into my chest. I had no more room for self-pity. I had done it all. I had worked out, tried new hair, new clothes. I had even gone so far as to get Botox. The only conclusion I came to after a few months of being refused in the skimpiest of lingerie was FUCK HIM. FUCK HIM. I had tried to make my marriage work. He was more interested in seeing it fail. Our relationship was too far gone from what it used to be. There was no trust, and definitely no lingering love. I had spent hours crying over him, now I just wanted my freedom. And freedom was becoming more important than comfort. I had to get out of this and soon.

I sipped my wine, thinking how completely unsatisfying it all was. I had waited until the age of twenty-nine to get married. It seemed the sensible thing to do after a few months of dating Alex. I couldn't even remember the last time we had made love or fucked. My last attempt to keep the home fires burning had failed miserably.

"We aren't a couple of fucking horny teenagers living out a fantasy, Vi. We aren't making a porno, and what the fuck are you wearing?"

I gave up that day, throwing every single negligee I owned away and burying any remaining hope. Sex with Alex was never exactly hot. It had been enough because I had honestly loved him.

Drinking the last of my glass, I poured myself another. Sex, now there was something I was tired of living without. I had my trusty toy. God, how I loved that thing. Battery maintenance promised endless minutes of pleasure. The thought alone had me wanting to reach for it.

I was thirty-two years old, sitting in a big, beautifully

decorated house, imagining the next session with my vibrator. I heard the shatter of the wine glass before I realized I was the one who had thrown it.

This was not my life! This was not who I was. This shit… this waiting, much like my marriage, was over!

Things were about to change and change today. First, I had to come up with a plan.

§§

Sex, or lack thereof, was what set me off in the kitchen. I missed it. I wanted it. I needed it, but why? I'd never really had sex like most adults. Well, those adults who I envied, which included anyone who was having their needs met at this point. I abstained from having my own affair because, for a short time, I held out hope. Now that my mind was made up on divorce, I no longer had to justify my reasoning. Sex was a necessity for me. I had waited long enough. My body was starving for touch, my lips bankrupt from a lack of kisses. While a relationship didn't appeal to me, at least not immediately, the thought of a good hard fuck made me insane with want. Not that I'd ever been satisfied sexually.

My experience consisted mainly of missionary, with a few sporadic moments here and there in various positions. Alex was not well endowed and had by no means made up for it throughout our years together. I wondered what it was like to be with a man with a big cock. I moaned at the thought, never once having an orgasm from a man's dick. My girlfriend, Molly, told me that without a vibrator, I might never have one. She insisted girls who came with men inside them were either porn stars with amazing acting skills or had been divinely gifted in that department. It was a myth to me, an orgasm from a man's cock. I'd had fantasies for years about the possibilities of sex. All of it interested me, especially the kink. Alex would look at me as though I was insane when I suggested anything out of our norm. I would get hot and bothered reading my dark, erotic romances and begged him to try some scenarios with me. Looking back now, I could see why he thought it a little strange. It just wasn't realistic.

Do these people really exist, the people that explore the forbidden? Of course they do, but where were they? Certainly not on the outskirts of Savannah, GA. I laughed at the thought. I'd do good to find a decent looking, well hung, hardworking man in this area, period, let alone one that would explore my sexuality with me. Then again, what if? I mean, surely the insatiable and erotic sexual cravings of people are not limited to only large cities.

Where in the hell would I look for something like that here?

Of course there was the web, but some, or most, of those sites had a virus attached. I'd delved into porn a little when my imagination couldn't do it for me and I needed a little extra something. That got old as well. I was tired of watching. I wanted the experience. Pouring myself another glass of wine, I ignored the shattered glass on the floor. Who the hell would care about the mess anyway? After all, it was only me here.

§§

Hours later, after watching Jimmy Fallon, my curiosity brought me back to the web. Fuck it; I'd been the well-behaved, jilted wife long enough. I wanted to know what was out there, especially those like me who shared the same curiosities. I would love to know if any other women in Savannah had a fascination with kink. After a few hours of searching, I stumbled upon a site advertising a local, adults only page. There was a large triple X on the screen and a flashing advertisement of what looked like a bar in or around Savannah, but my excitement was stifled when I realized there was no address. After a quick Google search for the bar, named The Rabbit Hole, I came up empty, and gave up. Yawning, I threw my tablet beside my pillow and laid my head down to watch *Nightline* when I heard a ping.

I looked at my tablet to see an incoming message asking for

the password. After careful thought, I had nothing. I typed my plea.

Hint?

Rabbit Hole.

Not helpful at all. Shit. The possibilities were endless. I studied the XXX on the screen and saw an Alice in Wonderland cartoon encased in them. Inside the rabbit hole, in the middle X, was Alice kissing another Alice on the cheek as she held her pointer finger to her lips.

Making the best guess I could, I keyed it in.

Don't kiss and tell.

I was immediately redirected to the homepage, asked to create a username—Blue_Alice—and started navigating my way around.

It was a chat room, and from the subject matter floating in boxes around the screen, it was definitely a no holds barred kink fest. Perfect! At least the curious vixen inside me wouldn't have to show her face for now. I sat for hours in the various chat rooms reading the conversations. Most of them consisted of people hooking up and then agreeing to email in private. Great, hours on the site and I had only gotten a little hot reading what appeared to be an open and unashamed twosome having really kinky message sex. I could read a book and get hotter than this. I was just about to grab my trusty silver bullet and a new erotica book when I received an incoming message.

MadHatter: What are you doing here?

I froze, feeling completely busted. I shook my embarrassment off quickly. I had knocked on the damn door. Why not have a little fun?

Blue_Alice: Looking.

MadHatter: For what?

Blue_Alice: Anything but what I'm doing.

There, honesty. Honesty was good.

MadHatter: Why so blue, Alice? Bored housewife?

Blue_Alice: Fuck you.

MadHatter: So, I'm assuming I'm correct?

Blue_Alice: Maybe. What the hell does it matter?

MadHatter: We don't do married here.

Blue_Alice: I am getting a divorce.

MadHatter: That's not a new one.

Blue_Alice: Keep your boring ass chat room.

MadHatter: Temper, temper.

Blue_Alice: I could do a better job turning people on than this bullshit.

MadHatter: Wow, you really need a thick cock in that sassy mouth.

Blue_Alice: And I suppose you're the one who will be giving it to me?

MadHatter: Why not me?

I felt my cheeks grow hot and took a deep breath. Okay, now we are talking here.

Blue_Alice: Fine…talk to me.

MadHatter: Why are you here?

Blue_Alice: You already asked me that.

MadHatter: And you didn't give me a good enough answer.

I thought about it. Going into this with honesty would be the only way I would truly get what I wanted. But is this what I wanted? What if he was some nasty, fat perv with bad skin and greasy hair? Then again, he may have thought I was some nasty troll with a huge gut and overgrown forest in my pants. I shook my head, indignant at my own stereotyping. *Not cool, Vi.* This whole scenario meant taking a chance. I had been teetering on the edge of this for years, if I was honest with myself. I wanted to be fucked ruthlessly, worshipped and tortured, brought to levels of sexual awareness I'd only dreamed about. I was sure—no, positive—I had an undiscovered fetish or two. Honest, I'll be honest.

Blue_Alice: I want to explore a part of me I've kept hidden.

MadHatter: Why?

Blue_Alice: Because I don't have anything to lose.

MadHatter: That's dangerous.

Blue_Alice: That in itself is why I am interested. I want to be fucked in ways I've only imagined, and I'm tired of only feeling half full. I have cravings and I'm ready.

A few minutes later, I was sure the conversation had ended, then a ping.

MadHatter: I'll be in touch.

Blue_Alice: Wait!

Okay that seemed a little desperate.

MadHatter: What?

Blue_Alice: Who are you?

MadHatter: I'm the guy with the thick cock you'll be wondering about tonight while you play with your toys.

Blue_Alice: Charming.

MadHatter: I can be.

And he was gone, if it had even been a he. For all I knew, it could have been a she. This too fascinated me. I thought of women and my sexual boundaries when it came to them and decided one leap at a time. Although women appealed to me from the waist up, I had no desire to explore the waist down. Then again, I'd really never had the opportunity.

§§

The next day, I brought my iPad on every single errand with the chat room queued up. He could see me. He knew I was waiting. I looked desperate, but I needed this! I felt it in every part of me. I needed to be sexually free. I'd slept with six men in my thirty-two years. Two one-night stands, one when I was in college and the other right before I met my husband, Alex. The rest were boyfriends and not one of them was a freak, well not in the sense that I wanted them to be. A few got me off with their mouth, but it wasn't earth shattering. It was more or less a struggle and an enormous amount of effort with constant murmurs of "Are you close?" during what seemed to be rigorous work. So, I rarely got off.

I had, as the mysterious messenger predicted, taken my toy to bed last night, imagining the man behind our brief chat. I was hot in a way I hadn't been in months at the possibilities alone. This had to be explored. I felt like I was a sexual creature on the verge of finally introducing myself. Once I was home, I unpacked my groceries, praying for the fucking iPad to ping. Just ping! When I got nothing, I decided to forgo cooking and treated myself to dinner at Tubby's, a nearby seafood restaurant on River Street. I sat on the balcony watching the boats glide down the river while the sun set. Couples passed by below me on the busy street holding hands and smiling while I dined alone. Minutes later I got my usual message from Alex letting me know he wouldn't be home tonight and I rolled my eyes. Why did he even bother at this point? God, how I hated him.

Later at home, I thought about looking up some listings to show. I had a real estate license I rarely used and knew it was getting close to time to put it back to use. I was good at it, and I enjoyed it, but when my marriage fell apart I dropped it completely. I had stayed at home for a month solid after hearing Alex's first conversation with one of his mistresses. I didn't need to see anything. The prick had no issue talking openly with her behind his office door. If you are going to cheat, at least have the smarts and decency to hide it. The devastating thought that he didn't care enough to hide is what really drove the knife into my heart. A few months after I had questioned him about his distance, I realized he had no intention of revealing his indiscretions to me. He was simply that fucking stupid. I heard every word he uttered to those women. It was eerily close to the way he used to speak to me. It hurt me horribly at first, now it just made my stomach turn. Why the fuck was I still here? What more reason did I need? He cheated; our marriage was over. I hated him. Why didn't I just ask for a divorce?

PING!

A wave of adrenaline shot through me as I looked at the screen. It was an address. It was obvious why. It was an invitation, and one that came too soon for my comfort.

Well that would be a hell no. I wanted to at least have a conversation longer than a few short sentences before I agreed to a rendezvous.

Blue_Alice: Hello?

No response came. I already knew the address would be my only message tonight. It was a challenge. He wanted to see what I was made of. If I was willing to step out of my comfort zone. All the reasonable reactions raced through me.

What kind of person barely introduces himself then gives an address to a total stranger?

Then again, what kind of person tells a complete stranger they want to be fucked six ways from Sunday?

I stared at the address for what seemed like an eternity. Okay, I could drive by. What was the harm? I would just look around, scope the place out. I could do this. Throwing my blanket off my legs and retiring my yoga pants, I took a scalding hot shower. I Googled the address with a towel wrapped around me, fear creeping into my thoughts. My search, of course, showed only results with possible directions. It had to be a home address. He gave me directions to his home? I shook off the towel, covered myself with scented lotion, and took in my body. I had long legs and curvy hips, a little extra weight made them even more pronounced. My breasts were pushing a C-cup, and though they weren't perfectly proportionate to my hips and ass, I was fine with them. I pulled out a thin black sheath dress that collared at the top, hugging my neck snugly, slipped on my spiked red heels and put on my best face. Thick eyelashes and perfectly lips later, I ran my hands through my dirty blonde hair that I'd ironed straight. I was ready.

After two small glasses of wine and a mini-breakdown later,

I corked my bottle and made my way to my car. *You can do this, Vi. You can also back out at any time.*

My cell had no issues navigating the address. My GPS estimated my trip to thirty minutes, and in thirty minutes I could be in the midst of possibly the best or worst situation of my life. Then again, I couldn't imagine anything worse than the one I was already in.

I had enough heart left to give. I just didn't give a damn enough to use it. This wasn't about my heart; this was about a thirst I'd fought long enough. This would be good. This could be my something to look forward to.

Come on, Violet, divorce is not death and you've got a lot of living to do.

ACKNOWLEDGEMENTS

Stacy Hahn, you are the epitome of what a friend should be. I'm sorry you got stuck with me (LOL). I would be so lost without you.

To my amazing PA's Bex and Christy, Thank you so much for dealing with my shit and supporting me. You are my rocks.

Julie Kerchof (seriously, Julie, you make me happy), Lina Linalove, Cindy Gordanier, Robert Williamson, Jessica Call, and the rest of my crew., thank you so much. It's just amazing to have you rocking my books daily. Your support means everything.

Christine from The Hype PR's, thank you so much for teaching me the art of finesse, and for all of your amazing help.

Daizy Zorman, you rock my socks off. Thank you for loving me and my dysfunction.

And to all the bloggers who have given this new series a chance and have taken the time to post a review, thank you so much. I really can't believe how lucky I am.

ABOUT THE AUTHOR

USA Today bestselling author and Texas native, Kate Stewart, lives in North Carolina with her husband, Nick. Nestled within the Blue Ridge Mountains, Kate pens messy, sexy, angst-filled contemporary romance, as well as romantic comedy and erotic suspense.

Kate's title, *Drive*, was named one of the best romances of 2017 by *The New York Daily News* and *Huffington Post*. *Drive* was also a finalist in the Goodreads Choice awards for best contemporary romance of 2017. The Ravenhood Trilogy, consisting of *Flock*, *Exodus*, and *The Finish Line*, has become an international bestseller and reader favorite. Her holiday release, *The Plight Before Christmas*, ranked #6 on Amazon's Top 100. Kate's works have been featured in *USA TODAY*, *BuzzFeed*, *The New York Daily News*, *Huffington Post* and translated into a dozen languages.

Kate is a lover of all things '80s and '90s, especially John Hughes films and rap. She dabbles a little in photography, can knit a simple stitch scarf for necessity, and on occasion, does very well at whiskey.

TITLES BY KATE STEWART

Romantic Suspense

The Ravenhood Series
Flock
Exodus
The Finish Line

Lust & Lies Series
Sexual Awakenings
Excess
Predator and Prey
The Lust & Lies Box set: Sexual Awakenings, Excess, Predator and Prey

Contemporary Romance

In Reading Order

Room 212
Never Me (Companion to Room 212 and The Reluctant Romantic Series)
The Reluctant Romantics Series
The Fall
The Mind
The Heart
The Reluctant Romantics Box Set: The Fall, The Heart, The Mind
Loving the White Liar

The Bittersweet Symphony
Drive
Reverse

The Real
Someone Else's Ocean
Heartbreak Warfare
Method

Romantic Dramedy

Balls in Play Series
Anything but Minor
Major Love
Sweeping the Series Novella
Balls in play Box Set: Anything but Minor, Major Love, Sweeping the Series, The Golden Sombrero

The Underdogs Series
The Guy on the Right
The Guy on the Left
The Guy in the Middle
The Underdogs Box Set: The Guy on The Right, The Guy on the Left, The Guy in the Middle

The Plight Before Christmas

Made in the USA
Columbia, SC
13 July 2025

60516931R00200